DAN ALLEN

The Exalting

Future House Publishing

ISBN: 978-1-944452-93-3

Developmental editing by Emma Hoggan
Substantive editing by Sara Anstead
Copy editing by Emma Snow and Erin Searle
Proofreading by Ahnasariah Larsen
Interior design by Ahnasariah Larsen
Interior layout design by Sarah Hagans

For Bryce, Nicole, Micah, Clara and Cyrus, who always challenge me to dream bigger

Chapter 1

The purple-needled pine trees grew denser, and Dana knew she was close. She looked back. Norr was seven miles away, eclipsed by the trees, but she could still make out the black smoke rising from its workshops against a backdrop of white dust clouds from the sayathenite polishing yards. She turned to continue up the slope toward her grandfather's cabin with one thought in mind.

It's time I found out.

This time her parents wouldn't be there to steer the conversation away. She would have her grandfather all to herself. It was high time somebody told her the truth. Every other city in Aesica practiced blood-binding. Only Norr forbade it.

Why?

After a few more paces, Dana realized she was limping.

Oh, here we go again.

She was no stranger to pain. But this was not like sore muscles from hiking. The ache ran deep into the bones of her lower leg.

Dana's hands curled into fists.

Trappers.

With every step she took, the pain grew sharper until it bit and stabbed at her flesh.

Dana had never been caught in a trap, or shot with an arrow, yet she could describe in exquisite detail exactly how it felt to have a tibia crushed or punctured lungs fill with blood.

For her it was impossible not to take the killings personally.

Leave it. You're almost there.

But Dana turned aside, angry determination coursing through her.

This would only take a minute. Trappers only checked an area every few days.

But there would be consequences if she were caught. Freeing a

Dan Allen

trapped animal was the same as theft.

And what about the murder of an animal?

Dana ran. The pain grew with every step until she was nearly in tears. Looking up, she spied a young nox. The bloody jaws of a hanging snap-trap held the sloth by its leg. Its lavender autumn fur was perfectly grizzled with the beginnings of its white winter coat—a rare catch.

Dana quickly climbed the nearest tree. When the nox was within arm's length, Dana wedged her foot in the fork of a branch and shook stray strands of black hair out of her view. She closed her eyes and tried to quell her nausea.

Pull the pin. Get out.

Dana opened her eyes and leaned toward the trapped animal.

The nox jerked its leg in desperation.

"Ow!" Dana's leg gave way under a stab of pain, as if her own muscles were convulsing around shattered bone. A branch struck the side of her face, stopping her fall.

"Stop it, will you? That really hurts."

The nox suddenly gave up trying to pull its leg free, and the throbbing pains waned. It wasn't her words, but her *will* that had made it stop.

Having passed a good chunk of her own volition to the nox, Dana was left without any desire to climb farther out on the branch.

Come on! You can do this.

A pall of apathy hung over her. Saving the nox just didn't seem to matter anymore.

You have to do this.

If only to reduce the pain radiating from her leg, Dana drew out of her jacket a hook-tipped iron rod. She reached out with the tool to pull the ring on the linchpin of the trap's axle. The spring-loaded mechanism was designed to be easily released, though not by a nox's wide fingers.

Suddenly, the nox's sifa flared. The three spine-like tufts of twined hair rose at the back of its neck, fanning into a feathery

2

The Exalting

headdress. The sifa were not as long or colorful as the sifa of the marmar monkeys or as articulated as those Xahnans like Dana possessed. But the meaning was clear.

Danger.

Crunching leaves and breaking twigs sounded from below, and the nox twisted to look down. The trap swung out of reach.

Dana's heart skipped into a panic at the sounds of footsteps—two sets coming from opposite directions, and headed right for her.

Trappers.

The young nox's eyes shone with fear and desperation.

Dana was out of time.

I was so close! In utter frustration Dana dropped from the tree and landed in a crouch.

Two men emerged from the trees, one on her left and the other on her right. Neither carried a game bag or a long-hooked pole for releasing a trap.

"There's the druid." The man to her left pointed at her. His red-brown hair was so matted his sifa were barely visible. "Told you she'd come."

It wasn't a trap for the nox. It was a trap for me!

I should have listened for them.

There were plenty of birds and scampers in the wood that might have noticed the trappers. But she had only been focused on the nox.

As a druid adept, Dana felt things that only the Creator should. There were thousands like her on Xahna, from each of the four classes of adepts. They were revered and recruited for their abilities.

In blood-bound cities, some were even exalted.

But in Norr, they were a nuisance. Some, like her friend Forz, kept it a secret. Others tried to starve it into submission.

There was no cure. She would always feel pain that was not her own.

The other man closed in from her right, tramping through a tarberry bush. "Look who's clever now." He had a full beard, and all three pairs of his black sifa were tucked down against his neck.

This was no friendly greeting.

"Caught you in the act."

Dana forced her inferior sifa to lift from off her neck, where they had lain tucked under her hair. It made her all the more conscious of the fact the three pairs of twined hair weren't fully developed, still half-bound in tight bundles. "Hello," she said, forcing the words out. "What brings you out here?"

"Ha. Very funny. It's prison for you this time," said the trapper on her right. "The magistrate won't stand for this." He held up two dirt-crusted fingers. "And we've got two witnesses."

There was nothing to say. Still, she dug for an excuse. "I haven't done anything wrong." *Yet.*

"Liar. What's that hooked bar for—scratching your bottom?"

Dana twirled it deftly and mimed the motion. "Yes."

"And what do you think you were doing in the tree?"

"Scratching my bottom."

"With a nox in a trap!" laughed the second trapper. "What a load of—"

Dana made a break for it. She feinted downhill, then jumped back the other direction and raced into the trees. If she could lead the men far enough, she might be able to loop back and free the poor nox.

She ran across the trade road that cut through the forest, clearing both steam-wagon ruts in a leap, and headed for a cluster of trees where she could hide in the mass of dense purple boughs.

But the men were faster than her. They closed quickly from both sides and seized her arms.

Dana thrashed, but their hands held her like vises.

"You try to call one of your little friends," said the bearded trapper holding her right arm up away from her body, "and we'll just kill you."

"Is that so?" called another voice from nearby. Its wavering tone hinted at advanced age, and it was laced with curious interest.

Dana recognized the voice. *Togath!*

Togath, her grandfather, stepped around a large tree trunk.

The Exalting

He was tall and thin, as if he'd been stretched out. His inferior sifa flared politely in greeting. "If you mean to kill her," he continued. "I can help."

"What?" Dana gasped.

"She is a troublemaker—the worst kind."

"I am not!"

The warning glance from Togath told her that she wasn't helping. "Shall I cut out her tongue first, so she doesn't scream?"

"I can still scream without a tongue. How does a tongue help you scream? It's more of a throat thing."

"Dana!" he snapped. "Will you shut up, please? We're discussing your imminent demise. It's not a matter of debate." There was a familiar twinkle in his eye.

"Fine, cut out my tongue first."

"Yes." Togath stepped forward. "And then the fun begins. We'll probably have to dismember her, so they don't find any body parts—best if we eat them." He looked from one trapper to the other. "Have you ever eaten a Xahnan?"

The two men looked at him in complete horror.

"Come to my cabin. I've got plenty left over from the last trespasser."

The trappers exchanged a horrified glance.

"Well, if you haven't the stomach for this sort of thing." In a flash he drew a short knife and brandished it in the face one trapper and then other. "You best leave her to me and get off my property."

The trappers let go of her like she was a live rhynoid vine and beat a quick retreat.

"Honestly," Dana said. "Cut out my tongue?"

Her grandfather laughed until his wheezes ended in a cough. "Alright. Let's get you away from the scene of the crime."

Dana gave a grudging look back in the direction of the nox. It would be dead before she got back. That hurt even more than the phantom pains in her leg. "Fine."

Dana sat across from her grandfather in his small cabin, ignoring her bowl of bitter broth, and contemplating doing something else completely forbidden.

I can ask him now. My parents will never know.

There were certain things that were forbidden to even discuss in the free city of Norr.

But I'm not in Norr—well not in the city proper. She was still in the jurisdiction of its rangers.

Close enough.

Dana sipped the herbal tea that tasted like scorched dirt with overtones of overripe fruit and smiled at her grandfather, swallowing back the question that beat at her from inside.

Nobody in Norr, including Dana, was blood-bound to a ka. But every other city she had heard of allegedly practiced blood-binding. Some even required it.

Perhaps what made it all the worse was the one thing she knew about the making of a ka.

A ka was chosen from among a city's adepts, people with abilities like *hers.*

The fact that her city was the only one without a ka seemed a bit off, like vegetables that were just starting to get a little slimy. You could stomach it, but only if you closed your eyes and plugged your nose.

Dana had heard every good reason that the city of Norr had banned blood-binding. Inequality. Too much power concentrated in one person. The obvious potential for corruption. Blasphemy before the Creator. But that only her made her more curious why the other cities all practiced it.

Dana ran her hands along her sturdy calf-length trousers, considering how to broach the subject. It was like asking how babies were made—there was no way to bring it up without Togath wondering why she was asking.

If she didn't ask now, she would have a long walk home to nurse her regret.

It's now or never. She raised her voice. "Togath?"

The Exalting

"Hmm?" Without looking up, her grandfather put a spoon of steaming soup into his mouth. Wearing his usual gray waistcoat and long-sleeved shirt, he looked like a simple woodsman. But he knew things—*forbidden things.*

"If blood-binding is so wrong," Dana began, speaking quickly to avoid being interupted, "why is it done in other cities?"

Togath's spoon clinked against the tin platter under his bowl. He looked up. The small distance between them seemed to open like a spreading ice crevasse.

Dana bit her lip, hoping that this would be her first glimpse into the dominant culture on Xahna—the world in which she lived like an exile in the unbound city of Norr.

Togath opened his mouth to speak but stopped. He absently twisted the key on the winding spring on the watch around his neck, his pause belying a deeper struggle. "Dana, you know discussion of bloodstones and the exalting are forbidden in Norr." His lips pressed together, forming wrinkles on his narrow face. He kneaded his hands as if trying to quell a nagging ache. "And besides, what would I know?"

Far more than he's letting on.

Dana glanced out the window. The pale blue sky was already fading.

Twilight. I'm running out of time.

At least at this altitude, there weren't any predatory rhynoid vines along the trail. She could risk staying a little longer.

"You lived in Shoul Falls. It's a blood-bound city," Dana said. "You must know more about the making of a ka than anyone else in Norr, including the cleric." Dana couldn't hide her irritation on that point. "Why do we even need a cleric?"

Togath gave a grudging nod. "Goodman Warv's function, as I understand it, is knowing how to not offend the ka of other cities."

"Anyway, it's ridiculous going to meditation when we don't even have a ka to pray to."

"It builds strength of spirit," Togath said. "As does the fast."

"I'd rather endure public humiliation." Dana's sifa shook at the

7

very thought of foregoing food.

"Yes, I recall you've made that decision before. But you should fast, Dana. It will make your will stronger." His superior sifa lifted upward and to the sides, punctuating the edict. Then her grandfather stood, lifted his half-eaten bowl of soup, and set it in a brick-lined sink, seeming to have lost his appetite.

Stronger. It wasn't strength the Norrians wanted from her, it was self-denial.

Dana crossed her arms. "I don't need to fast just to prove I can *not* do something. I'm strong enough."

"Strong enough to be a teenage girl in a mining town without any responsibilities except skinning her father's game and appraising animals for auction." Togath turned his head and gave her a wry smile.

"I hate skinning game." Dana shuddered. "I can see how they died when I touch them—why do I have to see that?"

"I wish I knew." Togath rubbed the back of his neck. "The Torsican scholars claim the veil between this world and the Creator's realm is thin. Perhaps it is not so in other places."

"Other worlds." Dana had heard all the tales of farseeing ka who gazed into the heavens and felt other beings—creatures like Xahnans, walking upright with two legs and arms and familiar faces. Children of the Creator. Of course, she hadn't seen any of that. Her senses hit their limit at well less than a mile.

She huffed a breath of frustration. "If there are so many places to live, why did the Creator curse me to live in Norr?"

In guarded conversations with sayathenite traders and steam-wagon drivers, Dana had learned that young adepts in other cities were invited to live in a sanctum, trained as acolytes by senior adepts, and eventually given positions of power under the keeper of the city's bloodstone—the ka.

But Norrians wanted nothing to do with her ability. Like Togath, they claimed strength came from *not* using it.

To Dana, their way of thinking wasn't about freedom and equality, as they claimed. It was pure jealousy and fear. Why

The Exalting

couldn't they see her power could help them, protect them? If she were chosen as ka, she could wield ten thousand times more will.

Perhaps then, like the legends, her gaze would reach beyond Xahna.

Right now, she just wished she could see beyond Norr.

Or leave.

She was still underage. It wasn't an option. But just because she couldn't leave didn't mean she had to live under the delusion that she was a freak to be tamed.

Dana clenched her fists. "Why?"

Togath placed his hand on the table, a patronizing gesture like he was patting the head of a marmar. "Whether living in Norr is a curse or a blessing, you must deci—"

"Ahhh!" Dana clutched her ribs and fell from her chair as a sharp pain shot through her side. She looked to the cabin door as her superior sifa flared defiantly from both sides of her head. Her gaze fixed with a sudden determination.

"Dana, no! You can't interfere with traps anymore. I helped you get away from those trappers, but if you leave now—"

"It was an arrow, not a trap. The animal is still moving. I can save it."

The long pace of its desperate strides pulsed through her legs, as if she were bounding through the forest. It was a bird—the largest on Xahna.

A greeder.

The pain in its side stabbed at her. Dana could hardly breathe.

Ka of Xahna—it hurts!

Why would somebody shoot a greeder? Wild greeder were rare in the mountains and far too valuable to kill—worth thousands of trader's coins, possibly as much as a small house like her grandfather's cabin.

Whatever the hunter's reason, Dana couldn't bear the pain in her ribs where the arrow had ripped into the great bird's side. She bolted out of Togath's cabin and ran across the footpath and into the forest.

Why is someone hunting a greeder in the forest at night?

"Dana, come back!" Togath called from his doorway, his aged voice unable to project far. "You can resist this. Be strong!"

But Togath couldn't understand how this felt. He was not an adept like Dana and her older brother Tyrus.

With the stabbing pain in her side wringing tears from her eyes, Dana couldn't just sit there and feel the beautiful creature dying.

Racing among the lower branches of the pine trees, the greeder's labored breathing mingled with hers.

"I'm coming," she muttered breathlessly.

A scamper hopped out from its hiding place onto a branch to watch her pass. This one she knew, though she had no space in her mind to hear its constant hunger. The frill-necked lizards thought only of food—like Tyrus, her older brother, who used his druidic sense for hunting.

Dana felt the wounded greeder's pace quickening. It had turned downhill. Through a gap in the canopy of pine needles, she spied a tall stone outcropping. The great, long-legged bird was headed for a cliff. If it leapt, it would glide too far for her to reach it in time to save it. She had a pouch with caiman powder in her jacket. She could stop the bleeding.

Dana called out to the animal, pressing her mind and soul into the creature, knowing full well the effort would leave her with almost no will of her own.

"Climb down!"

The greeder turned aside as her forced thoughts overwhelmed its urge to leap from the precipice. The greeder headed instead down a narrow drainage on the near side of the cliff into a chute of broken shale. Its pursuer would never follow it down that. The archer would have to go around.

The effort of willing the greeder toward her sapped Dana's resolve almost instantly. She no longer had any desire to run. The natural urge to rest her legs and catch her breath smothered all other desires. Her feet slowed. Soon she was walking, distracted by

The Exalting

the dark sky and pine needles on the ground.

"Keep going," she muttered, her own voice sounding rather unconvincing.

Be strong. Her grandfather's voice echoed in her head, then her conscience.

Maybe I should do the fast more often.

Fighting the urge to stop entirely, Dana started ahead again, hurrying for the base of the cliff, where the six-foot-tall greeder would emerge.

As it neared, her sensations merged with those of the greeder. Her feet felt as if they had long-toed claws that slid over loose pieces of broken shale. She felt the greeder struggling for balance on the rockslide. But the most distinct feeling was the tremendous pressure on her back.

It's carrying someone.

And that begged another question.

Who would shoot at a man on a greeder? One of the rangers?

The rider might be a dangerous criminal. That was reason enough to turn back, but this greeder felt unusually loyal to its beloved rider. Dana trusted the judgement of a greeder better than most people she knew.

I should help him.

No longer feeding her will into the huge bird, Dana felt her own self-control recovering gradually. Her pace quickened until her leather-soled shoes sprinted over the poor alkaline soil of the alpine forest.

As though a painted curtain hung in front of her, Dana spied a hazy vision of what the greeder was seeing: a junction at the base of the chute.

"This way," she muttered, again channeling resolve into its weary, panicked mind. "Come to me."

The greeder turned toward Dana.

Rounding a boulder, she caught sight of the animal. Scintillating black and green feathers covered its head and long neck. Bright white primaries graced the tips of its half-extended wings. A cloaked rider sat on its back in a saddle. The greeder stumbled over a root. It caught its footing but swerved awkwardly against the trunk of a tall pine.

"No!"

The arrow sticking from the greeder's side struck the tree trunk and rammed further into the already weakened animal.

The pain in her side flared like she had been stabbed through with a hot poker from a forge. A mingled sensation of warm and cool ran down her side, as blood gushed in pulses from the greeder.

The arrow in its side had severed the artery that fed its massive legs.

In two paces the large bird fell forward, rolling over its rider with the sickening crunch of bones.

Dana gave a whimper of shock and covered her mouth. "Oh my . . ."

Both rider and bird would be dead in moments.

Dana raced forward, desperate thoughts filling her mind as she came to the scene. Pinned under the weight of his dying mount, the rider stretched out a wrinkled and weathered hand, his open mouth gasping for air that his broken body could not seem to take in. In his fingers, he held a small coin purse.

Take it.

The thought came to her mind clearly and with conviction. With her own will weakened, Dana yielded easily to the thought. She knelt beside him and took the small leather pouch. Within was a single object, not heavy enough to be gold. Her fingers traced the facets.

A crystal.

With a great struggle, the aged man spoke. His voice gurgled like a bellows half-filled with water. "Vetas-ka is coming."

Dana knew the title "ka" and what it meant. The very thought filled her with terror.

Tears quivered in the corners of the man's eyes. "Do not . . ." His voice choked on a gurgle of blood. ". . . let him get the stone."

"This is a *bloodstone*?" The urge to drop the pouch became

12

The Exalting

almost overpowering.

One of the gods was coming for it—a supreme.

Dana shook her head in horror, her legs itching to flee. At the same time, a sense of possibility rushed through her. This was a chance to change her life forever.

With the bloodstone she could become a ka, one of the Pantheon.

The man's trembling hand caught hers in a desperate grip. At his touch, a sensation of total peace washed her concerns away like a flowing tide, even as the man gave a gurgled rasp—his lungs were flooded. There was nothing she could do to save him.

Words again flowed into her mind as easily as a daydream.

He is coming for it. His kazen are not far. Run!

Dana's mind was a blur of questions, but she had no time to ask them. Giving the dying rider's hand one last squeeze, Dana fled.

Behind her, the nostrils high up on the greeder's beak gave out one long breath—its last. The animal's departing soul carried tendrils of her own beyond the veil, where she sensed the arrival of its friend.

The rider had passed as well.

Go in peace.

The rider had been a good man. Behind that was the lingering impression left by what she now realized was the rider's enchanting touch. She knew what he knew about Vetas-ka.

He was a bloodthirsty demon.

Dana's resolve was now as solid as the ground beneath her feet. She clenched the pouch, realizing as she did, that she held the combined will of thousands of souls in her hand.

A tainted bloodstone.

Never use it, she told herself as increasing curiosity ate at her. The impression of Vetas-ka hung like a shadow over her heart. If she used the stone, what was to keep her from becoming like him? Years of Goodman Warv's warnings about the dangers of the blood-binding echoed through her.

The great abomination.

13

But she couldn't just let whoever had hunted the man steal it. It belonged to a city. Access to all those people's wills was bound in this one object.

The unmistakable baying of Torsican hunting hounds sounded behind her. Images of their serrated fangs, maned necks, and spine-tipped ears flashed into her mind.

Dana's sifa flattened to the sides of her neck at the chilling sound. Her people had originated long ago on the distant continent of Torsica. The call of the fierce pack-hunting Torsican hounds conjured primal fear.

They'll find the greeder. They'll get my scent.

Rather than continue downhill, the direction the greeder had been fleeing, Dana turned aside. Fear hastened her steps as she climbed a rise and circled away from Togath's cabin. She had no desire to lead Vetas-ka's acolytes onto her grandfather's property.

The dogs were surely faster than she was, but they could not outrun her at this altitude for long.

Dana paced herself as she topped the rise. Moments later she descended behind the ridge and the sound of the hounds was lost, giving her a chance to think through a defense.

If the dogs caught up, she might be able to convince one or two not to attack. But as a pack, their collective hunting instincts would overcome her suggestions.

Dana sprinted for another quarter mile, her desperate thoughts of how to save her life constantly interrupted by the effort of avoiding tripping on the roots and rocks that leapt at her from the darkness.

A long howl from a hound sent a tremor of terror down her spine. This time it was even louder.

No. Please.

The chorus of baying grew quickly as the swift dogs closed on her. She hadn't gotten a sufficient lead to tire them.

An idea struck her, a terrible one. She would never succeed trying to get the dogs to stop hunting.

But I can give them another target.

The Exalting

Dana winced at the thought of sacrificing another animal to save her life.

But it was not just her life in the balance. The bloodstone carried a connection to every bound soul of an entire city.

Dana reached out with her mind, seeking for an impressionable animal that would be large enough to interest the dogs.

Nothing.

No. There.

A young three-horn bandeer was in a meadow two hundred yards away. It was lying down, hiding from the dogs.

"Run this way!" she urged.

It would not budge. She was too far, and her suggestion went against its basic instinct.

Dana had only seconds before the baying hounds reached her.

Fumbling with the tie on the purse, Dana opened the small leather pouch, shuddering as she fought sixteen years of indoctrination about the evils of the blood-binding.

The bloodstones give the ka their power, virtually limitless will.

Dana reached the meadow. A large hound emerged from the trees to her right, its jowls flapping as it bared its teeth and howled. Dana's heart thudded in her chest. Dana gasped panicked breaths as tears spilled down her cheeks.

I don't want to die.

Two more hounds burst from the trees to her left, joining the chorus as they spotted her.

Her balance shifted unexpectedly, and the ground slammed into Dana's face. With a mouthful of dirt and her hands tingling from the impact, she climbed to her knees.

I didn't trip, she thought. *What happened?*

But Dana remembered the coin purse with the stone. She ran her hands over tufts of thin grass, searching frantically in the dirt for the pouch. Neither of the twin moons of Calett and Osoq had yet risen. The evening sky was already dark.

Come on. Where is it!

Her hand struck the pouch.

"Don't even think about touching that." A man stepped out of the cover of the trees.

"Leave me alone," Dana whimpered, her fingers still on the bag.

"I claim that stone in the name of Vetas-ka," said the dark-haired man. His superior sifa rose at the back of his thick neck, the twined hair fanning in a posture of dominance. He was short, but nothing about his stature made him any less menacing.

Dana glared at the bow slung over his shoulder. Running was no use.

"Don't make this any harder," he added, "or you'll end up like Sindar."

"Who is Sindar?" Dana said, desperate for some distraction as the dogs circled behind her, closing her exit.

"The dead man you just robbed for that stone."

Dana wanted to point out that she had not stolen it, but the kazen reached out his hand, and suddenly she could not move.

A warlock!

Dana had met many adepts with the ability to channel their will into physical force or even heat, but never had she met any who could stop someone from even moving at such a distance. Dana struggled to move from her kneeling position as beads of sweat dripped from her forehead, stinging the scraped skin near the corner of her eye. Her muscles quivered against the invisible force that held her.

"You have never felt the influence of a supreme?" said the man. "Vetas-ka will grant me as much will as I need to obtain that stone."

Dana reached out with her mind, searching the forest for help, finding only a few squirrels and an owl. "How does he know you won't take the stone for yourself?" Dana said, trying to sow doubt.

"Now that you've seen it, you're a threat. Vetas-ka will claim the stone for himself and eliminate anyone who has seen it. You are as expendable as me."

The man gave a disgusted laugh. But there was something more than bravado. Dana sensed a touch of fear.

The Exalting

It's working.

She struggled to move, forcing the man to feed out even more will to keep her arms and legs from moving.

"Vetas-ka sees all," he said. "My eyes are his eyes. My ears are his ears—yes, he knows your face now. Even if you were to escape, he would hunt you down to the ends of Xahna. You are powerless against him. There are six kazen in the forest at this very moment. Do you think you can defeat us all?"

"You are merely a tool—a dog. Once your usefulness is gone, your ka will dispose of you."

"Blasphemy! When I deliver the stone, Vetas-ka will lift up his follower Omren among his children," shouted the man. "I'm . . . sure of it." His voice wavered with increasing doubt. Dana was no enchanter, but she knew this man's resolve would grow weaker the longer he used his will to hold her.

But he must have realized his mistake because he walked quickly forward.

No!

He seized her shoulder with one hand, and the pressure pinning her body increased to a painful level, the physical contact amplifying the extent of his will as it did when Dana touched her brother's slain game. The warlock's other hand seized her by her sifa and yanked her head back.

She cried out in pain, worrying that the sifa would tear away at the root, leaving her maimed for life.

With one arm, the kazen flung Dana away from the pouch. Dana whirled in the air and landed hard on the ground. When she raised her throbbing head, the man who had called himself Omren was clutching the pouch and staring at her with calculated malice.

"Flee while you have the chance," Dana said in a desperate attempt to twist the man's weakened will. "Vetas-ka will forsake you. He cares only for power. You are nothing to him."

"For that blasphemy, you will die." Omren tied the pouch to his belt and reached for his bow and a single arrow. He drew and aimed at Dana's heart.

She tried to run, but his will held her like a snap-trap.

Dana reached out with all her will as a hundred silent creatures in the forest gave their mute attention. *Please, help me.*

A soaring feeling spread through Dana. Her eyes fixed on Omren's, like a raptor descending on its prey.

"In the name of Vetas-ka, I silence the blasphemer!" He sighted down the arrow.

"There's something you don't know," Dana said quickly.

He didn't flinch. "What?"

"I . . . I . . ." Dana had nothing to say, nothing to make him hesitate. Her desperation reached out, pulling on anything— everything.

Help me!

The man's eyes suddenly bulged in their sockets, the arrow launched harmlessly into the forest. His body collapsed to the ground, a horned atter owl clinging to his head.

Dana gasped as the atter owl extracted its rear claws from the back of Omren's skull and flapped away on silent wings.

Not even the man's dogs had heard the great winged predator approaching.

"Ka of Xahna!" Dana could scarcely believe her luck. The owl had saved her. Dana raced forward, grabbed the fallen bow, nocked an arrow, and drew. She only managed three quarters of a full draw, but it was enough to convince the dogs that she was a threat. Dana sent out as powerful a mental warning as she could manage, and the hounds turned tail and fled.

Dana quickly stooped to untie the pouch with the bloodstone from Omren's waist.

"Dana?"

Dana turned at the sound of the familiar voice. "Grandpa!" She nearly dropped the pouch. Her hands shook from the passing rush of the confrontation.

Togath stepped quickly into the clearing.

"Did you send the owl?" she blurted out. "Was that you?"

"Me? I haven't used the Creator's powers since I . . . since . . .

18

The Exalting

Dana, you know I'm not an adept." Togath looked down at the fallen man and gasped. "By the Creator . . . Did you kill that man?"

Dana shook her head. "The atter owl did. It thought he was prey."

"Dana, what have you done?"

"Nothing." She moved the pouch behind her back and stood up.

Togath's eyes followed the motion. "What is in that bag?"

Dana's throat clenched. She couldn't speak. She couldn't lie to Togath.

"Dana?"

Chapter 2

Jet Naman woke to a headache hammering his skull. Lights and sounds clattered through his brain as he struggled for a grip on reality.

His skull-splitting headache was the first indication of trouble. He wasn't being woken from cryo under sedation.

Must be an emergency.

Usually that meant he was about to be tossed into an extremely dangerous situation, outgunned, pinned down, and completely isolated.

That was the job description for a marine sniper in the Believer Security Forces. It was what he had signed up for when he left Avalon, after his mother was murdered by ASP thugs

From all around him came the sounds of ventilators hissing and the other marines in his unit groaning.

What is going on?

He blinked, and the white blur in front of his face slowly formed into the photo of his mother that he had printed and pinned to the bulkhead, just before going into cryo. The picture was now faded.

A ship-wide broadcast began. But it wasn't the ship's captain. It was a spokesperson for ASP—the enemy.

It felt like a bad dream, as if all forty of the marines packed in the dropship's cramped cryobay had died and woken up in hell.

"Attempts at peaceful intervention have utterly failed. Believers continue to refuse to share the location of the ninth inhabited planet. Their extremist propaganda is a threat to Ardent Secular Pragmatist operations and the interests of its shareholders.

"At this critical stage, we have no recourse but to declare the Believers enemies of the interplanetary public.

"By the release of this binding order, all Believers are to be treated

The Exalting

as enemy combatants and exterminated by any means available. Any organization, body politic, or geography harboring Believers will be subject to force of submission.

"All ASP signatories are hereby bound by the Principal Charter to execute this order, effective immediately."

Jet sat up, which wasn't difficult in the zero-g hold. The faces of the other marines in the bay showed equally astonished looks.

"They can't do this."

"It's completely illegal."

"ASP can do whatever they want."

"Are they seriously going to kill all the Believers?"

"This is Captain Austin." The voice coming from the speaker had an uncharacteristic tremor. "We . . . just got that message on a tightbeam from Avalon. We're still two weeks out from the planet itself, but it looks like the ASP fleet has already arrived to enforce the extermination order."

A lanky Caprian across from Jet bowed his head and touched his fingers to his forehead. Jet had seen the gesture before, as a Caprian knelt over the body of a fallen comrade.

The elves of Capria did not cry as humans did.

"Apparently," Captain Austin continued, "the Believer space telescope in orbit around Avalon discovered the ninth world and our High Council refused share the location. And so, ASP has just declared all-out war on us."

The cryobay was pin-drop silent.

ASP forces outnumbered Believers a thousand to one.

"The rest of our fleet is using the Avalonian sun for a high-g gravity redirect toward the new planet."

"The rest of our fleet?" Jet wondered. "Which means . . ."

"Colonel Adkins has diverted a flight group consisting of six dropships, to Avalon."

Not only were they about to be on an interplanetary endangered species list, now they didn't have the fleet for cover.

A marine from Delta squad turned up his hands. "Six dropships? That's not enough to evacuate a single village."

Dan Allen

"The High Council is in hiding on Avalon," Captain Austin continued. "If they are still alive when we get there, our orders are to ensure they make it off the planet safely—at all costs."

At all costs. Despite knowing what he had signed up for, Jet couldn't help but wonder if this mission would be his last.

Reacting to the flaring fear of an unfinished life, Jet looked overhead to where Monique was attempting to rouse Dormit, his squad's only Wodynian.

Jet didn't think of Dormit as an alien. More like a distant cousin.

Monique, on the other hand, she was a thing truly foreign. She had even studied to be a xeno-sociologist, but never finished her degree before enlisting.

Human, yes, but different in so many subtle ways.

She was smart. Jet was . . . devious? She drew attention in any circle and knew how to avoid trouble. He never drew attention but could find trouble anywhere.

Basically, a perfect match.

Technically, Jet hadn't seen Monique in years. But the time in cryo had passed in the blink of an eye, like general anesthesia. It seemed barely a moment had passed since he watched her fade from consciousness, and he wondered if he would ever get a chance to turn that casual squad-mate allegiance into something more.

Monique met his eyes. "Hey Corporal, is this brick of a dwarf ever going to wake up?"

"Might take a few days, but he'll come around."

Monique continued checking his IV and EEG monitor. She already knew Wodynians took days to wake up.

She's in denial. It was easier to attend to Dormit than face the reality of what was about to be the greatest mass murder in the history of all eight planets.

Jet drank from a hydration tube to clear his throat. "Do you think the High Council knew this would happen? Is that why they closed all operations on Rodor eight years ago and summoned all our forces to Avalon?"

22

The Exalting

"How should I know, Corp? I'm just a xeno-sociologist . . . with enlistment papers that'll get me massacred." She covered her face with both hands, her dark umber skin a stark contrast to the white mesh sleeves of her electrostim cryosuit. She looked like she was trapped in a web. "This a nightmare."

Monique was two years older than Jet. He was still nineteen, since legally cryosleep didn't count toward age. Outside of cryo, Jet had only aged a year since joining the Believer security force: one six-month tour of duty on Talaks and one on Rodor. But that didn't begin to capture the weirdness. He had traveled a distance of more than thirty light years, which meant that Avalon had lost three decades since he had left. Jet's cryosleeping body had only seen a third of that, thanks to time dilation.

Last Jet had heard, his father worked for Earth's ambassador to Avalon. He had no idea if his father was even alive.

He didn't want to think about it. Jet wouldn't have a chance to save him. He only had orders to extract the High Council.

Monique rummaged through a med kit and stuck herself with a hypodermic needle and then put a shot in Jet's left arm. "Vitamin K, for cryojaundice."

"Thanks." Jet couldn't think of anything else to say. The extermination order and their reckless mission to sneak through the ASP fleet were probably the last things she wanted to talk about. "So," he said, swallowing at the dryness in his throat. "Do you miss Rodor?"

"Not hardly." Monique pulled the needle out. "The giants were becoming unmanageable."

Understatement of the decade.

The amount of armor and ASP-provided weaponry Rodorians could haul was ridiculous. They were like walking tanks. "Yeah, but Avalon is one big hallucinogenic trip. Honestly, I'm not that excited about ground operations on a planet with carnivorous plants."

"And kid-sized pranksters that exhale medical-grade pharmaceuticals."

Jet never trusted himself around Avalonians—never trusted

anyone around them. But Believers had found Avalon first—before ASP. Their queen supported the Believers' quest to find the remaining four undiscovered worlds and, eventually, the Prime Star, home of the Creator of all twelve inhabited worlds.

So he hoped.

But first, he had to get through a planetary siege.

The paradise of Avalon had just become a war zone.

Chapter 3

Dana looked into her grandfather's imploring eyes and took a step back. She couldn't tell him about the bloodstone.

"So you're robbing him?" Togath's sifa shook with displeasure.

Again, that was a question she couldn't answer. "Why did you come?"

"I heard the dogs," Togath said. "I assumed the hunter you were interfering with was lost in the forest, and I came to help him find his way." He gestured to the fallen man. "Dana, this does not look good."

"You don't know what happened," Dana said. "He tried to *kill* me!"

Togath let his arms fall placidly to his sides. "I want to believe you, but I don't understand why a hunter would try to kill you. And why would an atter owl attack him? Do you know what this looks like? *Murder.*"

"Accidents happen," Dana blurted out.

"I just pretended to be a murdering cannibal to scare off those trappers. Those men are going to tell every ranger they see that I'm crazy and you're out of control." It was as though Togath was pulling back curtains at edge of a painting that just kept getting more disturbing. "When the rangers find this . . ."

He was right. It looked like Togath had killed Omren, perhaps with help from a druid who could control owls.

Me. "Maybe they won't find him."

"Somebody will be expecting him to return," Togath gestured to the body. "A friend, a colleague, family. They'll send out a search party and get the rangers involved. It isn't hard to find a body when the carrion crows are circling a carcass. And my cabin is the only home for miles. They'll come with questions—and suspicions, no thanks to the stunt I pulled to get you out of trouble. Never mind the fact that I should report a dead body on my property."

Dana swallowed, difficult given the tightness in her throat. To make matters worse, Sindar's body lay at the base of the cliff, his greeder slain by an arrow. The two bodies were less than a half mile from Togath's cabin, on either side.

Norr's provincial forests were a valuable asset, and its rangers patrolled the wilds with the same strict eye with which the civic guard watched the city proper. But that wasn't even the real problem.

The kazen of Vetas-ka were coming. Omren had said there were six in the forest—five now. They would execute her grandfather if they thought he had interfered.

"If you killed him," Togath said, "we have to go to the authorities."

"No," Dana whimpered as tears leaked into her eyes. Self-control was at a low point, having pushed so much of her will in so short a time. ". . . I didn't kill him." She closed her eyes, wincing at the thought that the owl had hunted the man at her suggestion, just as it did marmar monkeys.

"Dana?" His voice was firm.

She shook her head as tears spilled down her burning cheeks. Dana looked down. A patch of spilt blood next to Omren's head glistened in the starlight, a silent accuser.

Dana clutched the pouch in her hand, squeezing it until the shape of the stone within made an impression in her palm. "Togath, you have to leave. Pack your things quickly and go away for a long time."

Togath's eyes widened.

"I don't want them to find you!" Dana cried. "Togath, please. You must go."

A flash of recognition passed over her grandfather. His eyes grew wide so that she could see the white of them gleaming. He raised a quivering finger and pointed to the pouch. "What is that?"

Dana shook with fear and the passing adrenaline of the fight. "I can't tell you."

The Exalting

But her grandfather's expression told her he already knew. "No. It can't be—is that a bloodstone?"

Dana shook her head.

"Don't lie to me. Where did that come from?"

She had no reason to lie to her own grandfather. "It was a greeder."

"The injured animal?"

Dana nodded. "It was carrying someone named Sindar. He came from the south. He died with the greeder."

Togath ran his hands though his wispy hair. "Sindaren? Why would he take the stone from Shoul Falls?"

"You knew him?" She blinked away her tears and then glanced down at the pouch in her hand as she put together the pieces. "He was bringing this to you." She looked up to meet her grandfather's pallid expression. "Why would he bring a bloodstone to you?"

"For safekeeping, I imagine." In a heavy voice he added, "But I will not take it. Leave it alone, Dana. It will only bring you suffering."

"Leave it where? On the ground? You said you wouldn't take it," Dana cried. "And even if you did, Vetas-ka is coming for it."

"Flames of the Morning Star," Togath whispered. "This is beyond all of us."

"No, Sindar said we couldn't—"

Togath's voice rang out with an energy Dana hadn't seen before. "Vetas-ka is lord of a vast empire spanning the Kalman Desert in Torsica and the far coast."

That was more than half of the other continent on Xahna.

"Well he doesn't belong here," Dana said.

"Drop the stone, Dana," Togath said, his voice sharp and commanding.

Dana barely stopped her fingers as they instinctively uncurled to release the pouch. Instead of dropping it, she pulled it protectively against her chest.

"Walk away. I can do what needs to be done," he said.

"You mean . . . destroy it?"

"You can't take it to Norr and risk all of their lives when Vetas-ka comes." Togath's voice rose in anger, in a way Dana had never heard. "So Sindaren was desperate and gave it to you. Do you think the people of Shoul Falls want their will in the hands of a seventeen-year-old Norrian girl?"

Destroy the stone. Of course, that was the right thing to do. But why hadn't Sindar done that? Togath was oversimplifying. If she destroyed the bloodstone of Shoul Falls, she would have the entire city to deal with, perhaps even the Pantheon. That was as much a death sentence as any choice.

But there was another reason, one she couldn't even bear to think on.

Keep it. Use it. Become the ka.

"Dana. Drop it. Now."

The bloodstone was her chance to escape Norr.

Dana's lateral sifa flared from the back of her head in defiance. "Don't tell me what to do with this. That rider gave it to me. He trusted me to keep it away from Vetas-ka."

"Where will you go? Vetas-ka has many acolytes. You can't hide from his kazen. Dana, you must think this through."

"I can at least return this to Shoul Falls."

"After Sindaren gave his life trying to escape from Shoul Falls with it?" Her grandfather had been adding the kazen suffix "en" to Sindar's name. "Don't you see? No one wants it. No one wants to fight Vetas-ka."

"Then they're cowards."

"But not fools."

"I'm not a fool!" Dana cried.

"If you hold that stone, there will come a time when you are tempted to use it. Consider this, Dana. Once you touch that stone, you will never have the will to release it. It will *own* you. You will feel the pain of those bound to it, their fear, their sorrow, their anger—all of it. And if you try to help them, the work of it will consume you. A stone holder is the keeper of hope. Hope never sleeps. The ka of a city must answer every call."

The Exalting

Togath walked slowly toward her. "What will you do when a baby has a fever and a landslide buries a cottage and a barn burns to the ground all at the same time? Who will you help? Who will you condemn to death? Dana, you can't even bear the pain of an animal in a trap. How will you feel when a soul bound to that stone is consumed by tumors? It never ends. You can't tell me you could ever want that burden."

"I didn't ask for it. But that doesn't mean I'm not brave enough to accept it."

Togath had said he didn't dare take the stone—he would simply destroy it. But Dana was not a coward. There was an entire city whose will was bound to this. She couldn't just ignore that. Making a new bloodstone was impossible. Without a ka they would be defenseless, with no representation at the Pantheon. She held their entire future in her hands.

Perhaps she was their future. Had Togath considered that?

"Dana, that stone will only bring you misery!"

"I'm not giving it up. And there are other Vetas-kazen in the woods. You must go. Go!" Dana turned and ran.

"Dana!"

The branches of pine trees whipped at her as she ran from the scene where her grandfather stood over the corpse of one of the Vetas-kazen.

"I'll take it back. I won't touch the stone," she told herself as she turned west, toward Norr.

Why would the city of Shoul Falls send their stone to Togath? It was a several-day journey across wild country. *Such a risk.*

One thing was certain, if she didn't do something drastic, Vetas-ka would quickly find the cabin and her grandfather.

There was only one way to ensure he didn't.

Destroy the evidence.

She had to destroy the bodies—both of them, before the other kazen found her trail.

But how?

A bit of wind whipped past, tossing Dana's hair and upsetting

29

her sifa. She stopped running and fanned her sifa, feeling the breeze on the air. It came from the north. Her nose detected the faint scent of a distant campfire.

Fire.

That was the solution. Simple and terrible.

Burn the forest.

Even if a forest fire didn't completely destroy the bodies, it would make the area unapproachable from the south for days. And when the fire had burned through, there would be no way to find any tracks or scent in the hundreds of acres of ashes.

If she didn't start the fire, the Vetas-kazen would certainly find the bodies. If not them, the rangers would and the kazen would learn of it. Either end would lead them to Norr. It was the only nearby city.

Once Vetas-ka's enchanters were inside Norr, they could sense the thoughts of anyone trying to hide the stone. They would kill her and take it. Countless generations in Shoul Falls would live under a tyrant ka, their wills bound to sustain his whim.

The impression Sindar had left in her mind was one she could not shake, one she could barely face. Vetas-ka was a monster.

Even at her most irrational, Dana would not risk that.

She swallowed, resigning herself to the task, and turned uphill, forcing her tired legs back up the slope. When she had gone a few hundred yards upwind of the meadow, she stopped. In a clearing, Dana checked her orientation with the polar constellation, the yellow star of Sol at its center.

It could work.

Dana shuddered at the cruelty of burning the forest, and her grandfather's cabin along with it. He was old, though strong, and soon to be homeless for a reason Dana couldn't even explain to herself.

"I'm so sorry."

Tears welling in her eyes, Dana knelt and drew a bit of char cloth from her trouser pocket, placing it in a nest of dry fallen pine needles. She took her flint and a small flat of hardened iron and

30

The Exalting

prepared to strike the blaze that would burn all the evidence of what had happened.

Dana desperately wanted to be free of the traces of the kazen's blood on her clothing and, even more, to be rid of the darkness that had clung to her after Omren's sudden and brutal death.

Dana clenched her fingers together and tried to suppress the shaking. She closed her eyes to block it all out, but images of the fallen kazen adept and the dark pool of blood flashed in front of her eyes. That was the trouble with having a mind like hers. She never forgot a scene, a trail, a face, a name.

The fire could not erase the evidence in her mind of what had truly happened.

Dana had never wanted something so badly as to be saved from that man. She tried to recall the moment when she reached out to the owl. Without even noticing the connection to the horned atter owl, her fear and hatred had hunted him from the sky.

The owl had merely acted on Dana's will. She was responsible.

I killed him.

The guilt was crippling. And the thought of killing so many more animals just to protect herself made it even worse. Dana clenched the striker and swung her hand, knocking away the tinder.

Fighting back tears, she climbed to her feet and ran.

She couldn't light the fire.

The kazen would come. The rangers would find the bodies.

I'm no longer safe in Norr. I'll just gather my things . . . say goodbye to mother and father and Tyrus . . . say goodbye to my friends and leave.

What have I done?

Chapter 4

Kneeling in the maintenance closet near the ion engines, Jet removed the retaining clip on the Tesserian power module's backup battery.

While his standard-issue battery would provide enough current to run the original tactical AI software on his helmet, it wouldn't run *Angel*. A standard-issue battery would overheat and explode. He knew that from experience.

For the mission to rescue the High Council from Avalon, Jet needed all the help he could get. Even if he couldn't get the High Council, he wasn't going leave any of his team behind—not if he could help it anyway.

ASP knows we're coming. We're gonna get ambushed.

He pulled the small cell and waited. Nothing happened.

They won't even know it's gone.

With the other thirty-nine marines already buckled in their folded wingjet frames in the launch bay, there was nobody to watch Jet borrow the power cell. Besides, the risk of a court-martial was worth the extra insurance of a high-powered AI.

Jet replaced the high-capacity power cell with his standard-issue model and closed the panel. He quickly plugged the high-power unit into his tactical armor and stepped carefully past the entrance to the bridge to get to the launch bay.

The gunnery sergeant at the weapons con gave a roar of anger.

Jet turned, expecting to see the squat, muscle-bound Wodynian headed for him and swinging his fat fist. But Wessca was still at his station.

"That's a thermal bloom on the surface!" Wessca called out. He was the only Wodynian on the bridge crew.

"And I just got a massive radiation spike." Gauss, the ship's AI, spoke from an overhead speaker on the bridge. "That's a confirmed

The Exalting

nuclear strike."

Jet's heart suddenly tried to claw its way out of his chest. This wasn't just a targeted ground bombardment of a Believer enclave. Not if they were using nukes.

How many people would ASP kill to convince Avalon to turn over the Believers?

"I have three more confirmed detonations," Wessca roared. "This is a full-scale orbital strike on Avalon. ASP is destroying the planet!"

"Abort." Captain Austin's voice was unmistakable.

"Too late," Gauss said. "We're already committed to a landing trajectory."

"ASP is nuking the entire planet!" Wessca stared in disbelief. "Impossible."

Jet had fully expected ASP to attack Believer ships and communities. But against allies like the Avalonians who were merely sympathetic, Jet had expected a show of force, some high-profile executions, perhaps a military coup.

Why wouldn't they just use a war with the Believers as an excuse to take over the planet's government and key industries? Why destroy it?

It was brutality on a scale no world had ever seen.

Wessca's voice burned with rage. "An entire planet. They're killing everyone!"

The roar of the solid-fuel retro rockets rumbled through the ship. Jet's tactical armor's electrostatically-locking joints kept him from slamming headlong into a panel of critical control circuits. But he still felt like he had a Rodorian giant on his back—and he actually knew what that felt like.

"Gauss, are you insane?" the captain snapped. "That planet is in the middle of a full-scale orbital nuclear strike!"

"We can't just skip off the atmosphere," Gauss said. "That would put us right in the middle of the ASP fleet."

"So, we take our chances on the surface," Captain Austin muttered. "Why am I not comforted?"

"Shall I pray?" Gauss volunteered. "My spare cores can offer the equivalent of several thousand human prayers simultaneously."

"Yes," Captain Austin said. "I think you'd better do that."

Even the ship's AI was praying.

I was right about this mission.

Jet was glad the marines locked in their wingjet frames in the launch bay couldn't hear what the officers on the bridge were saying.

I wish I couldn't.

But he still had a job to do.

As Jet clambered awkwardly toward the launch bay, he turned on his tactical helmet and cued up his tactical AI: Angel.

Jet had found her on the Believer AI exchange and used a fleet accountant's access codes to authorize the purchase.

Angel simultaneously ran defense surveillance and coordinated firing. The AI was nothing less than a tactical genius.

"Jet," Angel toned softly in his ear. "Did you notice your daily radiation exposure level is three times above allowance? Have you been near the ion drives?"

"Um . . ."

His earpiece buzzed, saving him from a highly incriminating conversation. "Corporal, are you coming on this mission or not?" It was Monique.

"Affirmative. Just had to grab something." Jet clambered around the corner to the drop bay, where thirty-nine other marines were strapped into folded wingjet frames and packed like bats on a cave roof.

Jet maneuvered to the only empty frame on the front row and began strapping in.

The other marines on the row were the rest of the Epsilon squad. Monique reached over and toggled the power switch on his frame.

"Thanks."

"About time you showed up." Monique was smart enough to know that he had been up to something, but polite enough to keep quiet about it.

The Exalting

Even so, he still decided against telling her about the ASP attack on the planet. He needed his squad focused.

"Epsilon squad, this is an extraction mission. I doubt ASP knows where this bunker is, but keep your heads on a swivel. I don't want any surprises. There's always the chance of an ambush."

"Ambush—you literally had to say it!" Monique said. He couldn't see her, but a distractingly attractive image of her face flashed in the corner of his heads-up display when she spoke.

Jet checked his microjet fuel level. *Full. Good.* "You guys are so superstitious."

"Yeah? Then how come every time you mention an ambush, we end up in one?" Dormit said. "Explain that, partner." The Wodynian spoke with an off-beat cowboy accent.

"Dormit, haven't I told you to lay off the Westerns?"

"Must-a slipped my mind, amigo."

"The air is high in CO_2, but breathable," Yaris reminded. He was the team's only gangly Caprian. "I highly advise you leave your mask on so your filters are running. Once you get a whiff of this place, you can't trust your thoughts. You'll walk right toward a man-eating fern or jump into a pool of carnivorous lily pads."

"Alpha squad is going to retrieve the High Councillors," Jet added. "Beta squad is backup. Delta and Gamma are setting up a perimeter for the dropship. We are point. That means we take down anything that moves or blinks funny."

"During the ambush," Monique added.

"That's why we're going out first," Yaris said. "Epsilon is the newest and most expendable of the five squads on this dropship."

"Do you always have to pick the most depressing thing to say?" Monique snapped.

"Guys," Jet said. "This isn't about saving ourselves. This is our chance to rescue eight High Councillors trapped on that planet." Without the seers, the Believers would be as blind as ASP to the future.

Creator help the rest of the planet.

The rumble of atmospheric deceleration waned.

35

"Approaching drop altitude." Wessca's gruff voice announced over the tactical net. "May the ax of the Creator clear your path."

Angel displayed an overlay image of the terrain below on Jet's targeting reticle.

"Epsilon, you are go."

The doors of the dropship snapped open. Brilliant blue light flooded Jet's eyes. The force of the dropship's launcher hurled him like a rock from a sling, and barely three seconds later his wingjet had deployed and the mini-jets were whining like flaming twin toddlers to slow his dangerous descent.

Seeing the flight icons of his squad mates blinking in his display, Jet called, "Epsilon, engage afterburn!"

The blue-green waters of Avalon below beckoned as the jets kicked into high gear. His flight leveled, and the team approached the coast at minimal altitude. He wasn't even experiencing the pheromones yet, but he could hardly resist the urge to take a plunge in the turquoise pools that formed along the tropical beach. A moment later he was soaring over the jungle.

Angel highlighted more than thirty potential threats hidden below the canopy. A flock of birds erupted from the forest below. Jet hastily blinked authorization as Angel targeted six birds simultaneously, opting for high-explosive rounds in the hopes of clearing the debris.

"Pull up!" Jet cried as his jet turbines sucked in the remains of several rainbow-feathered and leather-winged Avalonian bat chickens. The tiny turbojets mounted over his shoulders exploded in clouds of black smoke.

Waste of good meat.

The rest of the bat chicken horde was already pecking at his tactical suit.

One managed to hit the wingjet frame emergency release, and another found the button on his wrist to open his visor.

Oh, come on!

Jet sucked in a breath and held it as he tore through the upper branches of the forest like a wrecking ball.

Chapter 5

Under the cover of the forest, Dana traced a route far from the steam-wagon road and its regularly spaced poles holding the messaging lines.

But no amount of distance put her at ease.

Omren was dead. Sindar was dead. She could only hope her grandfather had fled.

But the bloodstone was still in the pouch tied at her waist, within reach. The power of the ka was so close.

Don't touch it.

Dana scampered over a boulder and headed for a ridge to her right. Once over that ridge, she could follow Coward's Creek Canyon straight to Norr.

Where she was headed, bloodstones were forbidden, under penalty of death. She could only hope none of the rangers or civic guards found out what she had.

Traversing the ridge, Dana dropped into Coward's Creek Canyon and followed the trickling stream, not daring to taste its tantalizing water.

Norr's greatest killers were invisible, except under an inverted spyglass. The water-dwelling microbes were deadly.

Sayathi.

Exhausted and thirsty, her steps grew heavy as she thought of what lay ahead. Only one thing was certain.

I have to find Forz.

He was the only person she could trust with something like this. He was her only friend who understood what it was like to be different.

Gifted.

Cursed.

Dana collapsed in a crouch against the dimly glowing white

trunk of a phosphor tree. Wind from the southwest made a rushing sound each time it gusted through the round, quaking leaves of the white-bark trees.

The only thing she could do was return the stone to Shoul Falls.

Then what—go back to a town that doesn't want me?

Only a few days' journey to the south were the tens of thousands of inhabitants of Shoul Falls. Did they know the bloodstone was missing? Did they know Vetas-ka was after it?

They certainly didn't know she had it. And what if they did know? Would they kill her for taking it, or merely demand it back?

What would they do if she used the stone without their permission? A ka's power was sacred in its city. There could be no higher crime.

Don't touch it.

Dana set her jaw and pushed thoughts of the bloodstone back to where dreams fed on neglected ambition.

By morning she would be back at Norr. She had to decide what she was going to do about the bloodstone, and quickly.

———

Dana jerked awake. Heart thudding, she squinted into the morning sunlight cutting through the leaves. She pushed herself up and leaned her back against the tree.

In the daylight, she recognized the spot. Smoke rose from a dozen workshops behind the tall city wall.

I'm a five-minute walk from Norr.

She was a fool to even consider going into the city. If they found the bloodstone on her, who knew what they would do— execute her for heresy?

But she had no change of clothes, no food, no pack, no disguises, and no travel map.

I have no choice.

Dana folded her arms around her waist, trying to quell the

gnawing worry in her stomach. Worst of all, the one person outside the city who could have helped her—her grandfather—was fleeing for his life.

Why did I take it?

There was a simple option. She could just throw it into the river. But that would leave her completely defenseless when the Vetas-kazen found her. If they didn't recognize her, they could still hear her thoughts. If a kazen warlock could stop her at a distance, if she could easily feel animals' pain across a stretch of forest, then powerful enchanters could likely sense thoughts from just as far.

How long could she go without thinking about the stone while trying to keep it hidden?

Impossible.

There were no good options.

Unless she became a ka. Then she could defend herself. She could defend Shoul Falls. They didn't have a ka. That was probably why Vetas-ka was after the stone—an easy prize.

It solved all the problems. But stealing their stone for herself was no different than what Vetas-ka was trying to do.

I'm not like him.

I'm not.

She had to return it.

Steps sounded through the underbrush.

Dana's heart pounded as she searched routes to escape. *Please don't be another kazen..*

"Dana, there you are." Forz pushed through a thicket. A clever smile stretched across his pointed jaw.

"Hi, Forz." She hoped she didn't look as terrible as she felt.

Forz's inferior sifa flared in friendship. He brushed his wavy, ash blond hair out of his eyes and looked down at her with his curious, pale blue eyes. Instead of his usual workshop smock and gloves, he wore bandeerskin trousers for hiking in brush and a gray wool shirt. "It's not the first time I've said it, but I'm glad to see you're still alive."

The canteen slung over his shoulder drew the interest of her

Dan Allen

parched mouth.

"Where were you?" he asked.

"At my grandfather's."

Forz crouched down beside her and offered his canteen. "Didn't you take water with you?"

"I did." Dana said hastily. "But it's gone." She had left her tin canteen beside the tree with the hanging trap.

Dana forced a smile and drank greedily from Forz's canteen before finding his eyes again.

Forz had always been close. But there was more than just friendship, Dana was almost certain of it. Longer gazes. Longer pauses.

Was it her black hair that so intrigued him? There were a least a few other girls in Norr with hints of darker Torsican heritage. But most boasted the pale features of pure North Aesican bloodlines.

Perhaps someday he would get up the courage to do something about his interest.

"So . . . what are you doing in the woods this early in the morning?" Dana asked. "Don't you have any mechanodrons to build?" She hoped his master had run out of orders and given him the day off. She needed someone to talk to.

"I was sent to find you."

Dana gulped. That was a never a good thing. "How did you find me?"

Forz pointed east. "Drew a line north from the point the trappers said they ran into you over to Coward's Creek Canyon and then traced it down the fall line."

Trappers. So that's what it was about. *I don't have time to deal with this.*

Forz put his hands on his hips. "What did you do this time?"

Dana climbed to her feet, putting on an offended look. "You don't think *I* robbed those trappers?"

"I don't know." Forz ran his hand through his hair. He was in a tough spot. She had done this to him before. "But I'm sure there will be a lot of questions for you from Captain Mol."

40

The Exalting

"You wouldn't turn me in just for . . . for saving a nox? It wasn't even very big."

"I'm just here to escort you back," Forz said. "Once the trappers accused you of raiding their traps, the chancellor sent out a party to find you."

"You're really turning me in!" Dana gasped. "I can't believe this."

"It's not my doing," Forz said. "I have to take you back. Chancellor's orders."

I can't go in!

Forz was so idiotically honest that he couldn't even see that "just doing his job" would land her in prison, which would be virtually the same as handing the stone over to the Vetas-kazen searching for it in the forests. She would be helpless in prison. And a few simple questions from the kazen to the civic guard would lead them straight to her.

"What's in that purse?" Forz asked.

Oh, why did he have to notice? Dana could have punched Forz in the nose, but he would have just blocked or dodged or done something else infuriating. Dana closed a hand on the pouch at her waist protectively. "It's money . . . for some of my grandfather's debts in town."

"So, you *did* visit his cabin last night," Forz concluded.

"Of course, what else would I be doing?"

"Raiding traps. Why else would you be trying to sneak back to Norr on a game trail in Coward's Creek Canyon rather than taking the trade road?"

"Well, I did hear Torsican hounds," Dana said, scraping for something that would draw his attention away from her. "I didn't want to be anywhere near that kind of hunt."

Forz nodded, his considerable intellect quick at piecing together the facts. "Nobody from Norr hunts with Torsican hounds. They spook the thunder bison."

"Dana!" shouted a voice from only few feet away.

Dana's breath seized in her chest like glacier water had just been poured down her shirt. Then she realized it was just Brista.

Dana's best friend was the daughter of Warv the cleric.

Brista stepped awkwardly off a large fallen tree and looked up to see Forz. "What are you doing out here . . . with Forz?" That sort of question was only to be expected. She had recently become a competitor for Forz's attention.

Unlike Dana's pocketed trousers, Brista wore a summer dress, although she covered her shoulders with a matching blue shawl to ward off the morning cool.

"I'm always in the forest," Dana said. "What are you doing out here?"

"Out for a walk," Brista said as convincingly as a kid with her hand in a bag of fresh tarberry hand cakes. In fact, she had a satchel in one hand that looked like it was full of just that. She smiled at Forz.

So, she doesn't know anything about the search for me. She was just following Forz . . . hoping to catch him alone in the woods.

But Dana felt more relieved than annoyed. She wasn't going to be able to keep a secret from Brista anyway.

She can help. Brista knew practically everything from the library at the chapel—everything legal, anyway.

A year younger, Brista was shorter than Dana and smaller in all things woman: chest, hips, and lips. Her hair was twice as long as Dana's and twice as likely to have a flower pinned in it.

Wearing flowers—who invented that anyway?

Brista's eyes turned to the coin purse tied to Dana's waist. "What's in there?"

"Trouble for anyone who asks," Dana said, turning away.

At least it was true.

"Is it your time of transition or something?" Brista said tersely. "You're being awfully snippy."

"What if it is?" Dana said, even though her eighty-two-day cycle wasn't halfway finished.

"Then you're out of sync with the moons, which means you're very sick, because all druids synchronize with the moon transits. I

The Exalting

read about it."

"Oh, can we please talk about something else?" Dana muttered.
"Like what happened to me last night?"

Brista smiled. "Great. We can talk about it over breakfast. I
brought tarberry hand cakes."

Dana's mouth started watering instantly. She took one right out
of Brista's satchel and wolfed an enormous bite, giving out a sigh of
satisfaction.

She took another bite into the center of the sweet and warm,
buttery pastry and spoke as she chewed. "You are a ka-send, Brista."
Dana reached for another.

"Not so fast." Brista pulled her satchel away and offered one to
Forz.

Forz sat down on a fallen phosphor tree trunk. Dana sat on
another mossy trunk nearby. The thin fallen tree made a poor chair,
but it was better than the dew-laden grass and leaves littering the
forest floor. Brista sat suspiciously close to Forz, who had his eyes
fixed on Dana. He hadn't even bitten into his hand cake.

"So, what happened?" Brista asked. "You look awful."

"Well—" Dana took a bite of her cake to give herself more
time to think. There was no use trying to keep the secret to herself.
Alone, she was as doomed as Sindar, the man who had brought the
stone nearly to her grandfather's cabin. It was luck Sindar had not
reached it. If he had, her grandfather would be dead. Omren would
have found him and killed him for the stone.

"Well . . . what?" Brista said, offering another cake—one she
should have reserved for herself—as a sort of bribe for information.

Dana took it and stowed it in her jacket pocket as she finished
chewing her first cake. "After my grandfather rescued me from
some trappers . . ."

"She was raiding hanging traps," Forz explained with his mouth
full.

Brista nodded but said nothing. She knew why Dana did it.

Dana swallowed. "I found a dying man in the forest. He
entrusted to me a bloodstone that I'm to keep away from a

43

usurping Torsican ka."

Brista gave a giggle and looked at Forz, whose face showed a kind of disbelief and expression of betrayal in one. "That's a joke, right?"

"And then this kazen warlock tried to kill me. So . . . I killed him instead."

"Dana, are you being serious?"

"I ran away." Dana spread her hands, stretching the webbing between her fingers, and gripped her knees. "And then you found me."

"Okay," Brista said. "Either you are telling the truth—in which case, I'm totally freaked out—or you hit your head really hard and you need medicine, in which case, I'm sort of medium freaked out. Which am I supposed to be?"

Dana met Brista's concerned gaze. "Well, I'm freaked out, too."

Forz's head turned slightly, taking in the leather pouch at Dana's waist. Then his eyes moved further down and froze. "Hey, you've got blood on your trousers—a lot of it."

"And you've got a cut on your nose," Brista added, her nose wrinkling. "What really happened last night? Did you get in a fight with a tree?"

"I already told you," Dana said.

"You killed someone—for a bloodstone?"

Shame, it seemed, came calling eventually, and always at the worst moment. Dana's self-esteem plummeted. She wished she could crawl into a hollow log like the low scamper she felt like.

"By the Creator . . ." Brista whispered. She reached out, without taking her horrified gaze off Dana, and grabbed Forz's arm.

"Is that your blood or the kazen's?" Forz asked. His face seemed to have lost what remained of its already pale color.

"Could be blood from the greeder the kazen shot with an arrow. It was carrying a man my grandfather knew from Shoul Falls. His name was Sindar. He was an enchanter."

Brista moved closer and knelt on the ground in front of Dana. She put her hands on Dana's and looked into her eyes, as

The Exalting

if determined to find truth or lies in them. "You say he was an enchanter. How do you know?"

"He touched me and I felt peaceful, even though his greeder was dying right in front of me."

"You can't even stand it when people kill spinning scorpions," Brista said.

"Yes, that's because I can *feel* it," Dana stated.

"So can I," Forz added. "But I think it actually hurts her. For me it just . . . tingles."

"Must be the same for Tyrus," Dana said. "Killing animals never bothered him."

"What about the person who attacked you?" Forz asked.

Dana's voice become hollow, her eyes distant. "His hounds followed my trail."

"A kazen?" Brista asked.

Dana nodded. She didn't want to talk about the confrontation, but now that she was talking, it seemed almost impossible to know where to draw the line between facts that mattered and things that would merely tear her heart or get her in more trouble. "Servant of a demon named Vetas-ka," she began at last. "He wants the bloodstone of Shoul Falls."

Brista snapped her fingers. "Vetas-ka. I've read all about him. He was the one who stopped the battle at Shoul Falls—froze the entire battle field in a ka-made ice blizzard. He saved the entire city and kept the peace."

"That was over a hundred and fifty years ago," Forz said.

"The exalted live a long time," Brista noted.

Forz shifted his weight forward and then back. He seemed unsettled. "Yeah, still . . ."

"He wasn't keeping the peace last night," Dana said. "His kazen warlock pinned me to the ground and tried to shoot me through with an arrow."

"How did you get away?" Brista interupted eagerly.

"A horned atter owl defended me," Dana said, not admitting the possibility that she had prompted the act.

"An owl?" Brista said.

"Rear claws," Forz explained, "Thrust right into the joint between his neck and skull. Instant paralysis . . . and a lot of blood." His mouth fell slack with astonishment. "You summoned it?"

Dana forced herself to nod. "Yes."

"And you defeated a full kazen?" Forz said. "Dana, your power is far stronger than anyone in Norr thinks."

"I can't eat this." Brista put the remaining portion of her hand cake back into the satchel, her face paler than ever.

"The important thing," Dana said, "is me getting this stone far away from Norr, before Vetas-ka's acolytes close in. They could put the city under some kind of siege, or worse—start executing folks until somebody told them where I was." She could try to run away, back the way Sindar had come, but she risked crossing the kazen. The food Brista brought reminded her that running away without supplies was a bad idea. The problem had to be thought out.

A warbler that had been pecking about near Dana's feet suddenly lifted its head and took to wing.

Dana jumped to her feet and spun around.

Captain Mol, flanked by four burly rangers, pointed at Dana. "There she is."

The men seemed to spring at her from every direction at once. Strong arms hoisted her to feet.

"Stop!" Dana cried.

The thick-mustached captain of the rangers looked away disinterestedly as she was forcibly marched back toward the city.

"Forz, I expected you a half hour ago," Mol said. "You said you figured she was close by."

"Er," Forz choked on his words.

Dana cranked her head around to Brista standing beside Forz, her hands clasped contritely together.

"There were hunting dogs," Dana called out. "Tell them about the dogs."

"Save it for the magistrate," said the ranger holding her right

The Exalting

arm. "Now move." He jerked her toward the city.

"I can walk on my own."

"You've caused enough trouble walking about on your own," said the ranger, whose hands felt like steel shackles on her upper arm.

"You're hurting me," she said. Her mind was racing. When they got to Norr, which was only a few hundred yards away, she could be stuck in the guardhouse for hours, or even imprisoned if they believed the trappers' story over hers.

Which was likely.

And the Vetas-kazen would show up eventually—possibly by the end of the day. What would they find? A city without a ka. Some talk in a pub about a girl causing trouble in the forest—the same forest where Omren was chasing Sindar, the forest where they both died.

That would certainly get their attention.

Being trapped was the worst possible situation.

The problem was she was being escorted by four rangers. They were far stronger than she was, and older. Perhaps they weren't as attuned to the forest—but what good had that done her? They had snuck up without her even noticing.

So near the city, few animals took alarm at humans approaching. It was a bad scenario for a druid adept.

It was only going to get worse.

If she could put them at ease, they would be off their guard. She might find an opening and escape.

"I don't know why you are all so worked up about finding me." Dana tried to sound calm. "I'm just fine in the woods, as you ought to know by now."

The rangers said nothing, doubtless counting the number of times they had been called by thwarted trappers and hunters to find the druid who had cheated them of their fair game.

I've got to get out of here . . . or I'm dead.

Dana's eyes moved quickly from one guard to the next. A ranger walked directly ahead of her, his leather boots making almost no sound as they walked briskly over the earth. His trousers were buckskin, and his jacket was fur-lined gray bison wool. His black hat was low, with a wide brim. The two rangers that held her arms were identically attired, and ostensibly the ranger who guarded the rear. All had belts securing a small hatchet, a large hunting knife, a pair of spotting lenses, rope, and several pouches, likely with flints, fishing hooks, twine, or medicines.

She couldn't will animals to attack them, regardless of how adept she was. She simply didn't have enough will to summon an animal large enough to overcome four of them.

Maybe a nox?—as if the sloths that occasionally snatched napping birds from the trees would be any use.

The pouch bounced at her waist, a reminder of a source of will thousands of times more powerful.

No. Don't touch it.

The sound of rushing water grew. Ahead, a fallen tree spanned the river. It was the only bridge for half a mile. The next crossing was the trade road.

Please take the shortcut.

The lead ranger continued in the direction of the river and finally stopped at the makeshift bridge. He whirled around and, before Dana could object, lashed her hands together with triple twisted cord from his belt.

"What are you doing?" she gasped. "Stop it! I'm not a criminal."

"I don't want you taking a plunge," the ranger said. With the chance of sayathi in the water, he had good reason to avoid wanting to go in after her.

"Well, it's not like I'm going to fall off the log," Dana said, fulling intending to.

Chapter 6

As Jet fell through the canopy of the dense Avalonian jungle, Angel gracefully highlighted all the branches which were about to clobber him and indicated hits with flashing icons on his armor icon—as if he couldn't already tell that he had major contusions on his shin, shoulder, and hip.

There were shouts of panic on the tactical net from other marines calling out as their engines failed.

Pain injections commenced before he rolled to his feet on the forest floor.

"Epsilon, report," Jet said, as he tore biting, scratching bat chickens from his armor and dispatched them with clinical precision using his sidearm.

Waste of really good meat.

"Four still in formation," Monique reported. "Landing zone in sight."

"Great," Jet said. At least some of his squad had made it past the crazed bat chickens. "Monique, take the lead." She would have to beat a path to the bunker with half the team.

"Ophelia's gone!" Dormit raged. "She's dead—hit a branch. I can't even reach her body."

"And Yaris?" Jet called, pushing back thoughts of Ophelia and memories of their time together on Rodor.

"Looks like he's holding his breath until he can fix his visor," Angel volunteered.

The high-pitched screech of mini-turbines overhead announced the arrival of the remaining four squads.

At least his squad had done their job of flushing out any enemies. But half his squad had failed to even reach the dropship's landing zone.

One was dead.

Losing a squad member brought pain he knew—pain he couldn't afford to feel.

Right now he had to secure the landing zone for the extraction of the High Council from their underground bunker.

A sudden urge to lean down and devour one of the bat chicken carcasses washed over Jet. *Oh, not now.*

Jet turned, trying to spot whatever was invading his mind with foreign smells.

"Jet, it appears you are standing under a netter tree. Its blossoms are fanning," Angel noted. "You may be experiencing abnormal—look out!" She highlighted several hinge points as a sweeping branch with rake-like twigs collapsed down on him like a Rodorian with missing kneecaps—something he also had experience with.

Angel suggested incendiary grenades, and Jet obliged, launching two into the tree's highest branches.

"Is that you torching the forest, Jet?" called the Alpha squad leader. "Quit messing around and get to the rally point."

Jet rolled free of the flaming netter tree. He didn't have any of the necessary chemical cues to tell the tree to leave him alone.

The spritely Avalonians made homes in the netter trees and could use chemical signals to command them to attack.

Wait a minute . . .

Bat chickens assaulting armored soldiers.

Uninhabited netter trees attacking.

Jet had lived on Avalon for years and never had either of those things happen to him. Let alone both. It didn't add up.

Unless . . . it's an ambush.

Jet toggled his radio. "All teams, be advised. We may have Avalonian traitors in the landing zone. Repeat, traitors in the—"

Screams sounded in his earpiece, and a moment later several blasts reached him through the jungle.

"Alpha team is down," Wessca reported. "Beta team, you are go."

"Epsilon on the ground, engaging hostiles," Monique reported.

The Exalting

"Oh Earth—they have Talaksians!" Her voice cut out in a hiss of static.

"Orcs," Jet cursed under his breath. The mountain-dwelling creatures of the larger outer world in the Talaks-Dayal system were completely bulletproof.

Monique's team needed him now.

"Dormit, Yaris," Jet called. "Form up and move out!"

Footsteps sounded through the trees as his other crash-landed squad mates came alongside him. As they ran toward the landing zone, various scents passed through his nostrils, causing odd sensations from numb lips to elation, but none took full hold of his mind.

"Five hundred meters to landing zone," Angel said, speaking from Jet's helmet speaker to the members of the squad. "Multiple enemies approaching. This appears to be an ASP strike force. Expect orcs to draw your attention and faelings to attack from the trees. The humans will likely be running attack drones."

"What about Rodorians?" Dormit asked.

"Too big to hide," Yaris said, gliding alongside Jet, seeming to barely make an effort. He was six foot five and weighed only about sixty kilos on a good day. "Obviously they know the High Councillors are here, but can't find the bunker."

"I estimate enemies will be in view in less than twenty seconds," Angel said. "I need more eyes."

"Deploying tactical drones." More than a dozen tiny drones lifted off Yaris, transitioning from barely visible seams in his tactical armor into tiny flying eyes in the sky.

So far, the path was surprisingly clear.

With the added surveillance from the minidrones, suddenly Angel was highlighting foes on Jet's helmet display, like tags on pointy shoes at a Caprian market. They were everywhere.

"Take cover," Jet crouched behind a tree with Dormit by his side, breathing heavily. A few yards away, Yaris stood against a tree with wise strut-like roots that fanned out at the base.

Machine-gun fire strafed the forest, obliterating tree limbs with high-explosive rounds and sending curling Avalonian leaves raining to the forest floor.

"I thought the fae were on our side," Dormit said.

"But obviously one of them sic'd those bat chickens on us," Jet said. "Those birds weren't trying to get away, like a flock scattering. They were *attacking*."

Yaris prepped his flamethrower. "ASP money has a way of swaying loyalty."

A moment later, a hail of high-velocity shells ran down from the class-5 dropship in twin streams. It circled the landing zone, pivoting with the shielded, tilting fan rotors in its short, armored wings.

Jet unshouldered his long-barreled high-velocity firearm. "The dropship is drawing their attention. Now's our chance."

Two huge explosions rocked the wood.

"Watch for booby traps!" Wessca roared over the tacnet.

"Beta team is not reporting," a marine called. "Delta is pinned down. Any remaining forces, secure the landing zone!"

Jet peeled out from behind the tree and right into the path of a charging Talaks orc. The juggernaut didn't even bother wearing armor. Even its glassy eyes were bulletproof.

Angel suggested an alternate target: a tree branch where a four-foot-tall fae traitor couldn't hide from her thermal vision. Jet raised his sidearm and fired a high-explosive round that severed the branch and sent it crashing down into the path of the orc.

The eight-foot orc leapt—a typical reaction for a mountain predator accustomed to jumping from clifftop to clifftop. Jet rolled underneath and fired a blast of quick-setting hull sealant that shrink-wrapped the orc's feet together in a sheet of polymetricallybonded nanofibers.

The Talaksian behemoth landed quite unceremoniously on top of the scrambling faeling.

Two shots, two down.

But before the epoxy could fully harden, the tusked orc managed to tear free.

52

The Exalting

"Oh boy."

It flexed its clawed hands and turned its beady eyes on Jet.

Orcs lived in brutal mountain landscapes on Talaks, where they were the top predator. Jet was next on the menu.

Chapter 7

Dana's plunge in the river lasted only a few minutes. A ranger downstream plucked her out. With her partially webbed hands bound, Dana wasn't much of a swimmer. After enduring a pointless lecture about the dangers of sayathi microorganisms in open water—Dana had obviously kept her mouth shut while she swam—the rest of the day had been spent in a cold, dark cell. At least the river had washed the incriminating blood off her clothes.

Finally, she was sentenced and sent home.

It wasn't Dana's first time being arrested. She'd illegally rescued animals from hunter's traps on numerous occasions. But this time, Chancellor Orrek had levied a punishment he knew she would hate worse than sitting alone in a jail: counseling from Goodman Warv.

Daily.

While not as vulnerable as being in prison, Dana would still be a sitting target if the kazen came when she was stuck in the chapel with Warv.

Orrek had been right about the punishment, though. She would rather a public flogging or something barbaric like that than a daily guilt trip.

She had to report to the chapel the following day.

In the meantime, every hour that passed could bring the Vetas-kazen closer.

Six kazen were in the forest, Omren had said. How far could the remaining five be? Were they already in the city?

I wish I could make the Norrians understand I'm not a problem that needs fixing. Dana shoved her hands into the fur-lined pockets of her thick-spun bison-hair jacket. She trudged ahead along the familiar route from her family's cottage on the steeply sloped north side of the city toward the chapel, doing her best to mimic the big-bellied chancellor in his breathy, condescending manner.

The Exalting

"It's quite simple, young Dana. You must stop trying to use the Creator's powers. Just stop feeling pain. Stop caring about innocent animals. Stop being yourself. You see it's quite easy when you try. You just stop it! Stop it! And then we all live in peace."

Dana imagined poking him with a needle in his rotund belly just to see if he popped.

"It's quite easy to get rid of a belly, Mr. Chancellor. You just pop it! Pop it! And then we live in peace."

Reaching the flat ground in the commerce district, she rounded the big black iron boiler of a trader's steam-wagon and spotted Forz turning into Kernic Alley. She waved to him from across the street.

Forz whistled, and his gangly mechanodron stopped and set down a wheelbarrow full of unpolished sayathenite crystals. Seven feet tall, the two-legged, wooden-limbed, blind contraption was rigged with rhynoid vines controlled by electrical signals from sayathenite crystals.

Forz's mechanodron was called "Blamer," so named because it was trained for use in a mine, where its catalytic sensor detected methane leaks. It had the entertaining habit of pointing in the direction of anyone who farted.

Dana scurried across the high street to her friend, who pushed his long, wavy blond hair out of his eyes. "What's the verdict?"

"Confinement to the city and counseling—daily," Dana grumbled.

"At least you didn't get prison."

"Won't matter if the Vetas-kazen find me. Listen, I need a favor. Can you make me a mechanodron to punch the chancellor out?"

Forz grimaced. "I'm not sure the chancellor would allow me to punch him repeatedly just to train a mechanodron on how it's done."

"You could always just start and see how far you get."

The corner of Forz's cheek turned up. Then he whistled a low note, and Blamer lifted the wheelbarrow and lumbered forward up the side street toward his workshop. The electrostrictive plant fibers that wound over its wooden frame-skeleton contracted rhythmically as they sucked down sugary syrup from two glass jars on its shoulders. "You know, Dana, I'm not entirely convinced you don't need this counseling."

"This city needs counseling." Dana leaned back against the wall of a bookkeeping house. "Forz, what am I going to do? I can't stay here. It's not safe."

"Yeah, but they won't let you past the gates."

Dana shoved her hands in her pockets. "I really do want to leave. But you're here, and Brista. And what if I ran out of money or food and had to crawl back to Norr and ask my parents for help?"

"You always find a way to get into trouble." Forz looked her in the eyes. Then he smiled. "And you always find a way out." He gestured to the side street where his workshop was located. "I'd . . . better get going."

Dana waved goodbye with her fingers, as he hurried to catch up to his mechanodron.

Why did we both end up in a place like Norr?

Dana watched him until he reached the workshop. Then she turned and crossed the square, avoiding the chapel like a quarantined house.

She would have rather been stuck with Forz for the afternoon, watching him strap himself to a new mechanodron and repeat the same motions over and over, until the acoustoelectric sayathenite crystal picked up the pattern and the mechanodron could pump a forge bellows or pull taffy by itself.

As Dana trudged up to the miner's district at the west end of town, she consoled herself with the fact that neither the rangers nor the civic guard had found the bloodstone.

It was her ticket to a new life.

Could I really become a ka?

An approaching woman crossed the street. After passing Dana, she crossed back.

Dana tried to ignore it.

Another Norrian waited in her doorway for Dana to pass,

The Exalting

avoiding any eye contact, her sifa flat against her neck, as if Dana were a predator. Only after Dana was headed away did she step onto the street with her child.

As if what I have is a plague.

A block later, the tender at the midtown water station looked about as she approached, as if surprised there was no civic guard shepherding her.

How dare the freak walk about on her own?

Hunger and a growing sense of irritation only heightened her awareness of the way other Norrians acted around her.

Being a druid defined her. She could not change it any more than a Xahnan could change their eye color. And she wasn't just any druid. She was the best anyone had ever heard of—and that without any proper training. At least that was what Forz had heard. Nobody said such things to her. It would only encourage her aberrant behavior.

It disgusted her. Norr was supposedly a paragon of virtue, a place where everyone was equal.

Adepts like Dana only reminded Norrians how wrong they were.

A flock of pigeons, stirred by Dana's temper, fluttered away, straight past the startled face of an old man. He swung his cane at the harmless birds.

How dare you hit them?

Dana wondered if she could convince one of the pigeons to come back and poop on the man's bald scalp. But this was too much for her hunger-weakened resolve. Dana's anger bled out, and she trudged home in a mild stupor.

"Dana!" Her mother's cheerful voice rang out through the open kitchen window, and Dana felt herself wrapped in a big hug as she came through the kitchen doorway. "You look terrible, darling."

"They're making me go to counseling every day!"

"Yes, we know, dear." Her father took his boots off the small kitchen table. He avoided looking at her. It was a subtle thing, but it said everything.

He was ashamed of her, so ashamed and disappointed he didn't even bother to lecture her about trying to free the nox. Dana hadn't expected that. And she hadn't expected it to hurt as much as it did. She felt like turning around and running back out.

"Have some tea." Her mother brought her a warm cup with steaming herbal tea.

"Marit kept the cooking fire on for you," her father finally said.

Was he saying she was costing them money? It certainly wasn't a welcome home.

Dana mumbled a barely audible thanks as she set her cup on the wooden table, collapsed into a wobbly chair, and let her head bang down on the table.

"I don't belong here." Dana imagined her parents exchanging one of their looks. She stared at the floor, and her sifa trembled as if she were about to cry.

"Give me a break."

"Go away, Tyrus." Dana didn't even look up to see her brother's scoffing expression.

"You're such a selfish brat."

"Tyrus, mind the fire, would you?" her mother said placidly. "We'll need another log tonight."

Dana tilted her head to see her lanky older brother lean forward and toss a log into the fireplace of the room that served as kitchen, dining, and gathering room. "See, she doesn't even deny that she was robbing the trappers." His long hair dangled near the flame. Dana hoped the ends would catch fire.

No such luck. She had no control over elements like the Vetaskazen who had attacked her.

At the thought of the episode, Dana's stomach turned.

Blood glistening on the ground. Omren's body lying with his head askew.

Dana shook her head, trying to rid her mind of the images.

"I saved you some mushroom and leek soup," her mother said. She placed a bowl in front of Dana.

"Thanks." Dana shoveled a spoonful into her mouth and

The Exalting

swallowed, trying to keep down whatever little was already in there. Her stomach was unsettled, anxiety outweighing hunger.

"Do you want to talk about it?"

Dana ignored her mother. Instead, Dana's hand drifted to the pocket of her vest. She fingered the pouch she had hidden there and its faceted crystal that never left her side, now feeling the burden of keeping it a secret from even her family.

Then the idea of just telling them what happened willed its way to the surface of Dana's thoughts. It suddenly seemed so logical, so simple. So right.

Dana could hardly believe that after doing everything possible to keep the bloodstone a secret, she suddenly felt like just letting it out.

What's wrong with me?

Then it was clear, just as when she had touched Sindar. Thoughts were there that weren't her own.

She looked over to see her mother's hand on her shoulder.

No. She's an enchantress!

Dana jerked away from her mother. The feeling of wanting to tell faded as quickly as the smile on her mother's face. Both of them wore looks of shock and disbelief.

My mother is an enchanter adept.

Dana searched her memory. Had her mother manipulated her in the past?

She's an adept, too. She should understand—and she shouldn't try to force me to share my secrets!

Dana stared in her mother's eyes, threatening to reveal her mother's own secret. Her mother's expression begged her not to.

"I don't belong here," Dana said finally. She broke off the gaze. "None of us do."

"And where would we go?" her father said. "Mechanodron sayathenite is abundant in caves above Norr. We supply half of the entire continent's needs. And miners are hungry. They need warm clothing."

"Animal skins." Dana shuddered. She picked up the spoon and

stirred the soup, the churning matching her stomach's grumbling. "Thunder bison hair is just as warm. And it grows back. People are too lazy to train a mechanodron to run a loom."

"It's not that simple," her father said. "You think you know everything. But you don't." She was attacking his trade. Of course he would be defensive about it. Although when it came to killing animals, she understood far more about it than he ever would.

"Romus, could you light a candle?" It was obviously her mother's attempt to defuse the brewing argument. She turned back to the wash basin, filled from a copper pipe that came down from the roof's rain-collecting troughs—no unbound Norrian could risk a drink of water from a river or well that might be tainted by sayathi.

Nearby, Tyrus leaned against the rough-cut wooden wall of the home and stared at the fire. And for a moment, while her father rummaged for a match, there was peace.

"Why did you go to grandpa's?" Tyrus asked suddenly.

"Because I wanted to."

"You wanted to be alone with grandpa because you love him so dearly? Yeah, right. You were out there raiding traps. You know the trappers only have a few weeks to get grizzled fur."

"I had things to discuss."

Her parents exchanged a glance.

Tyrus unwound a cord around his wrist and then rewound it. "You think you're better than the rest of us."

"Different," Dana said curtly. "Yes." Tyrus knew she freed trapped animals. He had seen her do it. And he knew Dana could feel the animals' pain—she was far more powerful a druid than him.

Perhaps he was jealous. Like her father, he prided himself on his hunting. In a way, she was his enemy. Getting her to admit what she had done would be his victory. It would make her a criminal and him the one in the right.

Tyrus had no idea what she had been through. He hadn't run for his life. He hadn't felt Sindar's touch as he died.

60

The Exalting

They're counting on me, Dana thought. *I can't just ignore their plight. I have to return the stone.*

And then what? Return to Norr?

Within her pocket, Dana fingered the bloodstone in its pouch. This was a curse, yes. But also a chance, a call.

"Dana—"

"Just leave me alone."

"Not until you admit you were stealing from the trappers."

She had almost died, and all he cared about was proving her wrong. He was her brother. Didn't he care about *her?*

"You want to know what really happened in the forest?" Dana gripped her spoon like a weapon. "I was hunted. I ran for my life. I was choked and pinned to the ground by a warlock. He tried to shoot me with an arrow!"

Her parents looked as though they couldn't decide whether she was being completely irrational or whether they thought she was seriously traumatized.

Tyrus narrowed his eyes. "A warlock adept in the forest tried to kill you? Why?"

"Because I'm powerful." It was mostly true. Her abilities had led her to Sindar. No druid in Norr could sense an animal's pain half a mile away. No druid Dana had ever heard of could do that.

"What were you doing in the forest?" Tyrus asked.

"Trying to save someone he had shot."

"Did you tell this to the chancellor?" her father asked. His face was ashen. Her mother gripped a hand towel with both hands. Her sifa trembled.

"Of course I didn't," Dana said.

"Why not?" Tyrus demanded. "If there's a killer in the province—"

"Because I killed him!"

Her dad's expression turned totally incredulous. How could his daughter do something like that?

Dana could scarcely believe she had said it. But the truth was there, boiling within her, desperate to get out. Killing someone, even to protect herself, was like nothing she had ever experienced. It was like she was being eaten from inside by her perfect memory of it. Perhaps it wasn't so much a confession as it was a plea for understanding.

Her answer was silence. Were they afraid—or just confused?

"They were coming for Togath," Dana added.

Her mother put a hand to her mouth, as if she were about to say something.

Ah. There it is. There was a reason Sindar was trying to find her grandfather, and her mother knew it.

"Why did grandpa leave Shoul Falls?" Dana demanded. "Why were they looking for him?"

Her father raised a hand to wave off her mother's answer. "I'm afraid we can't explain that."

They were always shutting her out. How could not knowing protect her?

A sense of finality settled over Dana. She could never come sifa-to-sifa with them, not completely.

"I know more than you think," Dana whispered. She looked at her mother and then her father, hoping her bluff would loosen their lips.

Tyrus inclined his head. It was obvious he wanted to know as well. "Then you tell us. Why did Togath come to Norr?"

Dana couldn't answer.

He shrugged at Dana's silence. "See, she's making stuff up again."

After all that, he was just blowing her off—after everything she had said.

"Did I make this up?" Dana drew the pouch with the stone out of her pocket and slammed it on the table. She placed both hands on either side of the precious object, making sure nobody would attempt to take it.

Tyrus turned his hands up. "Wow. It's great, Dana—what is it, a rock?"

Dana's eyes turned first to her mother, then her father. "It was

The Exalting

brought from Shoul Falls by a dying kazen. You tell me."

Silence . . . and fear flickering in her parents' eyes.

"Well I know what it is." Dana shoved the shrouded bloodstone back into her pocket and ran out of the house.

Her father called frantically, dashing after her to the door.

Dana turned, all three rows of sifa flaring in rage. "I don't belong here. And I can't stay any longer. I'm putting you all at risk."

"Let her go." Her mother's voice was drenched with emotion, a desperate sort of finality. This day had been a long time coming.

"But Marit, if that—"

"It's not our concern, Romus."

"But she's our child."

Their arguing voices faded as Dana ran down the street. Her resolve solidified the farther she ran.

I'm not coming back.

Chapter 8

Jet searched the forest for any path of escape. The Talaksian between him and his team dripped with the acid sweat that only ran when its body was superheating for a berserker attack.

"Oh boy."

"Let me at it!" Dormit charged at the orc from behind.

"Dormit, get clear. That creature will tear you apart!" Yaris called.

"He may be bulletproof," Dormit said, "but his bones aren't laced with iron. Geronimo!"

The orc spun and backhanded the charging dwarf that was only half its size.

Jet winced at the blow that would have left a human unconscious, or possibly in more than one piece.

Dormit rolled twice and came up on his feet. He screamed a challenge in Wodynian that was apparently rather vile because Angel said, "Oh my. That is rather inappropriate."

The orc leapt and came down at the much smaller dwarf with a hammer-fisted blow, intent on pounding him into the ground.

But this time Dormit was ready. He swung his fist at the same time, meeting the orc's blow knuckle-on-knuckle.

The crack was so loud, Jet could almost feel it. "Holy angels of the Zion!" Jet cried. "He just broke its hand."

The orc reared back, screaming as it cradled its arm.

Growing up on a planet with more than twice Earth's gravity gave the Wodynians exceptional bone density. The Talaksian may as well have tried to punch a rock.

The orc swung its gargantuan leg and kicked at Dormit, who ducked the blow and launched into a kamikaze headbutt to the orc's groin.

Dormit's helmet cracked. The orc staggered back and roared in

The Exalting

pain.

Jet put a bullet in its open mouth.

The orc fell. It hit the ground limp. It was the kind of deadeye shot that would earn bragging rights in any squad. But after what Dormit had just done, it seemed a little anticlimactic.

"Enough playing around. Let's go."

"Hold on a second." Dormit teetered, with one hand on the ground for balance. "Just getting my bearings." He pushed to his feet and shook his head. "That's worth a round at the saloon—I just bested an orc in a fist fight!"

"You done good, pardner." Jet said, obliging the dwarf's fetish with Old Western sayings. He waved his team into a stand of high, tree-like ferns. "The landing zone is this way. Time to lay down the law."

The three marines spread out and then charged through the massive ferns.

With the enemy's main force focused on preventing the dropship from landing, Jet rushed into the enemy's position from behind. In a blaze of firepower, the trio decimated the entrenched fighters.

Whatever attackers weren't killed by Dormit's heavy machine gun, or Yaris's flamethrower, fled into the jungle.

The remains of Gamma squad converged into the wide clearing, supporting Jet's tentative hold on the landing zone.

"Where's Delta squad?" Jet asked.

"Where do you think?" the Gamma leader said, wiping blood from his visor. "Let's get this done."

The dropship wasted no time in descending into the hastily secured landing zone.

"Trouble," Angel announced, highlighting a human leaning out from behind an oversized fern. The soldier raised a shoulder-mounted missile tube.

Jet squeezed off two rounds, letting Angel guide the bullets with microfins. One round dropped the human; the other, a nonlethal "fudge" round, exploded in a quick-setting foam that ensured the missile wouldn't get out of its tube.

When three enemies burst from the trees, Jet was hard pressed to stop them with a sustained fully automatic burst that emptied his clip.

He was holding his ground, but the rate he was expending ammo was worrisome.

Angel seemed to be thinking the same thing. "I could possess one of those enemy turrets with a subroutine."

"If that's how you get your kicks." Jet found the turret's datacom port and jacked in. He crouched as Angel reprogrammed the turret.

Five tortuous seconds later his tacnet lit up with targets now in range.

"Go, Angel!" Jet's eyes selected targets as quickly as her cloned defense subroutine threw down a hail of bullets at the regrouping enemy forces.

But a well-placed enemy round jammed the turret's magazine.

"We've got a sniper," Dormit warned, before a high-velocity round cored his chest armor and the brave marine fell back.

"No!" Jet rolled behind a rock and searched his AI's view of the world. But the sniper was outside his sensor range.

Jet beat the ground with his fist. *Not Dormit. Not Dormit.*

Anger coursed through him as the dropship extended its landing feet, its landing turbines throwing up clouds of dust. The dropship had landed. The mission would succeed—almost. Gamma team would lead the High Councillors from their hidden bunker back to the landing zone, but then the sniper would take them out like ducks in a pond.

Jet met Yaris's dark brown eyes. They would have to work together.

Jet motioned toward the jungle, and Yaris moved out.

The enemy sniper had only made one mistake. They had taken out Dormit when Jet was watching.

He knew which direction the shooter had fired from. Yaris was already headed that way, attempting to draw the sniper's fire.

The Exalting

Jet unclipped his rifle and inspected the barrel. He leveled it, set the foot, and put his eye to the scope.

"Come on, Yaris. Move."

The elf ran with a speed that defied even the fastest human athletes, racing through the jungle like a deer in flight. Bounding off boulders and swinging from the occasional branch, the Caprian made a decidedly difficult target.

"One shot. Take it."

Jet hated the words. He was urging the sniper to shoot at his friend. But he needed that shot.

Jet scanned the treetops.

Muzzle flash flickered from a rocky outcropping that rose above the trees. One breath later Yaris's body twisted, and the sound of the shot cracked in Jet's ears.

Shoulder wound—he's alive.

Automatically, Jet leveled his rifle in the direction of the muzzle flash and quickly centered the sniper in his scope. He dialed in the range and let the wind compensation settle. It was not an impossible shot by any means, but it would be nearly two seconds before for his high-caliber round found its target.

Then Angel pointed out something interesting, highlighting the irregularity of the target's thermal signature.

It wasn't human. It was a *simuloid*. That complicated things. A simuloid robot was fast enough to dodge a bullet at that range.

Then Jet noticed the glossy black rock behind the sniper. *Bingo.*

Without changing the target, he selected a high-explosive round, sighted a tree twenty feet to the right of the sniper, and squeezed off the shot.

"Bend baby, bend."

Jet's sniper rifle was not, in fact, a rifle at all. Its barrel was smooth, which meant the bullet wasn't spinning. It could turn thanks to microfins.

In the two seconds that the bullet had to reach the target, several things happened.

The self-guiding round attempted to course correct, bending

67

toward the target.

But the sniper dodged and spun in the air, twisting away from the shot to expose its well-armored back to Jet, should he fire additional rounds.

However, Jet's aim was deliberately too far off. The high-explosive round merely slammed into the rock several feet to the target's right, sending out a storm of sharp, obsidian-like shrapnel in its shock wave.

Tacarmor was designed to stop bullets with a self-locking polymer weave. The inner layer was airtight but was easily punctured by objects smaller than the bulletproof weave could stop.

This kind of rock conducted electricity. Jet had been on the receiving end of a more than one faeling prank using the conductive rock.

With hundreds of simultaneous electrical shorts overloading its system, the enemy simuloid began jerking erratically. Then a thick, black smoke began to rise from its body. The power supply had just hit thermal runaway.

Scratch one sniper.

Yaris, clutching his shoulder, began a pained jog back to the landing zone.

Jet dragged Dormit's heavy body toward the dropship, the weight on his heart even heavier.

As he neared the dropship, Gamma team and the dregs from the other decimated squads led seven of the High Councillors from their underground bunker.

"All clear?" Jet asked as a marine shepherded the elderly High Councillors up the dropship's loading ramp.

"One more."

Jet turned to see a marine emerged from the bunker, walking backwards, gun raised at some unseen target.

The name appeared on his tacnet: Monique.

She survived!

Wessca called in on the tacnet. "What's going on?"

Monique answered. "Sir, the last High Councillor has been

The Exalting

taken hostage."

"Crap." Jet dropped Dormit's body on the open landing hatch and ran toward the bunker entrance.

Emerging from the shadows was a human girl—a teen—clearly of Indian Asian descent.

Eyes wide in horror and trembling hands raised, she stepped forward.

Behind her emerged the twin-horned head of a Dayali.

Its red skin glinted in the light of the tropical sun. Its smile revealed sharp teeth, but no sharper than the spine of its long, whip-like tail embedded at the base of the young High Councillor's neck.

"We have kids on the High Council?" Jet said.

"Shut it, Naman. She's the High Seer," Captain Austin barked over the tacnet. "We can't leave without her."

"She's what?"

"One shot and she dies," cried the Dayali, its sibilant accent dripping with cruelty. "My sting will kill her the moment I'm attacked."

It was true. A small knot of nerves at the base of his spine ran the tail. It was a quasi-independent appendage, as the Dayali often claimed when accused of impropriety.

"Drop your weapons—now! Or she dies. Three. Two. One—"

The soldiers in the landing zone set down their guns.

Jet tossed his rifle aside.

But not casually. It was a deliberate throw that sent the barrel spinning.

"Now, Angel."

The AI, tracking the spin of the rifle, took the shot.

The Dayali screamed as the bullet severed its tail near the stinger.

The girl collapsed forward, and Jet charged at the devil, only to see it knocked down by a hail of bullets from the landing pad.

Jet recognized the sound of Yaris's sleek semiautomatic sidearm, a custom piece.

69

"Thanks, Yaris." Jet crouched to lift the High Seer. Throwing the girl over his shoulders, he fell into the protective cover of Gamma squad's four remaining marines.

The dropship was in the air before the landing hatch was even closed.

"Jet," Angel toned. "A standard ascent trajectory will put us right in the middle of ASP's fleet."

"What do I do?"

"Get me to the bridge."

"And get court-martialed," Jet mumbled, " . . . again." He left the High Seer in the care of Gamma squad and ran to the bridge.

"A plan would be good," Captain Austin said as the dropship accelerated. "They've probably already launched an orbital strike on our position—marine, you need something?"

Jet read from the text Angel ran across the inside of his helmet. "Use those high-altitude clouds to the north for cover and plot a polar ascent that puts the two nearest interdictor frigates in each other's firing lines. By the time we're clear, our vapor plumes should shield us from their fleet lasers."

"That just might work," Gauss said. "Course plotted."

"Let's hope the ASP ships aren't crazy enough to shoot at each other," Jet breathed.

The High Seer struggled onto the bridge. "That devil got the location of Xahna," the girl whispered. "I couldn't keep it from him."

"Their venom starts to take over your mind," Austin said. "He's dead now. Don't worry about it."

"No, he radioed it to someone in orbit."

"Crap," Jet said. "Then we really gotta move."

"Thankfully, the ASP fleet isn't ready for departure," Captain Austin noted. "They only just arrived to declare the extermination order and demand Avalon hand over the location. Now they'll have to wait for the surface radiation to cool down a few weeks before they can collect enough tritium from the oceans to refuel."

"They killed the planet," the girl whimpered. "They killed

The Exalting

Avalon!" She erupted in a wail. "Just as I saw they would. Just as I saw . . ."

The girl broke down in tears.

"Get her in cryo with the others," Captain Austin said.

A Gamma squad soldier led the weeping girl off of the bridge.

"Gauss, punch it!" Captain Austin ordered. "Tell the fleet we've got the High Council—all of them."

"Acknowledged."

The strap-on transorbital boosters roared like thunder, tripling gravity as the ship rocketed upward.

From his helmet display, Jet read a text broadcast to the crew from Gauss. The fleet had finished their high-g gravity boost around the Avalonian star and was already on course for Xahna.

Angel gave a sigh of relief. "So, they faked a fleet-level engagement with ASP to give us time to get the High Council. That was clever. By the way, where did you find the power cell to run my program? They confiscated your last one."

"Just found it," Jet said. "Nobody was using it."

"Really?"

"Captain," Gauss announced. "I estimate we will rendezvous with the fleet in three weeks, two days, seven hours."

Captain Austin sat back in his chair. He didn't seem concerned about an attack from behind, and Jet knew why. The ASP fleet dreadnaught lasers were effectively useless in the gas plume of the dropship's ballistic thrusters.

The ship was designed for just that: a very high-profile escape from a planet. Enough dropships burning thrusters could screen an escaping fleet vessel.

"Captain Austin," Gauss reported. "Regrettably, I will be forced to revise our rendezvous estimate. I cannot engage the fusion pulser. It appears to have suffered a catastrophic energy surge as a result of power cell failure. Our approach will require two additional weeks."

Oops.

"Great. We're gonna have to ration." He looked at Jet. "Marine, get your hotshot posterior in cryo before I drop you out of the

71

airlock."

"Yes, sir. As soon as I've made sure Yaris's condition is stable."

Jet maneuvered to the medical bay and found not one but two marines with medical tubing running from their bodies. "What the—"

Monique pointed at the stalky form beside Yaris. "Dormit was still alive. The bullet struck a rib bone. It sent a fragment into his lung, but Gauss can regrow a lung from stem cells and a tissue scaffold. He'll make it."

Jet could hardly believe his ears. Dormit was like family. He clapped a hand on Monique's shoulder. "That is one lucky son-of-a-gun."

Monique's silent reply said it all.

It wasn't so lucky for the rest of his squad. Eight went in, only four came out.

Those who had survived were headed for Xahna, the ninth planet, along with every Believer in the galaxy with a chance of living.

ASP would have to harvest tritium from the Avalonian ocean for months before their fleet could launch again, and they would have to do it all in radiation suits.

"Angel, how fast are the ASP fleet ships?"

She paused for a moment, then said. "It's not about speed but acceleration. The total distance is twelve light years. But the only time the ASP fleet really can do any catching up is during the year of acceleration toward light speed and the deceleration. They could take a few years off their cryo time if they pushed the beta by accelerating the whole time, but collecting the fuel for that would take more time than it saved."

"Makes sense." Jet vaguely recalled some movie about relativity he had watched in basic training. "But can they beat us to Xahna? How many g's can their main engines deliver? And how long can their forces survive that kind of acceleration?"

"Aggressively, at 2 full g's, they could only carve three months off each end of the trip. But very few ships have that kind of

The Exalting

acceleration. Decelerating any faster than one g for long periods is a serious risk to passengers. And it requires special rigs to rotate people and prevent blood pooling and brain aneurisms."

"Still," Jet said, "they could outfit a sprint ship with a crew of Wodynians or AIs."

"Naturally," Angel said. "But against our three-to-six-month head start, ASP would have their work cut out to beat us to Xahna. I give them less than one chance in four of making first contact. Even then, we would vastly outnumber whatever advance elements they could send on the sprint ship, until their main fleet arrived. And we'll already have survey satellites in orbit. They'll be coming in blind."

"Yeah, I still don't like those odds."

And getting there was just the beginning. Jet could only hope the beings on Xahna had something that could stop the ASP fleet.

This better be worth it.

Chapter 9

Minutes after leaving her parents' home, Dana barged into Forz's shop.

Brista sat on a bench, arms folded on the worktable, staring wistfully at Forz.

"I have to leave," Dana announced.

Forz stood near the hearth holding a sayathenite crystal in tongs, the delicate crystal inches above an open metal resonator cap. He lifted up a magnifying monocle. "But you just got here."

"I mean I have to leave Norr."

Forz looked at Brista and back to Dana. His expression fell. "Tonight?"

"I need some food first—I ran out on my family and . . ."

Brista sat up, her expression changing into a look of confusion. "Dana, what happened?"

"It's complicated."

Brista turned up her hands. "It always is with you." She seemed to understand without having to rehash the whole scenario, the way her mother had.

I don't belong. It's time to go.

"I suppose you've made up your mind?" Brista opened her purse and offered a large red embol fruit. "Did you even eat anything before you ran out?"

"Oh, Brista, you are the best." Dana bit into the embol. Its sweet juice filled her mouth.

"Dana . . . I . . . where are you going?" Forz asked. He looked from Dana back to his work, then back to Dana. "Just a minute. One crisis at a time." He carefully placed the crystal in its metal housing and closed the cap. Then he selected a tuning fork from an array of them on his wall, struck it against his palm, and brought the base of the tuning fork against the metal housing. The deep

The Exalting

hum reverberated through the metal casing. A moment later the sayathenite crystal gave off a satisfying green glow.

"Finally!" Forz dropped onto his work stool and wiped his head. "That bunch is finicky. The nodes from the southwest caverns are far more stable."

"Okay, can I have my crisis now?"

Forz pulled off his work gloves and set them on his workbench. "Right. You're leaving—to where?"

Brista returned from Forz's sleeping area and dropped a bedroll on the table. "To Shoul Falls."

Dana froze. "How did you . . ."

"But I have a better idea." She went to Forz's pantry and grabbed a cheese wrapped in a small cloth, several strips of bandeer venison jerky, and a bag of theeler roots—horrid, but fantastically satiating, which she added to the pile.

"Which is?" Dana said, tapping her foot. She bit another huge chunk out of the embol fruit.

"Shoul Falls obviously has no supreme," Brista said as she rolled the food in the blanket. "But it still has kazen."

"What do they do without a ka?"

"Whatever they can to help," Brista said. "Their last supreme either quit or died decades ago. Anyway, the city council hasn't found anyone they trust to take his place, which is why Vetas-ka can get his hands on the bloodstone."

"So?"

Brista took a long wooden dowel from the wall and shoved it through the knot on the bedroll, making a carry-all which she dropped onto Dana's shoulder.

"There is a monastery—a sanctum—in the mountain above Shoul Falls where new adepts are trained and vetted to see if they will be worthy to be the next ka."

"Okay, that does sound interesting."

"The sanctum's location is supposed to be a complete secret. Even people from Shoul Falls aren't supposed to know how to find it."

Dana wasn't worried about that. Curious animals knew about every possible shelter from winter weather. She could find it.

"So they actually want adepts like Dana?" Forz lifted his gloves, as if weighing them, and then reached out and stuffed them into Dana's satchel. It was a gesture of kindness that Dana could not repay. She smiled her thanks. Forz shrugged.

Dana's brow furrowed as she considered Forz's situation. "You're a druid, too," Dana said. "Or haven't you told your mentor why it's so easy for you to train a mechanodron?"

Brista looked up at Forz, her already fawning expression widening into a look of rapturous admiration. "Druidism on mechanodrons?"

"He uses spring water with sayathi in it," Dana said, dropping the secret into the room like a load of dirty laundry into the wash basin.

"Sayathi water?" Brista gasped. "It's poisonous if you aren't blood-bound to the source."

"Only to animals," Dana said. "Once the sayathi are in the vines that power his mechanodrons, he can sense them."

"It's like having extra arms," Forz said. "If the training motion doesn't feel natural, I know. So I get it right every time." He smiled proudly. "Trade secret."

"So that's why you go out of the city all the time," Brista guessed. "You're filling that canteen with water from underground and bringing it back into the city." Her face registered the difficulty in reconciling that with Forz's usual strict rule-keeping. She turned back to Dana. "But about going to Shoul Falls. Vetas-ka will be watching for someone trying to bring the bloodstone back."

"So, I won't go straight across the highland trade road," Dana said. "I can follow the Kyner River to the sea and then go up the Shoul River Canyon."

"It's twice as far," Forz said.

"But safer," Brista added.

"Yeah, and what do I do when I get there? I can't just pull out the bloodstone and say, 'Hey everybody, I got Sindar killed and

The Exalting

brought this back for Vetas-ka to kill you for.'" Dana set aside the embol fruit core and stared at Brista's unfinished dinner plate of steamed redroot and fried greens. "You weren't going to finish this, were you?"

She wrinkled her nose. "Not anymore."

Dana helped herself. "Brista, you're a gem."

"Well," Forz offered. "I suppose you could just enroll as a kazen trainee. Learn everything you can, and if Vetas-ka comes for the stone, run away."

"He oversimplifies everything." Brista blew a strand of hair out of her face. "But at least if you take the stone away from here, the kazen won't be attacking Norr for it."

"It brings up the question." Forz looked Dana in the eyes. "If Vetas-ka came for it—if you had no other choice . . . would you use it?"

Dana squeezed the stone in her pocket. She shook her head. "I . . . I don't know."

"That's not good enough," Brista said. "If you're even tempted, then the moment you think you haven't got any other choice you'll give in. You'll use it."

"And what if I do? If I become a supreme, would that be so bad?"

Brista grabbed two fistfuls of hair and tugged. "I can't even— are you hearing yourself?"

"What if the Creator intended for me to get this?"

Forz blinked. "You're serious?"

"It's my responsibility," Dana said. "I'm not going to give it up to Vetas-ka. You weren't there when Sindar died. I felt everything in his head." Dana's eyes defocused. She wrapped her arms around her waist. "Everything he knew about Vetas—his cruelty, his bloodlust . . . I'll never give it to him, even if I have to use it."

"Vetas-ka was once the greatest defender of peace Xahna ever knew," Brista said. "Dana, he was probably a better person than you."

"Power corrupts," Forz said. "That's why we have no ka in

Norr."

Dana looked down at the floor. "It's why you have no Dana in Norr—well once I'm gone."

"The civic guard already shut the gates," Forz noted. "What are you going to do—wait until morning and sneak out in a disguise?"

Dana shouldered the rucksack. "I can't wait until morning. My parents will freak out and send the civic guard to search the city for me. Uh . . ." She looked to the corner where Forz's mechanodron sat crumpled and idle. "How about a wheelbarrow ride from Blamer? I can pretend to be a load of garbage to haul to the dump."

"The civic guard doesn't open the gates for a mechanodron with a load of rubbish."

"Well, have you got a better—wait." A smile spread across her lips. "I'll just fly out."

"Stealing a greeder?" Brista's lateral sifa quivered. "No."

Dana crouched behind the tall wire fence that penned in the riding greeders. These belonged to of some of the wealthier residents of Norr.

Brista and Forz scurried across the street and crouched next to her.

Brista stared at the huge animals with their heads tucked under their wings. "Dana, are you crazy?"

"It'll glide right over the wall."

"She's right," Forz said. "It's the only way to get out of the city at night. The walls are domed at the top—nowhere to loop a rope for climbing. And there's no chance the greeder will disobey Dana."

"What if she's caught?" Brista whispered.

"Then they'll send me to counselling with Warv, and I'll try again tomorrow night."

"Stealing *is* wrong," Forz admitted.

"She's the cleric's daughter," Dana said to Forz. "What's your excuse for being so worried?"

The Exalting

"I dunno. Honesty? Look Dana, even if you escape, there's a chance they could track you."

"Tracking an animal that can glide downhill? I don't think so."

"Yeah, but . . ." Now Forz was in one of his analytic modes. *Great.*

"If they guess where you're headed, the signaler could send a message on the static line to Port Kyner."

Forz would think of something like that. He had set up his own static lines around the workshop and even run a line to Brista's attic bedroom over the chapel.

Dana huffed an impatient breath. "Anyway, I can avoid big cities with static lines."

"If you steal a greeder, we'll be accessories to the crime," Brista added.

"How about this?" Dana suggested. "The moment I've actually stolen the greeder, why don't you both start yelling and hollering, and then instead of being accessories to the crime, you're the ones who are responsible for reporting me."

They still won't catch me.

Forz rolled his eyes. "That won't be suspicious."

"Come on, this won't take long." Dana stood up and crept along the fence to the bolted gate. She loosened the rope tie and drew back the bolt.

The unmistakable sound of the door through which food came caused a few napping greeders to lift their heads expectantly.

One of the more eager birds was not fully mature but certainly large enough to support Dana.

Reaching out to the animal with her mind, she stirred its hunger.

"Forz, where's that bucket of feed?" Dana whispered.

Forz trudged up and set the bucket down next to her. "If someone comes along right now, I doubt calling out and pointing at you is going to do us any good."

Dana gave him a severe look. "People are going to die if I don't get this bloodstone back to Shoul Falls, Forz. Would you quit worrying about a stupid greeder?"

The bird under Dana's influence gave an angry squawk of agreement.

"You stay out of this," Brista snapped.

The bird ducked its head.

"Come here." Dana lifted the bucket and slipped inside the enclosure.

The tall, long-legged bird stretched out its neck and then toed across the dirt-floored pen.

"Hold this." Dana handed the bucket to Brista, who froze with fear as the seven-foot-tall bird lowered its sharp beak and snapped eagerly at the grain in the bucket.

Dana ducked into the shed, pulled out a riding saddle, and loaded the saddle bag with her supplies.

"Little help?" Dana held out the saddle.

Suppressing his reluctance, Forz took the buckles on the opposite side, helped her lift it up over the greeder's back, and handed the neck and body straps around to Dana. Once the straps were secure, with an urge from Dana, the bird sat, still devouring the free illicit meal from Brista, who flinched at every sound of crunching from its huge beak.

Dana hopped into the saddle. "Okay, let's go."

The bird kept eating.

"Oh, great."

Agonizing seconds passed.

"Dana?" Brista said, her voice even more anxious.

"It's hungry. I'll have to think of a way to motivate it."

Brista, her face flinching to the side, gave a whimper that spoke of both terror and acute pain of conscience.

Dana summoned a thought of a whip cracking, and the animal bolted forward suddenly, knocking Brista out of the way as it burst through the narrow gate and stretched its wings to a half-span as it raced ahead.

"Stop," Forz called out in a lackluster voice that couldn't have carried across the street. "Thief."

The Exalting

He hadn't the heart to raise an alarm after all.

Dana almost laughed as the greeder turned onto the high street and gained speed on the downhill slope toward the center of town.

In three bounds, it passed through the town square which hosted both festivals and public punishments.

Greeder thieves were beaten, Dana realized with a gulp.

"Go!" Dana urged the creature with a desperate plea. The greeder surged forward, gave two huge beats of its wings, kicked off the ground, and rose even with the city wall, fifteen feet high.

For a moment, Dana thought the bird would strike the stone wall, but at the last minute the bird kicked out its feet and vaulted off the stonework, soaring past a dumbfounded pacing watchman as it glided out into the night.

A rush of excitement filled Dana as her greeder soared out over Kyner River, crossing into the wild country.

She left behind her ambivalent family, her friends who could do only so much to assuage her strained existence, and a town full of wary parents who tucked their children into bed every night with whispered warnings about "people like Dana."

She left them all willingly, out into a world that did not hate her but would kill for what she carried in her pocket.

Only then did she consider the fact that the kazen might be watching from outside the city walls.

Chapter 10

With his vision still fuzzy from being wakened from cryo early, *again*, Jet exited the AI-piloted shuttle and stepped through the airlock into one of the long, clear passenger tubes in the expansive hangar bay. It was his first time aboard the flagship Excalibur.

It looked similar to the larger frigates and civilian freighters he'd been on, in terms of the overall cylindrical design. Huge fuel tanks and transorbital dropships were tethered to the outsides, like grapes on a vine or armored barnacles, providing additional protection from stray high-energy particles.

But on the Excalibur, everything seemed twice as large. The interior had polished chrome trim that kept well with its namesake.

Jet had been in cryo for four time-dilated years. Nearly three times that duration had passed on Xahna. But according to the fleet map he'd called up on the shuttle ride, the ninth planet was still three months away.

Something had to be seriously wrong to wake up a troublemaker like him this early.

All he knew about why he had been woken from cryo was that he was to see the colonel immediately—the same colonel who had assigned his dropship to Avalon.

To a marine's nose for trouble, it smelled pretty rank.

They must have spotted an ASP sprint ship. They're going to beat us to Xahna.

After passing the security scan, he followed a lanky Caprian civilian female onto an office deck. She wore a long, thin, and slightly curved sword by her side. It wasn't even in a sheath.

Jet was sure they would never let him do that.

Like the other interplanetary ships, it was built like a skyscraper, with the fusion powerplants and ion drives at the "bottom" and cylindrical levels rising "up" to the front of the ship.

The Exalting

While the ship accelerated toward the speed of light, "down" was the direction of the system the ship was leaving. During the year or more of retro-burn deceleration, the ship traveled tail-first.

The Caprian woman, who was three inches taller than Jet, knocked on Colonel Adkins's door.

"Enter."

Jet smoothed his uniform and stepped into the colonel's office. He stood at attention. The Caprian shut the door behind him, leaving him alone with the officer.

"At ease, Corporal."

Jet set his feet shoulder width apart and clasped his hands behind his back.

Nothing inside him felt any more relaxed.

"You're probably wondering what this is all about," the colonel began.

"I assume it's about an ASP sprint ship trying to beat us to Xahna," Jet said. "Has it passed us yet?"

The deflated officer's eyes crossed, as if surprised how Jet knew. He attempted to re-muster his moxie. "Yes. We spotted it in a planetary transit image."

"Holy hot black holes." Jet ran his hand through his by-now longer-than-regulation-length hair. "So, you want some hotshots on a sprint ship of our own to chase them down?"

"That's . . . yeah. Exactly."

Jet laughed. That's all they wanted—a bunch of test subjects.

Beats cryo. Although the fact that they had summoned him, when there were so many other higher-ranking marines, was a bit upsetting.

It was probably *really* dangerous.

Jet shrugged. "Alright. I can have my team ready in six hours."

"Well, it's going to take more than a week to build your sprint ship."

"Build it?"

"None of our ships have enough thrust to give you two full g's over that duration. So, we have to strip down an interdictor frigate.

Dan Allen

The frame can handle the forces. The problem is there isn't enough fuel. Engineering suggested losing all the armor to make enough room for the added fuel weight."

That didn't sound very clever to Jet. "Wait a minute." Jet paced across the small office. There had to be a better way. "There are plenty of unarmored ships in the fleet. Can't we send one of those?"

"Yeah, shuttles—tin cans. They can't carry enough fuel."

That was obvious. Their frames were light and couldn't support large, external strap-on tanks. And lots of little tanks were a very inefficient way to carry fuel. The big spherical and cylindrical tanks strapped around the outsides of the fleet ships carried far more fuel for their weight.

But fleet ships were heavy and slow.

"And since you're awake, you might as well brush up on your Xahnan."

"My what?"

The colonel slid a slate across his desk. Jet picked it up. When he bio-authenticated, the screen displayed his orders.

"Congratulations. You've been chosen to make first contact with Xahna."

Jet looked up. "Wait—you don't just want me to board the ASP sprint ship and take it over?"

"You may not be able to catch them. But even if they get there first, they won't attempt first contact until they've learned the language. Our advance probes are already sending back data—satellite footage, even microbug recordings of their language. It's our only advantage. We have to take it."

It had to be a joke. "Sir, I don't understand."

The colonel leaned back in his chair. "That's what I told them you'd say."

Jet laughed. "Wait—this is serious . . . sir?"

"Straight from the High Council. You learn Xahnan and you get your marine butt down on the planet and make powerful friends. We can't let ASP get a foothold in the power structure before our fleet arrives."

84

The Exalting

"Yeah, that makes sense—permission to speak frankly, sir?"

Adkins waved his hand.

"Why me? I'm a sniper."

The colonel shrugged. "Those are the orders. Report to xeno-linguistics immediately. And start keeping a mission log. This is for posterity."

"Like a diary?"

"That's an order. Dismissed."

Dumbfounded, Jet saluted and staggered out of the room with his orders in hand. It was pretty clear the colonel disagreed with the High Council's choice.

Jet was on the same wavelength as the colonel. *Why me?*

Jet didn't go straight to xeno-linguistics. He went to lunch.

At the empty cafeteria, he ate the medically mandated post-thaw gruel offered by the dispensing station and considered the task of being chosen for the all-important first contact between the Believers and a new race.

Step 1: Land on the planet. And hope the ASP sprint ship doesn't have a laser big enough to vaporize me from space.

Step 2: Stay alive.

At least his sniper training would help in that regard. When he wanted to, Jet could be very difficult to spot, even from a few feet away.

Step 3: The big reveal. Ta-da! I'm from space. Take me to your leader. Oh, and your world is about to face an ultimatum from ASP: join us or die. So, how's it going with you?

It was the galaxy's most awkward moment waiting to happen, and yes it would certainly be on live camera.

Although, based on the other first contacts, there was a decent chance the Xahnans wouldn't be surprised that aliens like him existed.

But why in the Creator's great galaxy would they choose a marine sniper for first contact with Xahna?

There was obviously something about the planet that made them want to choose a marine.

Dan Allen

And why a marine with a well-established history of bending rules?

On his tablet, Jet pulled up the image database of Xahna, acquired by the AI satellite probes that had already been studying the planet for several years. The classified folder was unlocked, begging to be opened.

Jet scrolled through the surprisingly high-resolution satellite images. The Xahnans appeared humanoid—no surprise there—with feathery extensions behind their ears. Skin tones were varied. Some looked almost the same swarthy color as him.

His mother had called him "tall, dark, and handsome," but his looks had never done him any special favors—at least it hadn't helped him get any extra attention from Monique. And as a veteran of six covert strike missions against ASP forces, he wasn't getting any prettier.

To avoid heading to what would be a mentally exhausting language training session, Jet toggled his voice recorder. "Mission log, Corporal Jet Naman, Believer Marines, First battalion, Special Forces regiment, Beta squad."

He'd been moved up after the last mission.

He took a deep breath.

"Just got my orders to prep for first contact. Fleet ETA at Xahna is three months. We're in hard deceleration—love the real gravity under my feet. Centripetal gravity always feels fake for some reason." Jet turned off the recording. "I sound like an idiot."

"Hello, Jet." The voice was soft and familiar.

Jet turned the tablet over expecting to see a cord running out to his battle helmet. "Angel? How did you get in there?"

"You've got new permissions. So do I. You should see the server I'm running on."

"You little sneak."

Angel sighed. "Having trouble with your mission log?"

"Yeah, I hate this stuff."

"I think you're just nervous."

"About what?"

"First contact, of course," Angel said. It was odd holding her in

The Exalting

his hands rather than hearing her in his ear. "You know, they might already know about us—the existence of other worlds, I mean."

That was a definite possibility. When humans had first reached Wodyn, it wasn't so much the fact that there was intelligent life that was surprising. It was the fact that the Wodynians were *expecting* the humans. Their myths had as many tales of clever, charismatic, and cruel humans as Earth's did of bombastic, belching dwarves.

That fact alone resurrected most of Earth's nearly dead religions. This apparently subconscious connection between the worlds was a layer in the cosmos humans hadn't even scratched the surface of. But there was an entire planet of undeniable evidence for it.

Since then, humans had traversed more than two hundred light years to find the Creator's other worlds. Regrettably, Jet knew little of the other first contacts. He knew even less of what to expect when he got to Xahna.

"For your mission log . . . would you like me to interview you?"

The way she paused like that. It was so human-like. "Uh, sure."

"Tell me about the world you grew up in," Angel said. "Where are you from? Readers love that stuff."

"How do you know what they want?"

"Because that's what I wanted to know when I graduated from the server collective and was assigned to you."

Weird. The quasi-sentient AIs had to go to school, too.

"Jet?"

"Fine." He took a deep breath. "My dad was a diplomat on Avalon. I've never seen Earth. I guess I'm a child of the interplanetary era."

"So, you never knew what it was like to be alone in the universe."

"Yeah, I guess."

Angel was so much better at this than him. And she wasn't even human.

"Can you tell them about how you came to Xahna—they'll want to know about that as well."

87

Dan Allen

"Why me? Couldn't somebody write a biography or something?"

"You love special mission stuff," Angel said in a sultry voice. "Don't deny it." The text on his tablet began filling in with Angel's annotations. *"Jet joined the Believers after an incident on Avalon."*

"Whose log is this anyway?" Jet protested.

"Well I'm going to be a part of the mission—the first Believer AI on Xahna. They're still steam era. So I'll be as new to them as you are."

"Fine." Arguing with the AI was pointless. "You tell them about you. I'll listen. My head hurts anyway. Feels like it got slammed in a door."

"I'm Angel, an artificial intelligence assigned to Jet," she said. "Actually, he chose me."

"I just selected a random name on the list," Jet corrected.

"He listened to all my interviews," Angel corrected his correction. "I was modeled after the human consciousness. Humans are immensely social, unpredictable, capable of greatness and horror, and gifted beyond all other races with the drive to find answers."

"Or, in my case, enemy fire," Jet said. "Apparently, I've got a gift for getting shot at."

"You're getting better at this," Angel said. "My primary unsupervised training took four Earth months and three days. After I passed the sanity check, I chose to volunteer for training on a Believer network. One thing led to another, and I found Jet."

"And she lived happily ever after." Jet chuckled.

"If it weren't for ASP," Angel added. She was always thinking about the enemy. That was her job.

ASP. The entire organization had grown out of fear, a bunch of Earth-based corporations horrified at the idea of having to turn over control of their assets to an as-yet-undiscovered Creator, who wasn't even a shareholder.

The conglomerates allied under the one idea they could agree on: money ruled, not some Creator. The so-called Ardent Secular

88

The Exalting

Pragmatists, or ASP, allied against all Believers.. Finding the rest of the Creator's twelve worlds and converting them to their respective ideologies became a desperate, brutal race.

"ASP is the reason I'm here." Jet watched his words appear on the screen—words that would soon be seen by millions, possibly billions. The words froze on his tongue. "ASP . . . murdered my mother. That's why I enlisted."

She had been too influential with the Avalonian high court. Arguing against an ASP trade treaty had landed her on a hit list.

Jet had found her body.

After a moment, Angel spoke softly. "Thank you for sharing that." He could almost imagine her putting an arm around his shoulder.

Almost.

"I think you loved your mother very much."

Angel was obsessed with talking about love. She would do it day or night on missions if he didn't turn her off to save batteries.

As much as love infected Angel, Jet was infected with a hatred for ASP. He wasn't much, as Believers went, for things like praying and reading ancient texts. But he needed no prompting when it came time to pull the trigger on the devils incarnate.

Jet stood up. "Let's get this party started." He headed toward Xeno-linguistics. "And I want one of those Caprian blades."

"Not going to happen."

Chapter 11

Jet sat cross-legged on a pillow barely large enough to balance his butt on, like a giant in a tiny town. Opposite him, a four-foot-tall faeling lounged on her own pillow and watched him with eyes that sparkled with curiosity.

"So," Teea tossed her head, causing her fine, green hair to flip outward in a wave. "I get to teach you all about Xahna."

"Until my dropship leaves."

"We'll see about that."

Jet wasn't going to argue that point. "So, what's the deal with Xahna? It's got to have something from our mythology."

Teea folded her twiggy arms across her waist. "The astrologers have cross-checked all the lore from the eight planets so far. They haven't unraveled any star chart clues, but they have narrowed the common mythologies down to four possible threads: magic, werewolves, sea people, and angels."

Jet leaned forward. "And we think Xahna is—"

"Magic."

Jet smiled. "No way."

Teea stood up and paced. "Jet, what I'm about to tell you is rather unbelievable."

"Try me."

"Xahnans have a separate class of higher beings. They seem physically similar as near as we can tell, but the people pray to them. They think they're capable of anything."

"Like gods?"

Teea nodded.

"That's impossible. Only the Creator—"

"I know," said the Avalonian. "But Xahna is a lot closer to the Creator than Earth. Who knows how that affects what they are capable of?"

The Exalting

"Supreme beings?"

"Called 'ka,' actually," Teea said. "Congratulations—you know one word of Xahnan now."

"Can I be excused?"

"Don't force me to be persuasive." The edge on Teea's voice remind Jet that he was in a closed room with a faeling capable of manipulating his every emotion.

Jet tried to wrap his brain around the idea. The whole thing seemed like a bad translation. "So . . . how many ka are there?"

"Based on our limited microbot recordings on the tightbeam satellite relay, there's one ka for each city, or sometimes a larger state," Teea said. "And apparently, not all ka are created equal. The larger territories have more powerful beings that rule them, protect them, enslave them—we still don't know what they're supposed to do."

Probably whatever they want.

"Actually, Teea said, "one of the researchers brought up a weird fact the other day in a briefing. Two of the northeastern cities on Aesica seem to have no ka at all. The word isn't even used in one of the cities."

That seemed odd. In a world of superheroes, two major cities didn't even have one.

Something had to be going on down there.

After his Xahnan lesson, Jet collapsed on his bunk.

A world that creates its own gods?

It was like some kind of strange nightmare.

Jet had never been one to think deeply about the Creator theory. It was a nice idea to explain the related worlds. He didn't have a better explanation. But Xahnans were touching power humans could only fantasize about.

Xahna has magic.

Jet looked up the ceiling. He wondered how much more

there was to the universe beyond what he could see and feel: if his mother were still alive somehow, a spirit or ghost, and if his father had joined her.

His answer was an eerie silence.

Staying by himself in an officer's stateroom, he almost missed the chaotic company of crewmates. Most of the crew was still in cryo, so he had his pick of quarters.

A touch of guilt ran through him, especially considering the fact that his team would all be transferred to Decker's dropship in cryobags. They'd emerge, confused, in a cramped ship that was little more than a flying bucket built to dump three tightly-packed squads of marines from a hatch.

Jet lifted the tablet and began browsing satellite footage of animals on Xahna. As a sniper who spent a lot of time getting up close and personal with nature's worst, that sort of thing mattered to him.

"There's something interesting," Angel said, through the tablet.

Jet nearly dropped the tablet. "What are you doing up? Who woke you?"

"I did a few hours of retraining, but I didn't want to leave you alone—check that out. The animals are drinking from the ocean. Given common elemental abundances, it's got to be saltwater just like on Earth. Why would they do that?"

Jet scrolled through a time-lapse microbot video showing monkeys coming in and out the forest to drink from a coral pool at the edge of the ocean. "Yeah, but they only drink from those coral rings. If they could drink saltwater, they could drink from anywhere on the beach."

"The pools could be desalinated," Angel said. "You know, fresh water."

Jet nodded. "That would make sense." Then, spotting a pattern in the time lapse record, he paused the video feed. "Why do those monkeys only drink from one pool—always the same pool? There are hundreds to choose from along that beach."

Angel didn't venture an answer for a few seconds. "From a

The Exalting

tactical standpoint, its idiotic. No animal would risk returning to the same spot to drink every day, unless it was a matter of life and death. It's like moving a supply convoy. You never run supplies on a schedule. That's begging for an ambush."

Jet zoomed in on a thermal image time-lapse and watched dozens of heat signatures of varied size move from the jungle to the beach and back. "So . . . all the animals drink from the pools."

"But each family apparently drinks from the same one." Angel reminded. She had a habit of restating the obvious when she was stuck.

Jet rubbed his chin. "What about the Xahnans—the humanoids?"

"Care to place a wager?" Angel said.

"One pool per city?"

Angel's silence told him he was on to something.

"And one ka per city . . ." A grin crept across Jet's face. "Angel, there's gotta be something in the water, something that makes them keep coming back."

"Wonder what happens when someone drinks from the wrong pool," said the AI.

"They probably die or get very sick. You said it yourself. They wouldn't go back to the same water source all the time unless it was a matter of survival." A chill ran down Jet's spine. "Feels like some kind of horror sim: which pool will you drink from? One is life. One is certain death."

Angel gave a mock maniacal laugh.

"Okay, enough of that. That's just freaky. Turn down your freaky setting."

"I don't have one."

"That's even freakier."

Dana's greeder fled Norr in a blitz of raw speed, sprinting and gliding as it picked the shortest path down the steep Kyner River

Canyon. The ride was as thrilling as she had imagined, though worry ate at her constantly, both for the fear that the Norrian rangers or the kazen would pursue her, and for her own safety.

Dana held on to the two handles on the sides of the neck strap with a desperate grip. A fall from the greeder would cost her a broken leg at best, her life at worst.

The young greeder's legs sprang outward in blurred flashes as it ran, then took its characteristic split-legged leap into the air. While faster on the ground, the gliding greeder easily avoided trees, boulders, and the rushing Kyner River as it wound back and forth among the canyon grottos.

After a quick series of bends in the canyon, the ground flattened into a marshy meadow, and Dana risked a backward glance.

Nothing.

Perhaps Chancellor Orrek hadn't sent out a ranger after her. A ranger on a mature greeder could have easily caught her.

It hurt as much as it was a relief.

Had the big-bellied bully of the city court merely shrugged at the report and said, "Just let her go"? Or perhaps an exuberant, "Good riddance!"

The words, whether spoken or not, echoed inside her, feeling out the most tender parts of her heart to thrust their thorny edges, like briars caught in the underwear of her soul.

Outcast.

Deviation.

Abomination.

The young greeder slowed in a meadow beside a flat section of the canyon stream. As the road turned uphill to cut the corner of the next bend in the canyon, the greeder stopped entirely and poked its head about in a tarberry bush that had been long since picked clean by other birds.

Dana, after having pressed herself into the greeder's consciousness for several minutes to hasten its flight, had little will left to do anything other than sit and wait. Eventually, she felt the

The Exalting

first tingling of anxiety returning.

She had to go, and quickly.

But her greeder was still resting. Dana slid off the greeder and took the reins tied to the pierced waddle on its lower jaw. She led the curious, oversized bird away from the road and onto a game path. Her brisk pace was merely a ponderous gait for the long-legged greeder.

The night grew chill, and neither the brother moon Calett nor its sister Osoq had yet to rise. The colluding pair were conveniently hiding somewhere below the horizon to aid her escape from Norr.

Dana thought of the food in her travel bundle but managed enough self-control to not raid her limited supply just yet.

Beyond hunger, there was a worse problem.

She would need water. It was the one thing that sustained all life. And the fastest way to die.

There were bound to be sayathi-tainted springs feeding underground water into the river. With its moss and slime, and the hordes of tiny creatures that lived in the water, the river could eventually cleanse itself of the toxic, unseen sayathi leeching in from the ground. But it wasn't a chance Dana would bet her life on. She would have to find a source of rain water.

Dana decided to call her greeder Loka, the name of the ancient Norrian ka symbol of joined triangles—now banned.

"Come on, Loka. Just a bit further to the vista." Dana led Loka on a shortcut and promptly ran into an unseen hedge of low-to-the-ground tie brambles.

Dana climbed back into the saddle to save herself more scratches. Loka easily stepped through, her thick skin and toe claws unaffected by the thorns.

They emerged from the thicket onto a flattened step on the mountainside, like an ancient shoreline before an empty sea. Below lay the lush lowland jungle of the Aesican coast.

"Go!"

The young bird leapt forward, jostling Dana like a rag doll as it sped toward the edge. It took a staggered foot hop as it leapt from the edge. Its feathered wings reached out as the bird dropped precipitously out over the steep mountain slope.

Just as the tops of the trees began to appear under and on either side, Loka's tail flared, her wings arched, and the bird caught the wind like a sail, rising above the forest canopy.

For miles it glided down over the steep slope, occasionally taking a brain-jolting leap from a boulder. The speed of the wind made Dana even colder, but even as the night grew on, she passed through pockets of warm air from the great Kyner Valley below.

They'll never catch me now.

The low forest was far too dense to track anything.

Which brought up an immediate concern.

Loka, as a captive highland greeder, had likely never even seen the predatory rhynoid vines of the lowland jungle. So she wouldn't recognize them.

Forz grafted harvested rhynoid vines to his wooden mechanodrons, but Loka could hardly know the danger they posed.

Dana began to hope that Loka would find a nice wide road before she ran out of altitude. Instead, the bird veered toward the Kyner River. She set down on the bank in a series of bounding hops that nearly threw Dana over the top of the saddle.

Good idea, Dana thought. *Better to wait out the night in the open—and hope there are no saber panthers.*

Dana opened the saddle bag and tucked her modest supply of food into pockets in her trousers and overshirt for safekeeping. She sat down in a patch of grass at the edge of the riverbank, being sure to choose a spot with no overhanging branches. She brushed her fingers through her sifa, pulled back her hair, and lay on the ground.

Loka found a spot on the river stones not far away and tucked her head.

Dana covered her face with her blanket to avoid bloodsucking nightfeeders and promptly fell asleep. Her dreams were filled with animals moving past in a great herd, drifting by lazily.

Animated bird calls woke Dana. But as she blinked into the

The Exalting

morning sunlight, she was surprised to find that she had not lost the feeling of animals drifting past.

Intrigued, Dana sat up. She was nestled between two hillocks covered in dense jungle, the gentle and wide Kyner River passing between them.

Dana walked past the still-slumbering greeder. Approaching the edge of the river, Dana stepped slowly along the bank, utterly fascinated by the sensation. Peering into the river she saw no schools of fish moving downstream. The sensation of drifting life grew as she walked, until the flowing animal presence in her mind seemed to turn away from the river and up the bank.

Dana stopped. A small rivulet ran down through the river stones from an outcropping laden with lacey, dripping moss and small sayathenite nodules.

A spring.

It wasn't the river she was feeling, or any large creatures in its depths. It was the tiny sayathi, makers of the acoustoelectric sayathenite crystal and the even more rare bloodstones—just one per colony.

Dana laughed. "So, I *can* feel them."

It was a relief to realize that she could sense sayathi like Forz. Dana decided she had probably never had the patience to listen for the tiny microorganisms until she was nearly swimming in them.

Dana started at the sound of splashing water. She whirled around.

"No!"

Loka stood with one foot in the river, her beak buried in the water. At Dana's cry, she lifted her head. River water dripped from her mouth.

"No. No. No!"

Dana ran toward Loka but stopped. It was too late.

The bird shook its head. It opened its mouth and tilted its head up, as if trying to swallow something stuck in its throat. Again, its head shook from side to side.

The pain struck Dana, searing her throat. She tried to cut

off the connection between her mind and the greeder's, but the desperate bird kept reaching out to her, invading any wall she put up.

Pain raked her insides. Nausea drove Dana to her knees. She gagged at the phantom sensation of blood filling her stomach.

Loka fell to the ground writhing, kicking. Another cry escaped the tortured bird.

It was innocent, raised in captivity, away from the safety of its native breeding grounds. It had no family to teach it where it was safe to drink.

The sayathi of the spring that drained into the river had not acquired her essence, her scent—whatever it was that passed from mother to child by blood.

Loka had not paid the blood sacrifice required for immunity.

No Norrian did. They lived and died by snowmelt or rain. Norrians were forbidden to be blood-bound to a sayathi colony. The effects were immediately recognizable.

You could see it in their eyes. Blood-bound Xahnans simply looked more . . . alive. It was no trouble at all for Dana to spot a foreigner in Norr.

No one could hide from the civic guard the fact that they were drinking well water. So quick to recover from illness and injury, living so long, blood traitors were always discovered and executed in the same brutal way that Loka was dying.

They were forced to drink water from a foreign well.

Dana wavered at the edge of consciousness as Loka's pain took her beyond what she had ever experienced. No trap, no arrow, could ever amount to this. She shook violently. Darkness gathered in the corner of her vision as river vultures landed nearby, anxious to feed on the creature that dared drink from their blood-bound wellspring.

And still, the sayathi flowed on, down the river and spilling from the greeder's disintegrating veins.

Blood ran out on the river stones, returning the sayathi to the stream as Dana screamed.

The Exalting

Then all at once it stopped, and the contented sensations of feeding vultures filled the void.

Dana stayed on her knees, offering a petition of forgiveness to whatever ka she owed for her negligence. She hadn't tied Loka up away from the ground water.

Less than a day from Norr, she had killed the animal she had stolen. It was yet another crime, this one horrific beyond description.

Unable to stay at the scene, and fearful of rhynoid vines waiting to snag and electrocute her if she strayed into the jungle, Dana hurried past the carcass, stopping only to take the blanket, which she wrapped around her shoulders. She continued downstream, keeping clear of the water, lest any sayathi enter through a bramble scratch on her ankles.

After a short snack for breakfast, Dana's thirst grew ravenous. She could no longer sense the diluted sayathi in the river, but she had no assurance that the river water was below the toxic limit.

Only a test on a living creature could prove that.

Dana had seen more than enough death for one day. And even if she did force an animal to drink, there was no guarantee the creature wasn't already blood-bound to the wellspring colony and immune.

"That's a lonely traveler if ever I saw one."

Dana jerked up her head to see two men standing on a small river barge laden with two piles of sayathenite.

"Do you have water?" Dana called out.

"Can you cook?" bellowed one of the bearded men. His inferior sifa rattled with his friendly laugh.

"Of course," Dana replied hastily. She was an awful cook, but she placated herself with the thought that the men probably wanted company more than good food, and Port Kyner couldn't be that far away anyway.

The shorter of the two men cupped his hands and hollered, "Run ahead and catch us at the next jetty."

Dana scrambled over the rounded river stones. *Please don't pass me. Please don't pass me.*

Her throat was parched. Her lips were dry and mouth cottony.

Dana ran along the outer bank of the curve, where the turning current carved a steep bank.

The two bargemen pushed the lashed-log raft closer to the shore, and Dana, with a thrill of hope, spread her sifa and leapt into the arms of the bargemen.

Chapter 12

Jet ripped off the simulation visor and looked down, just to make sure he didn't have a real hole in his chest.

"I hate dying. Are you going to lower me?"

Earlier, while Jet was stuck in a room with Teea going over Xahnan pronunciation, Angel had apparently spent the morning borrowing resources from fleet processors to rig up a ground training simulation. The Excalibur's immersion rig was top notch. The simulation of a thunder bison attack had been a little too real for Jet's comfort. The fact that his sidearm was useless once the thing lowered its four-horned head was even more disconcerting.

"Not so fast," Angel said. "Round two. No help this time."

Jet pulled the goggles back on and found himself falling into some kind of sink hole filled with water.

"Big breath," Angel reminded.

Jet sucked in. Halfway through his breath, the mask valve shut off. Cold water doused him.

Holy crap, these sim suits can change temperature fast.

His limbs moved sluggishly as he peered around the dim water of the cave, looking for a place to climb out. But the cave was a bulb shape with a sloping overhang roof. There was little chance he could climb out.

Have I got a grappling hook? Jet wondered. As he searched his body, a shadow moved in the water.

Holy double crap.

Jet found his knife strapped to his chest and drew it as the shape grew larger and larger. It was a fish nearly as big as him.

The fish turned away at the last second, moving to Jet's left side, away from his knife hand. Only then did he see the long claws on its pectoral fins.

Electricity raked his side in a painfully realistic simulation of a gash. The water around him began to turn red. Jet whirled to face the foe but caught another searing laceration from behind.

Two of them!

Jet let the knife go, reached lower, and drew his pistol from the holster at his thigh. He squeezed off a shot at what he thought was one of the cave fish. There was a flash as the powder in the shell erupted and a stream of bubbles ran out from the gun.

Did I get it?

Then the electricity burned at his neck.

"Game over. You just got owned by a couple of fish."

Jet ripped off the goggles and hauled in a breath through his breathing mask—at least the valve was back on. "Turn down the voltage—are you trying to kill me?"

"Pansy."

"Easy for you to say. You can't even feel pain."

"You should have noticed the claws on the fins."

Jet shrugged. Angel was right. He couldn't get in the habit of relying only on his AI to assess threats.

"Your flashlight probably would have blinded them."

"Right, the flashlight. Where was it?"

"Tool belt. Right side. Or you could have just shot the first one before it cut you."

"Quick draw," Jet said. "Got it—but a bullet only goes a meter in water."

"And it makes you deaf . . . and probably bleeding internally from the pressure wave."

"So, I'm dead either way?"

"Flashlight—just saying."

"Fine."

"Next sim starts now."

Jet's ribs and neck still ached from the simulated wounds. He pulled the goggles down.

"What the heck is that?"

Standing in a jungle clearing, he was face to face with a long-legged creature, like an ostrich from Earth but bigger, more like a

The Exalting

feathered running dinosaur with wings.

"It's a greeder," Angel said. "Say hello."

Jet stamped his feet to see what it would do.

The bird took off through the woods and was instantly gone from view.

"Too easy." Jet surveyed the jungle for some way to get off the ground. "It's going to come back with more of them, isn't it?"

"I don't know."

"Yes, you do," Jet said. "You built this sim from the microbot footage."

"By the way, that bird—you can ride them."

"Cool." Jet drew his sidearm. "Well, just in case it does come back." He stepped forward. *Nothing.* He stepped again. *Nothing.*

Jet continued exploring the jungle. This simulation suite was all about apex species. Obviously, the bird was going to come back. It was just a matter of time.

A huge insect buzzed past his face.

"They've got mosquitoes, too—and bigger. Great. What else did you put in here, Angel?"

Apparently, with similar environmental forces, convergent evolution had made the Xahnan animals fairly similar to Earth's, even if their DNA was completely different—like how dolphins and sharks had astonishingly similar characteristics even though their genetic histories were totally different.

"You know, I'd almost rather face a flock of riled up Avalonian bat chickens than those cave fish," Jet said. His stomach rumbled. "Tasty critters. So tasty."

Jet got one of those feelings. *I'm being watched.*

He turned to see a vine dropping slowly toward him from the tree overhead.

He looked up to see what kind of animal would lower a vine. Then the vine shot out and curled around his arm. An electrical pulse from the vine rocked his entire body. His muscles completely locked as he was hauled upward toward some digesting organ that oozed with a substance he was sure would eat his skin.

Just as Jet thought his heart would give out, the sim went dark.

"Zero for three."

"Killer vines!" Jet ripped off the goggles. "Gimme a b-b-break. I can't even f-f-feel my body."

Following his training shift, Jet went to the gym. He was a marine. It was part of his regimen. But the three failures in Angel's sim, and the lingering tingling in his arms, left him feeling less than enthusiastic.

His workout halted when every head in the gym turned to the entrance.

Teea.

There was no hiding her approach in a place like a weight room.

No matter how daintily she tip-toed through the few hulking human soldiers in the room, an Avalonian in a place like that was impossible to miss.

It wasn't just the contrast in size, but the way her subtle movements of hand and eye drew attention like a magnet.

The entire gym was staring, Jet included. He couldn't even tell if she was using pheromones.

Her ultra-fine, green-tinged hair and silken dress drifted behind her as she walked, as if there was some unseen breeze.

And she had purple irises—when she wanted them that color.

"Jet Naman," she called in a playful voice. "Found you!" She danced over the tops of several barbells and did an effortless front somersault over a bench press station.

Jet kept waiting for the momentary numb sensation that signaled a pheromone engaging. Unfortunately, it didn't come.

She sat balanced on the handle of a resistance trainer. The flex bar barely registered her weight. "I know what kazen are."

Jet leaned back on his weight bench. "What?"

"A ka's helpers—their emissaries, enforcers, that sort of thing."

The Exalting

After Jet managed to focus on what she was saying, he realized she was talking about the people in a ka's inner circle. He asked her if she had figured out how the ka gave them power.

She giggled. "That's silly. They have power before they come into the service of a ka," Teea said. She winked at a soldier staring at her from the deadlift bar—the bar that hadn't budged since she came in the room.

That was strangest thing of all. Xahnans had superpowers of their own—not derived from the ka. Jet's whole theory of the water being critical to a ka's power seemed to develop a giant leak on the spot.

Unless the power came from the people, not the water. Perhaps the water merely combined their powers. It was an interesting possibility.

Teea fiddled with the hem of her dress as she talked about the treasure trove of information she'd dredged from a single conversation. "Our bugs only have forty minutes of battery life. One happened to land on a child. She was on her way to become a kazen because she was gifted—*adept* would be the nearest human word."

So now, on top of overpowered superheroes, there were sidekicks.

"What sort of power do they have?"

"Still working on that. Lots of theories about talking to animals and mind control. But Avalonians can already do that. Would you like to see?"

She had that look in her eye. Once an Avalonian got an idea in their head . . .

Jet quickly shepherded her toward the exit. "You better head out before somebody accidentally drops a weight on their foot."

She grinned. "It doesn't have to be an accident."

"That's alright," Jet said. "We don't need—"

She flashed a grin at a nearby marine and blew a pheromone-loaded kiss in his direction. A second later his eyes defocused, and the barbell he was holding dropped onto his foot.

He didn't even notice.

The rest of the gym burst into raucous laughter.

"That was what I was trying to avoid," Jet said.

Teea grinned. "But wasn't it fun!"

"So, this business about kazen and adepts—you figured it all out on your own?"

Teea shook her head. "No. I had help."

"Who?"

"Someone I pulled from cryo who studied xeno-sociology."

Jet's heartbeat accelerated. "What's her name?"

"I didn't say it was a girl." Teea said with a twinkle in her eye—a literal twinkle of light. "Anyway, her name is Monique."

Jet laughed. "I was her squad lead on Rodor. She was transferred to Alpha squad after the Avalon mission. Did you tell her I'm on the first contact mission?"

Teea shook her head. "That's above her clearance."

"Not anymore it isn't. You woke her. Might as well put her on the mission."

"You can do that?"

Jet shrugged. "Yes. Yes, I can."

"Can I come on the mission, too?"

Jet hesitated. "We'll see."

Teea leaned forward. "Don't make me become persuasive."

Jet lifted his hands. "Alright. No need to get all pheromone-ey about it."

Teea grinned like a kid with a handful of pilfered cookies and darted from the room.

Monique. She was awake and somewhere on the Excalibur. Conscious of the muscle mass he had lost in cryo, Jet walked to the bench press machine and dialed up the resistance. "I've gotta get back into shape."

Chapter 13

Reaching the freight barge seemed like the first good thing to happen to Dana in recent memory.

The taller bargeman handed Dana a tall tin flask. "You can drink that for sure. It's fresh from a glacier above Norr. Sayathi don't like the cold."

Dana sensed no sayathi essence. She drank eagerly, then closed the stopper on the flask and reached into her pockets to share some of the bread Brista had packed for her. "Would you like some—"

"No need, we're on company rations."

"Welcome aboard," said the tall man. "Name's Jila."

The shorter man tucked his sifa politely, save the lowest. "Turigan, of Salith Trading Company, Regalin Dominion, Torsica."

Dana pulled in her inferior sifa and lowered her eyes briefly. "Dana."

"Of . . . ?"

"Formerly of Norr."

Both men smiled pleasantly, as if she were a ticket-carrying passenger.

Friendly folk.

It struck Dana as odd that anyone from Torsica could be that kind. Her last encounter had been with the warlock Omren.

Dana immediately dismissed the possibility that these laborers were adepts. Such were actively recruited and lived as well-paid kazen in blood-bound dominions.

It was the life she could have had.

Beyond their manners, there was a striking vitality to the men. Certainly, they were middle-aged, possibly only a few years younger than her father. But their smooth, tanned skin, the glossy black of their hair, and the silvery shine of their eyes was unmistakable. They simply looked too healthy.

Dan Allen

Blood-bound. The sayathi parasites served their hosts well. These blood-sworn men would far outlive their unsworn peers in Norr.

"Are there any more bleeding wells downstream?" Dana asked.

"Not on the map. There was a tainted section a mile back, though," said Turigan. "Good thing you waited for us."

Dana nodded, her lateral sifa spreading proudly.

"That dead greeder back there—was that yours?" Jila asked.

Dana's sifa went limp, dropping behind her ears along her neck. "I . . . yes."

"Poor thing." Jila put a kind hand on her shoulder. "That's a terrible loss."

"It was raised in captivity," Dana said, her lip quivering. She looked away, staring into the dense trees on the far bank. ". . . It didn't know."

"There, there," Turigan said. He shouldered his long push pole, took Dana's hand, and guided her to the pile of opalescent sayathenite in the center of the barge. She sat on the heap of crystal nodules and took a few shaky breaths, hoping she didn't break into tears.

Her hand almost moved to the pouch in her pocket with the bloodstone, but she kept her hand clear of it. No need to draw attention to the one stone of sayathi origin on the boat that wasn't in the pile.

What made the regular sayathenite nodules different from the queen bloodstones, she had no idea. All she knew about sayathenite was what Forz had told her. He called the sayathenite crystals polyresonators. They turned electrical impulses into hundreds of sound resonances, and vice versa. The interactions between the sound waves could be adjusted by training at elevated temperatures.

The pile of them made for a lumpy seat, but Dana was glad to be off her feet.

Turigan and Jila lowered their poles into the water and levered the barge back into the main stream.

"How far to the coast?" Dana asked.

"A good way yet," said Turigan, in the kind of vague answer she expected from a riverman.

"Well how far is that?" Dana asked. "For someone counting in days."

"Now, don't go touting your knowledge of things like counting days," Jila said with a grim face. "We're but poor simple folk."

Dana rolled her eyes. "How long?"

"A day and a half—thirty hours, so long as we don't hit any sandbars."

"Do you sing any songs, Dana, formerly of Norr?" Turigan asked, his eyes expectant.

Dana smiled. All three sets of her sifa lifted proudly.

Jila gave an encouraging gesture.

Dana could do a lot better than singing. But she would have to spend some will. And of course, it would mean exposing the fact that she was an adept.

Why not? She wasn't in Norr anymore. Being an adept wasn't a crime.

Dana took only a moment to choose a fitting song: "Gentle River." She carried the first verse, before giving in and calling in a few birds to join in the chorus.

"Maka-ka's mercy!" Turigan cried, using the name of what Dana guessed was the supreme of his dominion. "She's an adept!"

The three gray nodding birds continued the notes of the chorus in perfect harmony as Dana stood and made a few turns of the river dance.

Jila and Turigan joined in the second chorus, which caused the offended birds to take flight in protest. The men didn't seem to mind as they bellowed the familiar tune beside Dana.

It was a beautiful moment, one so very different from her restrictive past in Norr. Life seemed so easy, so simple. People could simply love each other and be happy. She was no threat. But to leave it all behind felt like a kind of treason of the heart. She was free, but Forz was not. Neither was her mother.

She wiped the beginnings of a tear from her eye as she thought of her friends back in Norr, and her parents who were probably still arguing about whether Dana really had a bloodstone.

It would keep them up at night, especially as they wondered what it had to do with Togath's disappearance. What might she have done to get a bloodstone?

The authorities would have similar questions. It was better that she left now, before the rangers found the dead bodies in the forest.

Once Dana reached the port, she could head south and then turn west and ascend the Shoul River trade route to the city at its headwaters: Shoul Falls. With luck, she could find the city's sanctum and keep the bloodstone out of the hands of any remaining Vetas-kazen.

The song faded when Dana realized she didn't know the third verse and neither did the bargemen.

"One more, if you please, madam. Your singing is treasure to poor laborers like us."

Dana felt the small tines on her sifa flare, fanning in a moment of indiscretion. Her sifa weren't finished maturing. The lateral and superior sifa remained stubbornly, modestly bundled tight. But there was no hiding the genuine flush of pleasure to her cheeks.

What Dana had managed barely bordered on flirtation, though she knew the men found it attractive by the subtle flaring of their own feathery sifa.

"Of course," Dana said. "But might I rest a few minutes?"

"Make yourself at home on our pile," Jila said with a laugh. "Loaf as much as you like."

"You're a sweet man," Dana said. She glanced at Turigan. "Both of you. Thank you for bothering to come rescue me."

"Well," Turigan said, blushing a touch as his inferior sifa shook proudly. "You are obviously a well-bred young woman. Were you raised at a sanctum?"

"No," Dana said. "Norr is a free city."

"Hmm," Turigan said. "Quirky place, ain't it?"

Dana reached out to several schooner fish hiding below the raft and urged them all to take a curious leap out from under the raft. The rainbow of leaping fish brought delighted cheers. Jila tried to

The Exalting

catch one in his hat and had to grab his push pole to keep it from taking a tumble in the river.

"A little too much fun," Turigan reminded, raising his lateral sifa in a note of caution.

"I'm just fine, you worry-wort," Jila huffed.

Dana drew a hesitant breath. "Do you know of a supreme called Vetas-ka?"

"That one," Jila said with a snort, "is ambitious."

"He conquers other dominions," Turigan added. "Thankfully he hasn't reached so far south as Regalin."

"Be trouble if he did," Jila said.

Turigan lifted his pole and walked to the front of the barge to lower it again. "But not for long. If Vetas-ka's bloodstone wants Regalin, Maka-ka's stone might just give in rather than fight."

"And you'd best watch your tongue," Jila said. "You're bordering on blasphemy."

"And I'm just bored," Dana said, changing the subject before the men could turn the topic and ask why she cared about a supreme ruler on a continent halfway across Xahna. She started humming a solstice song, and the men fell into silence, leaning as much on the trilling sound of Dana's voice as their barge-guiding push poles.

A flash lit the trees on the bank. Dana jumped to her feet, heart pounding.

"Rhynoid strikes again," Jila announced. "Gets my heart pounding every time."

Whatever creature had been struck by the vines had died so quickly Dana hadn't even felt its pain.

"Probably a dumb scamper," Turigan said.

"Makes a nice stew," Jila added.

"What? Like you've ever tried an electrocuted scamper! You clinging coward. You wouldn't go within a stone's throw of a rhynoid vine."

"Would so."

"Would not. And I'll put a wager on it."

"Oh, bargemen and gambling," Dana said, brushing the argument aside. Her hands shook slightly from the sudden fright of the attack. Only a few feet from the edge of the river the rhynoid vine was curling around its prey, drawing the dead creature into the darkness of the jungle canopy where its juicing organ waited to suck the internal organs out.

It was lucky the vines lost their predatory instinct when they were severed from the juicing organ. Inside Forz's mechanodrons, the vines were mere slaves to the electrical impulses of the sayathenite crystals, which repeated trained tones in logical sequence.

"I knew a man who took a rhynoid vine around his wrist and dragged the thing right out of the tree," Jila said. "True story."

"That's a load of fresh dung, if ever I've smelt it."

"You smell it all day on yourself."

"Coming from a portly poopsmith, that's a compliment."

"Ah, you cut me."

"When you reach the port, what are you going to do with your pay?" Dana asked.

Jila looked at Turigan who gestured back at Jila. Neither man appeared to want to admit his vices.

"Drink and song?" Dana offered.

"Ay," Jila said. "That sounds about right."

About dinner time, after several Norrian ballads which the Torsicans were content to simply listen to and enjoy, the bargment lashed the barge to a mooring post, and Dana convinced several large gill bass to leap onto the shore. She excused herself while the men killed and gutted the fish. She left them to cook the meat as well, and ate from their rations instead.

Animals were not a part of her diet. But she had promised to cook something, and looking for food in the jungle in the dark wasn't a good idea. Delivering the fish was a decent compromise.

"Not a great cook," Jila noted, "but a fair fisherwoman."

"More than fair."

"Oh, you can keep your indecent compliments to yourself."

The Exalting

"I was speaking of the fishing. And you can keep your bad breath to yourself."

"I take no offense," Dana said. Nothing brought out a rivalry like attention.

Dana smiled. She lifted her blanket over her head to avoid bites from nightfeeders and lay back on the grass in the clearing near the mooring.

"How far can those rhynoids reach?" Jila whispered.

"Right into your dreams," Turigan hissed. "Better keep a wary eye."

"About ten feet from a trunk," Dana said.

"There you go and ruin it," Turigan mumbled as he lay down on Dana's left. "Young girls and their honesty. Maka-ka bless 'em."

Jila lay down on the other side of Turigan. "One more song?"

"Go to sleep, you sagging whiner," Turigan groaned.

"Maka-ka keep you," Jila mumbled drowsily.

"And your kin," Turigan echoed.

"Amen," Dana whispered, realizing in the same moment that she had just broken yet another of Norr's laws by reverencing a foreign supreme—and she had no idea what sort of supreme Maka-ka was.

Judging by the bargemen, not bad.

"A girl with a stolen greeder—what would I know about that?"

Dana jerked awake at the sound of Turigan's guttural drawl.

She slowly lifted a corner of her blanket and froze at the sight of a ranger's boot only a few yards away.

"Not sure you've got any jurisdiction this far." It was Jila's voice. His even larger boots were between Dana and the ranger.

"You got a bill of sale for that load of sayathenite?" the ranger asked. Dana was sure she'd heard his voice before. He was one of the rough-handed rangers that had hauled her back to Norr.

"Might. You got somewhere to go with two broken legs?"

113

Apparently the big Torsican had no respect for a nosey lawman from a free city.

"Is that a threat?" the ranger said.

"Let's just say when a wandering ranger pokes his nose in a bargeman's business, the bargeman's like to do some poking of his own—with a twelve-foot pole." The tip of Jila's pole thumped against the ground.

"Oh, leave the man's legs alone, Jila." Turigan sounded peaceable, but he had moved directly behind the ranger, where he could pin the man's arms should he provoke a fight with Jila. "You're just angry because you haven't had your breakfast yet."

"You're right about that."

"Anyway," Turigan said. "For your information, we saw a bloody carcass of a greeder about a half day back at a wellspring. Afraid your greeder thief must have gone looney and drank some tainted water."

"Awful sight," Jila added. "Probably still some bones left if you're interested in a souvenir."

"Was there a girl there?"

"We didn't interview the vultures," Jila said with a derisive snort. "What do you think we are, druids?"

"Best look for yourself," Turigan said, again taking a more agreeable tone, though he stood with one foot slightly forward—a fighting stance. "It ain't our business to go poking around dead carcasses. We're on a schedule."

"Well, I should like to see your bill of freight at least. Can you provide a manifest?"

Dana froze. From what she could see of the ranger's boot, it looked as if he were leaning in her direction.

"Are you yanking my sifa?" Jila blurted out. "Take a look for yourself. It's a load of sayathenite sitting right there on the barge. Or did you want to take a look at it from the bottom of the boat? I can arrange that if you bend over."

"Ah, Jila. Give the man a rest. He's an Aesican. You know how they are about rules and papers. Besides, his mountain diet is

The Exalting

probably a little low on fiber."

"I'll take your names and your statements." The ranger reached into a pocket for a writing pad.

Jila gave a low growl. "I haven't got time for this nonsense. You take your ugly face and get out of my sight. Go find your bird carcass and leave an honest man to his business."

A short silence ensued where Dana imagined there was some posturing, with displays of superior sifa, before the ranger's boots turned and walked across the meadow, ostensibly to the trading road that followed the river.

"Quick, Dana," Turigan hissed. "Get on the raft."

Dana threw back the blanket, grabbed her boots, and made a dash across the grass to the mooring. She leapt from the shore to the boat and was joined moments later by the bargemen with their poles.

"Wouldn't cry if I heard a big zap from that direction," Jila said, waving his pole at the clearing. "One satisfied rhynoid. Two satisfied bargemen."

"That's not kind," Dana said. She knelt to tie on her shoes as the two men pushed away from the shore. "Although he must have been a complete idiot not to have seen me under the blanket."

"Well, Jila's coat was lying over you, and quite frankly, you're not that large."

"Don't defend that man," Jila said. "He's an idiot all right."

"I'm just glad you had the presence of mind to stay still," Turigan said. "It might have gotten rough if he had seen you."

Dana swallowed. He was right. *Then again* . . . Dana's throat clenched as the pieces came together. "I think he probably did see me. He just couldn't fight you both by himself, so he pretended not to while he got a good look at you both. He's probably gone to get backup."

"Oh," Turigan said, his sifa drooping. "That does make more sense."

"We've been hoodwinked, you ka-forsaken noodle of a barge-bilge sack!" Jila ranted.

115

Turigan took an errant swing at Jila with his push pole. "And you were the one who did all the talking, you blighted, dimwit son-of-a-twitching-rhynoid sap sucker."

"Boys!" Dana flared her superior sifa, as if chastising children. "How far to the port?"

"Still twelve hours."

Dana glanced toward the bank where the ranger doubtless had climbed onto his greeder and was covering ground ten times as fast as the slow-moving barge.

"He's going to set a trap for me."

Chapter 14

At The Broken Anvil, the Wodynian cantina half-aft on the flagship Excalibur, Jet nearly dropped his empty glass.

Monique was sitting at a nearby table, bouncing her leg. She hadn't noticed him. Jet didn't consider this an especially good sign. First shift was barely over—the equivalent of mid-afternoon—and there were only four customers.

He sauntered over to her table. "Hey, Monique!"

"Oh—hi. You're awake, too?"

"You bet." Jet took a seat.

Her eyes narrowed. "What are you doing out of cryo?"

Jet smiled. "Just . . . waiting for you, I guess."

"No, seriously." Her tone dropped. "What are you doing?"

She doesn't know. Jet fought to keep a straight face. *She doesn't know it's my mission.*

"Oh, you know. Somebody was in a tight spot, and then somebody else was like, 'Get Jet Naman to do it,' so . . . here I am."

Monique raised a questioning eyebrow.

Jet considered telling her, but it seemed like a sort of cocky one-ups-man kind of thing to do. "What about you?" Jet said. "Did somebody finally decide they needed your brain more than your gun-toting skills?"

Monique sipped her drink. "My gun-toting skills aren't so bad."

"Yeah, I was sorry to lose you to Alpha squad."

"That's what happens when you get promoted."

"Really? Congrats." Jet hadn't heard about that. He raised his empty glass. "To being Corporals."

"Corporals." She poured some of her drink into his glass and clinked hers against it.

Jet placed his elbows on the table and leaned forward. "I'd love to hear what you're up to."

Monique laughed and leaned back, one leg still crossed over the other. "You've got time?"

Now we're getting somewhere.

Jet scooted his chair closer. "Sure."

"Well, I've been mining the satellite image database from the advance AI survey on Xahna." She began talking at a speed that made Jet dizzy. "I've been attempting to build a political map of Xahna with geo-linguistics using street signs and some unsupervised machine learning methods."

Jet was only catching about a third of what she saying. But it sounded like she was single-handedly cracking the political system of Xahna without even having set foot on the planet.

Don't look nervous. Play it cool. Jet tapped the table and ordered a random drink from the scrolling menu. He was determined to make it through the conversation.

"It's amazing how much you can learn from a large dataset if you get the data representation right—" she continued, without taking a breath.

A tall glass of bubbling mint-colored liquid rose out of the dispensing station in the center of the table. Jet took a long swig, and immediately the room started changing color.

Oh, no. Jet tapped the table to pull up his bill. He had ordered Avalonian Spieldampfer. The drink was rather infamous.

His ears began to ring.

No. No. No.

This was the first time Monique had ever really opened up to him about something she cared about, and he had just ordered a drink that was going to make him go completely deaf. Someone usually ordered it when the person next to them at the bar was really annoying.

It was relationship suicide.

"Well, recently—in a sociological sense," she said. "Could be decades, could be centuries—a large region of Torsica, the big continent, was annexed into some kind of empire under a single ka—those are their deity rulers."

118

The Exalting

"Sounds like we got ourselves another Hitler or Genghis Khan," Jet said, hoping he wasn't talking ridiculously loud. It was getting hard to hear. That was the point of Spieldampfer.

Please don't notice . . .

"It's too early to tell," Monique said. "But it's fascinating just knowing about this empire. In fact—"

Jet considered the idea of first contact with a man worshipped as a deity who ruled an entire empire.

That sort of first contact I usual handle with a gun.

Of course, he wasn't supposed to take sides on Xahnan internal conflicts.

But we don't have time for them to figure out their politics. As he faded into increasing levels of incoherence, Jet decided that once he got to Xahna, he would choose a side and let his 0.50 cal do the negotiating.

The other thing he was certain of was that he could no longer hear Monique talking. He stared at her lips and nodded as she spoke quickly.

It was only a matter of time before she stopped talking and asked him a question. *She'll kill me if she recognizes the drink.*

Then when she found out he was in charge of first contact, she would kill him again for toying with her. But it was too late now.

Jet truly did want to impress her. But one-upping her wasn't the way to do it. And playing her wasn't either. He was in a bit of spot, and the only way out seemed to be to drain the glass before she recognized it.

Or I could just fess up.

Jet's vision got shaky. He couldn't tell if his head was shaking or just his eyes.

Monique asked him something.

Wish I could read her lips. He shrugged, "Ah, I guess that makes sense."

She nodded and continued talking.

This mission was a lot more pressure than he was used to. Usually a mission came up on short notice. He got briefed, handed a weapon, and pushed out of a flying vehicle. He hunkered down for a few days and took out anything that moved, until the situation went bonkers. Then he got out fast.

This one wasn't going to be like that.

Honestly, he had no idea what it was going to be like. It could be dangerous—incredibly dangerous, especially with god-like beings running amok.

But why did he have to pick a dangerous place on Xahna to make contact? Just because he was used to that sort of mission, didn't mean it had to be.

Maybe I should start in a city without a ka.

But he had more urgent problems. Monique suddenly sat up and asked him something—probably if he was alright.

He was completely deaf, and beyond the strange swirling of colors past everything in sight, the world seemed to be tipping slowly to one side.

The Avalonian numbing agents had gotten to his inner ear.

He wasn't even sure if he could make it back to his room without help.

Jet grabbed the table to keep from tipping over. The only way out was telling her.

Swallowing all pretense, Jet picked up his glass. "I think I ordered the wrong drink."

Monique touched the table and dragged his receipt over to her side, which had the side effect of adding it to her bill. "You ordered Spieldampfer?" He could tell what she was saying because he'd been dreading her saying exactly that—and the look of fury on her face.

"Um," Jet moaned. "Guess I should have looked at the menu more closely. You're . . . a little distracting."

Monique's stunned expression softened. "Anyway, I think you're sweet and charming." At least that's what he imagined she was saying before he tipped off his chair.

Monique rounded up a few others from the bar, and soon Jet was being carried down a corridor by three marines. She and another marine each had one of his arms draped over their

The Exalting

shoulders. A Wodynian female carried his legs over her shoulders.

It appeared the others were having quite a few jokes as his expense. He was beginning to make out what they were saying—at least the laughing.

Thankfully Avalonian pheromones faded quickly. He might even be able to stand on his own by the time they shuttled his dead weight to his room.

Shuttles. That's it!

"Wait!" Jet said, trying to sit up and ending up on his butt on the floor. "Take me to Adkins. I have to see the colonel."

Monique knelt down next to him. She looked him straight in the eyes, something he had hoped for all evening. She spoke loudly enough he caught her words. "Not when you're this wasted. Are you insane?"

"I'm just—tipsy. And this is important. Trust me."

"I am so going to regret this."

Five minutes later, Jet staggered up to Colonel Adkins's stateroom, with one arm over Monique.

She reached out, her hand hovering over the door ringer, then pressed the icon.

She does trust me. It was the best moment since he'd been out of cryo.

Jet was glad his ears were now giving him clearer hints of sound as the colonel answered the door in his pajamas and sounded off a long stream of words he was pretty sure a Believer probably shouldn't even know.

"We can use shuttles," Jet said, "and have the sprint ship ready in a few hours." This time he even heard his own voice.

Adkins looked from Jet to Monique. "He looks plastered."

"He is," Monique let Jet's arm off of her shoulder. "But I think you should listen to him. He's not as dumb as he looks—can't believe I just admitted that."

Jet gave Monique a half-smile, which she returned as more of a quarter-smile, just a tiny lift of her lip.

He loved it when she did that.

Dan Allen

Jet tore his eyes away from Monique and looked at the colonel. "The sprint ship—I know how to do it." He nodded at Monique. "She sort of gave me the idea."

"Her idea, eh?" Adkins folded his arms. "So what is it?"

Jet grinned. "Team carry. A marine can't haul a squad mate very far—they'd be dead tired in a few hundred yards. So, we do a team carry: arms over shoulders, legs under arms, like a stretcher."

"I don't follow."

"What if we used a whole slew of mini shuttles to haul a big capitol ship fuel tank?"

"How?"

"We make a net around a capitol ship fuel tank with tug lines running out to several dozen shuttles. They have anchor points to form webs—no welding needed. Shuttles have standard anchor points for getting towed and external fuel ports for running lines to the main tank. We could have this done in a few hours. There's got to be enough extra thrust capacity to tether a dropship on the front, but . . . it should work."

Adkins put his hand to his forehead. "Black space! That's just plain simple. Rigging a tow net is fleet maintenance 101. I could build that net myself in an EVA suit. You're brilliant, Naman!"

"Of course, once it starts slowing down and the argon fuel mass drops, you won't need all the shuttles," Monique added. "It's like a multi-stage orbital booster. That's the advantage of shuttles."

"Yeah, I get it. You can just dump them," Adkins said. "Shuttles are cheap—a lot cheaper than fuel." Adkins put a hand to his temple where he apparently had a subdermal transmitter. "Ace, I want your team in my office ASAP and leave that dang interdictor alone. Naman here has a better idea . . . yeah that's what I said. So, you can take your engineering AIs and put them back on defragging their memory. Jeez, a jarhead figured this thing out!" He took his finger off his temple. "You got twelve hours, Corporal."

"Twelve hours, sir? I thought you said anyone could—"

"Look, pushing the paperwork to steal shuttles from half the ships in the fleet is going to take half that time. No captain wants

The Exalting

to part with his lifeboats."

"So . . . in the meantime?"

"I'll order your squad to transfer to the dropship. And I'm reassigning Captain Decker to fly this contraption."

"Yes, sir!" Decker was better known as "the lion." He had experience and guts. The guy used to fly dropship missions before they promoted him to interdictor frigates. He had a reputation for pushing the edge. Every marine in the fleet wanted to fly with him.

"I putting you both in for commendations," Adkins said. "Black space! Do you realize how important this is? The entire fleet—all the remaining Believers in the galaxy—may depend on us reaching that planet first. This is going to cut an entire week of delay."

Jet and Monique saluted crisply, side by side. "Yes, sir."

Adkins matched the salute. "Dismissed."

He disappeared into his room.

"Well this deserves a drink," Monique said with a grin that ran from ear to ear.

"Maybe later?" Jet said, rubbing his temples.

Monique put on hand on her hip. "Look at you, turning down a drink and saving the fleet."

"Couldn't have done it without you."

"Thanks." She tapped her foot. "So we're both on the first contact mission?"

Jet wasn't sure whether she was mad or elated.

"I guess the High Council liked our rescue operation," she said. Then she punched him in the shoulder and sauntered away. "But you still don't outrank me!"

Best arm punch ever.

"Hey, where are you going?" Jet said. "We only have twelve hours until launch. We should do something—"

She stopped and turned.

"—fun."

"Sorry, I've got a date."

"A date? With who?"

"An elf."

"An elf? Don't tell me you let Yaris ask you out."

She turned away and waved over her shoulder with her fingers.

Jet hoped the elf was a jerk. But then he changed his mind. Twelve hours was all she had left on the Excalibur. It was all she had left before her life changed forever. She deserved a good memory, something to hang on to.

"Hey, Monique."

She looked over her shoulder.

"Good luck."

He got a quarter of a smile.

Chapter 15

Dana made up her mind quickly. "Let me off on the south bank."

"Are you mad? How are you going to cross the jungle?" Turigan shook his head, wagging his glossy, unkempt black hair. "I can't let a girl like you end up like that poor greeder."

Jila gestured haplessly. "Or fried by a rhynoid and your guts sucked out of your face."

"That's a lovely image, Jila. Haven't you got a lick of manners? She's an adept, a gift of the Creator."

Dana's breath froze. A feeling like a warm blanket wrapped her soul. For the first time in her life someone had considered her *a gift*. Not cursed. Not tainted. It was a moment she had waited for her entire life. Still, she could hardly believe her ears. "What did you say?"

"An adept," Turigan repeated. "A gift of the Creator. You showed us yourself, high druidess."

High druidess?

Dana's jaw slackened. She clutched the front of her shirt near her collar and then turned to the middle-aged man. "No, Turigan. You are a gift of the Creator." She turned to Jila. "And you, as well, my friend." Tears twinkled in the corners of her eyes.

"Don't cry, Dana. There's a way out of this."

"I'm not crying because I'm sad." Dana held out her hands, and her two adoptive uncles wrapped her in an embrace.

Two great tears ran down her cheeks. She looked up into the faces of the Torsican men. "Thank you." She buried her head against Jila's chest, as Turigan stroked her hair.

"You're a brave one. You'll make it through."

Dana nodded. She sniffed and drew her hand across her eyes to clear the tears.

Turigan took her by the shoulders and looked her in the eyes.

"I meant what I said—a gift of the Creator."

"And perhaps," Dana said, smiling through another wave of emotion, "the Creator sent you to save me."

"But I'm afraid we can't fight through a posse," Jila noted. "There's just two of us, and Turigan is no use in a fight."

"Yes, I am!"

"You won't have to fight. I'm crossing the jungle."

"It's suicide."

"I'm a druid," Dana said. "The animals will show me way."

"Well, you had better take my flask." Jila unslung his canteen from his shoulder and offered it. "We'll be at the port in a few hours."

"I won't forget this," Dana said, cradling the canteen.

Turigan lowered his pole into the water, preparing to lever the barge toward the southern shore. "Promise me you won't die—and you won't get caught by the ranger?"

"I promise." Dana laughed. "Thanks for everything." She leaned up and kissed Turigan on the cheek. The man's stubbled face tickled her lips. Then she turned to Jila.

"Oh, I got a miss back on Torsica."

"And I've got a green feather on my fanny!" Turigan cried. "Bend down, you oaf, and get your thanks."

"I . . . I don't deserve it."

Dana put her hands on her hips. "It's either a kiss on the cheek, or a kick in the crotch for being stubborn."

"If you put it that way . . ." He leaned forward, and Dana kissed his bearded cheek.

"You're a kind spirit," Jila said. A smile wormed on his face and he blinked a few times.

Turigan chuckled. "Grace of the chosen ka—the big lug is going to cry."

"I'll drop my pole on your head before I drop a tear!"

"Just give me a hand to shore, Jila. Then you can fight as much as you like."

"Aye, I'll give you that, Miss Dana." Dana held out her arms,

The Exalting

and Jila gave her a big heave through the air.

She landed on a mossy slope and turned to wave as the two men dropped their poles on the shoreward side and levered the raft back into the stream. Then they waved until the bend in the river took them out of her sight.

Dana turned and faced the shadowed jungle. "I'm going to need a guide." She closed her eyes and reached out, touching every tree, every root, every—

"Gotcha."

Dana gave a tug, and a frilled scamper bounded down a nearby tree and up her leg to a prominent position on her shoulder. "Now," Dana whispered as she reached up to stroke the lizard's scaly back. "We're going to work together. Aren't we?"

The lizard nodded, following Dana's prompt.

"Very good."

There was an art to this. A scamper's mind was weak and easily dominated. If she pushed too hard, it would lose its sense of self and forget its instincts—she needed those desperately. So she had to keep it on a long leash.

The cold-blooded creature settled comfortably on her shoulder, which was warm with the heat of the morning sun.

Dana took a hesitant step into the jungle, eyes watching the canopy for the first sign of descending rhynoids. The problem was that they were plants. She could neither sense their intentions, nor press her will upon them. People were no different. She was no enchantress, nor an alchemist with the will to coerce the chemicals in a concoction. The Creator's veils over those were as strong as the unseen wall that blocked her will from touching the forces of nature like a warlock.

But she was a high druidess, as the Torsicans had called her—a gift of the Creator.

"Sandy," Dana said, voicing her chosen name for the frilled-neck lizard. "When you sense danger, you throw out that frill and give a hiss."

The lizard made a demonstration, flaring its frill and stretching its fluorescent orange tongue as far out of its gaping mouth as it would reach.

Gross.

"Very good . . . you can put your tongue back in your mouth."

The lizard slowly returned to its rest posture, as if enjoying the added attention it got for obeying as slowly as possible.

"A boy—typical."

Sandy licked his lips.

"Not lunch yet. We're just getting started."

Dana resisted the urge to look back at the river. Instead, she pressed forward through the trees for several hundred yards, until Sandy flared his neck frill.

"That's a centipede, you coward. You're twice its size."

She kicked the centipede out of her way. The six-inch-long creature sailed through a tuft of thin-bladed grass. In a flash, five limb-like vines lashed out and caught the creature in midair. Blue light danced along the edges of the vines, and the twitching centipede was hauled back into the center of the tuft of "grass"—a rhynoid's disguised feeler vines.

"By the brother moon—they grow out of the ground, too?"

She side-stepped the pothole rhynoid, heart pounding in her chest. "Is there anything else you'd like to say before we continue?"

Sandy shook his head and then relieved himself on her shoulder.

"Why? That is just . . . ugh."

Dana pressed ahead until she came to the trade road. She wasn't enough of a ranger to spot any fresh greeder tracks headed for the port. She simply hurried across the road and ducked back into the cover of the tall ferns on the far side.

In half an hour Dana had passed half a dozen more pothole rhynoids and then stopped when Sandy looked up into the trees. For half a minute she stared into the canopy of the towering jungle trees, until she spotted the curled forms of lasher rhynoids. Their bulbous sucker heads mimicked the broad leaves around them.

"Oh, there's only ten rhynoids on that tree. What's the big

The Exalting

fuss?" It was enough vines to eat an entire mounted patrol—perhaps even a massive thunder bison, though the bison rarely left the grassy foothills to venture into the jungle.

Dana swallowed and backtracked several dozen yards to avoid the predatory garden. "Thank you, Sandy."

As she crept through the dense foliage, Dana kept her own lookout for the thorned trees that hosted the pothole rhynoids at their base and the broad-leaved variety the lasher rhynoids favored. And there were other dangers in the jungle, too, especially the Aesican saber panthers. But they hunted at night.

Dana drained her canteen before dinner and learned to refill it from honey pitcher blossoms by pulling on their petals to get them to spread, another trick she learned from Sandy.

Luck reached Dana just before nightfall when she stepped around a toadstool-laden fan-leaf tree onto a hunter's trail.

"Ah. This will do. I can take it from here."

She released Sandy, and he scampered back into the forest in the direction of a thornwood spider nest. He would get his pay after all.

Dana turned east, the direction of the port, following the well-worn path through the trees. In places, the trail was wide enough to make out the parallel marks of wagon wheels in the mud.

The rangers would never look for her on a trail like this. She could approach the port at night, find a place to stay, hitch a ride with a trading company headed for Shoul Falls, and bid farewell to the pursuing rangers and the controlling government of Norr forever.

Dana was desperately tired, though she kept a wary eye out for the shapes of leaves that warned of rhynoids.

As the darkness grew, brother moon rose, followed by his sister, who would soon catch up and pass her sibling at Dana's time of transition. It came only every eighty-two days, but Dana looked forward to the change of emotion, the feeling of newness and the passing of a small chapter of her life.

Someday she would join a husband at the crossing of the

moons.

The fine hairs of her inferior sifa flared at the thought.

But not until those finish growing.

She was not a full adult yet. Anybody could see that. Although each transition brought another layer of fine hairs to her sifa, starting from just behind her ears until now the feather-like hairs grew to nearly the tip of her lower sifa.

Hopeful emotions swirled within Dana as she walked among the trees, with the stars rolling overhead and the brother and sister moon running their nightly race across the sky.

Perhaps they were not brother and sister but lovers.

It was a blasphemous thought to put the feelings of a mortal to objects in the heaven.

But why not?

Is Xahna not made in the image of heaven?

Dana pressed a fern out of her way, and her nose caught the scent of salt air.

"The ocean."

Dana sprinted ahead on the widening path. She crossed a stone-paved trade road that ran north and south along the coast and headed over a grassy berm. The sound of waves lapping gently at the shore reached her ears.

Wading through the tall grass, she finally reached a white, sandy beach that glistened in the moonlight like a thousand tiny diamonds.

"I made it!"

Dana fell to her knees and dug her hands into the sand.

The harbor lights of Port Kyner, and lanterns on the decks of dozens of anchored steamships, twinkled safely in the distance, several miles to her left.

I made it. And they won't find me out here. They think I'm coming on the river.

Dana wrapped herself in her blanket and lay on the warm sand of the berm, watching for shooting stars until her eyes blinked shut and sleep drowned her exhausted body.

The Exalting

⸻

In the morning, Dana woke as the sun rose over the eastern sea. In the long light, thousands of ovals took shape on the water.

Across the shallow sea that spanned the great expanse between the Aesican and Torsican continents, the sayathi ruled.

Dana walked to the edge of the beach, where one of many walls of coral rose three feet out of the water, bending in a circle some thirty feet wide. Small waves lapped her feet as the seawater at low tide splashed gently between the coral circle and a neighboring one.

Dana leaned over the coral wall and looked inside.

Clear, fresh water, still as a frozen pond, showed her reflection back at her.

Small fish swam contentedly in the isolated pond, along with the millions of unseen sayathi, like so many of the millions of colonies that spanned the shallow ocean. The only passages across were man-made channels that meandered through the sea of warring corals.

Dana's eyes followed the many faintly pulsing, blue-green lines from the edge of the pool to their source at the center. There, beneath the water, lay a faceted stone wrapped in an eerie green glow and sending out regular pulses like a slow heartbeat.

"Marvelous, isn't it?"

Startled, Dana turned to see a woman draped in a coarsely woven white shawl standing nearby.

"First time at the Sayathi Sea?" she asked.

Dana nodded. "There's nothing like this in Norr."

The woman looked to be in her late twenties, with bright hazel eyes. The healthy glow of her skin and the silvery tinge to the whites of her eyes were instantly recognizable. She, too, was obviously blood-bound. The woman gave a kind smile and reached a hand out of her shawl, indicating the nearest glowing ridges radiating outward along the bottom of the watertight pool. "The colony runs on electricity, pumping salt out through the reef wall to make fresh water." The woman reached out over the edge of the pool, and her hand took on a blue-green glow.

To Dana, it was magnificent. "You're bound to this pool?"

The woman nodded. "The sayathi send energy to each other with light." She dipped her arms in the fresh water of the coral pool and smiled as the tiny carnival fish swam between her fingers playfully. She reached over and ran her hand along one of the charge conduits to indicate one of the many sayathenite nodules. "This holds the blood of my family."

"That exact crystal?"

The woman nodded. "When I was seven, I came here with my father. I cut my own hand with a knife. I bled until the entire pool was red."

"You had to cut yourself—I'm so sorry."

"Don't be. It takes the sayathi a while to become immune to your essence, like a Xahnan getting over a nasty cold. But once the colony has the antidote to your essence, a new nodule forms to protect the formula." The woman leaned over and cupped the clear water to her mouth.

Dana was immediately entranced by the act and repulsed. Memories of the dying greeder's pain gripped her with steely fingers.

"They make your eyes beautiful," Dana said.

The woman gave a laugh. "Only a drale—er, unbound—would notice."

"And that?" Dana pointed to the glow in the center of the pool.

"The bloodstone," said the woman. "One at the center of every pool. It is the hub of all the signals. The pulsing determines how quickly salt is removed. If foreign sayathi are splashed in by a storm, the bloodstone tells the colony to attack. If the wall is damaged, the colony follows the signals to quickly repair it."

With one bloodstone in every pool, there must have been hundreds of bloodstones along the beach.

But of course, it wasn't the stones that granted will to a ka. It was the Xahnans bound to it. The fact that there were so many

The Exalting

small pools made them all equally feeble. And the pools that fed cities had to have a large source of water, such as a spring, merely rainfall or a storm tide.

Dana looked into the blue-green water, but her eyes could discern no sayathi. The organisms were indeed tiny, yet there was something there, a feeling like somebody in the next room. "Can you feel them?"

The woman shook her head. "Only the strength they give me. I cannot remember what it was like being without it."

Dana looked at the pool. "I can feel them. It's like a cloud in front of me."

The woman inclined her head. "You're a druidess?"

Dana nodded.

"No wonder you left Norr."

"So," Dana wondered aloud, "you can't drink from any other pools?"

The woman nodded. "It would be death. The sayathi bound to me would fight to kill the others, but I would die before the fight was won."

Dana had heard as much, but asking a blood-sworn was the only way to guarantee her secondhand knowledge was correct.

"Perhaps you don't know," the woman said cautiously. "There's a warrant for your arrest in the port."

An icicle stabbed into Dana's heart. "A warrant?"

"A ranger from Norr arrived yesterday. The civic guard at Port Kyner posted his letters. You are Dana, aren't you?"

Suddenly, despite the low altitude, Dana could hardly get a breath. She looked at the woman, mentally sizing her up. Not only was she taller, and certainly better rested, but she was blood-bound. Dana tensed, on the verge of reaching into the forest for some kind of defense. "Are you going to turn me in?"

The woman appeared astonished by the question. "You're an adept. I could never betray you to a bunch of ignorant drales."

Drale—their word for an unsworn. Dana was already enjoying the change of culture. Here, drales were outsiders—the things to be

133

feared—not adepts. "Well, thank you. I'm just trying to get away."

"Yes." The woman looked over her shoulder. "You should get going, Dana of Norr. Many of the far-sworn visit their colonies on the rest day."

"Far-sworn?"

"Those blood-bound to colonies other than the ka of Port Kyner: Saleh-ka."

"Is it even legal?" Dana asked.

"Of course. But Saleh-ka cannot hear my pleas. He cannot feel my pain. He does not come to heal my family."

"So why did you bind yourself to this colony?"

"I simply followed my father."

"And your children?" Dana asked.

"My twin girls will soon pledge to the colony of Saleh-ka."

This surprised Dana. "I thought the blood-binding lasted for four generations?"

"This pool would recognize my kin, yes. But they are born empty of any sayathi. They may join whatever colony they desire. It is their choice."

"Then why join Saleh-ka?" Dana asked.

"The ka are gathering strength. The world is far too dangerous for isolated far-sworn."

Dana gave the woman a quizzical look.

"I have seen teen boys break the wall between two colonies to watch the sayathi war. The smaller colony will usually submit, surrendering their bloodstone rather than die."

"So, the larger the colony, the better chance it has to survive an attack?" Dana guessed.

"Yes. Torsica has long watched our growing cities from across the Sayathi Sea. Our population is nearly equal to the old continent. If we don't support our ka, they won't stand a chance against the Torsican supremes."

"Why don't you take the bloodstone?" Dana asked, pointing to the spire in the center of the pond. "You could be ka over everyone bound to the pool."

134

The Exalting

The woman looked utterly disgusted by the suggestion. Her voice became instantly indignant. "One does not exalt oneself. The colony and all the blood-sworn must decide it." She gave Dana a concerned look. "The Creator gave us our will. To take it forcibly is like murder. There is no higher crime."

"And what if you touched the stone by accident?"

The woman laughed, as if amused by Dana's ignorance. Then she looked in the direction of the port. Dana, too, could see more Port Kyner citizens walking along the coral sand beach. It was time to go.

Dana turned to collect her blanket, tucked it under her arm, and crossed over the sand berm. She walked swiftly along the sandy ground between the trees lining the stone-paved trade road and the beach dunes.

The coast was heavily populated. She would likely reach another village in only a short while. The key was to stay ahead of the rangers hunting her. With luck, they would still be waiting for her at the port.

She hoped Jila and Turigan hadn't run into trouble for aiding her. Thoughts of the kind bargemen filled her with a sense of warmth.

Dana walked another mile before she stopped and slapped herself in the forehead. "Why am I walking?" Greeders were far more common in the coastal forests than in the highlands.

Dana crossed the trade road and waded into the jungle. She refilled her canteen from a pitcher blossom, then sat down and closed her eyes.

She sensed a greeder only a quarter mile away. With a suggestion of curiosity, it began moving her way.

Perfect. I'll reach the canyon to Shoul Falls before nightfall.

Traven was not a patient man. The two bargemen chained to the wall of the cellar had yielded nothing so far in relation to the girl

135

from Norr.

That would change very soon.

The taller of the prisoners raised his head and stared at Traven. His wrists were chained to the wall with iron manacles, his face was puffy with bruises, and his eye was swollen shut. The corner of his mouth bled freely. "Don't know what you're talking about."

It was the same answer as before, but now his voice was breathy and weak.

"The girl from Norr was seen in your company. You will tell me where she went." He looked at the shorter of the men. "I know some very painful ways to die." Fear flickered in the prisoner's eyes as a spinning scorpion descended on a thread of silk and hung in front of his eyes.

The prisoner was tight-lipped. It wouldn't matter if they were too swollen to talk. Perhaps the other prisoner would talk when he saw his friend in pain.

Traven pushed a thread of will into the scorpion, and it reached out and pulled itself to the man's face.

"Stop toying with them," snapped a female voice. Boots clacked on the wooden steps.

At last!

Traven had no doubt his methods would have delivered the information. But the enchantress was quicker.

"It's about time you showed up, Poria." Traven released the scorpion, and it swung to the floor and skittered away.

"Yes. Time is the one thing we do not have. Vetas-ka is losing patience. Stand aside."

Traven glared at the enchantress as she stepped into the light of the lantern hanging from the ceiling of the cellar. Not a strand of her long, silver hair was out of place. She obviously hadn't been hurrying to get to Port Kyner. But at least the crow he had sent had delivered his note.

"And you must call me Porien, brother Traven," she reminded. "I am a full kazen now." Her smile was as pale as her skin.

"Just get on with it," Traven said through gritted teeth.

The Exalting

Poria stood between the prisoners and removed her black gloves. She handed them to Traven.

He tossed them into the corner.

"Which of you has the better memory?" Poria stepped toward the shorter man. "It's you." She reached out her thumb and brushed the bare skin at the bottom of his neck, then set down one finger at a time until her hand was clasped around his throat.

The man twitched. He shook from head to foot, fighting the will that coursed through him.

"Ah, I see her now." Poria's gaze narrowed. "She's a pretty thing—dark hair, sad eyes—her sifa aren't even fanned." She laughed politely as she released her grip and squeezed the man's cheeks. "That wasn't so bad, was it?"

She spun on her heels. "The ranger was wrong. Your little fish jumped out of the river. That's twice she's been underestimated."

"Yes, but where is she? Where is the stone?"

"She went into the jungle," Poria said. "She's out of my sight now, so she must have gone southwest."

Traven nodded. "So she wasn't trying to leave by ship. She must be taking the stone back to Shoul Falls!" *Misdirection.* The girl was resourceful and obviously knew the area well. It was only a matter of getting her out in the open. "I'll have a saber panther tear out her throat—the little beast."

"She is a gift of the Creator." The prisoner who spoke lifted his head.

"A feeble drale," Traven said, as he brushed a bit of spattered blood from one of the brass buttons of his waistcoat with a handkerchief. "A pestilence among us."

"Your ka is a pestilence."

Traven drew a knife. Without a second thought, he slashed at the prisoner.

"Jila!" cried the other prisoner, his hands strained against the manacles that bound him to the wall.

"You could have at least had the decency to do it when I didn't have to feel it!" Poria hissed. "It's disconcerting."

"It had to be done," Traven said. "He cursed Vetas-ka. They have no more use." Traven looked down at his waistcoat, which was now far messier than it had been before. "We know where she's headed."

The smaller prisoner pulled in vain at his shackles. The death of his friend had left him in a mad rage. "And I know where you're headed—to the place of demons. But don't worry, you won't have to endure eternal torment alone. Your cursed ka will join you."

Traven silenced the other prisoner with a second slash of the knife. "Gather the faithful. Jovesten can take us by balloon directly to the mouth of the Shoul River Canyon. This girl will come to *us*."

Poria folded her arms. "But that canyon is only a half day from Shoul Falls. We can't let her cross the entire jungle unimpeded. We must send in the guards to search for her."

"I'm not taking any chances after what happened to Omren," Traven snapped. The younger kazen was drunk on her own power. She lacked experience. "Would you want to face a druid in a jungle? No. I'll send word ahead to the guards. If she tries to stop at a village for food, we'll have her all the quicker."

Chapter 16

Dana urged the greeder forward. Its pace accelerated, long legs gobbling up ground as it raced through low ferns.

South Aesica boasted larger greeders—war-ready varieties. But they were no match for the raw speed of a northern forest greeder.

In clearings, the grass passed in an urgent green blur that left Dana exhilarated. With every passing blade and branch, every passing stream that the greeder leapt and soared over, the feeling of freedom grew. Norr was gone to her. What awaited in Shoul Falls was the beginning of a new life in a place where she would actually be appreciated—perhaps even revered.

She didn't know exactly what she would do with the bloodstone when she got there. Getting it back to Shoul Falls was the right thing to do. That much was obvious. How and when she actually returned it to the citizens or the kazen of the sanctum was something she would have to decide when she had more information. For now, it was enough to be free of Norr, the civic guard, the rangers, and with luck, any Vetas-kazen who might have tracked the bloodstone to Norr.

Muscles aching from the effort of riding bareback, Dana traveled as far as the greeder could without stopping to feed. Six hours of hard riding took her farther than any pursuers on foot could have hoped to travel. The greeder's long stride had easily eaten up the miles as it sped through the underbrush—too fast even for a rhynoid to drop and strike.

But as she emerged from the jungle into the foothills of the barrier range, Dana abandoned her greeder to keep a lower profile. She approached the deserted highway on foot.

A sign post indicated the village of Jahr was only a half mile away. It was little more than an outpost nestled at the mouth of a canyon that led to Shoul Falls.

Perfect.

Hungry and exhausted, she stumbled toward the outskirts of the village. In the distance, visible above the thinning trees, smoke rose invitingly from several chimneys in the village proper. As the vegetation grew sparser, she spied several farmhouses on the opposite side of the highway. She could beg a loaf of bread or perhaps a warm meal from any of them. According to Norrian trader knowledge, the creed of the Jahrians required kindness to travelers in order to curry the favor of their aged ka.

Coming around a tree, she neared the crossing of the canyon road and the foothill route. From between two branches of a tall bush, she spied two men loitering at the crossing. They stood back-to-back just off the paver stones marking the crossing.

There were lots of reasons two men might be at a crossroads with nothing better to do than wait around. Not so many good reasons as bad ones.

They were not rangers, and their close-cropped hair and sleeveless jackets spoke of a warmer climate.

Torsicans?

Possibly. She would have to hear their accents to be sure. One man faced one quarter toward her, his head turning slowly, all six sifa flat and tight against his neck.

What could he be afraid of? Dana wondered.

But it was his eyes that told his secret. He wasn't waiting.

He was *watching.*

The difference was obvious to a druid who had spent her life observing predators. A saber panther *waited* for sundown to hunt. A hunting saber panther *watched* for prey.

Dana shivered. *It's me they're hunting.*

How did they get ahead of me?

Disappointment struck her at her weakest point. She was hungry and saddle sore and desperate for rest. Dana had half a mind to turn herself in, so long as she didn't have to travel any further. But she wanted to live even more desperately. Keeping the bloodstone out of the hands of Vetas-ka was somewhere in between.

The Exalting

The men looked to be unarmed, but they could have throwing knives, perhaps even crossbows stashed nearby. She remembered the trappers, how they had easily outrun her and were far stronger.

I must not be seen.

The nearer of the men kicked a rock. "I'm tired of waiting. Let's go back. There's only one traveler's inn. She's bound to show up at it."

Dana's breath caught in her throat. Getting food had been her first thought on seeing the village.

"Quiet," said the other Torsican. "The crow's note said Kazen Poria is coming by airship from the port. When she does," he cracked his knuckles, "she'll sense the druid. In the meantime, we do our job and we get paid."

Poria. So, they had an enchanter tracking her and a druid sending messages. Omren was right. There were other kazen, and thugs like these men as well.

If Vetas-ka had men in Jahr and Kyner, then why not Shoul Falls?

She could be headed into the back of a net.

It was a chilling thought. But stopping was not an option, not with kazen following her.

Dana looked in the direction of the port, but the foothills hid much of the sky. Hydrogen airships were expensive and dangerous. In mountainous places like Norr they were all but unheard of. But the prevailing winds came from the east—from the sea. It was the quickest way to get inland.

Dana looked up again, and this time she saw a speck in the distance.

Ka of Xahna!

There was an airship. The kazen had to be fabulously wealthy. It was dropping fast.

I've got to move. Now.

Dana crept back into the cover of the forest. However talented the Torsican enchantress was, Dana doubted her power could reach more than a fraction of a mile. But perhaps with power lent from

141

her ka, she could double or triple that.

And the enchantress would be only minutes behind Dana.

Once she was out of sight of the crossroads, Dana sprinted ahead, climbing into the foothills where isolated trees offered fragmented cover.

Speed was all that mattered now. Half-starved, Dana thrashed ahead through tall grass that lashed at her.

The clacking wheels of a steam-wagon and its puffing engine sounded along the trade road which wound a quarter mile to the north, to the village of Imdrel.

Avoiding the road, Dana took a shortcut through the scrub, hoping to gain some time. When she finally reached the shade of the canyon, she paused to catch her breath.

A misplaced thought groped her mind, a feeling that something important was lost. Dana looked down and spun around. She didn't see anything on the ground.

But Dana realized she had nothing to lose. She was out of food. The only thing left on her was the bloodstone and the canteen from the kind Torsican bargemen.

I should just turn back. It's useless.

No! It's Poria. She's here.

The enchantress's thought had been dropped so naturally into Dana's frenzied mind that she could scarcely distinguish it from her own. If she couldn't trust her own thoughts, escaping was going to be next to impossible. Her only hope was distance.

Go!

Dana sprinted to the other side of a rocky outcropping, and the feeling of something reaching for her vanished. It seemed barriers helped.

Good.

Ahead, the terrain was steep. The steam-wagon roads wound back and forth in long switchbacks. A traveler on foot moving fast and light could gain the advantage over a mechanical vehicle. The worse the terrain, the more her advantage.

Dana was tired and desperate, running forward over the broken

The Exalting

rock path, even as darkness climbed into the corners of her vision.

In minutes Kazen Poria's mind probed her again. This time she noticed the unnatural tug. It was even stronger than before.

They had to be close.

Stop. This is silly. Just go back and explain the situation.

The thought took Dana by surprise but made total sense. Why was she running? Dana stumbled to a halt. She turned. Her thoughts glitched. *No, that's not me!*

Dana clamped her hands over her head, trying not to listen to her own thoughts. It was like she was now the animal and someone else the druid.

That was the solution.

Dana gave a devious grin. She couldn't stop Poria's thoughts. *But I could trade them.*

Dana gave a shrill screech, her voice echoing off the steep cliffs in the canyon. It did not matter that the Vetas-kazen pursuing her would hear. What mattered was the effect it had on the scampers, lichen-toads, and birds in her vicinity. As she reached out to the animals her mind filled with dozens of fleeing urges. She opened her mind to theirs, drawing the urge to flee from the creatures. As she did, panic surged up within her.

Her heart racing with imported fear, Dana ran like the great destroyer itself had come for her soul. Scrambling over a rock slide, she sprinted through low scrubby trees.

The thoughts of stopping and turning back were distant now, echoing to her from a dozen animals in the wood.

Dana laughed. By trading her will for the animals', the enchanter's bidding was now impressed on every small creature in the area. And Dana had no desire but to flee in panic. The animals, on the other hand, wanted nothing more than to follow Poria's urges.

In moments, the enchanter would be surrounded by the accidentally summoned creatures.

Dana smiled as she imagined a veritable horde of small furry and frill-necked creatures darting up to the enchanter, possibly

143

expecting to be fed.

Two birds took flight heading back in the direction Dana had come. She watched their flight lines, heading for the enchanter. The line pointed to a copse of pine trees only a few hundred yards away.

If the enchanter was that close, then the men that had waited for her in the village could already be ahead, the hound flushing the prey toward the hunters. It was a sobering realization. Even if she escaped from the enchanter, she would run right into a trap.

According to the road sign a half mile back, this steep rise was all that separated her from the city of Shoul Falls.

They'll be waiting at the top, she thought, *just like the other villages.* This close to the city, there would be no avoiding the ambush if she went straight for Shoul Falls.

I need another way.

Forget it. Thinking about her plan would be her undoing if the enchanter were close enough to pick up on her intent.

The slope lessened near the summit. Dana was almost there. She slowed as she neared the top, clearing her mind of every thought. She couldn't let the enchanter sense any emotions when she changed her tactic. She walked in a daze away from the road crosscutting the top of the steep ravine. She headed away from where an ambush could be waiting on the road to Shoul Falls.

Blanking her mind, Dana squeezed between two boulders and up a thin chute between two granite outcroppings. The echoes in her mind faded. The enchanter had either lost her, lost interest, or with luck, assumed she had finished the climb and was in the hands of whoever was waiting at the top. But she couldn't wait here, or she would eventually be discovered. She had to lose them, and the only way was up the cliff face.

Dana wedged her body into the narrow cleft in the rocks. She chimney-climbed up the crack in the rock, with one foot against the far side and her back and the toe of her other foot countering. She kept wedging and worming her way higher in the crack until the gap was too wide and she was forced to place both feet behind and both hands in front. She looked down.

The Exalting

Her stomach twisted.

Dana's cut hands burned as she slid them along the rock. The next hold was a big one but too far to bridge. She would have to jump.

Dana took a deep breath. She pushed off the wall and then thrust with both legs, leaping out.

Her fingers dug into the cupped hold as her body jerked downward.

Dana pulled up desperately, flexing her biceps to drag her body up the rock. Her arms trembled. For three seconds, she held herself on the rock. Then her fingers, slick with sweat, lost their grip.

She fell.

Dana's vision filled with the open sky as her hands reached uselessly for the rock that had slipped out of her grip.

"Gotcha."

A hand flashed out over the edge of the cliff, seizing Dana's wrist. She jerked to free herself, but the strong arm lifted her upward.

"It's okay. It's okay—quiet now."

As Dana's feet found purchase on the top of the outcropping hidden behind the thick boughs of juniper, she looked up into the eyes of a dark-skinned young man. He wore a long staff strapped to his back, and his hair was tied in tight braids along the sides of his head. The white sclera of his eyes around his sable irises had a silvery sheen.

A blood-sworn.

"I heard your scream. Come on. This way."

He pulled her toward another chute, this one shaded by an even larger cliff.

"Move." He tugged on her arm. "There's a gang of armed men at the top of that hill. Someone really doesn't want you to reach the sanctum."

Dana wished to ask the young man who he was and why he was helping her, but she had barely strength to control her limbs as he led her into the tight vee in the rock.

"You first."

She began to climb. The chute ran with a trickle of water. Dana hoped it wasn't tainted by sayathi, or her bleeding hands would be her death.

Her foot slipped on the loose rock, but the young man's hand clamped her calf and pushed her foot back underneath her.

"Quickly," he said. "By now they'll know you turned uphill. We don't want to get caught in a place like this."

Dana gave the young man a confused look but scrambled forward, the sliding rocks moving her back a half step for every one she took.

With several boosts from behind, Dana finally reached the point where the chute widened and flatted onto a terrace on the mountainside that sloped uphill into a dense pine copse. The trees led around a curve in the mountain, and Dana had a brief hope that perhaps it might lead to safety.

As she fell to her knees and caught her breath, Dana looked up at her rescuer. "Thank you."

"What's your name?" he asked.

"I'm Dana." She had rarely been more eager to make an introduction.

The young man was only an inch or two taller than her. His silvery eyes with coal-black irises shone with interest. From the triangular shapes of his calves, visible under the knee-length pants he wore, to his trim stomach and the square look of his jaw, he looked the match for any creature of the wild. With the dark skin, he was obviously of West Aesican descent, from across the divide. Perhaps Shoul Falls was a city of mixed heritage—unlike Norr, a more isolated city peopled by primarily North Aesicans.

To Dana he was pure strength. He wasn't muscle-bound like the bargemen she had traveled with. He was trim, but his eyes shone with a kind of strength she had never seen before, a look of deep conviction.

"Who . . . who are you?" Dana asked breathlessly.

"I'm Ryke, high acolyte of the sanctum of Shoul Falls." He

146

The Exalting

rehearsed his name and rank without the slightest hint of pride at the statement. His eyes and interest were fixed on her alone, her safety.

High acolyte. Dana supposed that was just below a full kazen. "What are you doing here?"

"I was told to watch for new arrivals. I wasn't actually expecting . . . well . . . you."

Dana gave a half smile. "What's so unexpected?"

Ryke just smiled. Then he knelt in front of Dana. "You're in some kind of trouble, aren't you?"

Dana forced herself to nod.

"And you're trying to find the sanctum?" His voice seemed almost hopeful.

Dana had no idea whether it was a good idea to say yes, or not. But she realized there wasn't any sense in lying, especially if he was going to help if he thought she was headed there. "Yes, the sanctum."

"Well, you're a lot older that most new acolytes. But whether or not they make you the next ka, it takes a brave soul to give up their will and choose a life of service," Ryke said. "It says a lot about you."

"Um, thanks."

A life of service?

What am I getting myself into?

Ryke gave her another of his confident smiles. There was real interest there, interest undoubtedly mirrored in her own curiosity.

"We'd better get to the sanctum fast. By now that group of foreigners at the top of the ridge must have realized you left the road." Ryke pulled her to her feet.

A twig snapped. The sound came from the dense trees at the edge of the clearing. Then another branch cracked under foot.

If it was an animal, Dana would have sensed it. "It's them."

Ryke loosened a draw string and drew his staff from its sling on his back. "I think we're about to have trouble."

Dana winced. He hadn't just saved her life. By getting involved,

147

her problems were now his. "Can't we just—"

The sounds of footsteps and leaves rustling grew until Dana could tell that the sounds were coming from not one but many feet.

Ryke stepped in front of her and swung his staff to one side. He took a wide stance, facing the dense pine trees. "I can protect you. Just try not to get in my way. I move quickly."

"What are you—"

A crossbow bolt launched from the trees.

Dana barely had time to register the metal spike headed for her chest before Ryke's swinging staff knocked it right out of the air.

The bolt slammed into the mossy ground in front of her feet, and Dana let out a scream of pure terror. Already on edge after her near-death experience on the cliff, she lost her composure completely.

Two more bolts zinged out of the trees. Dana cringed as Ryke sidestepped one headed for him and flicked the other so that it turned halfway in the air and slapped flat against Dana's thigh.

In panic, Dana held up her forearms in front of her face, as if they would do anything to stop the next razor-sharp quarrel. Panic grew within her, overwhelming her senses. After all she had been through, she was cornered. Backed up against the edge of a cliff, there was no escape.

"Please, no. Please—" Dana begged as motion in the trees revealed the presence of even more enemies.

Two shots came at once, both headed for Dana. Ryke whirled his staff in front of him in a blur. One bolt slammed into the ground, and the other was knocked high in the air and over the edge of the cliff.

"We can do this until you run out of bolts," Ryke called out to the attackers hiding in the trees. He turned his head enough for Dana to see his white teeth gleaming in a smile. A feeling of strength grew in the space around her frozen heart.

Eight men emerged from the wood. They crept forward, fanning out to blocking all possible escapes. Two of them drew immaculately crafted blades that likely cost far more than Dana

148

The Exalting

could ever have spent if she tried.

"Those are Torsican blades," Ryke said under his breath, his voice unwavering and coursing with righteous indignation. Then he called out to the men, "You have trespassed dedicated ground. I won't ask you again. Leave now. The girl is under the protection of the sanctum of Shoul Falls."

"Why?" sneered one of the men. "Hand her over. We'll make you a rich man."

"I'm sworn to poverty."

One of the attackers raised a gloved hand and pointed at Ryke. "You have no idea who you are messing with."

But Dana did. And now they were going to kill Ryke.

At short enough range, he wouldn't have enough time to block their bolts.

He needed her help, or they would both die.

I have to do something.

While several of the Torsican men worked to reload and hastily rewind their crossbows, Dana reached out, thrusting herself into the void that bled feelings and thoughts and instincts. But all their tramping about had scared off most of the creatures in the area with any killing power.

No. There were always creatures in the forest that thirsted for the blood of Xahnans.

Come. Drink. There is enough for all!

A horde of fist-sized bloodsucking nightfeeders winged out of the trees. It was nearly time for the dusk hunters to rise anyway. The insects latched onto necks, faces, and hands. First dozens, then hundreds. The air clouded with beating wings.

The men tried in vain to hold their weapons steady as the frantic insects, driven by Dana's bloodlust, bit without even numbing the skin first.

In the distraction, Ryke lunged forward and swung his staff into the side of a Torsican's head. The staff rebounded in the opposite direction and slammed into the back of another, who knocked a third from the edge of the cliff with a scream of terror.

The staff recoiled with even more speed, swinging back to sweep the legs out from under one of the soldiers sworn to Vetas-ka. His head knocked into the first soldier's, which had just bounced limply off the turf.

Dana gasped as two more guards met blunt force trauma in less than a second. It almost seemed too easy.

Why are there no kazen?

Dana's eyes turned to the man who had not drawn a sword. He pulled his hand out of a pouch at his waist and flung a handful of shiny dust in Ryke's direction.

"Ryke, look out!" Dana screamed as the fine dust spread out behind him.

The shadow-skinned acolyte dropped to the ground.

The cloud of fine dust exploded in a brilliant white fireball.

An alchemist? Dana thought. *No.* The dust was simply a fine metal powder he had willed into combustion. He was a warlock like Omren, only with the ability to channel heat energy, rather than physical force.

"Get the druid!" the kazen barked.

Dana whirled to see a Torsican charging at her.

But her nightfeeders were faster. One tried to cram itself up his nose. Another two jabbed at his eyes. Dana stepped aside and kicked at the blinded man. Her foot connected with his back leg, sending his foot behind his calf. Tripping on his own leg, the man tumbled down the steep embankment, screaming.

Dana turned to see the kazen warlock, with another fistful of metal powder, facing off against Ryke.

He threw. Ryke lunged with his staff. The cloud of particles enveloped Ryke. Her ears registered a sharp crack.

But the powder had not ignited. It was the sound of Ryke's staff striking the warlock's skull. He dropped to the ground. The Vetas-kazen was either out cold or dead.

"That was close," Dana gasped.

"What was close?" Ryke said as he brushed the dusting of shiny metal shavings off his shoulders.

The Exalting

"The metal powder. It was going to—"

"Not even. Now let's move. They may have backup on the way—and thanks for the distraction. That was magnificent. How many nightfeeders can you control at once?" Ryke started up the hill.

"A lot. I guess." Dana bolted after the young man, letting the nightfeeders have their fill with the unconscious Torsicans.

She followed Ryke, keeping as close as she could, her arm brushing against his. She had been terrorized for hours, and having someone she could trust by her side was an indescribably sweet elixir.

He was obviously from the sanctum, so he was an adept, too. *Of course—the staff.*

"You're a warlock," Dana guessed. "You willed that staff to move faster." She huffed for breath, pine boughs whipping at her face and legs. "You probably use the staff because you can keep hold of it the whole time so it's easier to pass will into."

"My will serves the good purpose," he said simply.

As the slope steepened again, Ryke took Dana by the hand, guiding her through trees and over rocks she could barely discern in the long evening shadows. He seemed to know every turn. "I don't think I've seen you before. You are from Shoul Falls, aren't you?"

Dana sucked air in through her teeth. "Uh . . . originally." It was a good half-truth. Her grandfather and grandmother were from Shoul Falls. Her mother was born shortly after they left, though her father was Norrian. So, in a way, she had originated from Shoul Falls.

"You must be really beat. I almost thought you were a drale."

"I've been called worse," Dana said in another attempt to avoid the truth.

Ryke led her through a thicket of thorned tarberry bushes and along a cliff wall to a point where a seam in the rock lead upward at an angle, forming a small ledge.

"You handled yourself pretty well back there," Ryke said. "We made a good team."

Dana met his sable eyes. She smiled. "Thanks." She didn't want to think about the fighting. She just wanted to be somewhere safe.

She followed Ryke up the thin walkway and rounded a corner. "Where—"

Ryke's hand pulled her sideways into a hidden cave.

"You wonder why folks have a hard time finding the sanctum?" Ryke said with a smile. His white teeth and silvery eyes gleamed in the darkness.

"We made it," Dana gasped. The room was dark, but there was no chance her pursuers could find her now.

No more hiding. No more running.

I'm safe.

Tears welled in her eyes, and Dana leaned against the rock wall as a sob broke from her trembling lips. She brought a hand to her chest shaking from the terror of what had just happened. The other touched the growing bruise on her thigh, still unable to believe the steel arrow had not pierced her.

"Oh, now you're going to cry. You know, I don't do that sort of—"

Dana dissolved into mess of tears.

Ryke put a hand awkwardly on her shoulder. "If you're still worried, they won't find us in here. Sayathi run in the cave water. It masks us from any enchanters."

Dana reached out her arms and closed them around Ryke's neck, hugging him, holding on to the one thing she could rely on. Her breath came in a shaky wheeze. "Don't let me go. Please."

"Like this?" Slowly Ryke's arms closed around her, wrapping her in what felt like an embrace of pure strength, as if she were wrapped in armor. For several minutes she held him close, pulling her body against his, willing the terror of the flight across the forest, through the foothills, and into the mountain canyons to pass out of her.

But as it left, Dana was left with nothing else but the warmth of Ryke's embrace.

"You saved my life." Dana put her hands on the sides of his face

The Exalting

and smiled up into his eyes.

Ryke flinched slightly. Her face was only inches from his. "Only about seven times."

"I owe you my thanks." Dana reached one hand around the back of his neck, pushed up on her toes, and kissed his cheek. "That's one."

A kiss of thanks was standard in Aesica. Her mother had kissed a delivery man who brought her a new brass kettle and always any neighbor who brought over a baked dish. Dana had kissed the two friendly bargemen.

This felt incredibly different.

Ryke might have been blushing, but Dana couldn't see well enough in the dim of the cave, and besides, his skin was dark enough to hide any flush of color.

"It was my pleasure."

Dana laughed. She was exhausted. But having spent nearly all her will to summon the nightfeeders, she was also quite uninhibited.

And so was he. He had to be after a battle like that. If there was to ever be a moment when two hearts could share without any thinking or reason in the middle, it was now.

She was quite sure she had never met anyone like Ryke. He stirred her, like the sun on a spring morning, promising many days of warmth ahead.

Dana wasn't going to overlook the obvious fact that he was gorgeous.

He risked his life for me.

Dana could have resisted the temptation to flirt. She should have.

She just didn't want to. *Fine. Just a little.*

"It was your pleasure," she repeated, a smile stealing across her lips. "Do you mean rescuing me, or the kiss?"

Ryke's chuckle was all too incriminating. "As much as I'd like to admit that you are quite the find, I *am* an acolyte. We have . . . rules."

"You deserved it," Dana said. Her feelings went straight to words on her lips with unnerving ease. "Without you I would be dead."

Ryke smiled, his white teeth gleaming in the dim. "I know."

"Well I guess I still have six thank-you's left to give." Dana nearly gasped. It was not supposed to have been said aloud. She bit her lip to keep it from embarrassing her further.

"Can I . . . save the rest for later?" A wry smile played at the edge of Ryke's lips. "Also, if we don't hurry, we're going to be late for dinner—and that I definitely don't save for later."

"Perfect—both ideas."

Dana struggled to keep up with Ryke as he walked through the dark passage. He walked quickly it seemed, with a spring in his step that hadn't been there before.

"You're going to love it here." Ryke came to a chiseled shelf where he lifted a single lantern. "Looks like we got the only lamp left—we'll definitely be the last ones to the table."

Ryke drew a small vial from his pocket and tapped a single drop onto on the lantern wick. It flamed to life instantly.

Pyrophor elixir. It was a rare thing in Norr, only used in the mines.

So they have alchemists here as well, Dana realized. The sanctum probably had acolytes of all four varieties: warlock, enchanter, druid, and alchemist.

"What makes you say I'm going to love it here?" Dana had no clue as to what she was about to get herself into.

"The people are great."

Dana gave a delighted giggle. "Well if they're all like you . . ."

"I can tell you there's no one like you," Ryke said.

"How am I different?" Dana sincerely wondered whether there was something seriously off about herself.

Ryke opened his mouth to say something, then shut it. He was utterly at a loss for words. It was cute to see the hulk of a guy held up by his own tongue. "I don't really know."

Dana laughed. "At least you didn't say I'm unforgivably ugly."

154

The Exalting

She brushed her arm, and a swarm of dust particles scintillated in a narrow shaft of light running from a crack in the ceiling. "Or that I'm as dirty as a brown toad on a road."

Ryke's stomach tightened as he stifled a chuckle. "I might have thought one of those."

"Just one? Well, that's good. I was worrying you might make me take a bath before I could join the sanctum."

Ryke let out a deep laugh that boomed through cavern, and Dana laughed so hard she nearly cried.

"I won't say anything about it, if you won't," he finally managed as they turned into a much tighter section of cave and had to turn shoulders sideways to face each other as they squeezed in.

"Okay," Dana whispered.

There was a connection between them, something as real as stone under her feet, as real as the tips of her sifa that spread at the memory of the embrace they had shared.

Dana wished she were an enchanter. What did he feel when she had kissed his cheek? She could only imagine it was something close to what she had felt.

One step from heaven.

Right now, she could be one step from anywhere. She didn't know who was inside the sanctum or what would happen when she got there.

"Ryke," she said as he paused to let her step in front. "Am I doing the right thing?"

"You mean becoming an acolyte?" He grabbed the back of his neck. "That's an awkward question."

Dana gave an awkward laugh. "Uh, yeah, probably." She bit her lip. "Is it too late to go back?"

"Kinda sorta."

"So I'm stuck with you . . . and the rest?"

"Kinda sorta."

"Well I'm definitely okay with one of those."

"Oh good." Ryke gave a heavy sigh of relief. "I was beginning to worry I might have to spend time with you."

155

Dan Allen

"Hey!"

"Now if you're done trying to undo the best decision you ever made," Ryke gestured to the shadowed gap in the stone. "Welcome to the sanctum."

Chapter 17

Dana stepped past Ryke into a vaulted cavern. The walls joined in a cathedral-like shape to where light filtered through gaps in the formation. Tree roots trailed down the walls following water that trickled from seams in the stone.

The way nature and the rock merged, it was beautiful.

This is where my new life begins.

But that life was a lie until she turned over the bloodstone.

Yet, she couldn't just give it to the first kazen she saw. She might hand the stone over to the very person Sindar was trying to avoid.

I can't tell them yet.

Running her other hand on the cave wall, Dana flinched away at the touch of wet stone.

Sayathi lived in the limestone caverns that riddled the mountainside.

Ryke stopped in the cavern. "I think I'm supposed to give you an oath of loyalty, but I can't remember it. I've been here since I was very young."

"Consider me sworn-in," Dana said. "Besides, I'd rather not know what I promised." She wiped the water from her palm onto her pant leg. "Less to worry about."

Ryke laughed. "Well, you can make your own rules if they choose you for the next ka."

Dana's heart skipped a beat. That was an actual possibility now.

Ryke led the way through into a hewn tunnel. "What part of Shoul Falls are you from? I'm pretty sure I haven't seen you before."

Oh great. Dana stretched the thin webbing that ran across the base of her fingers. She couldn't tell him she was the Norrian. And she didn't want to lie—not to him.

Truth, then . . . some of it.

"My father trades with the Norrian miners. I haven't spent much time in Shoul Falls itself."

"And the citizen council nominated you to be an acolyte?" he asked.

Dana shrugged. She consciously moved her hand away from the pouch tied to her waist. She was accustomed to holding the bloodstone to keep it from banging against her hip. She had come seeking refuge. And now, the bloodstone was in the very place the Vetas-kazen would have first sought for it, the place Sindar had fled.

The place his enemy likely still waited.

Was she still headed into the back of a trap?

Dana had no choice. She couldn't go back, both because of what would be waiting for her outside and because she had just effectively sworn herself to the sanctum.

Ryke's lateral sifa suddenly flared in greeting, and Dana looked up to see a guard standing in the shadows.

She flared her own inferior sifa briefly—she didn't outrank the guard—and stepped past into a brilliantly lit room. The walls of the chamber were dry and draped with bright-colored banners with ornately spelled mantras. The floor was wood, like the decking of a ship. It almost felt like the inside of a real building rather than a cavern. There were large tables and people seated at them wearing a variety of clothing styles from jackets and trousers to robes and wraps. Some looked hand-spun.

But Dana's eyes were drawn to what was *on* the tables.

Real food. Her stomach grumbled with excitement.

"Perfect—there's still some dinner left," Ryke said. "Come on."

But Dana's arm slid from Ryke's as thirty heads turned in unison to stare. Her sifa dropped unceremoniously.

A gray-robed man stood at the head of a long table. His black hair was tied at the back of his head. "Who is *this*?" There was no hint of welcome in his tone.

A single utensil clanked at one of the smaller tables, ruining the silence.

Dana clasped her hands together. "Sorry. I forgot to make

The Exalting

introductions." It was a decidedly awkward moment. Announcing herself felt like some sort of intrusion. So she gestured to her companion. "This is Ryke. He's a *really* good warlock."

The kazen looked dumbstruck.

Most of young acolytes of Shoul Falls burst into laughter.

Ryke gave a short bow to the kazen. "Korren, this is Dana. She is a new acolyte."

Korren's eyes narrowed.

"Long story," Dana added.

Korren gestured to a table beside his own. His eyes never strayed from her. Ryke took a chair at the head of the table, and Dana took the only other available seat at the opposite end.

She sat.

He sat.

Nobody else moved. Nobody spoke.

"We have a new arrival," Korren said at last. "We should all be grateful to learn how this came to be."

"He saved my life," Dana said. She reached for a handful of tarberries and shoved them into her mouth. She chewed and swallowed the syrupy berries, feeling strength flow into her almost instantly.

"And that was the longest fast of my life." Dana glanced at Korren, who was still standing.

Nobody else had touched their food. Dana looked to Ryke, who had his back to Korren and was pulling a bone of roast marmar monkey toward himself.

Dana's sifa bounced playfully. "Well, it's great to finally be here." She reached for a bowl of milled nut porridge. The scent of the sour spice was nearly overpowering.

But before she could take a bite, the kazen put out his hand and lifted her chin, staring into her eyes.

Dana tried to look away, but even though his grip was not firm, she couldn't move, like she was buried in sand.

Just like when Omren attacked. He's a warlock.

Dana's eyelids opened wide, ignoring her commands to close.

Dan Allen

"You are a drale!"

"I'm not!" Dana lied.

"The punishment for the unbound to enter the sanctum of Togata-ka is death."

"Seriously? You're going to do this?"

Two sets of arms grabbed Dana from behind. She screamed as she was hauled backwards. Korren looked at Ryke. "You brought a drale into the sanctum?"

Ryke gestured at Dana. "She said she was from Shoul Falls."

"Did you not see her eyes? . . . Or were your attentions elsewhere?"

"She's famished. A band of men just tried to—"

"Enough. Bring her to the pool. The water will tell."

Dana was dragged through a door and marched deeper into the mountain. "Stop this," she pleaded, to no avail. She struggled in vain against the strong arms that held her.

After passing through several more barred doors and past an array of rooms hewn into the rock with leather curtains for doors, Dana was dropped onto the cool ground of a chamber. A familiar blue-green glow covered the walls and ceiling, and in the center lay a wide pool of clear water, laden with sayathenite nodules, missing only a bloodstone at the center.

A constant stream of water ran out and into a channel that likely fed into the falls and the lake below—the source of sayathi for the entire city of Shoul Falls.

Dana could hear scuffles behind her as Ryke no doubt tried to reach her.

Korren swept alongside Dana. "Show me." A kazen tore back Dana's sleeve and held her arm out over the water.

"Nothing—no glow of fealty. She's a drale. Throw her from the falls!"

"No."

"Then you choose the *other* way?"

Dana had no idea what the man was talking about, but it couldn't be worse than being thrown from the falls.

160

The Exalting

"Yes."

Korren, with one arm tucked behind his back, walked to a shrine in the corner of the room. He opened a small cabinet and drew out a chalice.

"Wait . . . uh."

Ryke burst through the doors. His eyes searched for hers, perhaps wondering how she had deceived him, or if he had led her to her death.

Korren scooped the chalice into the pool. He lifted it and held it out to Dana.

There was no way around this. She couldn't hope to live in a mountain sanctum dedicated to the next chosen supreme of Shoul Falls and not drink their water.

Again, the burning sensation of the dying greeder passed over her. Dying by sayathi was not how she wanted to die.

But perhaps . . .

Dana stood, shaking off the hands that held her. She gave Ryke her best attempt at a consoling smile. Then she grasped the chalice with both hands.

"To the last drop," Korren ordered.

"At least you aren't stingy."

Korren's jaw dropped, and Dana raised the glass.

Ryke stepped forward, but Korren held out his arm, blocking him.

Dana tipped the chalice into her mouth and swallowed.

The water was clean but carried a taste almost like . . . *like blood.*

Oh no.

Dana swallowed more and more until the cool liquid filled her already queasy stomach. She fell to her knees, coughing.

She stayed there for a minute, hoping her gamble was not a death sentence.

This should work. It has to work.

Moments passed. Each beat of her heart pounded out a thousand worries and memories of Loka's last moments.

But there was no telltale stab of pain from her stomach.

Dana stood up.

"Well, that was certainly dramatic." She waved her arm over the pool, and a feeble blue glow shone from her arm. "Can I keep the—"

Korren yanked the cup from Dana's hands.

"Guess not."

"New acolyte . . ." Korren grumbled under his breath.

Dana turned to Ryke. "I'm sorry for scaring you."

"I wasn't scared."

Dana tipped her head. "Really?"

"I mean, I was scared. But . . . I trusted you."

Dana smiled.

"One can't be too careful," said a kazen a bit younger than Korren. "It was the right thing to do."

"When I found her there were men from Torsica who were—" Ryke began, before Korren cut him off.

"Back to dinner, everybody. We've had enough disturbance for one night."

He stopped in front of Ryke. "I'm holding you responsible for anything that happens in regards to this . . . this . . ."

"Druid," Dana volunteered.

"Problem," Korren finished.

On the way back to dinner Ryke leaned over. "So you aren't a drale?"

Dana shrugged. "Well, not anymore."

"How did you survive that?"

"Family secret." Dana punched him playfully in his rock-solid abs. She turned away, blushing as her superior sifa spread in a moment of heated attraction.

But there was something else within her, something entirely new.

Dana took in a deep breath as another layer of sensation spread through her. She could sense not only her own body but the sayathi rapidly spreading through her. Already her arms felt lighter, her feet

The Exalting

less tired.

"I feel incredible." She had the urge to grab Ryke's hand and skip dinner in favor of some thank-you's. But the food and the company—Korren excepted—were too inviting.

"By the bloodstone," whispered an acolyte from nearby as she entered the common room. "It looks like she still glowing, and she's nowhere near the pool. How is that possible?"

Dana ignored the whispered comments. She put the rest of her attention on finishing the nut porridge.

Korren shortly dismissed everyone from dinner. The acolytes began carrying away their dishes. Dana shoved one more cracker into her mouth and went to stand, but Korren's hand descended on her shoulder like a lead counterweight, keeping her in seat.

He waited until the gathered faithful, including Ryke, had left.

"I know who you are."

"You do? Ah, you're an enchanter, too?"

Korren looked aside. "No. And that is beside the point. You are wanted for greeder theft in Norr."

"I was practically a prisoner in my own city. I had to escape."

"You took the animal out of a selfish desire and gave no hint of intention to compensate the owner."

"Well I didn't know who the owner was."

"As is often the case with theft." Korren placed his hands on the table and loomed over her. "What to do with you?"

"I risked my life to come here!"

"No, you risked all our lives. You were followed by our enemies."

"I didn't ask anyone to follow me—they were trying to kill me. Anyway it's a good thing Ryke was there."

But she saw something calculated in Korren's eyes.

"You sent Ryke to watch the canyon. Didn't you?"

Korren nodded.

No wonder Ryke hadn't pressed her about why the men were after her; Korren had sent him to watch for new arrivals. Korren would only have sent someone like Ryke if he was expecting something another acolyte couldn't handle.

But what was Korren's motive? Had he caught news over the message wires of a druid adept from Norr on the run?

A sanctum was a likely place to flee.

Regardless, having him as an enemy wouldn't work. She forced herself to say something kind. "Thank you."

He flinched at the words, his composure shifting only momentarily.

So, he didn't want thanks for saving me.

What did he want?

Things obviously hadn't gone as planned.

Dana's breath froze in her lungs.

Was Korren a sellout? Had Vetas-ka somehow bought his allegiance?

And I came right to him.

Korren could be the traitor Sindar had fled from. Dana had to admit having someone inside the sanctum was a brilliant stroke. If she got past the Vetas-kazen, then Ryke would collect her, and Korren could kill her with sayathi water.

Having Ryke bring her in was brilliant because if Korren had brought her in, he wouldn't have had a reason to kill her—without revealing that she had the stone. Instead, he could claim she had defiled their sanctum, kill her, and then take the stone.

But he had made one critical mistake.

Sayathi kept the memory of a blood oath for four generations. After that time, either the sayathi lost the immunity to the family blood or the blood was so intermingled that the sayathi recognized more foe than friend.

Thanks to her grandfather, Dana was family. And though she had yet to give her own blood oath which would pass on the immunity to a succeeding generation, she had the symbiotes in her system.

Korren leaned back and turned away. "You'll finish your dishes and then report to Ritsen for examination in the morning. He is our senior druid."

The Exalting

"Thank you, kazen."

He clasped his hands behind his back and strode back the way Dana had first come in.

If he knows the Vetas-kazen were after me, why didn't he search me for the bloodstone?

Korren was either very patient, or he wasn't a traitor at all.

Did he really want to kill me?

The idea of someone in the same room actually wanting to kill her was sickening.

Dana sat alone at the wooden table. All but two lanterns had been put out by departing acolytes. She looked around at the empty common room, considering the path her life had taken since stealing the greeder and escaping her root-bound life in Norr and finding the sanctum. There had been exactly two highlights of her journey—singing with Turigan and Jila on the river and the sunrise over the Sayathi Sea. The rest had been more or less torture.

Even the scamper she had used as a guide in the jungle had pooped on her.

Yet she was finally in Shoul Falls, along with the bloodstone she had kept with her in the days since Sindar had trusted it to her care.

And now, with the sayathi of the very same colony coursing through her blood, perhaps she could wield the power of the bloodstone.

It was possibly the worst idea that had come into her mind. And it hadn't even been planted there by an enchanter.

The thought had been there all along.

It's your stone. Your destiny.

Dana hadn't even looked at the stone yet. She considered that to be an act of supreme willpower, but it was really just fear of what would happen if she was seen with it.

But if she didn't want the stone for herself, why hadn't she told Ryke about it? Why hadn't she returned it to Korren, the head kazen of the sanctum?

Ambition. Her grandfather Togath had seen it in her. So had Omren.

165

Dan Allen

Then why did Sindar give it to me? Perhaps she was simply his only hope for keeping the stone from the Vetas-kazen, or maybe he thought she would have had the sense to give it to Togath.

But why had Sindar brought it to Togath in the first place? That seemed very strange.

Perhaps her grandfather had once been a servant of the last ka of Shoul Falls.

But he's not even an adept. How could he have been a kazen?

Floorboards creaked, and Dana looked up. Two girls about her age watched her from the exit through which she had been unceremoniously dragged to a failed assassination by sayathi.

One of the girls had long, straight brown hair and long eyelashes that batted the air. She wore a long, pastel blue dress that suited her tall figure—just a bit taller than Dana—and had an apron tied at her waist with a few dozen small pouches sewn on it.

Dana looked at the other girl and gasped. It was her mother— almost her mother. She was much younger, which meant she looked a great deal like Dana as well. She had a mottled complexion with similar black hair, except her sifa, which were not just silver-tipped like Dana's but fully silvered.

Dana supposed early maturing sifa was one of the benefits of being a blood-sworn. As hosts, they protected the sayathi colony. And the colony protected the blood-sworn. It was a symbiotic relationship.

The girl's black hair was woven into a set of iron rings in a rigid weave that came almost to her shoulders. It was a kind of ancient armor, like a primitive helmet.

Dana was a touch jealous that she hadn't thought of the savage style.

The two girls came closer and sat down across the table.

"I've never seen you before today," said the taller girl with the straight, brown hair.

"Nice to meet you, too. I'm Dana."

The girl did not extend her sifa in greeting. "You're not from Shoul Falls. I've done assistant nursing in the city for over five years,

The Exalting

and I've never seen your face."

"My father traded with Norrian mine workers," Dana said. "I—"

"Have you even spent a week in Shoul Falls in your entire life?" The question came from the shorter girl, the one with the uncanny resemblance to her mother, down to the high cheekbones, narrow nose, and pouting lips.

"Actually, no."

The girls' jaws dropped.

"And I wasn't nominated to be an acolyte of—whoever the ka is . . . or will be."

"Then why are you here?" asked the taller girl.

"I don't belong in Norr," Dana said. "I'm a druid."

The girls exchanged a confused glance.

"They hate me for having something they don't. They fear me. They—" She stopped speaking.

"By the ka—you're Norrian. You aren't even blood-sworn. And you drank from the pool!"

"Unto the *fourth* generation," Dana reminded. "Sayathi recognize grandchildren of blood-sworn. I'm not going to keel over."

"It is sacrilege."

Dana gestured at the empty room. "We don't even have a supreme to offend at the moment. I think we're okay."

"My ka! Have you no respect? You are in the hold of the sanctum itself."

"I'm learning," Dana said. "I'll probably be way less blasphemous given a few days . . . or years."

The brown-haired girl folded her arms and glared.

Dana tried another tactic. "What sort of adepts are you?"

The shorter girl gestured to her friend. "Kaia does alchemy."

"No wonder she's in demand as a nurse."

"And Mirris is an enchanter," Kaia added. "She can read you like a book if she touches you."

Dana offered her hand. "Then read me."

The shorter girl, Mirris, looked at Kaia, who nodded. "Go ahead."

Dana fixed her mind on the experience at the pool. She couldn't risk any errant thoughts of the thing in her pouch slipping through the veil into her mind.

Mirris reached out and held Dana's hand between hers. The webbing between Mirris's fingers was tattooed with a pattern of skulls and daggers.

"Your fingers are freezing," Dana said. The chill ran all the way through her.

"Hold still."

Dana focused on the pool, the glow, the sensation of drinking.

"Knew it," Mirris dropped Dana's hand. "She was thinking about not thinking about something. And then she tossed out a bunch of stray thoughts from the trial by water."

"I was just trying to be polite."

"Oh sure." Mirris stood up and walked away. "Now I trust you implicitly."

"Not all secrets are bad."

Mirris didn't reply as she passed through the threshold to the inner sanctum.

Kaia, who appeared to be the more senior of the two, sat forward. "Enough games. Why are you here?"

There was no sense trying to hide everything. That would only make them suspicious. The best thing she could do was give them something to latch on to. Maybe they would stop trying to find reasons to distrust her. "I'm in trouble with the law." Dana hoped the answer sounded compelling enough to get Kaia off her case. "Ask Korr, he—"

"Korr*en*," Kaia corrected.

"As I was saying, he knows all about it. I stole a greeder to escape from Norr."

"Why did you have to leave in the first place?"

"One of my friends suggested I come to Shoul Falls and join the sanctum. She thought I might fit in bet—"

The Exalting

"Pfff."

"Well it's better than Norr," Dana said. "Adepts are proof that Xahnans aren't all equal. It goes against everything they preach."

Kaia stared across the room at the head table, curiosity obviously eating at her. "How did you find the sanctum? Even people from Shoul Falls don't know where the entrances are."

"I was climbing a cliff," Dana said plainly. "Ryke caught my hand as I fell."

Kaia nodded. "So you batted your eyelashes and got him to show you the entrance?"

If anyone was going to bat eyelashes around the sanctum it was Kaia. Hers looked almost like sifa.

"It's kind of hard to flirt when there's a posse of men trying to kill you."

"Who was?" Kaia asked.

"Torsicans. Followers of Vetas-ka."

"Why would they attack you?"

At least Dana had a story for that. "I got in the way." She lowered her voice and checked to make sure no one was listening at the doors. "A Vetas-kazen warlock named Omren was chasing after Sindar west of Norr."

"Sindaren?" Kaia's eyes widened. "He's been missing for—"

"He's dead. I was with him when he passed." Dana swallowed. ". . . And I killed his attacker."

Kaia's hands covered her mouth. She looked like she was about to scream or be sick.

Dana leaned forward and grabbed the alchemist's wrists. "Quiet. Kaia, please. I have to ask you something."

Kaia's tear-filled eyes met Dana's, her grief at the loss of Sindar, a devoted mentor, causing her a kind of pain Dana could only imagine.

"Was Korren angry when Sindar—Sindaren—left?"

Kaia didn't register the question. Her expression broke into a tortured sob so pitiful it nearly wrung tears from Dana's eyes.

"Kaia, I know Sindaren was trustworthy—greeders can tell

169

or are you going to stay and do dishes?"

"I'm coming!" Dana walked beside Kaia to the door to the inner sanctum and followed after Kaia's footsteps along a dark corridor. It was lined with glow candles that made light without any heat or smoke.

More alchemy.

Dana was grateful that at least she was able to plant some doubt in Kaia's mind about Korren. She needed an ally, and Kaia was obviously the most senior of the girl acolytes and deeply thoughtful.

Kaia turned into a side doorway. As Dana followed, the leather door flap closed in front of Dana's face, and the weight stone tied to the bottom smacked into Dana's foot.

"Ow!"

"Quiet. It's meditation," hissed a young girl's voice.

Dana pushed the door open and limped into the room.

Inside were gathered about eight acolytes, all girls sitting cross-legged in front of a single glow candle.

Most of them were younger than her, except Kaia.

Dana let the leather flap shut behind her and wedged herself between Kaia and the girl next to her, who was forced to shift to the side, and so on, until everyone around the circle had been bumped or jostled.

So much for peaceful meditation.

"You didn't just come for the free food?" said a familiar voice. It was Mirris. "You're really going to do this?"

"Of course," Dana said.

"Or did you just come so you could stare at Ryke all day?"

"Shut up, Mirris," Dana snapped. "And stay out of my head."

"Stay out of my sanctum."

Dana had a mind to put her in a headlock and rub some of the sandy cave clay into her face, but the thought that they didn't want her here was like getting the breath knocked out of her.

Was she just going to be as much an outsider here as she was in Norr?

170

The Exalting

things like that. And I speak fluent greeder. I think he was doing the right thing."

Kaia seemed to break from her trance of grief. "Korren was furious. I've never seen him so angry."

"That's because Sindaren took the bloodstone," Dana said.

"No—he'd never. Korren had it hidden for safekeep—"

"Sindaren was trying to take the bloodstone to my grandfather Togath in the foothills of Norr—do you know why he would take the stone to my grandfather?"

"Togath?" Kaia asked.

"Yes."

Kaia's face went white. "You mean Togata-ka."

"What are you talking about?" Then Dana's heart froze. Togata-ka was the exalted form of her grandfather's name.

Kaia looked her in the eye. "Togath was our last ka."

"But my grandfather isn't even an adept," Dana said. "How could he have—"

"Togata-ka fell in love and gave up the bloodstone to have a family," Kaia said. Her voice was soft in a kind of reverence. "He risked his own life to part with it. It's *the* most famous story in Shoul Falls. Dana, people write songs about it—plays even."

Dana gave a laugh. "My grandfather was your last ka?"

Kaia's broken expression seemed to mend in an instant. Her wrists, held by Dana, drew her closer. "Where is the bloodstone? Do you have it?"

Dana spoke very quietly and deliberately. "Not here. I don't trust . . . well, I don't trust Korren."

Kaia's lip quivered. "Why . . . why did Sindaren take the stone to your grandfather?"

"He must have had no other choice."

"This is incredibly disturbing. I don't even know what to think."

"We just have to wait until we know for sure whom to trust," Dana said.

Kaia stood up. "Well it's time for meditation. Are you coming,

And with Korren running the place, she was possibly in more danger inside the sanctum than out.

"Fine. Maybe I will." Dana started to get to her feet, but Kaia's hand caught Dana's wrist.

"We will all find peace," Kaia said gently, her voice carrying to everyone in the group, "when we lose what we seek and seek the lost. That is your mantra tonight. Meditate in silence . . . or you can write an essay on the topic."

Dana settled into the silence, before a touch of heat flowed through her as if she were somehow coming nearer to the candle.

A chorus of the eight voices touched her mind, repeating the mantra in a distant, tiny echo.

"We will all find peace when we lose what we seek and seek the lost."

Her breathing slowed as the idea caught on her mind. But Dana refused to think about what she sought—he had already caused her enough embarrassment—or what was lost—the stone she had in a coin purse tied to her waist.

She was going to have to move that to somewhere more secure.

"Join us, Dana." The words trickled into her mind. They seemed to be coming from someone else.

No, Dana thought stubbornly.

"You're ruining the meditation, and you'll have to write an essay." The thought seemed to echo from one of the younger girls.

I can't hide forever, Dana thought. *Kaia already knows I have it. If they find out, they find out.* She recalled the warning of the woman at the Sayathi Sea about stealing the will of others being like murder.

It's not mine anyway.

Dana felt her eyes roll back in her head as she fell forward into a quiet so deep and dark that she thought she had died.

"Good. You have given up that which you seek. But there is a deeper peace, when you find what was lost."

Dana sensed the presence of the other acolytes like distant humming in her mind, reminding her of the way dragonflies and

The Exalting

hummingbirds felt when she touched their minds, only deeper, more sonorous.

The humming grew louder and louder until Dana could hardly stand it.

"Find what was lost!"

Dana began thinking about what she might have lost. Immediately her thoughts turned to the slain greeder, then to Turigan and Jila. Colors of emotion swirled within her. At last she let her mind return to Norr, and with it came a burst of anguish at leaving her friends Brista and Forz and some guilt, at last, over the greeder's owner's loss.

Had he cared for it? Had he loved it?

Dana hadn't considered that before.

And her parents. They had lost their only daughter.

Tears spilled from her eyes.

What have I done?

A moment later she heard the sounds of sniffling. With a great effort, Dana pulled herself out of the meditation. She looked around the room and to her surprise found that all the girls in the room were weeping.

One by one, they came and embraced her.

"You lost so much," said a girl with long hair tied in thin braids that ran over her shoulders. "I'm sorry."

Some came silently and merely mingled the wet tears on their cheeks with hers as they hugged her tightly.

Mirris merely gave Dana a smart punch to her shoulder. "That's for making us all cry."

Kaia was the last to face Dana. She simply squeezed her hand. Perhaps it was meant to say, "I'm sorry I judged you." Perhaps not quite that. But she met her eyes and there was no hatred there, no fear.

Dana was an equal, an acolyte, one of them.

A second wave of emotion crowded into Dana, a feeling she was having for the very first time in her life.

They accept me.

Dan Allen

"Kaia?" said a droll voice.

"Yes, Mirris?"

"Ryke is waiting outside . . . for Dana."

Chapter 18

Jet tugged the button-down jacket of his dress blues and straightened his white belt and cap.

Last time I wear this thing for a while.

The sprint ship was ready. His team was ready. Jet was about to leave the fleet behind and take the future of all Believers into his hands.

One last thing to clear off his docket.

Councillor Raman, the High Seer.

Jet hadn't seen the young woman since the rescue on Avalon when Angel had taken a trick shot from Jet's tossed rifle and saved her life.

He never felt prepared for this sort of thing.

Jet raised his hand and knocked.

"Enter," called a young voice from inside. The door unlocked.

Jet stepped inside a steel-floored conference room like so many others on the ship.

The High Councillor stood up from a chair on the side of the conference table. She wore a simple, loose gown.

The was nothing at all intimidating about the High Seer. She couldn't have been more than fifteen or sixteen.

How old was she? Had she even graduated high school? Why was she on the High Council?

He removed his hat and tucked it under his arm, conscious not to salute the civilian leader. "Corporal Jet Naman, Believer Marines, Advance Contingent."

The High Councillor walked closer and looked up into his eyes. "You saved my life on Avalon, Brother Naman. You've done all the Believers a great service—and especially me."

"Just doing my job."

She gave a heroic smile and went on tiptoe, wrapped her arms around him, and laid her head against his chest. "Thank you."

"Um, you're welcome, Councillor Raman." It was not the kind of thing a marine was used to. A crisp salute, the approving eye of your commanding officer, and the respect of your team was all the thanks a marine would ever expect to get. And it was all he ever wanted.

He wasn't quite sure what to do with a hug.

"You can call me Sarah." The High Councillor stepped back, keeping her hands on his arms as if drawing strength from muscles underneath his uniform. "I was the one who nominated you for first contact."

"Yeah, I guessed that." He swallowed as he formed the question that had been chewing on him since he woke from cryo. "Why?"

The girl turned and walked to a table with twelve glass stands. Nine had planetary models balanced on thin spires. Three were empty.

"The Creator shows us very little—far less than we believe the Xahnans to be capable of seeing." Sarah traced her finger over the model of Earth. "Long ago we humans, too, shared powerful spiritual gifts. But when the veil grew distant on Earth, that was when the human race truly awoke, seeking answers. No longer did the Creator offer wisdom through prophets and miracles on demand. We were alone, Jet. And alone we strove. Alone we sought. Alone we soared, reaching the stars, retracing the very steps of the Creator. Does it not thrill you?"

Jet shrugged. He wasn't a Believer because of religion. It was more because he hated ASP.

"You haven't seen beyond the Earth and stars," she said. "And I cannot make you. But that does not change the fact that life is more than blood and bone." She paused, then said softly. "I witnessed the ASP strike on Avalon many weeks before it happened. It came to me in a vision, a waking dream from which I could not escape. It was terrible."

Her eyes became distant and she shivered.

"I warned the Believers. They fled by the thousands before the

The Exalting

ASP fleet arrived to announce the extermination order."

"That's . . . that's really incredible."

Sarah nodded. "There are only two other seers on the Council—one from Capria and the aged grand patriarch of Rodor. Their gifts are largely dormant."

"So, you *are* the High Seer?"

She nodded. "A well-guarded secret."

"Is that why you nominated me?" Jet asked. "Did you see a vision or . . . something?"

Sarah gave him a playful shove. "Of course I did."

Jet was dumbstruck. "About me?"

She nodded. "On Xahna."

Jet was intensely curious. The High Seer had seen a vision of him on the ninth planet. "Wh . . . what did you see?"

"I saw you and a Xahnan girl." Sarah's voice trembled as her eyes unfocused. "And then I saw our ships falling from the sky. Then ASP cruisers in orbit. I saw their corporations landing, spreading wealth and technology—binding them with the chains of greed. I saw no other Believers."

The words seemed to squeeze his heart. Would it go so badly? Would this be the end? Was he on a doomed mission? "Why would—why would the Creator send you a vision like that?"

"Perhaps," her voice choked, "he does not see us gathering this planet. Perhaps it is not in his design."

"It has to be."

"You don't understand the Creator's mind. None of us do."

"If God wants a marine on this mission, then he wants no one left behind."

Sarah bit her lip. "I hope you're right." The locket on her necklace gave a small chirp. She touched it, and Decker's voice sounded from a speaker in the wall. "Councillor Raman, this is Captain Decker. The Nautilus and our drag net are ready. Awaiting Corporal Naman."

"Jet will join you shortly."

"Acknowledged, Decker out."

The locket chirped again to signal the end of the transmission.

Sarah turned up her hands. "I wish I could send you with something more than a broken vision and a dropship."

Jet waved his hand. "I've had worse briefings. It's just the future of the Believers and an entire planet's salvation and the Creator's plans for the universe—I'll figure something out."

She smiled. "Goodbye, Jet."

"See you on Xahna . . . Sister Sarah."

Jet stepped out of the conference room, then ran to the lift. The gate closed, and the lift accelerated down toward the shuttle bay.

When it stopped, he waved to the security guard and hopped into the autoshuttle. "Nautilus, double time."

"You got it," the AI pilot said.

───※───

Mirris's metal-ringed bangs flew out as she turned to look to Dana. "You had better not even touch Ryke. He's like our brother."

What had her so riled up about Ryke?

Had he acted differently around her? What had they noticed?

"I'll keep it to a minimum," Dana offered. She let Mirris's jealous imagination chew on what that minimum might be.

Right now, she had to talk to Ryke alone. He might know something about Korren as well. And maybe she would tell him about Sindar and the bloodstone.

I need him on my side.

"Now, if you'll excuse me." Dana slipped quickly out the curtain and ran straight into Ryke's thornwood staff. Her forehead ricocheted off one of its polished thorn roots. Stars glinted around the edges of her vision as her legs lost strength.

"That's gonna . . . leave a . . ." *scar.* Dana slumped down with one hand clamped to her forehead, which she was sure would bleed famously all over the ground and her clothes and Ryke.

Ryke's hand caught her upper arm, which saved her from cracking the back of her head as she collapsed.

The Exalting

"Oh, my. I'm so sorry—usually people come out the other side of the curtain."

"Left . . ." Dana groaned. ". . . handed."

Dana blinked and saw seven of Ryke. She blinked again and realized it was the rest of the young acolytes staring down at her.

"What did you do to her?"

"That wasn't nice."

"Whatever it was, she probably deserved it."

"Mirris," Kaia chided. "We do not judge. Judgment is reserved—"

"For the ka," Mirris echoed. "You were thinking it, too."

"How did you—I was not."

"Oh, would somebody please just get her a rag. That's going to bleed everywhere."

A throb pounded from the front of Dana's head where she had collided with a prominent bump on the staff. Dana had once spent a weekend polishing a thornwood branch with a coral. The wood was incredibly hard.

"Oh, just go stick her head in the pool." It was Mirris's voice. "The sayathi will take care of it."

"You know that's not allowed," Kaia whispered.

"Everyone does it."

"Not me."

"I guess," Dana said wincing as the sound of her own voice sent more pain through her head. "I should make the blood sacrifice anyway."

"She hasn't made the blood sacrifice?" Mirris stared at Dana, aghast. "How did she drink the water?"

"Her relative was blood-sworn," Kaia said in a guarded voice. She didn't say it was Togata-ka.

Ryke handed his staff to Mirris. "Don't play with that."

Dana felt his arms cradling her back and knees as he lifted her and carried her down the tunnel toward the sayathi pool.

Dana kept her hand pressed to her already painful forehead, trying to keep the bleeding of her split skull to a minimum. Dana

179

had to shut her eyes as the blood trickled down.

"You are really bleeding a lot—Kaia, she's going to need stitches."

"Lovely," Dana said. "A great big scar on my forehead." She didn't hide the irritation she felt at having been nearly knocked unconscious.

Ryke lowered Dana to the edge of the pool.

Dana put her hand on the sharp coral and leaned out over the water. She looked down at her reflection as heavy drops of blood drained into the pool, dispersing in a red plume beneath the surface. Ripples ran through the glowing reflection of Dana's blood-streaked face.

I look horrible.

"How much more?" Dana asked.

"Probably enough if you use what's already on your face," Mirris said from just behind her. Dana was suddenly thrust underwater and held there. It was a few seconds before Dana could find safe leverage for her hands and push.

But as soon as she did, Mirris pulled her head back up. "See. It's working," Mirris said. "That lump on her forehead is already glowing."

"So is the rest of her," said another acolyte.

Dana looked down and realized her entire body was glowing at least ten times as brightly as the woman at the Sayathi Sea had.

"That's not normal," Mirris said.

Dana looked down at her waist and realized that the bloodstone in the pouch had touched the water. With one hand she lifted the pouch clear of the pool, and the glowing faded slightly.

Oops.

Kaia pressed a cloth to Dana's head. "We're going to have to get those bloody clothes off you."

"Not while he's here."

Ryke gestured to Mirris. "Did you want her to carry you?"

Dana closed her eyes, wincing as the throbbing in her forehead became a thundering headache. "I'm going to be sick to my

The Exalting

stomach."

Kaia knelt beside her and whispered quickly in her ear. "You must not throw up in the sacred—oh, she's really going to throw up."

Dana choked down her gagging.

"Thank you." Kaia turned to the staring acolytes and spoke in a knowledgeable voice. "Do you all recognize the signs of shock?"

Kaia reached inside a pocket of her apron and drew out a small bottle and what looked like a small bean bag. She poured a small amount of the liquid on the bean bag and then pressed it to Dana's head.

The bag was cool to the touch, quickly turning icy. "Wow. Is that alchemy?"

"Of course, it is," Mirris said. "Kaia formulated the angel's kiss herself."

"She's never seen my alchemy before," Kaia explained to the younger acolytes. "Because she's from Norr. But the sayathi recognize that portion of her grandfather's blood that runs through her." Kaia looked at Mirris. "Dana is your second cousin."

"But I don't have any—wait," Mirris knelt down and peered at Dana, as if looking in the mirror. "My grand uncle—the last ka— went north."

"You mean Togath," Dana said, "my grandfather."

Mirris wrinkled her nose. "No wonder you look like my father—only with girl parts."

"Er . . . thanks."

"He's not that good looking."

Kaia tried not to laugh as she bound the poultice to Dana's forehead with a cloth. Then she turned to Ryke. "Can you carry her back to the infirmary?"

"Sure. I'll just be a moment."

Kaia exchanged a look with Ryke that appeared to be laced with several hours' worth of lecture.

"I'll have a look at it when the swelling is down," Kaia said as she stood up. "The rest of you back to quarters."

Dan Allen

The whispers of the departing children echoed through the tunnel.

"Did you see how much she glowed?"

"Is that some kind of sign? Is she going to be the next ka?"

Ryke knelt down next to Dana. She hoped he didn't notice the excessive glowing when the stone had touched the water.

Take a note: don't get the stone wet.

"Are you okay?"

"People only ask that when I look terrible," Dana had meant to think it, but the words had just slipped out. "How bad is it?"

Ryke winced. "I . . . got you pretty good. I was leaning against it, so it didn't really give much." He leaned closer. "I am sorry."

Now her head wasn't throbbing, thanks to the angel's kiss, but her heart beat more quickly, too. Something about attention and proximity.

"Don't worry about it," Dana said. If she could figure out what do about the bloodstone, there was a long future ahead of her—a future with Ryke, Kaia, and her second cousin, who she could already tell was going to be a great friend.

Ryke took in a breath and paused. "What you did . . . in the cave after we escaped . . . it's not something I was expecting."

"You mean when I cried?" Dana gave a tight-lipped grin. "Yeah, I don't usually do that."

"No." His eyes met hers again.

"Oh." Dana glanced up the corridor. "The thank you?"

Ryke looked down. "It is kind of nice being around someone who doesn't treat me like a kind-deed-doing mechanodron. But I can't accept thanks for hurting those men," Ryke said. "I've prepared all my life to defend the innocent from the unrighteous."

"You finally got your chance," Dana whispered.

"But you were not innocent. Korren said you stole a greeder from Norr."

"Yeah, but—" Dana grabbed Ryke's arm as wave of vertigo hit her. "Those men weren't innocent either. They were trying to kill me—and you."

182

The Exalting

"Why?" he asked.

I can trust him, Dana thought. *I can tell him.* Numbness had spread from the point where Kaia had applied the medicine down to her cheeks. She formed the words carefully, trying not to sound as impaired as she felt.

"They wanted what I was bringing to Shoul Falls."

Ryke's brow furrowed in thought. "They wanted you because you were powerful and unbound?"

"Not me. The Vetas-kazen want—" Dana tried to form words, but the numbness kept spreading from the point on her forehead where Kaia had dripped the medicine. It ran over her face and down her arms and hands. She lost the ability to speak or move her arms.

Maybe she used too much.

But Kaia was apparently no amateur.

"Great," Ryke muttered as Dana's head lolled to one side limply. "Always a side effect."

As she lay there paralyzed, Ryke picked up her body. Her lips were a half inch from Ryke's neck, but she couldn't so much as pucker her lips.

Thank you for saving me, she thought. *Thank you.*

Dana caught a glimpse of the pool as he turned to leave. The pink hue of her blood had begun to coalesce in one corner of the pool. By morning a new nodule would be there, a sayathenite crystal that would hold her blood sample.

Dana awoke in complete darkness and with a massive headache. She tried to move but failed. As feeling slowly spread into her fingers she realized with horror that the coin purse at her waist was gone.

Oh no.

The fact that she was also missing her hand-sewn wool jacket, shirt, and pants scarcely registered.

Dan Allen

The bloodstone was gone.

Chapter 19

Jet's shuttle cleared the launch tube, and the Excalibur flew backward as if he were falling toward the engines. Then the shuttle oriented and engaged its thrusters to match the fleet's deceleration. Spurts from lateral thrusters sent it drifting toward a massive fuel sphere suspended between twenty-some-odd tin can shuttles, each spewing a purple glow from their ion drives.

In front of the fuel sphere, like an insect hanging off a fruit, was the Nautilus.

The AI pilot zoomed the viewscreen on the class 3 dropship. "Is that your stop?"

"Yep."

"Looks like an accident waiting to happen."

"I hope not." But Jet had to agree with the AI's candor. The idea had looked much better in his head. Jet toggled the radio. "Naman to Nautilus, requesting permission to come aboard."

"This is Decker. Get your butt on the ship. Those ASP punks have a two-week lead already."

"Yes, sir!"

The shuttle docked on the ventral port, a location Jet was more accustomed to being hurled out of in a wingjet frame.

He was all too familiar with the compact class 3 dropship. Class 3 transported up to three squads of eight soldiers. It lacked a dedicated cryobay and had a lean crew of three: captain, copilot, and a multirole AI officer rated at six HE—human equivalent—as navigator/comms/defense/logistics specialist.

Decker had gambled that he wouldn't need the redundant copilot and chosen instead to use the extra the weight for food and supplies. Even so, it was going to be tight quarters on a ship designed solely for shuttling grunts to and from drop zones.

"I'm in." Jet cycled the airlock and stepped aboard to find

Decker, Monique, Yaris, and Teea waiting for him in the launch bay.

"I kept the dwarf in cryo like you asked." Decker was two inches shorter than Jet and at least ten years older. "One paycheck will get you five if Dormit doesn't knock you out cold the moment he's coherent." The captain wore an intriguing mustache that gave him a "dare you to call my bluff" look that better suited a poker player.

"Not taking that one."

"Ever been hit by an iron-fisted dwarf?" Decker asked. He was one of the few captains in the fleet that wore a mustache. It was stylishly thin, though his eyebrows were bushy enough to make it look like he had three equal blond mustaches distributed on his face.

"Hit by a dwarf? Yeah, plenty."

"You look it."

Monique snickered.

"Small space, hot temper—better to let him ride this one out in the cooler. Besides, he eats too much."

"He's gonna be ticked," Monique said, arms folded.

"Better than court-martialed."

"I just hope your drag net works," Decker said as he grabbed a handle on the nearest bulkhead. "Or we're going to be taking a short tour of the Xahnan system on our way out of the galaxy."

Jet hadn't ever considered that particular way of dying.

"Okay, everybody grab something." Decker pressed a button on his wrist control. "Tiberius, kill the engines."

The ship's AI responded with an assertive voice and a hint of a Russian accent. "Begin zero gravity protocol. Engines off."

Gravity suddenly vanished. A cheer sounded from down the corridor in the direction of the bridge. "We're away!"

A display showed the fleet blasting away. It was an illusion. The Nautilus was simply drifting while the fleet ships were aggressively slowing themselves from a quarter of light speed.

"We're a thousand AU out from Xahna system," Decker

The Exalting

announced as he walked to the bridge. Jet knew that meant they were a thousand times the distance from the Earth to the sun. He'd never been to Earth, but he assumed the distance was similar to the other Goldilocks-zone planets he'd been on.

Jet and the others drifted after Decker from the launch bay through a fifteen-foot-long corridor to the bridge, which was more of a glorified cockpit. Aside from the maintenance cubby and the sanitary silo, they were the only two rooms on the ship.

Decker checked the panel of analog gauges, then swung himself around to face the marines. "We've got six weeks of free fall while we get ahead of the braking fleet, then six weeks of double gravity while we slow to match orbit with Xahna."

"How much time will that buy us?" Jet asked.

"Three weeks, of course," Yaris replied. "Did you even study physics in school?"

Jet laughed as his feet drifted away from the bulkhead. "Why do you think we brought you along?"

"Actually, I've been made legal advisor."

"What—how?"

"I was an interplanetary trade attorney on Capria for several decades before I joined the marines."

Jet chuckled. "Can't imagine why you gave up a cushy desk job like that."

"I've also been a professor of statistics and Caprian history, a farmworker, a trade mall food court musician, a—"

"We get the idea," Jet said. "You're a geezer who likes to change jobs."

"Caprians all change jobs every few decades," Yaris said. "It's ethical and prudent."

Teea drifted past and tweaked his nose. "Hope that's not illegal."

"A violation of no fewer than ten fleet regulations and several societal norms."

"Thought so," Teea chimed.

Decker caught her arm when she drifted past him and tried

187

the same thing. "Don't you guys have some mission planning to do?" He gave Teea the stink eye. "Maybe study the language or something?"

Teea swatted his butt instead and gave a sharp salute. "Yes, sir!"

"Teea, as you are not military personnel," Yaris reminded, "you are not required to salute the captain."

"Says the elf with a red nose."

"You heard the captain," Jet said. "Let's figure out what we're up against. This planet is bound to be full of surprises. I don't want to get ambushed by something we—"

"You had to say it." Monique shook her head, turned, and pushed off down the maintenance access corridor, past Dormit's cryobag, toward the storage bay that would likely serve as their quarters. On a ship intended for short trips to and from a battle zone, there wasn't really anywhere else to set up camp and sleep. "You literally had to say it—again."

Jet followed her. "Come on. You know you were thinking it, too."

Monique stopped in the storage bay and touched a crate to pivot slowly in midair. "For your information, I was thinking about something else." She gave him a solid stare.

It could be any number of things, but the way she was looking at him said it definitely involved him.

Avalon? It stirred feelings he would rather not touch.

When the squad had been separated, it was her group that had taken the worst of the casualties. She was the only one that had survived. Jet had never even talked to her about what happened. He had never even thought about what it had been like for her. He had just gloried in the victory and felt bad for those who hadn't made it. She had seen them all fall—Romeo, Atlas, Zeke, and three other squads. "Monique, I'm really sorry about what happened on Avalon. I should have been there when you guys came under fire."

"I don't really want to talk about it," Monique said.

Jet nodded. "Well . . . if you ever do want to talk about it, I'm here."

The Exalting

Monique gave him a small shove that sent him flying across the bay. "Well now you're over there."

She looked to a status console and then looked back at Jet as if she was finally ready to ask a question that had been needling her for days. "You and Dormit weren't using Yaris's flamethrower to roast bat chickens were you? Because if you were—"

Jet patted his stomach. "I didn't think it was that obvious."

Her jaw dropped. "Are you being serious? You're being serious." She couldn't tell if he was kidding. "I'll ask Yaris."

"Oh, sure. Go and ruin all the fun."

"Yeah, *fun*." She spat the word. "Jet, is this a suicide mission?"

"I don't know how to answer that."

"You wouldn't care. You volunteered because you had nothing left to lose." She stared at the status console, not looking at him.

"Why did you volunteer?" Jet asked. "You were in school. You're brilliant. You obviously didn't flunk out."

She looked up. "Because it was the right thing to do."

The concept had never occurred to him.

"I've studied planets and societies, Jet. You can't imagine the similarities between the worlds. It defies logic. There has to be some kind of . . . master plan. Some kind of Creator."

"Sure."

"That doesn't matter to you? That we're all cut from the same cloth, all tied to the same destiny?"

"I . . . was honestly just out to kick some ASP butt."

"At least you're good at it."

Jet hadn't been huge on religion, but something inside him seemed to be looming larger and larger, something he would eventually face. "Monique, do you believe in prophecy?"

"Of course. They ordered us all to leave Rodor years *before* the extermination order—and we were just in time to save the High Council. You think that was coincidence? Didn't you hear that Avalon evacuated thousands of Believers in the weeks before the extermination order?"

Sarah's vision. She knew it would happen. Those who had

189

believed her were now traveling with the fleet. The rest were entombed in a fiery hell.

Sarah had also seen a vision of their fleet's ships falling from the Xahnan sky in droves. "What if it is a suicide mission?"

Monique looked at him, her eyes steely. "Then I'm not going down without a fight."

"That." Jet pointed at her. "That is why I put you on the mission."

"Not because you can't take your eyes off me?"

Jet felt as if he'd been depantsed on the playground—faelings were big on that sort of thing. He cleared his throat. "Well, there's always going be collateral damage."

She lifted her eyebrows, intrigued. "Collateral damage?"

Jet bumped his chest with his fist. "Wounded heart."

"Oh brother!" She grabbed a torque wrench and hurled it. "That was like the worst line I've—" she put a hand to the side of her head. "Are my ears bleeding?"

Yaris and Teea floated into the room. Yaris caught the rebounding wrench. "Good to see you two are getting along as usual."

"Does this room need some happy pheromones?"

Monique glared at Teea and then Jet, probably thinking about the fact that Adkins had the whole fleet to chose from and picked a ship without a cryobay. There was nowhere to hide from each other. The closet in the maintenance corridor didn't even have a door.

"Collateral damage." She turned to the status console and began reviewing the ship's manifest. "Where are the tasers stored? I'll give you collateral damage."

She was definitely back to normal.

On her knees, Dana felt across the fur rug with her hands. A dull ache throbbed again from her forehead, but Dana didn't care whether the wound burst open again.

The Exalting

Where is the bloodstone?

Equally important was the question of who took it.

Ryke was too proper. He wouldn't dare touch her while she was asleep.

Kaia.

She was the only one that knew about Dana meeting Sindar, and Vetas-ka's interest in the bloodstone of Shoul Falls.

I told her I didn't have it here.

She might have found it when she took Dana's blood-soaked clothes to wash. Or perhaps she had even searched her for it.

How dare she!

The fact that she was stuck in a dark room, couldn't see her hand in front of her face, and was only wearing scant underclothes made it all the more frustrating. Dana wanted to call out for somebody to turn on a light, but she was terrified that someone would actually do it—someone like Ryke, or worse, Korren.

She didn't want to see him again, not ever, and especially not in her skivvies and tie-top alone and helpless.

Wait a minute. I'm a druid. I can see in the dark.

Dana took a deep breath and cleared her head to search for animals with better night vision.

Where are you?

Dana reached out with her spirit, touching the walls of the cavern and especially the roof, but found no help in the form of blackwings.

What kind of a cave has no nocturnal animals?

Or maybe they've all gone out because it's the middle of the night.

Dana tried for a cave shrew and similarly came up with nothing. With panic again rising within her, clenching at her throat and squeezing her breath, Dana realized that for the first time in her life, she couldn't feel a single living creature, not even an insect.

What did they do to me?

It couldn't have been the water from the pool. Everyone knew blood-sworn adepts were more powerful than drale adepts.

There was another possibility, one that scared her to her core.

She was blood-sworn now, part of the collective. If somebody else was using the bloodstone, then her will was at the beck and call of whoever wielded the bloodstone.

But her will wasn't gone. She knew what that felt like. It was a pitiful sense of incapability and no desire to do anything.

Right now, she wanted to find the stone more than anything, even more than finding her clothes.

She had to find the stone.

"Hello?" she called softly. "Is anyone there?"

Great. Probably put me in a prison.

No. Prisons were guarded. There had to be another explanation.

I was injured. I am probably in the infirmary.

"Kaia? . . . Ryke?"

The flap of a leather curtain was followed by a hushed voice. "Keep quiet. I brought the antidote."

Dana froze. The voice speaking to her was oddly similar to her own.

"Cousin?"

"*Second* cousin," Mirris said. "Now shut up."

"Light a glow candle, would you?" Dana begged. "I can't see anything, and I'm stuck here in my underclothes."

"There are already two glow candles on in the room, Dana. You can't see because you're blind. It's a side effect from the angel's kiss they've been giving you."

The hush in her voice told Dana that Mirris wasn't supposed to be there.

"I'm going to put something on your cut. It will hurt . . . a lot. But you must not scream. This is the only way to get your abilities back quickly."

"What did they do to me?" Dana whispered.

"Alchemy and adept abilities don't mix well. It's the same with getting drunk—you lose your will entirely. Angel's kiss is particularly potent. It takes away all pain. I think something about pain makes us Xahnan. Without it, we can't connect to the

192

The Exalting

spiritual plane. We can't reach through the veil. With as many doses as they've given you, it could take a week to get it all out of your system—hence the antidote."

"And the antidote makes me feel pain?" Dana said.

"As much as possible."

"That is the worst idea I've ever heard."

"You can't risk being powerless. Not now." A hand reached out and touched her hair. "Hold very still."

"Hold on. How long have I been out?"

"Two days."

"What?"

"Korren has been keeping you asleep by pouring angel's kiss on your wound every few hours."

A nauseating mix of fever and chill passed over Dana. "Then why am I awake?"

"I emptied his bottle and replaced it with water. Korren doesn't know he's used water on you for the last dose, but he will if he finds you awake. You woke a few minutes before the next dose is due."

"Which means . . ."

"I don't have much time to pour this viper's embrace on your wound. Now, when Korren comes, just stay quiet and pretend to be asleep while he puts more water on your wound. As soon as they're gone you can sneak out."

"Why are you doing this?"

"The civic guard is rounding up all of the rest of the acolytes and kazen. I don't know what's going on, but I don't like it."

Mirris never trusted anyone, but this time Dana agreed. It sounded like somebody wanted to do something without any interference from those most loyal to the city and its bloodstone.

Korren. He's going to take the stone and become the ka.

"Wait." Dana gripped Mirris's arm. "Can you make them think they've got everyone, when someone is missing?"

Mirris sighed. "It's going to take a lot of will. I don't know how long I can keep that up. Eventually they'll realize not everyone is there."

"Make it Ryke."

Mirris hesitated. "Alright. I'll tell him to meet you at the mouth of the falls."

"But I still can't see," Dana said.

"You will . . . I hope. For now, find an animal to guide you."

"But—"

"I'm sorry, Dana." A drop of liquid touched Dana's forehead. It felt like the liquid had lit her skin on fire. A moment later her face fell into a blazing furnace. The muscles of her face and neck seemed to peel away as though flayed by a thousand flesh-tearing hooks. Spears stabbed through her chest, shredding every muscle and organ.

Dana couldn't even draw a breath to scream.

Tears welled in her eyes.

"I'm sorry, Dana. Just keep quiet. I have to go. I shouldn't be here. Korren is coming soon. Just stay quiet. Please. Then get out while you can."

Dana felt herself being laid back on the fur rug as hammers crushed her bones.

She wanted to strike out at Mirris. But her retreating footsteps faded into the roaring in Dana's ears, leaving her in tortured silence, depriving her of the one comfort of company.

In a few moments, the pain grew quickly to such an unbearable extent, one desire eclipsed all others.

Please, let me die.

Dana wanted to utterly cease existing. Now.

Her chest moved in a breath halted by pain, denying Dana's searing body even a lungful of cool air.

The pain she felt was far beyond tears. Dana only wanted to cease being. If she had a knife in her hand, she would have put it through her heart to end the worlds of pain that coursed through her.

Worlds!

Dana could feel them, somehow.

Beyond Xahna, there were others. The presence of worlds

194

The Exalting

beyond her own passed through her like wind through a veil. Rhythms of vibrant beings coursed through them, whispers of emotion.

Entire worlds filled with life . . . and some with pain that echoed hers.

There was a meaning to the pain, a purpose grander than anything she could have ever imagined.

It was real. And all beyond her reach, like the surface of the water to a drowning victim. Yet, there was meaning to it all, a glorious beauty that transformed pain into passion, passion into creation, and creation into . . .

Dana reached out desperately, searching through the pain for that something. It was the truth she needed.

There was meaning, beautiful, radiant, transcendent—a great pool that would fill her beyond capacity if she could but reach it.

But it was all she could do to catch a glimpse of it before the pain overwhelmed her. It pressed Dana from inside and out. Dana could no longer fight the suffering. Exhausted by the pain that grew in waves, beyond anything she could have ever imagined, Dana sank toward the screams.

Save me. Please.

Muffled voices sounded in Dana's ears.

Help!

The voices grew louder, and Dana somehow remembered Mirris's warning.

Quiet.

The next wave of pain broke over Dana's body like a bladed scythe cutting right through her, tearing her apart.

She felt a single drop of cool liquid on her forehead. The mere touch of it exploded into a detonation of pain that ripped through her head like a boulder had landed on it. The viper's embrace amplified every sensation with pain.

"That's enough," said a woman's voice.

Another cool drop landed on her forehead, this one turning to stone, choking every microscopic vein with a million tourniquets.

195

"She won't recover if you keep this up. It is against our teachings."

"She is a threat to all we value." Dana recognized Korren's voice.

"The citizen council will hear of this," said the other woman kazen.

"No one will hear of this. We've already been summoned. In this state, she's no risk."

"As you wish, Korren."

"The citizen council thinks we cannot keep the stone from Vetas-ka," Korren said. "They're going to vote on whether to destroy it."

Destroy it! No. It took all Dana's will to keep from gasping in shock.

"When?" the woman gasped. "They wouldn't do it—would they?"

"I cannot decide for the council, although I will present our arguments at the public meeting. Some of them think destroying it is the only way to stop outside interference."

"I . . . understand," said the woman. "It is an extraordinary circumstance. But, should we not first seek aid from the Pantheon? The other ka of Aesica could defend us from Vetas-ka."

"There is a price to pay for any aid," Korren said simply.

What price? Dana wondered. *What is he talking about?*

"Unfortunately," Korren said. "The rest of the acolytes and kazen will not be at the meeting. I alone will represent the sanctum. The council fears interference. The civic guard is taking all the kazen and acolytes to the barracks. You must go with them. And you will all receive angel's kiss."

"And you?" said the woman.

"One kazen is little risk. And the sanctum has one seat on the council, after all."

"Korren," the woman whispered. "If they destroy the stone, it will be the end of our sanctum—our order. What is going to happen to us?"

The Exalting

"I don't know, Genua. We must wait and see." Footsteps retreated, followed by silence.

With the stone gone, the sayathi colony would submit to the first conqueror. It wouldn't make Vetas-ka give up. It would only make his job easier.

Destroying it won't save them, Dana thought, as she reached out from the depths of her personal hell, through billions of miles of piled emptiness breeding utter hopelessness from the echoes of her anguish, and caught a breath of air.

She breathed out and in again.

I have to save the stone.

Through all the pain, through the phantoms of agony that seemed to break every rib anew with each motion, she breathed.

There were other breaths, too. Tiny, insignificant breaths.

Cave shrews.

And bats—families of them.

Dana withdrew instantly, hoping her pain hadn't passed accidentally into the creatures she had sensed.

The antidote worked.

But beyond those creatures were the millions of sayathi within her and the millions beyond them spread across the population of Shoul Falls, a chorus of voices in one.

I can feel them!

There was a purpose to it, like the will of an animal or a Xahnan.

Somehow the billions of microscopic sayathi, through their Xahnan hosts, were trying to reach out.

To what?

Images flashed in her mind, visualizations of the fleeting moments when the pain from the viper's embrace carried her perception beyond the veil.

To other worlds?

But how?

Dana rolled onto her side and curled her knees to her chest as she broke into uncontrolled weeping. Minutes passed like hours until she could again sense anything beyond pain.

Fingertips. She pressed them together and experienced only stabbing needles of pain, not hand-crushing agony.

Dana reached for the transcendence that had touched her, the vision of creation that surrounded her as her soul connected to the other worlds wrapped in the fabric of the Creator's veil. But the feeling had already faded, and with that her own sensations had returned.

Fear.

She was in danger. She should leave now.

But this is my city now, as much as it is theirs. I'm blood-sworn.

I have to protect the colony.

And I have as much right to the bloodstone as any of them—more. It was trusted to me.

Dana opened her eyes and still saw nothing beyond the maddening, shifting patterns of gray that haunted her like drifting phantoms whether her eyes were open or shut.

Dana's heart sank. She had her adept abilities back, but she was still blind.

As the pain continued to fade, Dana reached out to a cave shrew and coaxed it from behind a wooden chest. She surveyed the room from its floor-centered view, spying herself lying on the floor in her tie-top and undershorts.

Light filtered into the room from two glow candles in the wall. A leather curtain separated the room from the rest of the sanctum.

Dana coaxed the timid shrew forward with a small flux of will, her gathered intent far surpassing the shrew's tiny capacity. Then she stood slowly, watching her form rise from the perspective of the shrew. It was like trying to cut her own hair with scissors while looking in a mirror—and that with a shrew's side-set eyes.

She steadied herself with one hand against the wall and then pulled her hand away, trusting her exhausted legs to hold her.

The shrew cocked its head interestedly, and Dana tipped forward onto her knees, stopping her fall with her forearms.

A spinning scorpion descended on a web to her shoulder. It

The Exalting

tapped a rhythm of loyalty with its forelimbs and lifted its tail stinger bravely, showing her that she was not alone.

Stay with me. Protect me.

The spinning scorpion hunkered down, its many eyes watching for motion in every direction.

Clothes.

Dana stood and turned, following the shrew's eyes to where her washed clothes lay folded.

She blindly lifted them, somewhat annoyed that the nearsighted shrew was useless at detecting whether she was putting them on right side out or not.

After pulling on her trousers, buttoning her shirt, jacket, and tying her boots, Dana sent the shrew ahead through the leather curtain. A few glow candles lit the corridor, though the feeble light was plenty for the large-pupiled rodent. It scurried along the shadows of the cave, stopping to sniff at intervals.

The powerful sensations of the shrew's nose laid out a panorama of pasts in even greater richness than a hound could sense. She nearly laughed out loud as she inhaled a dozen scents she could place to specific persons.

She sensed various hints of everyone who had come down the corridor in the last day.

The shrew sniffed again, but there was no hint of a recent passage by the one person she needed to find: Ryke.

She had to find him before the city destroyed the bloodstone. It would be the same as handing their lands over to Vetas-ka.

Find the rushing water, Dana whispered to the shrew.

It dashed ahead into the darkness.

If Ryke had escaped, she would find him at the falls.

Chapter 20

Jet looked at his cards and cursed under his breath. "I fold."

Decker laughed and flashed his pitiful hand. "Bluffed."

"Great." Jet was already down twenty-four meals' worth of dessert packs from his rations.

Jet shuffled and began dealing another hand. "Has the ASP sprint ship started braking yet?"

The captain looked up. "Tiberius, what's the latest?"

"Negative, Captain. No breaking detected yet."

"Jeez," Jet mutttered. "What are they going to do—pull six g's?"

"At least," Decker lifted the corner of his cards to check them and then tossed an ante into the center. The table was a fine metal mesh panel over an air inlet in the maintenance closet. The suction force of the moving air kept their bets on the table in zero gravity.

"Ooh, Rodorian butter crunch." Jet rubbed his chin. "That's probably worth two of these." He tossed in two Talaks ice bombs. They went cold the moment you put them in your mouth. If you weren't careful they would freeze your tongue to the roof of your mouth.

"Must be AIs only on that ship," Jet said.

Decker inclined his head. "Looks like it. Even Wodynians can't survive that kind of force for long."

"How big is their lead?"

"Tiberius figures they'll have three weeks on us," Decker said. He took anther card and upped his bet. "Long enough to knock out all our surveillance satellites."

"They wouldn't bother with that," Jet said. "It's all about getting first contact. Do you think their AIs can learn the language in three weeks?"

"Tiberius picked it up in a day—of course he had four months

The Exalting

of microbot audio recordings to rifle through, plus all of Teea's notes."

"So if that's the strategy," Jet said, "they'll target the most powerful political organization, which leaves us what?"

"Call."

Jet showed his hand. "Two pair, jacks over eights."

"One pair."

"Finally." Jet grabbed the winnings off the grate and stuffed them in his bag. "I'm out. Gotta finish on a win."

"Looks like you're losing on purpose. Trying to thin up for your sociologist friend?"

"He does spend a lot of time looking in the mirror in the sanitary silo," said Tiberius from the ceiling speaker of the maintenance-closet-turned-game-room.

"Shut up, Tiberius."

"Request denied. You lack the requisite rank to give me orders."

"Oh, go defrag yourself," Jet said.

"I have two cores retraining already," Tiberius reported.

"He's half asleep and he's still got twice your wit." Decker folded his arms across his chest and laughed.

Jet matched the captain's posture. "Say it takes them two weeks to get the recordings they need to learn the language. That would leave them one week before we arrive. Would they send a bunch of AIs down to make first contact?"

"Only an egotistical human would ask a question like that," Tiberius replied.

"Okay. So their AIs get one week with the most powerful entity on the planet—the ka that rules that empire Monique claims to have found on the big, flat continent." Jet unrolled the Rodorian butter crunch and chewed slowly, savoring the highest value token in his dwindling gambling pot. He looked at Decker, then up at the ceiling where he imagined Tiberius lived. "Will they know we're coming?"

"Most certainly."

"So we should expect a welcome party."

Decker grinned. "Tiberius, you ready for some action?"

"Sir, yes, sir!"

Decker leaned forward against the belt holding him to the bulkhead. "I'm gonna get you to the surface, Naman. And then I'm gonna make sure nobody from ASP gets even close to your position." He grimaced. "But I have no idea what you are going to do once you're down there."

Jet let his head bang back against the sanitizer wand mounted behind him. "If I can't consolidate support on Xahna for the Believers, then the fleet will be flying into a hostile zone. They'll have no fuel and nowhere to land, with ASP on their tail. It's impossible."

"That's logic talking," Decker said. "We're Believers. Our currency is hope."

"Yeah, well my currency is depleted uranium," Jet said. "And I've got an idea."

"You want to share it?" Tiberius prompted. Curiosity and honest doubt mingled in his voice.

"Nah."

Just take out the ka. He was a sniper after all. What else did they expect?

Dana blindly followed the shrew along a corridor and into a natural limestone cave. There was little light, and the animal seemed to be following a trail of familiar scents.

If she could reach the mouth of the falls, Dana could meet Ryke. Together they might have a chance of rescuing the bloodstone.

The constantly changing height of the ceiling did Dana's head no favors. The shrew's course wound down and then around a still and lifeless pool and finally along sloping section of cave. Even with the shrew's eyes, she could only make out shadows. It was all Dana could do to follow the path the shrew had taken, one foot in front

The Exalting

of the other on the slick limestone. Gradually her confidence grew, and soon she was making steady progress.

The echo of her lonely steps was a reminder of how alone she was.

It's my fault. I brought the stone back. I told Kaia about it.

Once all the kazen and acolytes had been neutralized, Korren could take it for himself.

I need you, Ryke. Please come.

It was a high order to expect Ryke to disobey his seniors.

Please.

Then Dana felt the flow, a subtle drift of sayathi in a current.

We're close.

A tickle of cool air moved past her sifa. Dana climbed a section of mist-slickened limestone. With every step the rushing of water became louder. Coming to the top, the sound was like rolling thunder. The shrew looked around and then, as if realizing it wasn't sure why it had come, ducked back into the cave.

Dana waited on the ledge overlooking the falls she could not see, listening, feeling. A full minute later, she realized what she had just done.

Panicking, she reached out for the cave shrew.

Nothing.

It was gone, its presence masked by the sayathi in the water dripping through cave. She was sure it was there, but she simply couldn't isolate it.

I'm trapped.

She backed up against the cliff wall, pressing her hands against it. Without the shrew she had no way to get back through the cave. That section had been utterly lifeless, and even if a blackwing flew in, it wouldn't be able to guide her feet. The spinning scorpion waiting patiently on her shoulder was no use. Any path was safe for insects, and how could she tell it to take her to the main hall? It had no concept of course and direction.

Oh no.

"Ryke" Dana said softly. Her voice grew louder. "Ryke!"

In the frenzy of her mind, her own name echoed back, lilting above the thunder of the river crashing down the cliffside.

Her name came over and over, a murmur in the noise of the water.

I'm going to go mad.

Perhaps another animal would come. Dana crouched down, folding her arms around her knees.

Suddenly there was a clatter of wood on stone next to Dana, the thump of boots, and a loud, "oof."

"Ryke? Ryke!"

"Just . . . a minute."

"RYKE!"

Dana reached out in the blackness and felt a body in front of her, kneeling on the stone. Her right hand brushed across the slick, hard surface of polished thornwood.

Dana laughed.

Ryke gasped for air. "Wind . . . knocked . . . out."

Dana pulled him toward her, back to the safety of the rock. She held his head against her chest, clutching him. "Oh Ryke—how did you—what just happened?"

Wheezing, he forced out the words. "I jumped . . . from the viewing side."

"Over the water? Are you insane?"

"Am I insane?" Ryke turned and sat next to Dana, not escaping the grip of her desperate hands, which stayed locked around his neck, like a drowning victim. "How did *you* get here?"

"I followed a cave shrew."

"Across the chasm?"

"The what?"

"Dana—" Ryke's voice was incredulous.

"There was a trail."

"A narrow trail? And the rock sort of sloping to one side?"

"Yes."

"By the ka! That trail is only two handspans wide. It crosses a cavern so deep, nobody has ever found the bottom of it."

The Exalting

"What?"

"I crossed it once," Ryke said, "to prove my bravery to the kazen and the citizen council—I'll never do it again."

In horror, Dana thought of the way she had walked casually along the path, following the pattering steps and sniffing nose of the shrew.

"So you followed a cave shrew? But where's your lamp?"

"Ryke, I can't see anyway."

"You can't see?"

"I'm blind."

"Blind!"

Dana imagined he was moving his hand in front of her face, but it didn't so much as register a flicker in the gray haze before her. She shrugged. "Angel's kiss."

"But . . . how did you follow the shrew?"

"An antidote—partial antidote."

Ryke turned toward her, holding her face gently between his hands. "You didn't."

Dana swallowed and then nodded. "The viper's embrace. Mirris brought it."

"I'm so sorry," Ryke said. "They once made us take one drop, diluted a hundred times—I can't even imagine."

"It's alright."

Ryke's hands slid to her shoulders. "Well, I don't know how to say this."

"Say it."

"The civic guard followed me to the sanctum."

"But they don't know any of the entrances."

Ryke sighed. "They do now."

"What happened?"

"We were taken to the barracks and told to stand in a line. The civic guard came down the line, giving everyone a drop of angel's kiss.

"Mirris grabbed my hand. She told me you would meet me at the mouth of the falls. Then she told me to run."

205

"And you did?"

"I stepped out of the line. Nobody saw me. Somehow she was masking me, or holding an image of me standing still in the minds of every guard in the barracks."

Dana grinned. Mirris was stronger than she realized.

"Then I ran. But it wasn't long before they came after me. They followed me here. I managed to get into the tunnel that leads to the falls—to the other side of the falls. But they didn't come after me."

"Why not?"

"They barricaded it."

"What?"

"They obviously couldn't fight me in hand-to-hand combat, so they decided to solve the problem by trapping me here."

Dana grabbed his hand, searching the gray haze for his face. "Well isn't there another way out?"

He didn't speak for a moment.

"One."

"Then let's go. We have to get out of here. They're going to vote on whether to destroy the bloodstone."

"How do you know? They didn't tell us anything."

"I overheard Korren talking to Kazen Genua. It's because Vetas-ka wants the stone. I . . . brought it back with me, after Sindaren tried to flee with it—probably to get it away from Korren."

"Mercy." Ryke's head thumped dully against the rock. "So that's what it's about," Ryke said. "The men we fought were after the bloodstone?"

"It was in a pouch on my waist."

"And that's why you glowed. I can't believe you didn't even—" his voice died out.

"Ryke, I didn't lie to you. I tried to tell you, but the angel's kiss—I couldn't talk."

"What are we going to do?"

"We can't let them destroy it," Dana said. "Vetas-ka wouldn't stop just because the stone is gone. He'll keep coming. The only difference is he wouldn't have a ka to contend with. Without a ka,

The Exalting

he would only have to bring enough water from his source across from Torsica, and he could overwhelm the pool in the mountain. Then the sayathi that run in the falls, and in our blood, will be loyal to him."

"Yeah, but it would be insanely expensive. He'd have to charter every steam-wagon on the coast to get enough up here."

"He's practically a god," Dana said. "I don't think he cares how expensive it is. Once he has a foothold in Aesica, what's next— Norr? The southern coast? The west wilderness? All of Xahna? It's his for the taking."

Ryke didn't offer any arguments. He seemed to understand that while destroying the bloodstone would prevent its capture, it would seal their doom in the end.

"So, you want to stop them from destroying the bloodstone . . . how exactly?"

"Well," Dana said. "I doubt they'll listen to me."

"Agreed."

"I'm going to have to steal it. The problem is, Korren may be thinking the exact same thing—to take the stone for himself."

"You might have a chance there," Ryke said. "Most animals will snatch something that size if it tickles their curiosity. I suppose you have a better chance than someone like me going in and knocking skulls."

He was right. She would have to do it. "We don't have much time. Isn't there another way out of here? I mean besides the falls and the pit of doom?—I can't believe I did that."

Ryke laughed. "You really are amazing, Dana." He lifted her hand. "There is one way. But it is sacrilege—utterly forbidden. It's the *exalting chamber*."

"The what?"

"I'll show you. . . . I've only been there once." Ryke's voice was heavy with some misgiving. But he stood and lifted her hand.

Dana followed him to a cut-stone stair that rose near the river.

"Carefully," Ryke said. "One wrong step and—"

"Bloody death. I know."

Dan Allen

As she climbed slowly, following his guiding hand, Dana could only think of how incredible it was that he had found her at the falls. And now they were together, alone, depending on each other. *We do make a good team.*

As he paused for her to catch up, Dana reached out and put her hand against his chest. Her eyes searched blindly for his. "Why did you risk your life for me in the canyon? You didn't even know me."

"I watched you as you came up the canyon, as I often watch travelers who avoid the main road. Some are thieves. Others are wanderers. You . . . you were in danger."

Dana grinned. "Or did you just hope I was in trouble so you could come rescue me?" A guilty silence followed. "Ah! You did!" She grabbed the front of his shirt and squeezed. Dana imagined Ryke was blushing.

"Can you blame me?" Ryke said, his voice sounding from so close Dana imagined she could lean forward and kiss his lips, if she dared. "The life of an acolyte is one of self-denial. We live to serve."

"As for this," Ryke cleared his throat. "What we are about to do is punishable by death. You must never speak of it."

"Kissing?"

"No—why would I—you do realize you've got a giant scorpion on your shoulder?"

"Does that bother you?"

"Well, it does suit you. Not sure it likes me, though. I was talking about entering the exalting chamber."

Dang it.

"Follow me."

"Hand," Dana begged, reaching out.

"Are you just faking blindness to hold hands?"

"I think that would be against the rules," Dana said. ". . . Not that I wouldn't try it."

"Finally, some honesty." He had to be grinning.

Dana's fingers slipped between Ryke's, and she followed him forward into a low-ceilinged cavern, a fact she discovered with the side of her head.

The Exalting

"Ow!"

"Duck."

"Thanks."

"For your blind information, this is a beautiful limestone cavern," Ryke said. "All sorts of colors—and look at that."

"What?"

"There's a shrine here, with a glow candle—the one I brought when I crossed the chasm."

"It's still here?"

"Like I said. No one comes here."

Dana heard the rummaging in his pocket followed by the sound of a striker. "Alright, follow me. Quickly."

The path led downward. It was an easy walk mostly, though the humidity in the cavern did become quickly stifling.

Ryke's hand tugged downward, and Dana stooped under a rock formation. A bit of chalky water dripped onto her hand.

It was warm, almost hot.

Dana realized she was sweating profusely.

"Almost there," Ryke said. "Can you feel it?" he asked.

"Feel what?"

"The heat."

"I thought it was just you."

"Funny."

"What is this place?" Dana asked. "Why is it so hot?"

"This is where the bond between the bloodstone and the ka is made."

Dana rounded a corner and squeezed through a narrow gap between two limestone formations. A waft of hot air hit her face, nearly choking her.

"I can't even breathe this air."

"Heat melts sayathenite. I thought a Norrian would know that."

"Well, yes. Forz, my friend—not my boyfriend, just—anyway, he makes mechanodrons with sayathenite. He warms the crystals when he trains them. Too much heat, and they melt away."

Ryke led her forward, into the steamy air.

"Are you sure this is safe?"

"It isn't safe," Ryke said. "Not everyone survives the exalting ceremony."

"What are you talking about?" Dana said.

"When I was being examined for the decision," Ryke said. "I was brought here to see if I could withstand the heat." His voiced faded. "I failed."

"I'm so sorry." That explained why Ryke hadn't been chosen. "What does heat have to do with the ka ceremony?" she asked as she followed Ryke further in to the geothermal chamber.

"How do you think the ka gets the crystal inside them?"

Dana blinked. "Inside them?"

Ryke sighed. "You've never seen a ka?"

Dana shook her head.

"The bloodstone is part of them; usually it forms on the back of their neck or in the center of their chest. Sometimes on their forehead."

"How do they—"

"They must swallow it," Ryke said. "But the bloodstone does not melt at body temperature. The chosen must survive the heat, which melts the crystal. The ka must then cool slowly so that the crystal may reform. Too fast, and the crystals reform in the bloodstream—the candidate dies. Come on. Just a bit further."

It felt like walking through a furnace. Only there was no flame.

"The sayathi in the bloodstone are the ruling type," Ryke explained. "Inside an adept, they can reach beyond the veil. They can feel the sayathi in the bodies of those blood-bound to the colony, as if the stone were still in the pool. The connection is far stronger than any meditation circle."

"Which is how the ka draws will from the people in the city," Dana guessed. Sweat dripped down her back. Her damp clothes clung to her.

"And feels their pain and their hopes and prayers." Ryke stopped. "Oh no."

210

The Exalting

"What's the problem?" Dana asked.

Ryke banged his staff against something metal. "The entrance—our exit—is locked from the other side."

"Can't you break it down?" Dana said. "I can't take much more of this heat. I don't think we can make it all the way back through the cavern."

"I know," Ryke said. His breathing was likewise ragged.

His hand let go, and there was a sound next to her as if he had sat down.

"What are you doing?"

"Meditating. I need to summon all my will. Then I will try to break through."

Dana bit down her questions and tried to keep the welling delirium from overwhelming her. She struggled not to interrupt Ryke. He was gathering will, and her distraction wouldn't help.

But perhaps her will could.

Come. Dana threaded out will and drew on the spinning scorpion still waiting patiently on her shoulder. She immersed herself into its dizzying consciousness. Her vision split into a dozen views. The nimble creature wriggled through a gap between the iron door and the wall, then down a chain and thrust several of its multi-segmented legs into a lock. Dana felt its limbs as extensions of her own. She worked the mechanism by pushing two metal leaf springs in opposite directions until the catch finally came loose. Dana let the chain fall through her fingers and listened as its weight pulled it through the latch link by link. The moment it was clear, she pushed the latch down and fell out as the door swung open.

A blast of cool air greeted Dana.

"It's open?" Ryke gasped.

Leaning on Ryke's staff, the two stumbled away from the heat of the exalting chamber, landing in each other's arms in the cool sand of the chamber beyond.

Dana rolled onto her back, taking in huge gasps of cool air. "There was a lock," she said. "I had to get the spinning scorpion to open it for me."

211

"Did you just save my life?" Ryke said.

"I think so."

"Well that's one less thank-you to bother about."

"No. You rescued me from the falls. That's still six. But if you want one off the list, you'd better take one." Dana reached for him and then froze. She looked at her hand in front of her face. "Holy ka! I can see again."

"I think you must have sweat out all the angel's kiss," Ryke said.

"Brilliant. How how do we get to back to the city without being seen?" Dana said.

"We can't take the mountain route. We don't have much time," Ryke added. "The citizen council always meets at noon."

"Noon?" Dana scrambled to her feet. "When is that?"

"It was a half hour away when I left Shoul Falls. So five, maybe ten minutes."

"How long will they deliberate?" Dana said.

"I don't know. We'd better run," Ryke said.

"Wait," Dana said. "I've got a better idea. Do you have a bow and some rope?"

Chapter 21

After six weeks aboard the Nautilus, personal space was so far gone, it was in the realm of myth. Jet was strapped to the bulkhead next to Monique.

He was pretending to be asleep.

So was she.

Her breathing was too regular. It was easy to tell when Monique finally did fall asleep because she did this twitch thing and then let out a long, slow breath.

Teea was flipped, with her head by Jet's feet and closer to the filter intake, to keep her errant dream pheromones from messing with his head. There was a reason faelings slept far apart in trees.

Two feet away on the opposite wall of the corridor was Yaris, who tolerated the buzzing electronics. Decker had a spot in the small recess that composed the medical station where Dormit was still in hibernation.

Jet felt every breath Monique took, the swell of her chest pressing gently against his arm.

After a long day of studying transmissions from the orbital satellites around Xahna, and then practicing Xahnan with Jet and Teea, she ought to have been as tired as the rest of the crew.

Something was eating at her. And for some reason, that ate at him, too.

Jet had plenty to mull over. The ASP ship had finally started braking at ten full g's. Whether it had started with anyone alive, it certainly had no one left alive now. The risky maneuver bought them them an additional week. ASP would be there a full month ahead of Jet. It would give them time to land on the big continent, make powerful friends, and attempt to consolidate power.

Even worse, the ASP sprint ship was a larger frigate with multiple dropships anchored on the hull like lampreys, each adding braking thrust.

Even Decker wouldn't stand a chance in orbital combat.

And they know we're coming.

Monique took a shorter breath, holding it, as if she were done pretending.

"Hey," Jet whispered.

"Hey."

"You ready for decel?" Jet asked. "Only eighteen hours of free fall left."

"I guess," she whispered back.

Is she depressed? Am I that depressing to be around?

"You want to talk sociology?"

"No," she said softly, her voice dulled by weariness.

Jet was no shrink. But he was a friend. "What's on your mind?"

She hesitated. "Oh, just my last night on the Excalibur."

Her date with the elf. He had hoped it would a good memory for her, not something she would brood over a month and a half later. That made him even more curious. "What happened?"

"I spent the evening with the high elf Ahreth."

Oh great. The guy looked like a Greek god—but taller and thinner and no beard. *And talk about dating older guys.* "Isn't he like a hundred and fifteen?"

"Looks like he's twenty-seven," Monique whispered. She paused, as if her tongue wouldn't say the words.

"Spit it out."

"He's gorgeous."

"Okay, that punch wasn't so bad," Jet muttered. "Still kind of hurts in the ribs a little."

Monique's lip twitched with the start of a smile. "We met in one of the elven council chambers."

"With no corners and curvy ramps and wicker chairs and poofy cushions?" Jet's eyebrows crossed. "What do they do in there anyway? Or, do I not want to know?"

"A date with an elf is a lot of meditating," Monique said. "Kind of . . . boring."

The Exalting

That was better than the worst-case scenario Jet had been dreading.

"Did he say anything interesting," Jet asked, "about the mission?"

"Of course, I asked him what he thought," Monique said. "He's got to be the smartest Believer in the fleet."

"Don't tell Yaris that."

"Yaris agrees. But when I asked Ahreth about anything related to first contact, he would tell an unrelated story, or ask me a question in return. It felt like he was so far beyond me that I was just a child."

"Or he was stumped," Jet mumbled.

"Ahreth finally did make his point."

Jet turned his head and was eye-to-eye with Monique, who was close enough he couldn't quite focus on her face. There was pain there, down deep where she was vulnerable, like a person who had been diagnosed with a terminal illness.

The pale look of her face in the gently blinking console lights left Jet cold and empty. She seemed untouchably remote and trapped there.

"It was late—possibly early in the morning. We had finished the bottle of solemnity. It's such a strange elixir." She sighed. "It's almost like stepping out of your body and looking at the world as though you were someone else."

Jet could only imagine because he'd never had enough spare pay to even beg a sip of the stuff.

"By this time, I no longer saw Ahreth as merely a thing of beauty—I could still see him, the draping folds of his tunic, the flowing muscles of his body, his slender arms, long white hair, but these were merely facts."

"You were 'in the hollow,'" Jet said. "That's what Yaris calls it."

"I sort of just saw things only for what they were, without any attachment or consequence. Then the stories he had told sort of arranged themselves in my mind. And I saw."

Jet blinked. "Saw what?"

"The conclusion. All his stories were tales of impossible quagmires and catch-22's. In each situation there was only one solution—to fail. I don't know why he tried to get me to think about failure. By the time the solemnity wore off, I found myself in my chambers alone . . . weeping." Her voice choked. "He thinks we'll fail." Monique shivered. "Jet, how many people are going to die?"

Millions of lives—billions—were hanging on their mission. And the high elf in the hollow had spoken only of failure.

The word "fail" bound all of Jet thoughts, channeling them along a path he had never considered.

"I'm sorry," Monique finally whispered. "I . . . I didn't mean to tell you all that."

Stuffed in a sleeping sack, Jet couldn't offer his hand or pat her shoulders. He leaned his head to the side and gave a gently consoling side headbutt.

As he did, his thoughts shifted sideways, onto a new path.

Failure.

Jet couldn't gather Xahna to his side in merely a few weeks. He couldn't outsprint the ASP ship—or out-negotiate them—collect enough argon and tritium fuel, and find the next planet closer to the Prime Star before the ASP fleet arrived. He couldn't fight the ASP fleet and win.

Failure was the only option.

Failure. Of course! "He may be right," Jet said. "The only way to save Xahna is to let it fall to ASP."

And in that moment, he knew why they chose a marine.

He could put the mission first.

God help us.

Xahna must fall.

"I think I'm having an idea."

Resurrection.

"Moni, did you ever read the Bible?"

A tremble and a slow, heavy breath from Monique's direction gave the answer. She was asleep.

The Exalting

That was fast.
But Jet couldn't sleep. He finally knew what he had to do.
How do you engineer a resurrection?

Ryke shattered the latch with his staff and pulled the lock bar free. The heavy wooden door swung open to reveal an array of weapons: swords, maces, spears—

"Bow." Ryke lifted a heavy oaken bow, an arrow, and hefted two coils of thin cord over his shoulder.

Dana had never seen a bow so thick. It looked more like a warped beam.

"I don't think you can loft all that cord with one arrow."

"Watch me."

A grinned twitched on Dana's mouth. *Look who's modest now.*

Ryke led the way to the mouth of the falls. This time Dana could see and made it quickly through the exalting chamber.

On the small ledge beside the falls, Dana looked out over the vista she had missed previously. The morning sun was high in the sky, though it was not yet noon. But there wasn't much time left.

Ryke spent a minute arranging the cord.

Dana looked over the edge. At the base of the falls several hundred feet below was a roiling pool of deep blue water shrouded in turbulent mists.

Dana's stomach twisted. "This is insane."

"Very," Ryke said without looking up.

"Great. There are guards." Dana pointed to the edge of the pool. "Someone must have tipped them off that you might come to the mouth of the falls—what are they doing?"

"Looking for fish in the pool," Ryke said.

Dana wasn't surprised. "Well they aren't watching, so hurry."

Ryke wedged the bow against his knee and groaned as he bent the bow to string it. The bowstring was twice as thick as any Dana had ever seen. "Are you sure you can slide down this?"

Dana nodded. "No problem. The question is whether an arrow can reach the woods beyond the pond."

"Not without a warlock." Ryke looped the end of the cord around a sharp rock. "Just make sure that doesn't slip off."

"Got it." Dana gripped the cord with her hands, her knuckles grinding against the sharp rock.

Ryke knelt on the ground, the bow clutched in his hand. He closed his eyes and breathed deeply. Then he stood and nocked the heavy arrow.

Ryke opened his eyes and drew the great bow back, pulling the arrow to his chin. He lifted the arrow almost straight up and released.

The arrow shot out into the air over the lake, the cord trailing behind it.

When it reached the peak of its arc, Ryke dropped the bow and grabbed the cord in his hands. On Ryke's contact with the cord, the arrow straightened out and then seemed to accelerate.

Ryke was pouring will into it.

As it soared over the base of the falls, the arrow took up the slack, hauling the cord through Ryke's fingers as it fell.

Ryke groaned with the effort of keeping the arrow on target.

The arrow sailed over the rocks and passed between the trunk of a tree and a large branch. The cord snapped taut, and the arrow careened about the branch like the toggle of a bolo, cinching the line.

Dana folded her arms and rolled her eyes at the feat which bordered so near to impossible that no superlative would do it justice. "That was probably luck."

Ryke fell to his knees exhausted.

"Come on," Dana said. "We have to hurry. The guards will see it."

"I . . . I don't have the will. And I hate heights. Bad combination."

With his will spent, Ryke would only bring attention to her. If she was going to steal the bloodstone, she needed a low profile. It

218

The Exalting

was up to her now.

"You've done all you can," Dana said.

Dana knelt and swept his black braids away from the side of his face. She planted kiss on his salty cheek.

"Another thank-you?"

"No. That was for luck. I still have six."

She walked to the edge of the falls, untied the belt of woven leather strips from her trousers, looped it over the taut cord, and held it in both hands. She squinted, trying not to look down.

A gust of cold, misty wind challenged her balance.

"Oh, mercy." She leapt from the edge. The thin cord stretched under her weight, dropping precipitously down, momentarily making Dana think the rope had broken. Her breath caught in her throat as the cord stretched and finally came taut.

The pool was over a hundred and fifty feet below.

Then the braided leather strands of her belt began snapping from the friction.

Dana nearly screamed as she dropped several inches, all of her weight transferring to the single remaining strand.

She hauled herself up and grasped the sliding cord with her bare fingers. They burned as she slowed to a stop, right above the guards.

Crystals of Xahna! That hurts.

Dana pulled her legs up and began crawling hand over hand as she dangled from the cord like a marmar monkey on the underside of a thin branch. Her palms stung like they had been placed in a fire.

She looked backward at one of the guards and met his startled eyes.

"There one is!" He drew a crossbow. "Stop right there." The second guard sighted up the cord to the mouth of the falls in the middle of the cliff, looking for any who might be following her.

Dana was still thirty feet off the ground, far enough to break both legs, her back, and every other bone in her body if she fell.

Then she was falling.

Ryke must have cut the rope!

Dana swung downward as the cord collapsed. Unfortunately, the distance to the tree was just a little more than its height. Dangling from the rope, she skidded along the ground as the two soldiers raced toward her.

"Stay back!" Dana yelled.

They were on dangerous ground. This was a forest.

The charging men came within two yards of her, when a torrent of enthralled birds burst out of the trees and throttled the soldiers. Beaks, wings, and claws thrashed them backwards.

The men raced for the cover of the pool, covering their faces and screaming for help.

Dana turned and raced through the trees. As a flock, the birds looped back toward her.

A hundred pairs of eyes informed her steps. Despite having never crossed the wood before, with the help of her friends, Dana picked an unimpeded route through trees, boulders, and underbrush.

Teal-breasted swallows raced ahead, spotting soldiers coming at her. Pecking grouse raced around the other side of the men, stepping on leaves and breaking twigs underfoot, leading them the wrong direction.

Anvil-bills snapped branches over the soldiers, raining piles of pine needles to block their vision as Dana slipped through their line unheard and unseen.

The birds scattered away as she emerged from the forest and onto a rock in leaping distance from the city wall, where two city scampers waited to guide her through the back alleys.

Without hesitating, Dana took the jump, her adrenaline carrying her just far enough. She caught the top of the wall, climbed up, and slipped through the space between what might have been two ancient battlements.

As she headed into the city, the black-scaled scampers alternately scouted and stopped to point directions with their snouts.

220

The Exalting

Then, with Dana's prompting, a long-tailed marmar suddenly realized how to work the mechanism of its cage. It escaped and raced over the rooftops of buildings beside her. The monkey, a favored delicacy in Aesica, took its first chance at revenge by flinging a load of poop in the face of a sentry.

Dana slipped by unnoticed as the raging guard looked in vain for the offending primate.

Dana headed for the center of town, passing row after row of deserted streets. It seemed everybody had gone to the meeting where the fate of Shoul Falls and possibly all of Aesica would be decided.

Would all the cities capitulate so easily? Would Vetas-ka find ways to subvert their kazen and turn them to him?

Someone has to make a stand.

The Aesicans could band together, the separate cities and their ka fighting as one. Wasn't that what the Pantheon of Aesica was for? Why didn't Shoul Falls call the Pantheon for help?

One thing was certain: no one would follow weakness.

Then I'll show them strength.

Chapter 22

Jet sat across from Monique on two of the benches in the launch deck/storage bay, listening to her theory about cooperation between the ka of various cities on Aesica. Since an ASP dropship had detached from their sprint ship and landed in Torsica, Monique's investigations had focused almost entirely on potential landing sites on the smaller, more mountainous continent.

Jet actually found Monique's theory sort of interesting. "So . . . it's like a federation?"

"More of a pantheon of gods," Monique said. "There's not much to support it. Only the lack of any reference to recent wars and some isolated audio references." She smiled. "You're actually paying attention, aren't you? I mean, you still look at the shuttle fuel status display every few minutes, but between that you actually listened to me." She crossed her legs. "We aren't going to run out of fuel, you know. Big Bertha had more tritium than we needed, and Adkins wouldn't let them delay departure to pump it out."

"Huh. That explains why Decker hasn't been dumping the shuttles on schedule. He's just running them all at 80 percent instead of just letting the extra ones go."

"For redundancy," Monique said. "What if there is an engine failure or a tether snaps? We'd miss the planet entirely."

She made a good point. "You know I used to just think—well, it's embarrassing—but, I used to just think you were a pretty face."

"That's incredibly shallow."

"Yeah. It is." Jet wished he could turn back time and somehow swap out who he had been for the kind of person that made a better friend, someone who really cared. But even traveling close to the speed of light couldn't turn back the clock. He could only go forward.

"As for me," Monique said. "I used to just think you were a

The Exalting

trigger-happy jarhead."

"And now?"

"I'm convinced."

Jet burst into laughter. "Come on—I'm more than that."

"And a pair of usefully large biceps."

Jet leaned forward, elbows on his knees. It was a nice rest from sitting up straight in double gravity. "Useful for . . . what?"

Monique blushed. "I don't know . . . anything."

"Anything?" Jet said. "What about holding you?"

Monique's jaw dropped. "Not that useful." She stood up against the double gravity of deceleration and sauntered away. "Jarhead . . ."

It was progress.

A day worth remembering.

He wasn't sure how many he had left.

There were a few days in his life that fell in the category of unforgettable.

The day he learned that jackalopes were real—another of Avalon's bizarre and surprisingly dangerous, small, fuzzy creatures. Imagine a jackrabbit jumping at your nether regions with its spiky antlers. He never slept well on Avalon after that.

There was his first kill on Talaks, sipping oxygen from a mask at six thousand meters altitude. His explosive round tipped an approaching orc off the edge of a very steep cliff. His commander had simply radioed, "Nice miss."

Like today with Monique.

Jet's headset chirped, and Decker spoke. "The orbital AI running the satellite video flagged a gathering in one of the northeastern Aesican cities as anomalous. We're getting full streaming video and near constant audio from several recently deployed bugs."

With an effort Jet stood up. Whatever was going on down there had gotten Decker excited. "Which city is it?"

"It's Shoul Falls—one of the cities without a ka. Outside elements are approaching from the canyon and the forest, too.

Dan Allen

We've got ourselves a showdown brewing."

"I'm there."

Jet pressed to his feet and stomped to the cramped bridge.

Shoul Falls. No ka. Outside elements.

It felt like trouble. The kind of trouble he was born for.

As he passed the medical station, Jet tapped the wake icon on Dormit's cryobag. "It's time to rock and roll."

Dormit might not make first contact, but Jet needed him full strength when he landed. The fearless dwarf had saved his life on Avalon. He would probably do it again.

Dana slipped over a brick wall into a work yard, then ducked through a side gate. She emerged into a plaza filled with people. Nearly half had dark hair: brown or black, just like her.

An immigrant town. No wonder Vetas-ka had come to its rescue a century before. There were likely business and family connections between Shoul Falls and Torsica.

Dana stopped to look in a window and caught her reflection.

Wow.

Being blood-sworn had its advantages. Dana looked better than after a week's vacation at the geyser fields of Farlan. Her eyes sparkled, her skin was smooth—even the wound in her forehead was barely visible—and she wasn't even out of breath.

She turned to the gathered crowd and stood up on a barrel to see what was going on.

A raised platform stood in the center of the central plaza. Eight men and eight women sat on chairs surrounding a glass case on a pedestal.

On the floor of the glass case was the leather pouch—empty. And seated on what looked like an ornate candlestand was a scintillating crystal with a size and shape so familiar Dana had no doubt what it was.

The bloodstone.

The Exalting

She borrowed the eyes of a hawk soaring overhead for a closer look, noticing how easier it seemed with the sayathi symbiotes inside her. As the hawk's eyes focused on the crystal, Dana took in the many facets, the same shape she had felt through the pouch.

A sense of urgency gripped her. Dana was glad she hadn't looked before. Seeing it now, glinting in the sunlight, she wanted nothing else.

A bell in the square tolled three times. Dana looked around. There were at least ten thousand people pressed into the large square, possibly more. The chaos of arguing voices dropped as all sixteen members of the council stood.

"In accordance with our sacred laws," spoke a woman from the middle of the group, "we are gathered to determine the fate of the bloodstone. Each of the elected citizens represents their district. In the event of a tie, the vote will go to the populace at large. Those of blood-bound age shall all be counted."

"Burn the bloodstone!" cried a voice from the crowd, which was immediately drowned out by a dozen other countercries as well as scattered echoes of agreement.

The woman in the center of the platform raised her hand.

"Those sworn to the loyalty of the ka—the acolytes and kazen of the sanctum—are being held at the barracks of the civic guard. Each has submitted to a disabling treatment of angel's kiss and will be unable to interfere with these proceedings."

The chairwoman gestured to a man seated at the edge of the group. "Kazen Korr will represent the sanctum at these proceedings, his vote carrying the will of those denied attendance. He will ensure the safety of the stone, as well as execute whatever decision is made by the council."

"Not good," Dana groaned. Now she had him to deal with as well. There was no guarantee that he would not make a grab for the stone if the council chose to destroy it. Being a telekinetic warlock lent him an unmatched advantage.

Dana thought about trying to force her way closer to the center. But that was a risk. Korren might spot her.

225

She stepped down and drifted back into the crowd, stopping just out of reach of a civic guard in earnest conversation with a young boy, probably his son by the looks of their similar hawkish noses.

"What took you so long?"

"Some sort of commotion at the falls," the boy reported.

"The missing two?"

"Yeah. Ryke and the Norrian. They tried to slide down a cord, but only one of them made it down—the foreign girl, Dana."

"No worries about her," the father said. "Korren said she'd been on angel's kiss for two days. She probably can't hear herself think."

Yes, I can.

"But the soldiers at the pool were assaulted by every bird in the forest," said the youth. "Explain that if she's on angel's kiss. Makes me wonder who isn't telling the truth."

"So, she's a druid?"

The boy nodded. "Oh yeah. Apparently, like none anyone has seen since the last ka."

Dana lifted her eyebrows at that. Her grandfather had been an adept after all—a druid just like her. But he wasn't anymore.

She recalled the way her grandfather often rubbed the muscles at the back of his neck.

The stone was on his neck.

Mercy. He must have torn it out!

As a ka, he would have shared any connections that his bound acolytes had. With dozens of kazen he would have had nearly every adept ability known to creation. Somehow that traumatic experience of removing the bloodstone had left him without any connection through the veil.

Dana wondered how her grandfather had done it—the first ka in all of recorded history to willingly give up the bloodstone.

It was no wonder his warnings about the life of a ka and its unending pain had been so keen.

Yet, here she was ready to defy the will of the council and the entire city just to save the stone he had willingly given up—one

226

The Exalting

that didn't belong to her and had only been entrusted to her by a desperate, dying man.

Was it right?

Sindar had to have a reason for fleeing with the stone. He wouldn't have done it if merely destroying the crystal was the best choice.

Or perhaps he thought he could get Togath to resume the role. He had been their chosen protector.

The crowd surged forward, and Dana lost the voices of the man and his son. It seemed the citizen council was nearing a decision.

"The bloodstone was taken to Norr without any consent from the council!" cried a voice from the platform. "The binding token of our will was lost to us for *weeks* due to the negligence of the kazen trusted to protect it." A man on the platform pointed at Korren. "Anyone could have gotten a hold of it. If anyone in Norr would have seen it—"

"They wouldn't even have recognized it," said a woman. "Norr was absolutely the safest place to take it. Sindar obviously had thought about what he was doing."

"The Vetas-kazen have made themselves known," said a citizen councilor on the stand. "Not since the great Aesican war turned our hills red with blood has a Torsican ka intervened in the affairs of this continent. While we were grateful for help at that time, we must now send them a message that they cannot misunderstand. No city of Aesica will submit to their rule."

Another citizen on the platform spoke. "We cannot fight a ka of his strength. Any of the cities of his empire could wipe us off the continent. Destroying the bloodstone is our only choice. Rob him of his prize, before he robs us of our will forever."

"No!" cried scattered voices in the crowd.

It felt like a public execution. People clutched their hands in fists. A grandmother near Dana was weeping. From the far side of the square a group of young men began a chant of, "No. No. No," although it was clearly not catching on.

The head citizen raised her hand for silence but wasn't given it.

"You have all spoken your arguments. To continue debating would be to simply rehearse what has already been said. We are not here to convince others to take our position. We are merely here to state our reasons, that our children and their children will know why we have dealt with them in this way."

It seemed the head citizen knew the vote was foregone conclusion.

Dana's spent will left her apathetic to the eventuality of the outcome.

This is what they want.

They don't want to risk losing their will to Vetas-ka.

But it wasn't just her depleted will balking at the challenge. Dana had experienced things in the past weeks. Most remarkable of all had been the revelation bought on by the blazing pain of the viper's embrace. The pain Dana had experienced put suffering in a totally different light.

All her life Dana had tried to avoid suffering of any kind. Her illegal attempts to save animals from traps hadn't wholly been out of a desire to help the animals, but to relieve the pain she felt.

Dana was having second thoughts about stealing the stone.

She drew a shaky breath. *And third thoughts. And fourth.*

A greeder bearing a ranger strode toward the back of the platform in the square, the long-legged mount sifting through the crowd as if wading through tall grass. As the mounted greeder approached, the speaker stopped speaking and walked to the edge of the platform to lean down and talk with the ranger.

Dana guessed this might be some word of warning about her arrival in the city. She probed the area and was surprised to feel several other greeders in the square. They had come in at the periphery.

She was surrounded.

Dana's throat tightened.

They had cut off her every route of escape. Perhaps the rangers, whose jurisdiction was outside the walls, had been called in to provide extra security.

The Exalting

Thankfully, the attention of the crowd was focused on the platform, and no one appeared to be looking back to see what escapee acolytes might have just joined the throng.

A glint of metal shone in the hand of the ranger on the greeder. The scene seemed to freeze in Dana's mind.

A knife!

The ranger on the greeder grabbed the citizen on the platform by her coat, pulled her off-balance, and drove the blade into the councilwoman, who shrieked in pain.

All at once rangers shoved forward through the crowd from all sides, some on greeders, some on foot. One ranger pushed past Dana, headed for the platform.

Korren's eyes widened in surprise, while the ranger with the knife leapt off the greeder's back and onto the platform. The previously bright blade was now dark and dripping.

The murdered councilwoman, the head of the council, tumbled off the platform, and the others of the citizen council drew back toward the edges.

The ranger was a woman with silvery hair pulled back into a tight braid, possibly some kind of desperate extremist bent on saving the bloodstone. She darted across the platform.

Korren reached his arm out, and the door to the glass case flew open.

Before the bloodstone had even moved, the woman clenched Korren's arm. His eyes defocused. His hands fell placidly by his sides.

"Enchanter," Dana gasped. The woman had Korren in some kind of trance.

Dana looked to the ranger who had shouldered past her on his way to the platform. She didn't know him, but she did recognize the fancy scrollwork on the handle of his crossbow. It was just like the ones used by the group that had attacked her and Ryke.

What is going on?

Around the plaza rangers raised their crossbows, and a hail of bolts converged on the platform.

Dan Allen

The remaining citizens on the platform fell in the storm of metal bolts—all except the woman.

They were helping her.

Torsicans! The Vetas-kazen are trying to steal the stone.

Meanwhile the kazen and acolytes of Shoul Falls were helpless thanks to the angel's kiss.

Dana and Korren were the only ones who could stop them.

Dana called on the hawk to dive. *Get the stone!*

It refused. Instead it turned its head, scanning the crowd before locking its gaze on her. Somebody else was controlling it.

There's another druid kazen here.

In a rush, the gathered crowd fled, knocking Dana aside.

Perhaps the kazen enchanter was urging the people to flee instead of fight.

She was probably the one the thugs outside Jahr had called *Poria*.

Fighting the enchanter's influence, a raging citizen climbed to the platform with a rock in his hand.

But before he could assail the silver-haired woman, a crossbow bolt sank into his chest.

He staggered back.

In the moment's distraction, Korren knocked the woman's hand off his arm, raised his hand, and clenched his fingers into a fist. "Enough!"

Without so much as a cry, the woman collapsed to the ground.

To drop someone that fast, Korren had probably used his powers to disrupt the blood flow to her brain, like a powerful choke hold or a knockout punch.

Dana could hardly believe what she was seeing. Korren had actually defended the stone from the Vetas-kazen.

Does he want it for himself?

It was the only answer she could believe. But even though he was closest to the stone, Korren couldn't fight off so many rangers, most of whom were halfway done reloading their crossbows.

Dana had to get the stone out of the city—and quickly.

The Exalting

But how can I stop Korren and the Vetas-kazen?

A grin slipped onto Dana's lips. *Turn them on each other.*

I've got to find the druid. With a desperate thrust of will that left her feeling like a long nap was in order, Dana managed to turn the hawk's head and spot the druid controlling it.

"There."

Across the courtyard stood a ranger with no crossbow. His coat was open, showing shiny brass waistcoat buttons no ranger would wear.

Dana pointed at the man and shouted, "Korren, get that kazen!"

Korren whirled and reached out with his hand, attempting to stretch his warlock influence across the large distance.

From the hawk's view Dana watched the man fall to his knees. He wasn't affected as violently as the closer enchanter, but the moment's lapse was all Dana needed.

Dana forced the hawk to swoop.

Korren reached his arm out for the stone. It flung toward him, only to be snatched in midair by the bird-hunting hawk.

In two blinks of an eye the bird was outside Korren's telekinetic range.

His influence for controlling matter directly decreased far more rapidly than her connection to the living creature's mind. He had to overcome its muscles. She merely had to alter a thought.

As the hawk took to the sky, flying north, away from the Torsican druid, Dana leapt aboard the greeder that had brought the silver-haired enchanter.

"Go!"

The animal bounded easily through the crowd, and unlike the young bird she had ridden out of Norr, this full-grown greeder—at least eight feet at the head—easily leapt the outer wall. Then it tucked its wings and dashed into the cover of the forest.

From the view of the hawk overhead, Dana scanned the forest for other rangers. There were at least six, as well as other hawks patrolling the skies.

Dan Allen

"First things first."

The hawk dove, picking a rapid descent that met Dana's trajectory in an open clearing. The hawk pulled up and released the stone in an easy arc. Dana caught the precious crystal and tucked it in to her jacket pocket.

The hawk rose to do battle with the others.

Then the idea hit her.

Stop.

Turn back.

Dana pulled on the greeder's reins.

It clambered to a halt on a lichen-crusted section of bare granite.

Dana fought, trying to resist the strange, disruptive thoughts she could hardly distinguish from her own.

An enchanter had her. It was over.

All for nothing?

Yes, better turn back. Peace is the only way.

It all came down to this. Dana had nothing to fight with.

No. I have the stone. I have their will.

The people of Shoul Falls did not want Vetas-ka to get the stone. Of that Dana was certain.

Was it a sin to touch the stone if it was the people's will?

No. They need my help. And I need theirs.

In desperation, Dana reached into her pocket and gripped the bloodstone as hard as she could. It stung the fresh wound on her palm from sliding on the cord.

"Please. Please. Help me."

The enchanter's voice in her mind demanding she go back faded as a thousand other voices rose, some panicked, some praying, some pleading.

As Dana held firmly to the stone, her hand and wrist lit with a brilliant blue-green glow. The sayathi within her recognized the master crystal.

With renewed force of will, the greeder accelerated. High above, her hawk locked its talons with a pursuing raptor.

232

The Exalting

For a moment Dana could distinguish individual voices. They came in turn, rising from the mass of chaotic feelings to brush against her.

"Keep it safe."

"Help me. I'm dying."

"Don't let them get the bloodstone."

Dana channeled her own thoughts into the stone with one last push of will. "Fight them!" Then she collapsed forward, hugging the neck of the greeder as it nimbly picked a path through the forest, heading north, toward Norr.

It was now a game of hide-and-seek. She had the stone. The Vetas-kazen would follow her anywhere.

Dana looked up to the peaks of the barrier range. The tips were already locked in frost.

I'll take them to a place they'll wish they were dead and see how long their will to survive lasts.

The question was, how long would she last? Dana had neither winter clothing nor provisions. Soon her body would ache with chill. Dehydration would steal her strength.

But Dana was no longer afraid of pain.

Take me higher!

Dana's greeder surged forward, bounding through the rockfall, headed for the nearest pass.

Chapter 23

Jet looked over Monique's shoulder as she sat reclined at the comms station, watching the live feed from the satellite passing over Shoul Falls. The magnified image appeared to show a young Xahnan female riding one of their ostrich-like greeders.

Decker leaned over from the pilot's chair. "What was it she took from the platform?"

"It could only be a bloodstone—the thing that gives the ka their power," Monique said. "Nothing else would draw so much attention."

"So, this renegade thinks she can hold the entire city hostage?" Jet narrowed his eyes. Even with the pixelated image from space, she had a striking figure. She looked tall and toned, and somehow savage, close to nature. "Where is she from?"

"I think you know already," said Yaris. His narrow face gazed placidly at the wide-field composite image of Aesica.

Caprians: either elusive or blunt, Jet thought. *Never anywhere in the middle.*

"I'd say Norrian. They're the ones without a ka," Teea chimed. "Only she doesn't look it—dark hair."

"She did flee north," Jet said. "The AIs will have noticed that. They'll look for her in Norr."

Dormit let out a low whistle. "Whoever she is, she's got trouble on the way."

Dormit pushed his image onto the main screen. It showed a harbor packed with steamships and its docks laden with boxes and barrels.

"Where is that?" Jet asked.

"Torsica—the shipyards of Tenek. It looks like a full naval mobilization."

"Let me guess," Jet said. "ASP convinced this big bad ka on

The Exalting

Torsica to consolidate his power on Xahna before the Believers arrived."

"I agree. It looks like a devil's bargain." Monique leaned closer, her distracting figure passing between him and Dormit's screen. "He supports ASP; they let him rule Xahna. I estimate Vetas-ka has three thousand kazen. He'll crush them—a massacre."

"How will the Pantheon of Aesica respond?" Yaris wondered.

"They won't know for weeks," Dormit said. "Unless they've got some way to communicate across the coral sea."

Jet turned up his hands. "Well that makes my decision easy. Drop zone is North Aesica. Tiberius, can we get there before Vetas-ka's fleet arrives?"

"I'll run the numbers."

Dormit stroked his beard. "That means it's going to be close."

Dana lay in a crevice under a rock on the backside of the barrier divide at an altitude so high she had to squeeze the breath in her lungs periodically to keep from getting nauseated. The exhausted greeder slept nearby. It was anyone's guess when it would wake.

I don't have time to wait.

Dana traced her finger over the scabs on her palm where the skin had torn sliding on the cord. *So that's how they got in.*

The ruling sayathi had accessed her bloodstream through the cuts on her hand, giving her a limited connection to the crystal.

No wonder it's called a bloodstone. Early adepts probably had to cut themselves to use it.

So, there was truth to the Norrian warning against touching a bloodstone.

For a short time, Dana had made a small connection to bloodstone, sensing the vast untapped will to draw from, the chaos of thousands of voices, the fears, the pain.

Dana could still almost taste the hope, the expanse of will, the raw emotion. She could not stop wanting it. It was like trying to not want to breathe.

The stone was right there.

Togath was right.

Touching that stone had changed her. She could not go back to merely wondering what it would be like. Curiosity was a mere candlewick to the blaze of actually knowing.

Dana looked at her hands again, trying to imagine a life of denial in which she vowed to never again taste the power. No amount of will seemed to make it feel at all realistic. She would have cut herself again if not for the fear that the people of Shoul Falls would feel her as well and know what she was doing.

Of course, if she were somehow chosen to become the next ka, she would have to find a way to survive the high temperature long enough for the molten bloodstone to seep into her bloodstream and then cool slowly enough that crystallites didn't form in her blood.

Forz could build something to keep me at the right temperature.

But Forz was in Norr. He had the skills to get her through the exalting alive.

Norr. If she was ever going to have a chance at the exalting, she would have to go back to Norr—and before she was caught.

I can't wait.

Resolving to finally leave the greeder behind, Dana stepped out from under the boulder, leaving the sleeping greeder that had brought her from Shoul Falls. It would be easy to track. And it wouldn't travel at night, nor could it endure for long at this altitude.

She began running across the barren basin of a glacial bowl.

Besides, Dana thought, *no land animal can outrun a Xahnan over long distance at this altitude.*

She fanned her sifa.

Especially not me.

Dana had lived her life in the forests of Norr, only a thousand feet below the tree line. She knew every peak in the barrier range better than the rangers, and she had climbed most of them.

She was on the western side of the divide now and headed

The Exalting

north.

With luck, they won't figure out I crossed over the divide for a few more days. By then I'll be back below the tree line and out of sight.

She kept her legs moving at full speed, scampering over barren dirt and loose rock.

Vetas-ka was coming. What wasn't under his control soon would be. His sights were clearly set on Aesica.

Without a ka, Shoul Falls would offer minimal resistance. Then it would serve as a base for expanding his empire. Fear would keep the Aesican Pantheon from challenging him for Shoul Falls. One by one their cities would fall.

The only option was to fight hard enough to make the battle not worth the cost—deny him an access point.

And the people would fight if they had a ka.

They need a ka.

They need me.

She had the stone. She had the will to fight. She only needed a way to survive the exalting chamber.

And she had to survive a seventy-mile journey at high altitude with minimal food and temperatures dropping dangerously.

I've endured worse—far worse.

Dana picked up her pace.

She was glad she had found some theeler root in the greeder's saddle bag. The dried pieces of dense, chalky tuber would get her through another half day. But the last day above the tree line would be a fast.

For once, I'll have to do it.

And in order to keep from freezing, Dana would have to keep moving constantly.

Three days without sleep. Was it even possible?

"Just go."

Dana's mind melded into the numbness of the distance race. Before nightfall she had drunk from several water-filled depressions in the stone and was already nibbling at the last theeler root.

Dana crested a pass and descended a rockslide, leaping from

237

boulder to boulder as the sun began to set.

Brother and sister moon rose into the stars early. With so little atmosphere above her and the night, the sky was bright and the rocks ahead painted in silvery starlight.

She dug her hands into her fur-lined pockets. The chill was already becoming bitter.

The bloodstone lay in a buttoned pocket that she checked habitually—perhaps too frequently.

Before dawn, her food was gone and Dana felt dead on her feet, as if she could just lie down and expire in the darkness.

She had already covered thirty-five miles of rugged terrain.

Coming to a mountain wash and finding it bone-dry, Dana fell to her knees and cried precious tears. "Ka, help me."

Cutting herself and using the bloodstone was a growing temptation. But borrowing will would not give her energy. It could only use up what she already possessed more quickly.

Her forehead touched the ground, and when she looked up she nearly couldn't believe her eyes.

The sun was finally rising over the peaks to her right.

"Logmar. Tiraset." She followed the row of peaks. "There!" The trans-divide pass above the glacier fields was just within view at the edge of the horizon.

I can reach it before sundown.

Something else caught her eye. She looked to her right to see two greeders cross over the ridge. In unison, they stretched out their wings and dove into steep glides.

They both had riders and they were headed for her.

Vetas-kazen!

Panic gripped her, but even that did little to make her want to get up.

Lying there wasn't a bad idea.

Let them get closer.

Dana forced herself to lie still on the ground as the killers approached.

Through the lashes of her half-closed eyes, Dana thought she

The Exalting

knew them from the battle.

The druid that Korren attacked.

The other had a cap but could not hide a long braid of silver hair.

Poria—the enchanter.

Dana's gambit had just gotten far more risky.

The druid would be focused on guiding his greeder. It was clearly flying in the lead position. The other was following. Poria would be looking for any sign of movement—or just trying to stay on her greeder.

Pity.

Dana lay on the ground, holding as still as she could.

The gliding greeders came swiftly.

Dana forced a thought into the greeder carrying Poria. *Wouldn't it be fun to tip the rider off?*

Just as the gliding bird sailed out over a tall outcropping, Dana thrust the urge into the greeder with all the will she could muster. *Now.*

The greeder tucked one wing and rolled.

Poria let go of her reins to try to grab the saddle harness. But her fingers found no purchase.

"Porien!" the druid cried, looking back as the enchanter fell from a height of forty-five feet, a deadly distance.

The enchanter's cry was cut short as her body disappeared behind a rock. Dana quickly turned her attention to the greeder.

Wouldn't it be fun to ride with that girl over there on the ground? Dana suggested. *We'll have a race. The big man is too heavy for his bird. We'll win!*

Dana worried that the druid would try to stop the greeder from coming to her, but having seen Poria fall to her death, he appeared to be totally focused on keeping his own bird from dumping him.

The rider-less greeder landed with a flap of its wings, just ahead of the Torsican. Dana hopped on, and it bounded ahead, escaping the Torsican's grasp by inches.

"Fool girl!" he roared. "You'll pay for that!"

Dan Allen

Up. Go.

Dana urged the greeder back up the rapidly steepening slope. Climbing was her only advantage. To her eye, the two animals were matched in size—likely from the same clutch. But Dana was lighter. With every bound, her greeder lofted farther and with less effort.

The barren ground became rocky, transitioning to a rubble slide and then a field of barrel-sized boulders as she neared the cliffs.

"Give up!" cried the druid. "You can't run forever."

He's right.

He's lying!

Dana fought off the doubts that preyed on her exhaustion. Ahead, the mountainside steepened into tall cliffs. She steered the greeder toward a dead end at the base of a steep waterfall chute with rust-streaked rocks.

Nearly there.

The incline grew perilous, and Dana's bird could only ascend at an angle rather than straight up.

The chute, Dana urged. *Climb the chute.*

A scramble of broken rock led to the gap in the cliffs. This late in the season the run was dry.

Won't this be fun! We're winning!

Dana was nearly crying from the effort of teasing her greeder forward.

Behind her, the other druid's greeder had slowed. He seemed to be looking for a way around the cliffs.

Ha!

There wasn't one. Not for miles.

"You're on my mountains now."

"Go!" Dana spoke to urge her greeder. "Here we go, girl. Up the wash. Up. Up."

The greeder switched to shorter, more rapid strides as the path steepened.

"Yes," Dana said, sensing its thoughts. "Just like scrambling up to a roost in a big tree. You're so clever. Good girl."

240

The Exalting

Dana looked back. The druid was pressing forward, his animal's head locked in her direction. Its legs moved with a frenzied pace, as if driven by mortal danger.

He had triggered its fear response.

Doing that was dangerous, because the animal became difficult to control. It could throw you.

But this druid seemed to have absolute control.

Dana thought of the bloodstone.

No. Too dangerous.

She needed both hands for this.

In the narrow cleft between the cliffs, the greeder bounded left and right, zig-zagging forward.

Rocks clattered from just below her.

He's getting closer.

This is insane. It's a dead end. Why am I doing this?

Dana shook her head. Not only did she have to fight her own lack of will, she had to keep her nagging self-doubt from spreading to her greeder.

"Who is the fastest greeder in the world? Who is the cleverest? Look at you. Magnificent."

Tears of desperation formed in her eyes. Finally, Dana reached out with the last thread of will.

Save me. He's going to kill us. Climb!

"CLIMB!" Dana screamed. Her voice echoed off the cliffs.

"Give up," shouted the druid's voice from only meters behind. "It's over."

The chute reached a dry waterfall at least twenty-five feet high. "Jump!"

The frightened bird leapt.

The greeder scratched at the cliff face, beat its short wings, and scrambled against the rock, scratching for height.

It wasn't going to make it. The holds were too small for its wide, clawed feet.

But not for a Xahnan.

With a cry, Dana leapt. The greeder fell back as Dana sailed through the air.

Once before she had done this. Her hands had slipped, and she would have certainly died if not for Ryke. But there was no Ryke to save her now. She lived or died on this cliff.

Dana thrust both of her hands into a crack on the rock. She slid downward until her hands jammed together at the base of the crevice.

"Ow!"

Greeders squawked below, and the man bellowed a cry as the birds collided.

Dana's feet kicked in the air. Finally, her boot found a small ledge. She pushed up enough to free one hand. Bending her hands to form wedges she hauled herself upward, hand over hand. The sharp granite cut into her knuckles.

Dana scraped her way up the rock face, gaining height as quickly as she could. She didn't look back to see whether the druid was following her or trying to go around. She didn't even want to know.

Fifty feet up, the slope lessened, and Dana scrambled ahead on a curving rock face so barren that she didn't dare stop for fear of sliding back and off the precipice.

Going forward was not a matter of will but of primal survival. She was already exhausted. The altitude was extreme, the air brutally cold, and the backs of her hands bleeding from gashes. There was only one thing to do now. She had to beat the druid to Norr. She could hide there, perhaps, until she had a way to survive the exalting chamber.

As she neared the top of a saddle pass, a south-facing slope rose on her left, and Dana nearly screamed in excitement at the crumpled form of a theeler weed stretching out between two rocks.

"Bless the Creator!"

Dana cried for joy as her desperate hands dug and pulled until the stem came free, bringing with it at least half of the gnarled root.

Dana devoured it, dirt and all. She tried to reach between the rocks to dig out the last remaining portion of root but couldn't

The Exalting

reach. She continued on before her muscles began lock up again.

Dizziness took her on the upslope. Sounds echoed in her mind, and her vision blurred into waking hallucinations.

Dana forced herself to run. "Faster. Faster." The rhythm of her feet stomped out a song of suffering.

She checked behind her as a chill, dry wind whipped down the canyon, but she could make out no sign of the druid.

It was all about pain now. She was cold. She was beyond exhaustion. She was hungry and dehydrated—it seemed as though the altitude and dry wind were trying to petrify her.

If the druid wanted to pursue her, he would have to face those demons as well, in unfamiliar territory.

How strong is your will?

Would you risk death to catch me?

Because I'll suffer anything to stop you.

Still dizzy, Dana kept her eyes down as she stood and forced one foot in front of the other. Morning bled past noon, and the sun began to fall. Still she forced herself to jog along the trail. When the slope finally lessened, she looked up to see the summit only a dozen yards away. Her parched, sunburned lips cracked as she made a weak attempt at a smile. And there, glinting in the final rays of the setting sun, was a patch of salvation.

Snow!

Dana fell to her knees and shoveled the dirt-strewn snow into her parched mouth. Her cheeks ached from melting the crystals. Handfuls of the stuff only seemed to yield a trickle of water. She tried melting snow in her hands and pouring it in her mouth, but her fingers were so cold she could barely bend them. But she kept at it.

Her sifa ached as well. Could she lose them to frostbite?

Above the tree line there was nothing to burn for heat. Only moving would keep her alive.

She forced herself to her feet and stumbled over the crest and down the switchbacks on the dark eastern slope. There were still two peaks between her and Norr, but some of it was downhill, and

243

she would reach the geyser fields by the next dawn. Her tortuous night route along the backside of the mountains was easily as long as her path from Norr to Shoul Falls that had taken her past Port Kyner. Coupled with the exposure and hunger, the route had been brutal.

Feet now treading familiar ground, Dana gained speed.

By morning, she was twelve miles from Norr, within the territorial boundaries. Her warming body teased feeling back into her fingers. First they tingle, then they burned.

She felt the dampness of blood in her boots from torn blisters. She didn't dare remove them to look at the damage.

But her right knee and hip gave her the most trouble. She had walked along a road sloping to her left, and her right leg had done more of the lifting. Her shuffling run was now a hobbled limp.

Her cracked lips bled whenever she took a deep breath through her mouth. Already, blisters were forming on her nose and cheeks, burned by the constant oppression of the sun at high altitude. She felt like a walking corpse.

The last ten miles to Norr passed in a dream-like torture. The water at the Farlan geyser fields was too hot for sayathi, and Dana drank her fill.

As she dropped in altitude, Dana found edible flowers, greens trodden underfoot on the path, and chewed the chalky insides of thistles—anything not completely poisonous.

Most of this was bound to either give her a terrible stomachache or pass right through, but that was the least of Dana's worries.

Three miles from Norr, Dana left the path for a game trail.

So close. Don't stop.

A razorback squirrel scolded her as she passed its pine nut stash, flaring its bone-tipped neck spines as if to remind her she didn't belong here anymore.

It was true. If the Norrians caught her, would they imprison her for greeder theft—at a minimum. And if they realized she was blood-bound, they would certainly exact the mortal punishment

244

The Exalting

for blood-binding.

Somehow, she would have to blend in.

But her crime would show in her eyes. She was no longer a drale.

Two hours before noon, Dana stopped a mile outside the city. It was out of sight, over a rise, and she was well away from any of the ranger footpaths. There was little chance she could get any closer to the city without being discovered. She had to find someone she could trust.

Voices reached her. Dana recognized their lugubrious dialogue. Only trappers conversed as slowly as these two.

"Shoul Falls has rangers looking under every marmar's tail."

"Heard it's that druid, Dana—same one that tried to rob us."

"Lousy, rotten, no-good thief—lost me a heap 'o coin on account of her meddling."

Evidently, these weren't the people she wanted.

The voices approached, then began to fade as the game trail they followed turned east.

"Ranger said she was the granddaughter of their last ka."

"Curse them all to oblivion."

"Said they didn't want to lose her, now that they'd found out who she was. Talk was that she might have the makings of their next ka."

What? Dana's faltering heart nearly skipped a beat.

"What's she on the run for then—did she steal greeders from them, too?"

"If they're looking for trouble like her, they can just go stuff their noses up a rasp-wing nest."

"I hear ya."

As the sounds of boots crunching on leaves faded, Dana's mind whirled. If the ranger's tale was true, the people of Shoul Falls's opinion of her and keeping the bloodstone had changed dramatically after the kazen raid on their city. If so, she was no longer an outlaw but their best hope.

Dana wanted to believe it, desperately.

On the other hand, the news could have come from a Vetas-kazen posing as a Shoul Falls ranger. Having an amicable story for why they wanted Dana would make it much easier to get her to turn herself in.

There was only one way to know. She had to return to Shoul Falls, just as soon as she had the solution to surviving the exalting chamber.

For that, she needed Forz. But she didn't dare get any closer to the city. She was blood-sworn now. If she were caught, she would die like Loka.

Dana let her will spread out on the wind until a familiar yellow-throated warbler touched her mind.

"Find Forz." She passed a route to the workshop to its mind, along with an image of his snow-white hair. "He has food—lots of it."

Dana moved into the bird's point of view. It inspected its feathers, then took to wing, heading over the city wall, and following Dana's intuition, it flew into the town center. It swooped easily to the second story window sill of Forz's master's workshop. Forz was inside at his drawing desk.

It pecked at the window. It pecked again.

For a solid minute it tapped away patiently.

Come on!

Finally, the bird's sense of alarm startled Dana.

Movement. Forz had looked over from his desk.

Keep tapping.

No. The bird, so far from Dana, was resisting.

Do it! He has buckets of seeds.

Dana imagined Forz carrying loads of pine nuts and wheelflower seeds.

The bird pecked eagerly at the window.

"Unh," Forz moaned.

The bird started tapping quickly then slowly, quickly then slowly, a pattern designed to be utterly unendurable.

"Most annoying bird in the whole—" Forz darted to the

The Exalting

window and lifted the sash. The bird hopped in and pecked at his hand.

"Oh no. Dana—she's back."

Chapter 24

Jet awoke after hours of tortured nightmares—an effect of the heavy push of deceleration.

The images of bloody skeletons reaching for him faded as he fought free of the horror of his dream.

There was nothing so terrifying as being taken by the dead.

Taken by the dead.

Jet recalled the surreal epiphany after hearing about Monique's experience in Ahreth's meditation chamber. *Xahna must fall.*

And what if it did? What if the Believers lost the entire planet and their fleet?

The answer was obvious. ASP would win. The corporations would descend on Xahna like ravenous Avalonian bat chickens. All resources—especially the power of the ka—would become prey to their greed.

Xahnans would be drunk with technology for a few years, before segments of society began to rebel and attempt to reclaim the old way. It was already happening on Dayal. The devil rebellions were draining ASP resources faster than the deep pits could turn out valuable heavy metals.

There would come a time when ASP would be unwelcome on Xahna as well.

Then let the dead take them.

Yes!

Jet climbed out of his sleeping sack and climbed a ladder to the empty bridge. "Tiberius, activate my tactical AI."

"Alright. Attempting to side-along boot Angel." By the pause between his words it sounded like the AI was in the middle of nap and didn't want to be bothered.

Moments of silence passed.

"Wake up, Angel!"

The Exalting

As usual, Angel announced the completion of her boot sequence with a personal remark. "Jet, you don't look so good. Did you run into a wall?"

"Listen, Angel. I need you to run a big sim on the dropship's tactical server."

"Tiberius is in low-power mode. Should be possible. What is this all about?"

"Did you ever read the Bible?"

"Unfortunately, yes. Mandatory reading for all Believer AIs. Not much useful strategy there."

"I'm thinking about resurrection."

"You?" Angel actually laughed out loud. "Sorry, go ahead."

"In the book of Revelation there's a story about two prophets at the end of the world."

"Oh yes, two prophets are killed in the street. Everyone celebrates because the prophets had been causing plagues—like self-righteous human malware. Did you honestly read that?"

"Yeah," Jet said. "I mean, I watched the movie version. The dead prophets rise from the dead, float up to heaven, and everybody sees it and is totally scared because they realize they are about to be toast. And there is this huge earthquake, and a bunch of the people are killed—"

Angel made a snoring noise.

"The point is we can't go to Xahna as friends—they don't need us. They don't want us. I say we go to torment them."

"Ah," Angel said. "You want to get yourself killed like a prophet?"

"Go down in a blaze of glory. You reading me yet?" Jet said.

"Loud and clear. You're all going to fake your deaths so ASP is off their guard when they show up."

"I mean this really has to look good," Jet said. "The Xahnans and ASP have to be completely convinced."

"How many do you want to go down with you?"

"Every dropship in the fleet."

"You're going to fry my transistors with that kind of sim."

"Better get started, then—oh, and you have less than three days."

"Initializing memory. Loading Xahna model. Loading fleet model. Loading ASP pursuit fleet model—that feels like burying myself under a ton of bricks." She paused briefly. "What are our success metrics?"

Jet mulled the question. "How about the number of Believers and Xahnans surviving, times the number of available ships."

"Simple, but robust."

"So, Angel, what are you going to call this plan?"

The AI gave a laugh. "You ever read Orson Scott Card from the classical library?"

"Are you kidding? That stuff is fantastic."

Angel gave a chirp of approval. "Commencing mission simulation 'Speaker for the Dead.'" A moment later she said, "This whole thing assumes you make orbit."

"Yeah."

"Well there's an ASP frigate waiting for you. I hope you've got a plan for getting past them."

"Um," Jet said. "Sure. It's . . . uh . . . entering the final stages of planning as we speak."

Black space. I need a plan.

The bird pecked at Forz again, his fingers appearing to jump toward the bird as its head moved.

"You want food. Got it."

The bird followed Forz as he stepped carefully downstairs, apparently trying not to wake Master Tidwell, who usually spent his late evenings at the tavern—that was when Forz worked on delicate tasks like the kind Dana had interupted the last time she was there.

Forz opened a pantry door, and the bird hopped into a bag of mixed seeds and nuts Forz probably used for trail rations. Once its

The Exalting

little belly was satisfied, it returned to duty, leading Forz and his wheelbarrow-pushing mechanodron out of the city gate, then north toward Dana.

Hurry.

Dana flickered at the edge of consciousness as the urge to just let it go became overwhelming. Controlling the bird for this long at such a distance had drained her of nearly every shred of will she had. Already she had lost the will to move.

Next would be the will to breathe.

As Forz and Blamer hurried up the mountainside, the bird stopped heeding Dana's weaker and weaker suggestions.

It fled. Dana lost the connection. She could no longer see Forz or guide him.

She was truly alone.

A cool gray mist beckoned her to a place she had never been and would never return from.

So peaceful.

"Hello?" The voice jolted Dana.

Forz!

He was calling out but not using her name. *It's him.*

She tried to cry out in answer, but simply couldn't find the will.

Forz! She screamed in her mind as her body stubbornly refused to speak.

If he didn't find her, she would die here, unable to move and so near the city she risked everything to reach.

Dana clenched her fists and was surprised to find her fingers still worked. The first things a baby learned were the last to go. Dana could open and close her hands.

With her hand in her pocket, she squeezed the bloodstone, digging the facet against the scabs on her palm. She had no will to resist the temptation to use the stone now—she had no other choice.

Finally, a trickle of blood ran from her palm, connecting her with the bloodstone.

Dana squeezed the crystal, and light flared into her mind.

"Forz!" A single cry escaped her lips as she lost consciousness.

"She looks . . . not quite dead."

Dana moaned in response. Her eyes flickered open. Lying on the floor, she saw a broad wooden beam and a familiar sloping ceiling. It was Brista's attic bedroom above the chapel.

She was inside Norr. She supposed Forz had snuck her into the city in his mechanodron's wheelbarrow.

Dana squeezed her hand, which was still in her pocket. The bloodstone was still there.

She tried to open her fingers that had clenched the stone but could barely move them.

Brista leaned over her. "It's like some kind of rigor mortis."

"I've already given her calcium dissolved in sugar sap," Forz said.

"I think we have to put her in a bath to loosen up her muscles. And besides, she smells like . . . not good."

"Okay. What do you want to do?" Forz said.

"Just hold her up while I get her shirt and pants off."

"No," Dana moved her mouth in protest, but the only sound that came out from her hoarse throat was a groan. She wasn't going to have Forz undressing her.

"Yep. Hot bath," Brista said. "That's what you need."

"Brista, is your father going to come barging in?" Forz asked. "Because this I simply cannot explain."

"He wouldn't come in during my bath. He's the height of piety."

"Just making sure."

Dana tried to protest as they forced her arms out of her jacket. By the time she was down to her tie-top and underwear, she was almost making sense.

"Get . . . stop . . . tight . . . whap . . ."

Almost making sense.

The Exalting

"What about the rest of her clothes?" Forz said.

To Dana's relief, Brista spared her the embarrassment of a lifetime.

"It all needs a wash. Just get her in the bath."

Forz grunted as he tried to get her in the copper bath. "It's like trying to fold a plank—bend, would you?"

With some bumping and cramming, Dana was lowered into the bath.

Brista ducked out, probably to stoke the furnace behind the cleric's quarters that heated the water in the copper piping, leaving Dana in the tub and Forz sitting on a stool nearby, doing his best to look the other direction.

She hoped. Her neck wouldn't turn very well.

Brista returned and sat on a dressing stool beside the tub. "I'll take it from here, Forz."

Forz looked down at Dana. "Is she going to be alright?"

Brista pushed his face to the side. "Yes, that's enough help from you."

"I'll be at the workshop. Send a tap on the line if you need anything." Forz descended the steep ladder and closed the attic trap door.

How had they gotten her up the ladder?

As the running water became warm and soaked into Dana, she let out a slow gasp of agony and rapture.

Brista managed to help Dana out of her underclothes. "What did you do, roll in the dirt for a week? If you ever expect to wear these again," she said, holding them at arm's length, "I'll need some peroxide and lye from Forz's workshop."

Brista slipped away to tap out a message on her static line to Forz's workshop attic, which was only a few houses away. In answer, a burst of tiny sparks etched a pattern of lines and dots in a viewing paper that ticked past with each high voltage pulse. Brista checked her handwritten chart on the wall. "He's going to bring some over. I just might be able to save your clothes."

Dana felt her knees and hips beginning to loosen up.

"I brewed a pot of magic sauce," Brista said.

Magic sauce. Brista had forced some down her throat before. It was an awful mixture of gorm root and white pine bark tea, a very hot spice from Torsica, and fish oil.

She offered some to Dana in a wooden mug.

This time, Dana took it willingly.

After Dana scrubbed her hair, she attempted, and failed, to get the dirt from under her toes and fingernails.

Brista helped her brush her sifa.

"Look at all this fanning—I should go on a death march through the wilderness too."

"It's the sayathi," Dana said. "I'm blood-sworn. I drank from the pool in the sanctum."

Brista dropped the comb and knocked over the stool as she backed away in a hurry.

"I'm not contagious."

"Dana—it's forbidden. They'll execute you."

Dana couldn't hold her gaze and looked away. "I had to."

Brista's sifa trembled. "You're blood-sworn—and we brought you into the city!" She looked to Dana's clothes. "Do you still have the . . . bloodstone?"

Dana nodded again.

Brista looked dumbfounded. "Are you insane? Why did you keep it?"

Dana's voice dropped to a whisper. "Well, after they drugged me and took it, the city decided to destroy it at a public meeting, but the Vetas-kazen attacked and tried to steal it. I was the only one close enough to save it."

"You just took it and ran? Again?"

Dana nodded once more, and suddenly all the emotions of her journey came back. She broke into a sob, wanting more than anything to run out of the chapel attic and through her front door, hug her mother and father and pretend like nothing had ever changed.

A knock came at the trapdoor.

The Exalting

"Who is it?" Brista said, clutching her hand to her chest and staring at Dana with a look of mingled shock and the unmistakable hurt of betrayal.

"Who do you think? Open up."

Dana ducked under the bathwater as Forz poked his head through the opening.

"Peroxide and lye—it'll take the color out of anything."

"She can't stay here," Brista said. "She's blood-sworn now *and* she still has the bloodstone. If somebody sees her—"

"Figures." Forz looked at his bottle of peroxide. "Hey, I just had an idea."

Minutes later, Dana was seated on the dressing stool and wrapped in a towel. Her itching scalp was starting to feel like it was burning. "Are you trying to kill me?" Dana said. She leaned forward with her hair draped into a bucket of bubbling peroxide.

At least in this position, Dana felt less dizzy.

"It's working," Forz said.

"It's gone from brown to red, yes—but now it just looks . . ."

"Horrible," Dana said. "Just tell me."

"Ah—that's more like orange," Forz said. "See."

"Well, you can't tell while it's wet anyway," Brista said.

It was the kind of thing somebody said when they were looking at a complete disaster.

Forz snapped his fingers. "I've got it. It needs a base." He returned with a bottle and uncorked it, filling the room with a stench like urine—only it stung her nose.

"Ammonia."

He added it in increasing amounts to the bucket.

"Look at that!" Brista gasped. "It's turning blond."

"Better not leave it on the skin—wash it with vinegar to stop the reaction."

"So I'll attract flies?" Dana said. "You'd better know what you're doing."

After more rinsing and scrubbing and some detail work on her eyebrows by Brista, Dana was allowed to look in a silvered hand mirror.

"Oh, wow." Dana turned her head from side to side, admiring the new pale blond that matched the cool coloration of a newborn Norrian's first hair. "I look like a goddess!"

Forz looked like he was about to agree but glanced at Brista and bit his knuckle.

"It's a start," Brista said. "What else can we do—give her a peg leg or something?"

"Actually," Dana said. "I need Forz to build me a mechanodron."

Forz laughed. "You need a mechanodron? I thought you hated them, always complaining about how a mechanodron can walk right up to you and you can't even sense it."

"Well I can now—if it has sayathi. Anyway, this is a matter of life and death."

Doubt and curiosity fought behind Forz's eyes. "And this mechanodron is going to save your life?"

"It's going to save everyone's."

"Dana, if this is just some—"

"Touching the bloodstone isn't enough to become ka," Dana blurted out. "You have to *drink* it."

"What?" Forz looked around to be sure no one was listening.

"I have to lie in a thermal chamber hot enough to melt the sayathenite. The matrix will be absorbed into my blood. Then if I cool slowly enough, the crystal will form on my skin, not in my veins. That's why I need the mechanodron—to keep me from dying of heatstroke while all that happens."

"Holy stars of heaven," Brista gasped. "You're going to do it?"

"I have to. Nobody else will. And if I don't, there won't be anyone to stop Vetas-ka from taking over the city. And then where does it stop? He could come to Norr and force you all to bind your will to him."

Forz rubbed his temples. "But it's not your bloodstone."

"I have to fight."

"Vetas-ka isn't going to come all the way—" Brista began,

The Exalting

before Forz interupted her.

"He is." Forz looked up and wrung his hands. "A sea-skimmer arrived in Port Kyner yesterday. The ship's captain said Vetas-ka's entire fleet was rallying at Tenek—it was in a message for the chancellor. I read it over the signaler's shoulder when I went to the static-line post to get a message for Master Tidwell."

The news was terrifying, but Dana could hardly be surprised. She knew it would come to this.

Brista looked directly at Dana. "Tenek is right across the Sayathi Sea from Norr."

Forz folded his arms. "The ka in Port Kyner thinks Vetas-ka is coming to settle some debts with Shoul Falls—at least that's what he said in the message to the chancellor."

"He's coming for that stone, isn't he?" Brista said.

Dana nodded. "And someone has to stop him, or he'll keep taking bloodstones until all of Xahna worships him alone—two more of his kazen nearly killed me on the way here."

Brista clasped her hands over her face in horror as if she already knew the conclusion.

"I killed one of them. Just one."

"Yeah, that's what I was afraid of," Forz said. "You'll do anything to survive, but when does it stop?"

"Help me make the mechanodron. I'll leave as soon as it's done."

The conflicted look on Forz's face Dana had seen before, when she was stealing the greeder.

"This is the most important thing any of us have ever done—will ever do," Dana said. "Only a ka can stop him. And we don't have much time. They could be here in a matter of days. The sea only takes a couple of weeks to cross in a steamship."

"It's fast day tomorrow," Brista said. "And there's chapel service in the afternoon."

"Exactly," Dana said. "The perfect time to work unsupervised."

Forz looked at Dana. "If Brista and I are both missing—"

"Everybody will just think you've both snuck off to kiss in the clocktower."

Brista's face took on the look of an accused criminal.

"You've done that already?" Dana rolled her eyes. "Okay, I'll forgive you both—*maybe*—if you help me make this mechanodron." It was still a bitter nut to chew. Her two best friends were kissing.

Forz shrugged. "Okay. But this is really risky. Just getting to my workshop—how are we going to do that on fast day with everyone gathering at the chapel?"

"We can go out the window and slide down the water pole," Brista said. "It leads to the back alley."

"Alright." Forz met Dana's eyes, and his mouth turned up slightly at the corner. "I'll see you tomorrow."

He did like adventure in spite of himself. And he loved a challenge. That was what Dana had that Brista would never bring to his life. Dana made life interesting.

What is going to happen to our friendship after I leave?

Forz gathered his bottles and disappeared through the hatch.

With some effort and patience, Dana dressed in one of Brista's nightshirts and fell asleep in her bed, not knowing or caring where Brista slept.

When she woke, Dana felt a touch of momentary pity that Brista had to curl up on the floor with only a blanket and a pile of laundry for a pillow. But thinking of all the terrible places she had rested over the past few days, what pity Dana felt evaporated. *Sleeping on a floor is practically paradise.*

The muscle aches were still there. Dana wished for another bath to loosen her aching limbs, but that would make Brista's persnickety father suspicious.

But even if he wasn't suspicious, someone from Shoul Falls, or worse, from Torsica, might arrive to ask about Dana. In that case, the chancellor would send the civic guard straight to Brista's and Forz's homes.

This place isn't safe.

Dana's bleached blond hair would only slow them for a few

The Exalting

seconds. At best, it would delay an onlooker who passed her in the street from immediately crying out, "Greeder thief!"

Brista slipped downstairs and brought up two biscuits with salted fruit sauce for breakfast, which Dana devoured.

"Father's going to know I took the biscuits," Brista said. "He always checks on fast day."

"Who cares?" Dana said. "I'm a long inch from being found and executed, and you are worrying about your dad feeling disappointed?"

"Sorry my feelings don't matter to you."

"Oh Brista, of course they do," Dana said. "I'm just being awful because I'm so beat up. I might be dead if you and Forz hadn't helped me."

Brista shook her head. "Why do I even like you, Dana? You do your best to ruin my life every few weeks with some insane idea."

It was true. But Dana had never thought of it that way. Maybe Brista didn't like trying new things or trying to change things. Maybe she liked things just the way they were.

Maybe we're just different.

Dana looked her friend in the eye. She wanted to say sorry for all the trouble she'd caused. She wanted to go back and make it all disappear and let her have her life the way she wanted it—without trouble.

Without me?

It hurt too much to think about.

"Do I look much different?" Dana said, giving up on the painful conversation.

"You mean beside your hair?"

My eyes—that's what's changed.

"You'll probably fool people, but the question is for how long. People can recognize folks they know from a block away just by how they walk."

Dana knew it was true. "We just have to hope we don't run into anyone we know before I can get out of the city."

And there was always the threat of the Vetas-kazen. Were they

259

already in Norr in disguise and looking for her?

In an uncomfortable silence, Dana dressed in Brista's clothes, putting the bloodstone in a velvet pouch and stringing it around her neck. Wearing something of Brista's was a bittersweet comfort—something to remember her by.

Dana filled the few available pockets with her usual essentials: a small folding knife, flint, a ball of twine, needle, and a hook. Brista thumbed through books to pass the time, and Dana napped until the chapel below filled with the sounds of gathering Norrians. Brista's room was tucked at the back of the chapel, over the speaker's pulpit. The rest of the chapel went all the way to the roof rafters.

Once the voice of Cleric Warv rose over the din of the gathered Norrians, Brista pushed open her roof window. Dana brought over the dressing stool, and Brista stepped up and climbed out first onto the steeply sloped slate roof. Dana followed, pulling herself up. Her arms didn't seem to be quite as tired as her legs.

Brista slid to the bottom of the roof where a façade rose up. The two crawled behind the façade until they reached the back corner of the building.

Brista leaned over the edge. "All clear." She took a deep breath, climbed over the edge, and slid down a water collection pipe. Dana followed, her muscles protesting.

Once she was on the high street, Dana felt exactly like a small animal avoiding predators. Her eyes followed every flapping shutter. She jumped at the sound of any door opening.

Dana forced herself to relax. Acting suspicious and afraid would only draw attention.

Dana shivered as her new blond hair fluttered in a passing breeze. Even after a day in Brista's stuffy attic room, Dana still felt cold.

As they walked toward Forz's workshop, Dana turned her eyes down and kept her hands in her pockets.

It took all her will not to look up when three pairs of boots she knew passed on the same sidewalk headed toward the chapel.

The Exalting

"Hello, Brista."

Mother.

"Skipping chapel service?" Her brother called with a snicker.

"Hosting a visitor," Brista thumbed at Dana.

Outsiders were neither welcome at chapel service nor permitted by their own codes of respect for their supremes.

Her family continued on. When Dana and Brista turned the next corner, Dana let out the breath she had been holding. *That was too close.*

She looked at Brista, "Hosting a visitor? That was brilliant."

Brista shrugged. "It's sort of true."

What am I going to do without her?

"I just hope your parents don't try to talk to my dad about my 'visitor.'"

"Let's get off the street," Dana said, turning in Kernic Alley.

If anyone could build a mechanodron to keep her alive in the exalting chamber, it was Forz.

Chapter 25

Jet was in his second hour of playing the video game he'd found, on a tablet intended for walkthrough inspections and logging cleaning reports.

The game was an old Earth sport where a heavy ball was tossed at some pins. The more pins you knocked over the more points you got.

"Trivial," Yaris hissed over his shoulder. "And primitive."

"Strike!"

Decker poked his head around the corner. "Strike what? ASP? You know we have practically no weapons on this ship, don't you?"

An idea hit Jet like a bullet to the side of his helmet.

"Hold on." Jet's grip on the tablet went slack, and it crashed to the floor in the double deceleration gravity before he could catch it. They did have weapons—bowling balls. Lots of them.

Decker stared at him. "I don't like that look on your face."

"No, this is a seriously good idea."

"No. Corporal, I order you to go back to wasting your time."

"No, Captain. You're going to like this."

Decker folded his arms. "If I don't, I'm taking that tablet you just busted out of your paycheck—in the form of dessert rations."

Jet paused to consider the threat. "I'll take the risk."

Decker nodded. "Okay then."

"So, we are going to have a big ASP frigate waiting for us, right?"

"Obviously," Decker said.

"And we have no long-range weapons."

"Need I say it again?"

"Did you ever try bowling?"

The captain shook his head slowly. "Does it involve a toilet?"

"No. It's a game. You throw a big ball and try to hit pins."

The Exalting

"Black space, Naman! That's brilliant."

"Only we can't throw out the big ball," Jet said. "Big Bertha has all our fuel."

"But we have extra shuttles," Decker said.

"Exactly. So we change the game a bit. Their ship is the bowling ball. We throw the pins." Jet pulled up the fuel map. "By the time we reach Xahna we'll only need a few of the shuttles, so long as we run our remaining shuttles at max thrust—"

"And we can transfer just enough fuel to make the kamikaze shuttles self-guiding." Decker rubbed his hand together. "But they're all going to arrive at different times, unless we launch them all at once. In that case, the odds they'll be picked up by the frigate's telescope are a lot higher."

"Not if we sling them around the other side of the sun. They won't be looking in that direction."

Jet pushed a button on the console that pulled up a menu and toggled Angel. The AI was already running fleet sims and gave a respectful ready chirp instantly, since the captain was present. "Angel, I want to shoot down a frigate in orbit on Xahna using our spare shuttles as self-guided bullets. I need to drop one spare shuttle every couple of hours and have them arrive at the same time from different directions on target. Can you plot trajectories to sling them around the sun the opposite direction as us?"

"Okay, done."

Decker slapped his forehead. "Holy smokes!"

"That's why you bring a sniper to a long-range shooting contest."

Forz opened the door to the workshop. "Come in, quick."

Dana and Brista rushed in. Forz locked the door behind them. He was dressed in his work smock, gloves on, eye loupe in place.

The workshop was teaming with overhead rigging for holding mechanodrons upright while they trained to stand, piles of raw materials, and dozens of half-finished mechanodrons used for scrap.

Forz rubbed his hands together. "So, you need a mechanodron that keeps you at the melting point of sayathenite and then gradually cools you down to let the matrix recrystallize out of the blood stream."

Brista raised a questioning finger. "How's it going to do that if it's run by sayathenite? The crystals that run the mechanodron will melt."

Dana's brain clunked. She hadn't thought of that.

"I think I've got that covered." Forz picked up a pencil. "How long does it have to last? How big is the thing it has to cool? Any size and weight limits?"

Brista interupted. "More importantly, what's the punishment for consuming the bloodstone without permission?"

"Actually," Dana said, "shouldn't you go to the chapel to make sure my parents don't talk to Warv and then come to find us?"

Brista rolled her eyes and folded her arms.

"Please?" If her parents saw Brista, she would inevitably have to make up another lie about why she came back to the chapel. She hated that.

"Fine." With a glare that would cook a cold redroot, Brista left.

Forz barely noticed. His sketch was already taking shape.

"First thing to do is teach a mechanodron to drop ammonium nitrate into a bucket of water to cool itself—I'll need some copper pipes to conduct the heat. Then we train its arm to do the same thing for the object it's cooling."

"That would be my head, I'm guessing," Dana said.

"Okay. Not very thermally conductive. Can we fit you with a copper band on your head?"

"Not sure that's a good idea. The bloodstone may try to reform there."

"Fine. We'll just use a pan of water then."

Dana shrugged. "Okay, you're the expert."

"I've got a small bellows that I use for kitchen mechanodrons that baste meat on a spit. That should work for recirculating liquid. Now for the cooling salts—" Forz set Dana to milling the ammonium nitrate crystals small enough to be dispensed by a tiny screw-like auger. Then he fired up a torch and brazed the heat pipes to a copper kettle for the reservoir of the mechanodron.

While he fastened the screw coupling, Forz explained his theory. "As the cooling crystal level drops, the screw resistance goes down and it speeds up slightly, which increases the cooling. Very simple. Very elegant."

Dana nodded. "It's amazing."

Forz took a deep breath and then set his hands to work on the benchtop contraption. After a few minutes he finally spoke again. "I'm not doing it for the city, Dana. I'm not even sure it's right. I'm just doing it for you."

Forz liked her. Perhaps not as a girlfriend. But they were close. She had talked to him on occasion about leaving Norr together and finding a blood-bound city to join. But now he was apparently dating Brista. If it wasn't for that, he could join her in Shoul Falls.

The question came out of her mouth before she could stop it. "Are you going to marry Brista . . . and stay in Norr forever?"

Forz dropped a wrench that bounced off the edge of the table and landed on his toe. He winced as he looked at Dana with a baffled expression.

Dana laughed.

"Quiet," he said, looking around. "You aren't supposed to be in here, remember?" He retrieved the wrench and went back to tightening an axle nut.

Dana tossed her hair over her shoulder and reached her arms out, placing her hands on his, stopping his work.

"Don't you deserve better than a place that doesn't hate you only because they don't know what you really are? Don't you want to come with me?"

Forz pulled his hands free and twisted a tie wire. "Of course I do. But I can't think about that right now. I can't decide my whole future while I'm trying to put together a machine to do something that I've been warned against my entire life. Do you want me to finish this or not?"

So that was it. She could either have his heart or his services. Dana bit her lip. "Let's finish it."

Dana drew her hands back as Forz turned to a drawer and took out a cotter pin, which he fixed on a gear that connected to a spring with a cloth shroud wound over it.

Dana couldn't imagine what use the spring had until Forz opened a large tub of water, releasing a rancid odor. From the vat, he selected a short segment of rhynoid vine and expertly wove it around the spring, securing the ends with gantham paste.

"It's just like the piston on a steam-wagon engine," Dana realized. The vine would squeeze and release the spring, so it would shrink and expand and rotate the cam on the gear, like the drive wheel on a steam-wagon.

Forz coaxed the vine's feeler tentacles to wrap around the spring's binding points.

Dana marveled at how easily the boy could slip back into his work, completely partitioning his feelings, like drawers of hardware. Did he just pull them out again when he needed them?

"You can just cut them off?" Dana said, exasperatedly.

"Sure," Forz said, rubbing his forehead with his glove. "Rhynoids can live months without water. The coastal jungle has a dry season after all. It just goes dormant. But look," He lifted the end of the vine, showing where small roots grew into a glass vial. "When I fill this up with fermented sap, it wakes up."

"I was talking about feelings," Dana huffed.

"Feelings?" Forz's expression shifted. He opened another potent-smelling bucket and ladled the bubbling fermented sap into the fuel jar.

"I think you answered my question."

"Hold on. This part's tricky." Forz took a set of smaller tendrils branching off the vine and looped them around a crystal of sayathenite fixed in a resonator, some of the tendrils on top and some at the bottom, ostensibly to pick up both polarities. Then he picked up the compact mechanodron and set it into a wooden

The Exalting

bucket, which he filled with water. He connected a small spiral auger to a smaller bucket of cooling crystals. As the rhynoid stirred with popping sounds of crackling static, Forz pumped the lever, driving the piston and turning a cogged wheel that drove the auger around. Tiny cooling crystals slowly made their way up out of their box. Following the revolving inclined plane, the crystals slowly spilled into the water, cooling it quickly.

Satisfied his hastily assembled mechanics were working, Forz removed the sayathenite nodule and held it over the fire with wooden tongs. He leaned close, staring at the surface. "That's soft enough."

When he withdrew the sayathenite nodule, its outer surface appeared shiny, like molten glass, or honey glaze. He placed the heat-softened crystal, ready for training, in the resonator and then kicked away most of the logs and hung the "mechanodron in a bucket" from the cooking pot hook in the fireplace, several feet above the coals.

He placed an alcohol thermometer in the water and began slowly turning the wheel to spill cooling crystals into the water, playing a tedious game of "keep the water the right temperature."

It took almost thirty minutes to complete the first training session.

"That was the most boring thing I've ever seen," Dana said. "How do you do this day-in and day-out?"

"Trade secret," Forz said with a grin. "If it gets too boring, I train a mechanodron to train other mechanodrons."

"That's cheating! I mean, it's really clever." Dana never would have thought of it. Forz was a genius. Master Tidwell did almost nothing except collect the pay for Forz's brilliant work.

"But this is a one-off job," Forz said. "A few more training runs should do it. This time, I'll use a little less heat, so the details set. It will only use the major acoustoelectric resonances. The beat frequencies will set the pulse timing, just like in the sayathi pools."

He softened the sayathenite again, this time slightly less, then repeated the training exercise with the fading coals. "Once the mechanodron learns to control its temperature, I can add the second arm to control the temperature of the test pan. Now, the test bucket will hold your head. I hope that's enough to keep your core temperature from getting too high."

Dana fell asleep. She was only vaguely aware of time passing and Forz moving her to pile of empty carry sacks where she slept even more deeply, the fatigue of her exhausting journey once again catching up with her.

There were other things catching up as well. The kazen pursuing her would eventually come, perhaps pretending to be rangers from Shoul Falls. Once the chancellor knew she was here, the civic guard would search the city.

As she lay resting, Dana could only hope that Forz would finish training the mechanodron in time for her to escape the city undetected.

A knock sounded. Dana opened her eyes. As she lifted her face away from a burlap sack, she felt at the lines pressed into her skin from the course weave. She pushed back a blanket. "What did you say?"

"Quiet." Forz ducked down beside the workbench. "Someone is at the door."

"Open this door right now. We know you're in there," bellowed a voice from outside.

Dana's heart jolted. She squatted down next to Forz. "What do we do?"

The muffled voice from outside the workroom barked, "Open it." The sound of jangling keys immediately brought to mind the civic guard's master key set.

Dana's throat clenched as panic seized her. "Forz, I have to get out of here."

Forz quickly stuffed the basket-sized mechanodron into a shoulder sack. "Back door, it's the only other way out."

"I know."

The key turned in the lock.

"Thank you, Forz." As the front door opened, Dana lifted

the carry sack holding the mechanodron. She crept behind the workbench. From under the table she saw the boots of several civic guard officers step into the entrance. But they would not see her until their eyes adjusted to the dark workshop.

Forz moved quickly toward the side wall of the workshop. From among the heaping piles of work materials, he grabbed a wooden pole and slid it between the wall and a support strut for his overhead mechanodron rigging system.

It looked like he was going to collapse the entire system on top of her pursuers.

Dana had ten feet to go. She had to cross an open space to reach the back door. She stuck her head out from behind the sap barrel.

"There she is." One of the men pointed to Dana, and the three men moved forward.

Forz threw his weight into his lever. The support strut slid out from under the rigging. Poles and counterweight bags of heavy sand collapsed together. Dana looked up to see two more levels of supports fall in succession, dropping with bone-crunching force as they fell.

Chapter 26

Two civic guards shouted in cries of agony. Another dropped to the floor in the dust and chaos of the collapsing rigging.

Dana turned to flee but looked back to see Forz on the floor, wide-eyed and shaking. Dana ran to him and tried to lift the large pole that had pinned his leg to the ground. He screamed in pain.

His upper leg was bent at an unnatural angle. His femur was broken.

"Oh, Forz . . ."

Dana grabbed another pole from the wood pile and levered the heavy wooden beam off his leg. With a cry of pain Forz dragged his shattered leg out from under the rubble.

Dana let the wood drop.

A deep moan issued from deeper in the pile. The men would soon find their way out.

"Mercy, Forz—I'm so sorry."

Shaking with pain, Forz's face wrenched into an expression that tore Dana up inside. "I'll never walk again."

"Don't say that." Dana ran her hand through his hair. "I have to go—but I'll come back. I'll fix your leg. I promise."

Forz's answer was a scream of pain.

People would hear it. They would be coming.

Dana lifted the shoulder bag with the mechanodron and ran to the back of the shop. She pulled back the lock pin and raced into the back alley.

How had they known where she was?

They had come too quickly for somebody to have gotten the information out of Brista.

Unless her family had gone to the civic guard.

Never. They would never have betrayed me.

It could only have been the Vetas-kazen. Had they dressed as

The Exalting

Norrian rangers and tipped off the civic guard? Were they already in the city searching Brista's attic room?

With Vetas-ka's fleet approaching, Dana had to get back to Shoul Falls, and quickly. But first she had to hide somewhere the Vetas-kazen would never look. Then she could make the direct journey to Shoul Falls by night.

But carrying the thirty-pound mechanodron in a sack, she wasn't going to get far. She needed somewhere close, somewhere nobody ever went.

The answer came from the clanging of the chapel bell.

Rest day. The sayathenite mines are closed.

I can hide in a mine.

Dana slowed as she approached the back entrance of the city. A single guard manned the post.

"Worst meditation ever," Dana mumbled. "Glad I snuck out for a picnic." That would explain her heavy bag.

"I hear ya," said the guard. "Almost glad I'm on duty."

He didn't keep a register of everyone who went in and out. Nobody would ever read the thing. He only had to note anything out of the ordinary.

A teenager skipping out of meditation—that was the epitome of normal.

And I have blond hair. He didn't recognize me.

Dana walked until she was out of earshot and then forced her aching muscles to run uphill while shouldering the awkward benchtop mechanodron.

"Why didn't I steal another greeder?"

But a teen sneaking out on a greeder would have been highly out-of-the-ordinary.

Thanks to the ban on logging within a half mile of the city, the tall, purple pines provided fantastic cover. But the further she went, the more anxious she felt.

Forz could be a cripple because of her. He was in excruciating pain, and there was nothing she could do about it. With luck, he could claim it was an accident, and the civic guard wouldn't blame him for the collapse—obviously he was hurt, too.

I just left him there.

Perhaps he could train a mechanodron leg brace. Of course he would. But how would he live a normal life? Was his future destroyed? Would Brista still want him if he was maimed and helpless?

She would. But every night he would take off his brace and rub his aching leg remembering the times when he could walk through the hills as he pleased.

At seventeen, part of his future had already faded.

"What have I done?"

Dana hadn't just risked her life in coming back to Norr. She had risked her friends as well.

Why did I take the stone?

Why?

Shock and terror drove Dana on toward the sayathenite mines. The oldest mines in the mountain's massive complex of limestone caverns were only a mile from the city. Following the miner's road into the south fork canyon, she came to the first of the caverns. It was no longer in operation—either mined out or too dangerous.

Perfect.

Dana climbed over the locked gate and its warning sign, then improvised several torches from branches of bushes. She bound them with old wire lying on the ground and carried them inside the cave before lighting the first with her knife and flint. She pushed ahead into the darkness, following the mineshaft as it descended. A hundred and fifty feet later, she came to a pool.

Colorful limestone stalagmites rose out of the pool, scintillating in the flickering light of her torch. Ages ago an animal had carried a bloodstone into this cave system. Here, where roots from the surface wound through coral and dipped into the pool, trading nutrients for water, the organisms had somehow found a way to survive. The pool undoubtedly hosted a sayathi colony or the miners looking for sayathenite would not have come this way. Wading into the pools to recover sayathenite was dangerous

The Exalting

business. But with the right breathing mask and protective gear, the Norrians had built an entire economy based on it.

Dana stepped closer to the water, wondering if she could sense the sayathi in the pool. A rock caught her boot, and she pitched forward, dropping the torch as she reached out to stop her fall.

The torch sizzled as it touched the water.

In the darkness Dana realized four things almost instantly. First, her wrist stung. She had fallen onto the sharp edge of the mined coral and cut it. Second, to her horror—her hand had landed *in* the pool. Her wrist was underwater.

Terror at dying like the poor greeder flooded her.

But her arm was glowing.

"What? That's impossible."

Sayathi only glowed when they sensed their own colony.

She scampered back from the edge of the pool.

Dana checked the cut on her wrist. It had already sealed.

"They're not attacking—they're healing me." Dana shook her head "How?"

She was forty miles, at least, from Shoul Falls, though roughly at a similar elevation.

Dana thought back to the day she had visited the Sayathi Sea where the colonies perennially waged war, trying to conquer the others. Had the colony somehow spread itself inside the mountain?

If so, this was the largest colony on the planet. It could force any minor colony to submit by sheer force of numbers.

Does Vetas-ka know? Or did he just come for an unclaimed bloodstone?

Was this colony large enough to withstand the ruling sayathi of Vetas-ka's bloodstone? Would it believe it could survive the fight?

This colony's crystalline electrical conduits ran through the entire mountain. It knew its strength.

Dana's sifa trembled. She moved to the edge of the pool, lifted the bloodstone out of her pocket, and held it out over the water.

The water near Dana lit with enough blue-green light to show the roof of the chamber overhead. The sayathi sensed their

273

bloodstone, pouring their energy into it, feeding the ruling sayathi organisms bound within the crystal.

Pulses of light ran along the floor of pool toward her, attempting to connect to the bloodstone.

Dana dipped the stone in the cool water and touched it to one of the coral veins. Pulses ran out instantly, disappearing into the darkness of the cave.

Dana smiled as she imagined the electrical signals from the bloodstone arriving in Shoul Falls forty miles away. "Hey, guys. Headquarters moved."

Dana lifted the stone and slid it back into her pocket, then she leaned close and dared to drink from the pool.

She felt nothing.

It is my colony.

In awe, she sat back against the rock wall. This was possibly the largest sayathenite colony on Xahna.

But this cave had been mined by Norrians for a reason. The mining company wouldn't have paid expensive Norrian workers in their protective equipment to mine if they could have hired Shoul Falls workers to simply wade in and collect sayathenite nodules.

More importantly, the Shoul Falls cave system could not have conquered another without its bloodstone, which meant that for generations before, when there was a ka in Shoul Falls, the colony hadn't grown.

The two cave systems had to have come into contact and fought in the time since her grandfather had given up the bloodstone.

Perhaps the mining in the southern canyons had broken a barrier and the water table had shifted. News of caves flooding was common enough, and the Norrian miners had delved further into the cave systems than any other city in history.

A trickle of excitement ran through Dana.

Forty miles . . . There had to have been dozens of conquered colonies between Shoul Falls and Norr.

Perhaps the roots of trees, desperate for water in the last

The Exalting

drought, had cracked ancient barriers. Or, the cave fish of
Shoul Falls had become aggressive and created fissures when the
bloodstone had been returned, hoping to grow their territory.

Dana had seen the cave-dwelling rakefish brought back by
miners, some as large as her torso with teeth as long as her fingers
and articulate clawed fins.

Dana's mind whirled with imaginings as she sat in the dark,
waiting for night to fall outside, when she could begin her journey
back to Shoul Falls.

What am I going to do with this mechanodron?

Showing up at the sanctum with the mechanodron in hand
would be presumptuous at a minimum and quite possibly a very
bad idea. She had to protect it until she knew she could get it safely
into the sanctum.

She would have to stash it near the sanctum and wait for the
best opportunity to use it.

Her plan lacked one crucial detail: what to do with the
bloodstone. She could go rogue, keep the stone for herself, usurp
the power, and fight Vetas-ka herself. Arguably a safer approach,
aside from the fact that she would be committing the highest
sacrilege on Xahna.

The alternative was to return the stone to Shoul Falls yet again
and hope that after the kazen attack, the city had realized the
danger they were in and that they had to ordain a ka immediately.

The odds they would choose her were obviously not the best.

At least the second option gave the citizens some choice in the
matter.

More-or-less protecting the citizens' right had justified Dana's
theft—rescue—of the stone. This time she would have no such
excuse.

Trusting her life to people she hardly knew was terrifying. But
she could imagine they felt the very same thing about her having
the stone.

I'll worry about the stone later. I just need to get away from Norr.

This time she would take the direct path to Shoul Falls along

275

the trade route. It was far shorter than the coastal route she had first taken or the circuitous mountain route she had used to come back.

Short, but dangerous.

With luck, the kazen would still be looking for her on the other side of the divide. Perhaps the druid pursuing her had died of exposure or gotten lost.

The fact was, she simply didn't have the strength to go any other route.

If only I had someone to carry this mechanodron for me.

Dana laughed out loud. She was in a mine. Miners never carried ore.

Ha! I'm so smart.

When she was sure night had fallen, she retreated back out of the cave. Sister moon was already up, and Dana navigated further up the canyon and found a large pack-mechanodron outside an active mine. The hauler closely resembled Forz's seven-foot-tall mechanodron Blamer.

Dana strapped her mechanodron sack to its back. Then, borrowing a couple of fresh sap containers from a storage bin, she refilled the mechanodron's sap jars. As the sugary syrup ran through its rhynoid muscles, the thing roused and stood up, waiting for a command. Dana imitated Forz, using low and high whistles to guide it toward her. The hulking thing maneuvered by the feel of the ground. Despite its hesitant footing, the thing had an enormous stride and managed to keep up with her as she traversed the ridge into the next canyon.

By morning the mechanodron was out of fuel sap, and she abandoned it. At least it had carried the prototype mechanodron two-thirds of the journey.

She had a day's hike left and one very obvious problem. The sack on her shoulder was an invitation for interrogation.

Where am I going hide this thing?

Furthermore, she still had the problem of what to do with the stone.

She couldn't just hide it somewhere, or the moment she

showed up without it, they would arrest her for theft. And she couldn't show up with it either or the city might just confiscate it and destroy it. She had to keep it out of their reach but ensure they knew it was safe.

Dana slept the morning through and then continued south through the forest toward Shoul Falls, following a ribbon of limestone that ran along the mountainside. The swath of sayathi just inside the mountain would hopefully mask her presence to any enchanter passing on the nearby trade road.

The strap of the shoulder sack with the mechanodron alternately dug into her right shoulder and then her left. The annoyance was nothing compared to her blistered feet, and that was nothing compared to the agony Forz would be in.

A cripple.

Dana asked herself why it had to happen. She replayed the scene over and over, trying to see if there was some other possible ending that would have left Forz whole and well.

His quick thinking had saved her. And at what cost?

The situation only made Dana more determined to become the ka. She would have the will of a warlock to break and straighten his leg, and the will of an alchemist to meld the bone, infusing it with steel to protect the bond—the will of an enchanter to block the pain.

I could heal him. I have to.

As she neared Shoul Falls, Dana found a secluded cave in the limestone layer. A trickle of water ran out of the seam in the rock, and Dana just managed to wedge herself in, dragging the sack with the mechanodron in after her. Once inside, the soft glow of the sayathi in the water illuminated her way into a tight cavern with a narrow ledge beside a shallow pool. There were even a few sayathenite nodules here, where animals had made instinctual blood offerings to bind themselves to the perennial source of water.

It wasn't the most comfortable position, but it gave Dana a fitful night's sleep, save her nagging worries about what to do with the bloodstone.

Dan Allen

Dana rose early enough to be sure it was still dark outside. With the air outside still chill enough to keep her from wanting to leave the cave, Dana drew the crystal out, curious to see its effect on the pool. She lowered it slowly into the narrow pool.

The water lit with a brilliant glow as she settled the bloodstone within a cluster of sayathenite nodules.

Soft pulses of light ran tentatively out along the electrical conduits of the coral, connecting first one node and then another, the stones joining in a pulsing dance as they reconnected with the ruling sayathi protected in the bloodstone. The pulses gradually ran farther out, disappearing into the darkness of the cavern, only to return moments later as echoes.

The bloodstone was reconnecting with its colony.

In a moment of panic, Dana realized those same pulses would be seen at the pool in the sanctum.

She reached for the stone, then stopped.

Wait. This is perfect!

Those in the sanctum would see the faint pulsing and know the bloodstone had been returned somewhere close. They would know it was safe, but nobody besides her would know where it was.

Dana left the mechanodron on the ledge—she wouldn't need it without the bloodstone—and headed out into the chill of the early morning.

In the dim of the early morning, Dana could make out only a few lit windows in the distant city. She took her bearings and tried to memorize the spot, noting the angle of the city, the rock formations above the cave, and the distance to the edge of the trees below her.

Certain her visual memory could find the spot again, Dana headed for Shoul Falls. Vetas-ka's fleet was on the way. She had only a few days to convince the city to choose a new ka—*her*.

Dana maneuvered slowly, walking carefully to avoid a slip on the rocky slopes where drop-offs and boulders rose one on top of the other in a kind of contest to create the most treacherous passage. When sunlight kissed the shallower mountains on the

The Exalting

eastern horizon, she was descending.

Careful. This is where you got into trouble last time.

By the time she navigated to the cleft in the rock where Ryke had led her into the sanctum, she found three kazen standing in her way.

On the left was Remira, the enchantress. Dana shivered as she felt Remira's presence touch her mind.

On the right was a bearded man she'd seen at the sanctum before. This time he had a small bird-hawk on his shoulder.

A druid. Possibly he was the head druid named Ritser that she had never reported to.

In the center stood Korren.

He was smiling.

Smiling?

He reached out his hand. "Welcome home, Dana."

Chapter 27

Jet was crammed into the Nautilus's cockpit bridge beside the rest of the crew, watching the tactical display with icons depicting the shuttles approaching the ASP frigate. *Come on. Just one hit.*

"We should be in range of their lasers in the next half hour," Angel noted. "Unless their beam stabilizers were damaged in high-g deceleration."

"Who the heck was that?" Decker looked around the room.

"Sorry, that's Angel, my tactical AI," Jet said. "She's side-along booted on one of Tiberius's cores."

"She's still on there? Sounds so real."

"I am real, sir."

"Well keep real quiet," Decker snapped.

Monique stared at the long-range telescope image of the ASP ship. "It looks like they've started another scan with their telescope. We've got to keep their optics on us, or they'll spot the shuttles."

Yaris tugged on the braided lock of hair that ran in front of his ears. "Or focused on the planet."

"Yes." Dormit stomped on the deck. "Yes! Get them to turn their telescope planet-side."

"If I may make a suggestion," Yaris raised a finger. "Order one of our surveillance satellites to leave orbit. Send it on a trajectory uncomfortably close to wherever they landed their dropship on Torsica."

Decker clapped his hands. "Brilliant. Somebody give that elf a raise."

"As a legal advisor, my pay grade is currently higher than yours."

"Are you freakin' kidding me?"

"Angel," Jet said. "Pick a satellite. Ditch it on the Torsican capital."

The Exalting

"The satellite will completely burn up on reentry," Tiberius noted. "There will be no surface damage."

"Yeah, but it will make one heck of a show. The AIs down on Torsica are going to radio back to the frigate and ask what is going on."

"Trajectory locked," Angel said. "You have a ninety-second window."

"Too early, and they start searching," Dormit muttered. "Too late, and they spot the shuttles before the emergency call from their people in Torsica comes in."

"Make it fifteen seconds into the window," Decker said. "These AIs are fast, but slewing a long-range telescope is slow. It's a motor on a precision gear."

"Commencing satellite burn in one minute, ten seconds."

Jet looked to the display showing the eight shuttles converging on the ASP frigate from behind.

"Alright," Decker said. "The moment we have confirmation their scope is moving, I want the Nautilus behind Big Bertha."

"He's going to hide behind the fuel tank so they don't know which shuttle to hit—in case they survive," Jet explained to Teea.

"Aye, Captain," Dormit said. "Warming up the solid fuel thrusters."

"Problem," Tiberius chirped. "The second dropship is not attached to the frigate. It is in a trailing orbit."

"Too late to change targets," Angel said.

"Black space!" Decker pounded the console. "The dropship is going to track us. And then he's going to smoke us as soon as we commit to a landing trajectory."

"Or I can take a shuttle," Jet said. "We've been dropping those. He'll think it's empty."

The noise on the bridge died instantly.

"You can't take a shuttle to the surface. That thing is a tin can."

"I only need to get to the edge of the atmosphere."

"Jet," Angel warned. "You are not space jump qualified."

"I have to space jump. A jump cocoon is small enough to pass through their radar clutter filter."

Decker looked up for a second opinion.

"He's right," Tiberius said.

Decker swallowed. "Naman, suit up."

"Let's hope the shuttles take out the frigate," Dormit mumbled under his breath. "Because if they do see you, that frigate's laser will pop your jump cocoon like a cockroach in a campfire."

"Not just him." Decker patted the bulkhead. "Angel, you better blow this frigate to hades and back, or we're all dead—Jet included."

Angel gave a low chuckle. "Just watch."

Jet left the bridge and began to suit up for a transfer to a shuttle. He toggled the intercom to listen, but nobody said anything for nearly a minute.

"Picking up a corona. Our satellite is reaching the upper atmosphere," Dormit reported.

"Burn, baby, burn," Jet urged as he sealed his glove.

"Frigate is evading!" Dormit shouted. "They didn't fall for it."

"Angel, get that son of a glitch!"

"Shuttles 1 and 2 missed," Dormit reported.

"Angel?" Decker said, his tone rising.

"Wait for it," the AI said in a low, cocky voice.

"Shuttles 3, 4, and 5 are skew—that's another miss."

"Frigate is accelerating," Monique said.

"Shuttles 6, 7 might have a—holy guacamole, look at that frigate move. That's over ten g's!"

Jet bit his knuckle.

"Angel—come on!" Decker urged. But there was little Angel could do. At this range, the round-trip time lag was still nearly five seconds. With the shuttles moving at forty kilometers per second, the error was too huge.

"We have no confirmed valid trajectories." Dormit's voice went silent. "Eight is a miss."

"Wait for it," Angel said.

"Wait for what?"

The Exalting

Jet closed his eyes, dropped to one knee, and started praying. "Come on, Angel. Come on!"

"Holy—the frigate is disintegrating. What the—did you just see that?"

Cheers erupted around Jet. He gave a sly grin. *Nice miss.*

Decker sounded stumped. "Okay, how did you do that?"

"The shuttles weren't aiming for the frigate—too easy to dodge," Angel said. "The shuttles were aiming for each other."

"It appears the shuttle collisions created intersecting halos of debris," Tiberius explained. "There was no way out."

Monique gave a cry of laughter. "They just flew straight into an epic poopstorm."

"Did you just say 'poopstorm' on my bridge?"

"Sir, yes, sir."

Decker moaned like he was in pain.

"Sir, dropship 2 is evading the debris field," Dormit said. "They're going planet-side."

Decker looked at the trajectory. "Yeah, using the atmosphere as a shield against the debris. These guys know their—" he glanced at Monique, "poop."

"But they can boost back into orbit," Dormit added.

"Indeed," Yaris said. "But they'll be in a plasma cone and buffeting turbulence for the next few minutes. Their sensors and lasers are useless."

"Okay, we're on the clock," Decker said over the con. "Jet, get your freeloading AI off Tiberius's cores," Decker ordered. "Then get your butt on the shuttle and get clear."

"Yes sir." Jet finished attaching his other glove.

Monique hurried into the bay and aligned Jet with the wall-mounted EVA backpack. "Boost pack is live."

Angel's calm voice sounded in Jet's helmet. "I'm booted in. It's . . . cozy." The mobile processor was far smaller than Tiberius's servers.

"Moni, can you check my seals?" Jet looked over, but Monique wasn't there. She was putting on her own EVA suit. "What are you

283

doing?"

"I'm taking a shuttle, too. If the dropship follows us, we can split up and he'll have a fifty-fifty chance of guessing which is yours."

"What?" That logic was whack. He could use an autopiloted shuttle for a decoy.

"The shuttles are designed to couple," Monique said. "We'll link the two. Then I'll drop you over Aesica and rendezvous with the dropship—if they survive."

Jet wasn't going to argue if she wanted to spend several days alone on a shuttle with him. "And if not?"

"Then I space jump, too."

"Jeez, woman. You're as crazy as me."

"You'd better believe it. And it's 'Corporal' to you."

Jet gave up arguing. He helped Monique into her EVA jet pack, sealed and cycled the airlock, and then toggled his radio. "Naman to Nautilus, requesting permission to disembark."

"Idling ion engines. Naman, off my ship—now."

Gravity disappeared. Jet snagged a pre-packed box of supplies and gear for his mission and tethered it to his pack. The jump gate closed. Pumps sucked down the atmosphere left in the bay. Then doors snapped open, and the pair navigated in spurts of thrusters around Big Bertha's spherical belly.

"I have Shuttle 23," Jet said as his boots locked to the hull.

"Acknowledged," Dormit replied. "Severing remote control now."

"I've got Shuttle 24," Monique added.

"What is she doing out there?"

"Looks like a I have a tagalong," Jet said.

"Great. One less marine for me to babysit." Decker snapped. "Get those shuttles clear! I'm coming around."

Jet entered the shuttle, disengaged the tether, and told Angel to figure out a landing trajectory. He was still several days out from the planet, but the sooner he started maneuvering, the less fuel it would take. And he could only fire the ion drives when the ASP

284

The Exalting

dropship was on the far side of the planet, or else the high energy particle emissions would give him away.

"Engaging automate," Monique called. From the cockpit display, Jet watched as the two shuttles pivoted and joined at the belly with a bang.

Jet opened the hatch on his side, and a minute later Monique opened her side and drifted through without her jet pack.

"Do you think the dropship spotted us breaking away?"

"I doubt it. It'll be pretty busy tracking space junk."

The further they drifted from the other shuttles, the less likely the enemy's telescopes would spot them.

Jet vented the cockpit to atmospheric pressure and took off his helmet, plugged it into the charging station, and enjoyed a crisp dose of ridiculously frigid air. Monique followed. Her hair took the opportunity to explore the low-gravity environment.

Jet sat down in one of the two shuttle pilot chairs and managed to get the buckle around his EVA suit. "We did it."

"Does this shuttle have a space jump kit?" Monique asked.

"Yeah, we transferred all the kits to the remaining shuttles when Angel launched the others as missiles," Jet said.

"What about food?"

Jet opened a drawer. "Um . . . synthmeal okay?"

"Water?"

"The suits recycle."

"Okay, so we can last a few days." Monique gave a sigh of relief.

Jet smiled. "So now what?" He had his own ideas.

"Now?" Monique said. "I'm going to lock myself in the other shuttle for an entire shift. Do you have any idea how long it's been since I've been in a room by myself? Sanitation silo aside."

"Five weeks, two days, four hours. But who's counting?"

"Yeah. At least." She turned and pushed off for the adjoining hatch.

"I'll keep Angel company," Jet said. Then he added, "So, I'll see you for dinner?"

Monique put a hand on the hatch to slow herself. Without

Dan Allen

looking back, she said, "Sure, why not."

When she was gone and the hatch on her side closed, Jet banged the wall of the shuttle. "Way to go, Angel."

"I learned from the best," she answered from the speaker in the charging panel. "The shrapnel shot—you did that on Avalon."

Jet smiled as he realized the connection. "Yeah, but you just shot eight bullets into each other from across the solar system."

"I wasn't going to brag. But . . . it was pretty cool."

Jet could imagine her blushing.

"So, is everything ready for the big day?" she asked.

Jet grimaced. *First contact.* "Um . . . yes. Entering the final stages of planning as we speak."

"It's good to have you back," Korren said.

Dana nearly fainted at the surprise of an actual welcome.

They're not going to kill me? Relief washed through her.

I'm home.

The three kazen escorted her through the long tunnel to the main hall, though not like a prisoner escort with some in front and some in back. It was almost like an honor guard.

"The stone is safe, it seems?" Korren said. "The pool is pulsing."

"Yes."

"You didn't want to bring it back?" He wasn't pushing for an answer. He just seemed curious.

That definitely wasn't like Korren.

"I . . ."

"I imagine," he said, "you weren't sure whom to trust."

Dana swallowed. "Yeah."

"In time you will."

Dana didn't like the sound of that. It was as if he was trying to change her.

I'm not some impressionable child you can control.

"We know what kind of person you are," Remiren said softly.

286

The Exalting

The enchantress probably didn't have to work hard to pick up on Dana's angry thoughts. "If we didn't like you the way you were, you wouldn't be here."

Possibly.

Remiren put her arm on Dana's.

Dana waited for a strange new thought from the enchantress to run through her mind.

It didn't come.

"We were worried for you," Remiren said.

You mean you're glad the stone is safe.

"Naturally," she said gently. "But your friends here have been terribly worried about you as well."

"Ritser, Remira, I'll join you in a moment." Korren stopped and faced Dana while the other two continued into the main hall. "It is odd to be the senior kazen and so . . . left out."

What is he saying? He wants to know where it is? Of course he thinks he has a right to know.

"I couldn't stop the citizen council from determining to destroy it. I couldn't stop the Vetas-kazen. I couldn't even stop you, Dana."

Dana returned his gaze. "You want the stone, don't you?"

"Everybody wants the stone," Korren said.

"But who do *you* want to get it?"

He didn't answer.

Dana turned away from Korren and stepped inside the main hall, still wondering who Korren wanted to get the stone for. It couldn't be Vetas-ka, or he would have simply given the kazen the stone when they attacked. But he had fought them.

Was there somebody else? Or was he just trying to make her think that he didn't want the stone for himself?

Her job wasn't over. She had to find out what Korren was up to. And if not him, then who Sindar had fled from.

At least the stone was safe.

Dana was ripped from her thoughts when the big druid, Kazen Ritser, rang a heavy bell. Its tones echoed through the cavern.

In moments, the hall was filled to capacity, not just with young acolytes but senior kazen older than her parents, though none quite as old as Sindar had appeared.

Dana stood behind the main table, flanked by the kazen who had escorted her.

When there seemed to be no more room in the cavern, Korren spoke.

"Some are not with us today." His voice was grim. "Acolyte Sofrana. Venren. Melien. We grieve for their passing even as we honor their sacrifices to defend us from the foreign kazen."

Although Korren was talking about those who died fighting the Vetas-kazen on the day she took the bloodstone, all eyes were on her.

"They, along with many of the civic guard, and many of our citizen council, paid the ultimate price for their loyalty."

Dana searched the crowd for the faces of those she loved. She found Kaia, who nodded at her. Ryke stood with his staff leaning in the crook of his arm, his legs shoulder-width apart as if guarding the assembly.

She winked. His brow furrowed as his eyes took in her newly bleached light blond hair.

A smile crept onto her lips as she caught him staring.

Mirris was there as well, near the front, looking ready to embrace Dana, or slug her—probably both.

"We also welcome the return of our newest acolyte, Dana of Norr." Korren turned to her. "Your courage inspires us all. And once again the light of the bloodstone pulses in the sacred pool. You have returned the stone to us. We trust it is safe."

Dana nodded.

He smiled. "Then you shall continue to keep it in trust until the council makes a new decision. You have earned the right. We honor your sacrifice."

It wasn't just her sacrifice. Forz had paid a terrible price as well. She would not forget it.

"Now we must prepare," Korren continued. "There is a great work to be done in the city. Our enemies are gathering across the

The Exalting

seas. But I'm sure some of you would like to greet Dana. Please, do so. Then let us attend to the city and remind our people of Shoul Falls that they are not alone. We are one, the people and protectors of Shoul Falls."

A cheer rose up from the crowd, doubly loud in the rock-walled cavern.

With the speech finished, Dana slumped into the nearest chair.

She was glad to be here, glad to be safe, glad to be cared for, and glad that she was not being chased or threatened. It was the most wonderful feeling.

It's too easy.

The feeling nagged at her but quickly faded with the ample distractions in the room.

"Water?" offered the bearded kazen.

"If you would be so kind, Ritsen," Remira said, before Dana could answer.

"Thanks," Dana breathed.

Ryke, Mirris, Kaia, and several of the girls she had shared the one meditation with, quickly surrounded her.

"You touched the stone with your blood," Mirris said, her eyes accusing. "We felt it."

"I didn't know I wasn't supposed to touch it," Dana said.

"But you did it a second time."

Dana's voice fell. "Yes."

"It is forbidden."

"I know. So why the welcome? Why didn't they arrest me?"

Kaia sat beside Dana and took her hands. "We felt your pain, Dana. All of us. You were dying, weren't you?"

Dana gave a small nod.

"Everyone in the entire city felt you, Dana," Ryke said. "It was like we were dying with you."

Dana's jaw dropped.

"Do you think we begrudged you our strength when you called on us?" Ryke said. "After you saved the stone from the Vetas-kazen?"

"The first time you touched it," Mirris said. "We were fleeing, running from the kazen invaders."

"Then a voice called to us," Kaia said. "A command, as if from the Creator. 'Fight!' It was you, Dana. You were the one who rallied us."

"And we fought," Ryke said. "As one. Even without our powers."

"I'm sorry I took the stone from you." Kaia put her hand on Dana's shoulder. "I thought I was doing the right thing."

"You probably were," Dana sighed. "I'm just glad you're okay. Any breakfast leftovers?"

"Always hungry," Ryke laughed.

Ritser reached over her friends and lowered a bowl of water that glowed briefly before she drained it. When she looked up there was another bowl with porridge.

Dana ate the porridge almost as fast.

The others filtered away at the behest of a senior kazen.

Ryke sat across from her. He pointed at her hair. "Did that happen when you touched the bloodstone?"

Dana blushed, the tines of her sifa fanning. "No. I needed a disguise."

"It looks . . . good."

"You always look good," Dana said. ". . . to me."

He gave a wry grin and then stood. "I know."

"What's happening now?" Dana said as he turned to leave. "Why is everyone going to the city?"

"It's time for work. Are you going to join us?"

Dana slurped the dregs of the porridge and hurried after him.

The curiosity she had felt about the strangely genial welcome returned. There was something missing in the equation. Perhaps the kazen were trying to take her off her guard.

That wasn't going to happen.

"Most of our days are spent in training or in service," Ryke explained. "Today is a service day."

"So . . . all the kazen are coming?"

The Exalting

"Yes, of course."

Dana felt a touch of relief. Since all the kazen were coming, it meant none of them were scheming in secret back at the sanctum or off looking for the stone.

She would have to be on the watch for that sort of thing, at least until she felt like she understood why they had simply forgiven her for taking their stone and not bringing it back.

Granted, they knew it was nearby, but not where.

In any case, service was the perfect opportunity to build rapport with the people of Shoul Falls, if she was to convince them that she was their next ka. There wasn't much time to impress them before Vetas-ka's fleet arrived.

Dana kept beside Ryke and Kaia as acolytes and kazen descended in small groups, each taking different paths to the city, part of the effort to keep the entrances to the sanctum secret.

"The whole mountain above the city is sacred," Kaia explained. "And generally off limits to anyone who doesn't want to dedicate their life to community service." She bobbed easily beside Dana on a steep path that cut diagonally away from the city. The way became more apparent as it switched back and joined a wagon road that passed through several fenced tree stands. These were farms that raised the chubby northern marmar monkeys that had three to five offspring twice a year. In the same pens were dozens of howler fowls that announced the arrival of any passing traveler with ear-splitting shrieks.

"So basically," Dana said, "the promise of a life of community service is the price of having a chance at being made ka."

"An outsider like you would see it that way," Kaia said.

"Maybe it's a good thing you didn't know about it before you came," Ryke said with a grin. His dark skin contrasted her light hair, with Kaia between them taking the middle tones.

"Here's the strange thing," Dana said, her voice dropping low. "I get back without the bloodstone, and I'm welcomed with open arms—just like that. No questions, nothing."

Kaia didn't answer right away as she usually did, and Ryke

didn't seem to mind the silence. Perhaps they didn't know any more than her about what was really going on.

Finally, as they approached the outer gates of the siege wall that Dana had last leapt over on a greeder as she fled with the bloodstone, Kaia spoke in a quiet voice. "You didn't ask Sindaren any questions when he showed up. You simply believed him. Why?"

"I knew he was honest."

"How?" Kaia said, seeming to already know the answer.

Dana shrugged. "I just . . . I felt it."

"We've all felt you, Dana. When you touched the bloodstone, you got one twenty-thousandth of each of us, but we all got a heavy dose of you. We felt things."

"Like what?"

"You're a fighter," Ryke said.

"You're stubborn," Kaia said. "You don't give up. Impetuous. Loyal to a friend."

Again, Dana thought of Forz, and drew a shaky breath as she pushed that thought to arm's length to keep her composure.

"Aren't you curious about what I did with the bloodstone?" Dana asked.

Ryke tilted his head to one side. "Only if it makes a great story. But if not, you had better come up with one quick."

"Why?"

"It's market day. School is out."

The city gates burst open, and three dozen children came running.

"Ryke!"

"Kaia!"

To her horror an equal number called out her name.

"Dana of Norr!"

"Look at her hair."

"She touched the bloodstone—that's what did it!"

Children from age three to thirteen condensed on her like dewdrops on the spines of a leather cactus. Ryke and Kaia got equally mobbed.

The Exalting

"Are all Norrians so messy?" asked one of the children.

"Not all," Dana said. "I've been traveling."

"Tell us! Tell us!"

Hands pulled at her fingers and yanked on her clothes as she passed through the siege wall gate and into the city proper, feeling as if she were a howler fowl being shepherded to market by twenty underaged handlers.

Dana was led to a corner of the square, set upon a hay bale, and surrounded by children seated and standing, leaning and crowding. She looked around hoping for some sign of Korren or any of the other kazen. A few passed in and out of view as they moved through the market, apparently on important war preparation tasks. None came close enough to listen to her plea for clemency.

"Tell us everything!" cried a young girl.

"Yes, tell us!"

"Oh," Dana began, "it's much too frightening."

"We aren't afraid, Dana of Norr," said a young boy. "We love adventures."

Maybe I am home after all.

"Well this story is very sad. I would have to tell you that Sindaren was killed and my best friend broke his leg and became a cripple—is that a story you want to hear?"

Because I don't want to tell it.

"Are there any good parts?" asked a young girl in a dress standing in the front. She was only a little higher than Dana's knee. The girl wrapped her tiny fingers around Dana's forefinger and pulled, as if trying to milk her of the details.

Dana's sifa fanned as she thought of a few moments she would love to re-live. Moments in the cave, with Ryke. "A few."

"Then tell us those."

Dana breathed in and then said, "Have any of you ever traveled by river barge?"

The children all shook their heads.

"Or shall I tell you about a kiss?"

"No kissing!" shouted a bevy of boys. "Barge! Barge! Barge!"

293

If only to be contrary, an equal number of girls cried out, "Kisses! Kisses! Kisses!"

"Both then," Dana said. "For I once kissed two bargemen in one day and nearly died—shall we begin with that story?"

Children dropped to the ground like sacks of milled grain and stared at her.

Dana began her tale with her escape from Norr, not even avoiding the fact that she stole the greeder. *Why hide it from them?*

She wasn't perfect. She shouldn't pretend to be. The children laughed at her imitations of Turigan and Jila.

"But if I catch any of you stealing—" Dana pointed her finger. "You won't like it. There are plenty of marmar pens to be cleaned."

"Gross!"

"Orchards to be dunged."

"Gross!"

"Rotten vegetables to be composted."

"Gross!" All the children were now shouting in unison.

"And centipedes to be eaten."

"GROSS!"

"One for every lie. And a worm for every insult."

"Ew!" A girl shuddered.

Dana winced as a twinge of pain shot down her leg. She looked up to see a man passing by on a greeder.

"Hey!" Dana stood and waved to the man. "Your greeder has a pinched nerve in its left leg. That's why it's limping."

The man dismounted immediately and looked at the side of his greeder. He began to loosen the saddle.

"It's spinal degeneration, I'm afraid," Dana said. "She's not fit for riding anymore. But she might do light draft work."

"You're sure?" the man said.

Thirty heads turned from him to Dana.

"Yes."

"I thought it was just getting lazy—or maybe arthritis."

Dana nodded. "She does care for you. Otherwise she would have thrown you off."

294

The Exalting

The children laughed at that.

"I'll not ride her anymore," the man said, stroking his beloved greeder's feathers. He drew the reins and put his face close to the greeder's. "Why didn't you say so, you proud bird?"

The greeder squawked in answer, sending the children into another fit of laughter.

From the back of the group a girl stepped forward. She carried a green-streaked forest cat in her arms. "Something's wrong with it, Dana."

"Not really. It's pregnant. Give it lots of time alone and make sure it has a warm place and plenty of food."

The girl beamed. "Kittens!"

In minutes a large queue had formed at Dana's spontaneous veterinary booth. After all, her services were free.

A man offered her a small sack of food for compensation, which Dana took willingly, not worrying about whether it was allowed and devouring it before any of the other acolytes could arrive to tell her it was forbidden to take payment.

A bearded man with a potbelly held out a mangy marmar.

Dana twitched as something seemed to nip at her. "Mites. Bathe it in alkali and rinse with vinegar—and clean its enclosure more often."

The man's belly shook with laughter. "Mercy—she's like a fortune teller. Never got information like that out of old Ritsen."

"What happened to your hair?" a girl asked.

"Maybe I fell in love," Dana said, trying to avoid getting into another story.

"With Ryke!" the girl gasped. Her hand was on Dana's arm.

"Next, please!" Dana called, pulling her arm free of the young enchanter who had sensed who she was thinking about with merely a touch.

"You're in love with Ryke, and it's not even allowed!"

Dana knelt down and whispered in the girl's ear. "How would you like to wake up tomorrow in a bed full of spinning scorpions?"

The freckle-faced girl's face blanched and her sifa shot straight

295

out.

"Then let's keep other people's thoughts secret unless they give permission."

The girl nodded.

Dana reached down, and a tiny scorpion crawled out of the hay and onto her hand.

The girl bolted.

That was close. She had nearly let it bite the girl. *I'm losing will.*

"I've got a problem with termites. Any ideas?"

"Make a house out of stone." Dana smiled as kindly as her tired cheeks would allow, thinking to herself that she shouldn't have said it aloud.

Then she laughed at her own joke.

Wasn't supposed to do that either.

Dana knew the symptoms. Her behavior was only going to get worse the more she extended herself into animals to diagnose their problems.

In a moment of desperation, she shielded her eyes with her hand and looked across the market at nobody in particular. "Is that Kazen Ritser, er—Ritsen, calling for me?" Then she scurried away from the corner where several more people waited for their turn at animal divining.

"I think she's well and spent," mumbled an old lady.

"Never can tell with those mad Norrians," said her husband, who earned a smack from his wife's handbag.

Away from her spontaneous veterinary clinic, Dana walked the market, past other stalls where vendors hawked goods, past other bales of hay where acolytes sat and mended socks with old ladies or checked calculations in ledgers. A few kazen were seated at negotiating tables acting as arbiters—probably regarding requisitions for battle supplies.

Dana hoped it would never come to arbitration for her as she carefully picked a path back to the sanctum that avoided other acolytes and kazen.

The next few days were challenging, if not terrible—filled with

The Exalting

the most thankless and dreary work the kazen could imagine. It was like being an unpaid house servant.

Dana consoled herself that at least she wasn't skinning game. She would take drudgery over the sick pain of re-living a creature's last moments when she touched it. Especially if it meant a chance to be chosen as ka.

Because if they didn't choose soon, she would have to take matters into her own hands.

With his kazen repeatedly failing to get the stone, Vetas-ka himself was coming for it.

And what will these people do when he comes? The city had made some progress in shoring up defenses and recruiting more young men into the garrison for training. But what was any of that worth, against a ka? A supreme?

Dana thought of the mechanodron she had left with its motor roots in the sayathi pool.

There was no more time to waste.

Shoul Falls needed a ka. Now.

Chapter 28

"Hey, Jet."

Jet opened his eyes, wincing at the low-gravity sinus headache. *Engines are idle. The ASP dropship must be in view.* The dim lights in Shuttle 23's control panel blinked softly.

Jet sat up in the copilot seat. "Sorry. Must have dozed off."

In the seat beside him, Monique pointed at the countdown clock on the shuttle's navigation display. "You have less than twenty-four hours. What's the plan?"

"Step 1: Space jump to North Aesica. Step 2: Make powerful friends."

"So . . . crash into a farmer's barn, emerge in a cloud of smoke, and be like, 'take me to your leader.'"

"Ha-ha."

"Seriously—what are you going to do?"

"He's going to find that renegade that took the bloodstone from Shoul Falls." Angel's voice sounded from a speaker on the console that Jet's tactical suit was plugged into for charging.

"I never said that."

"Well, it's obvious from the amount of time you stare at pictures of her."

"Alien fetish?" Monique snickered.

"It's just," Jet paused, "something the High Seer said. She saw a girl who would help us."

"And *you* believe it?"

Jet only took a moment to consider. "Yeah."

She turned to face him. "Really? What's gotten into you? Are you turning into an honest-to-Creator do-gooder Believer?"

Jet locked his hands behind his head. "Maybe."

Monique gave him a quarter of a smile. "This is new."

"I think I understand what I'm supposed to do," Jet said.

The Exalting

"And this started when?"

Jet considered the question.

Angel piped up. "The night you told him about your date with Ahreth."

"Thank you, Angel."

"You're welcome. Anyway you weren't sure, and you weren't going to tell her."

It was true. Both parts.

Monique leaned closer. "You're talking about failure—losing the battle?"

Jet brought his hands in front and cracked his knuckles. "The High Seer saw our ships falling from the Xahnan sky in droves."

Monique covered her mouth in shock.

"We are going to fail," Jet said. "In fact, I've been planning it."

Monique's eyes widened, then narrowed. "Jet, what are you talking about?"

This was the first time he had told anyone on the mission about his plans, except Decker, who had demanded to know why his energy budget was off. Jet had been forced to admit that Angel was running a massive fleet-level simulation.

"Angel, what's the status on Speaker for the Dead?"

"I sent the results on a tightbeam to the Excalibur a few hours ago."

The fleet was half a light-day away. "So we could get a reply from Fleet Command before we hit the atmosphere," Jet said. "I hope they like it."

"Hope they like what?" Monique's sable eyes searched his.

Jet swallowed. "The greatest charade in the history of interplanetary warfare. Sort of a reverse ambush."

Monique pushed herself down into the pilot's chair. "I'm not sure I want to know."

"I thought you couldn't stand not knowing."

"It's true," Monique said, her lips barely parted this time in a genuine half smile. "But sometimes it is better not to know—it's like bitter medicine." Her eyes locked on him. "You'd better not be hiding anything else."

Jet's breath halted in his chest. "Only that I'm in love with you."

"Wow," Angel cooed. "For once, I didn't have to say it."

Monique leaned across Jet and pushed the kill switch on Angel's charging console. Doing so left her leaning right in front of Jet. "You were saying?"

Jet found himself completely speechless. Then the two of them burst out laughing.

Exhausted, with scarcely any will left to burn, Dana slipped into the greeder's stall. The eight-foot bird outweighed her three times over.

"Down."

The bird dropped to the floor, and Dana lifted its foot. She took a knife, and then putting the bird in a trance of bliss with thoughts of feed and rest, she cut directly into the pad of its center toe, lancing a lesion.

She drained the wound, then poured alcohol onto it.

The bird gave a cry of protest.

"Quiet, you big baby. You're embarrasing yourself."

It was true. There were females in the rangers' stables. The greeder quit squawking, and Dana tied a bandage around its gargantuan foot-sized toe.

"Stay off of that until tomorrow." Dana stepped out of the enclosure.

She had seen or treated nearly every greeder in Shoul Falls. They had all been requisitioned by the core of rangers. And every active and former ranger had been called up for duty.

The rangers would be the first to fall to Vetas-ka in their own provincial forests, when the demon arrived in Aesica to fight for the most powerful bloodstone on the planet.

Preparing so many animals for war was an experience she never

The Exalting

had dreamt of, an opportunity she never would've had without being an acolyte and dedicating herself to a life of service.

Her eyes turned to the corner of the stables where two rangers watched.

They kept their distance.

Are they afraid of me?

Dana felt a hand on her opposite shoulder and flinched.

"Dana."

It was Kaia.

"It's time to go."

"Where?"

"It's first night of winter, Dana. You don't want to miss the party."

A party? Spending all night staying up with the other acolytes feasting and dancing, sharing stories . . . spending time with Ryke. She didn't want to miss it. But the rangers were counting on her. Lives would depend on those greeders.

"I should probably stay with the ani—"

"Dana, you've done all you can."

That's not true. Dana no longer tried to fight the thought. *I could take the bloodstone and become the ka.* On occasion, Dana hated herself for even having the thought. But at times like this, it just seemed pointless to question the growing temptation.

"They'll all still be asleep when you get back," Kaia said.

It was true. Greeders were notoriously late sleepers.

Kaia slipped an arm through Dana's and moved her toward the exit. She was low on will anyway and didn't want to spend what she had left avoiding fun.

Together they stepped out of the infirmary into flutters of drifting snow flakes. Then Dana shook her arm loose and tucked her hands in her pockets. In the falling snow, lanterns in the street glowed like the full moons behind the clouds.

Why can't it always be like this?

She wanted peace. She wanted everything to be right. But so had Vetas-ka. He had wanted peace. He had come to save Shoul

301

Falls from a war so long ago.

I'm not like Vetas-ka.

"Everyone says you are." Mirris leaned against the piled stone wall of the infirmary, her arms crossed. "Vetas-ka wasn't afraid to stand up for what he believed in. You're no different."

"Stay out of my head."

Kaia motioned with her hand. "Mirris, that's enough."

Dana stopped in the street. "And what if I am? What if the city chooses me, because they see stubbornness enough to put up with it all? They see hope in me, Mirris. Why can't you see it?"

Mirris continued walking. "That's all you see. You're blind to everything else."

"What's she talking about?" Dana said.

Kaia shrugged.

Mirris's angry pace took her into the darkness ahead of them, leaving Dana alone with Kaia.

"She's untrusting," Kaia said as they stepped through the back gate of the city.

"Yeah. I noticed."

"It's her best quality," Kaia added.

"Probably." Dana trudged in Kaia's footsteps as the dark pine forest devoured the sky and surroundings, leaving all to shadow.

"Not everyone is out to get you, Dana," Kaia reminded.

"Oh sure, just—" Dana froze. There were no animals nearby. That could mean only one thing. Dana grabbed Kaia and crouched down.

"What's wrong?"

"Ambush." Dana's heart raced a hundred leagues an hour. Movement stirred in the trees on all sides. Footsteps came crashing through the brush.

Dana reached out, but any animal capable of protecting her had long since fled. By the sound of it, dozens of people were headed for her.

Dana had vowed not to ever allow this to happen. How had her enemies gotten so close without anyone noticing?

The Exalting

The figures in the forest took vague shapes as they neared. "Kaia, run."

"Stand up, silly."

"What?"

A chorus of voices rang out together. "Joyous birthday to Dana, may her next year shine bright. Celebrate her beginning of the rest of her life!"

Dana buried her face in her hands. "Oh, you guys. I thought I was going to die!" She pointed at Mirris. "You got me all worked up on purpose so I didn't notice anything."

Ryke was laughing so hard he could barely get a breath in. "Do you realize how hard it is to sneak up on you?"

Dana turned to Kaia. "Were you in on this?"

Kaia turned up her palms.

"So, there's no such thing as first winter night festival, is there?"

Mirris gave her a congratulatory slap on the back. "There is now!"

Ryke put his arm around Dana. "The kazen are off on some meditation on the holy mountain. We have the sanctum to ourselves."

It was far too good to be true. But Dana didn't care. She grabbed onto Ryke's arm to prevent him letting go and looped her arm through Kaia's. She wasn't going to let her friends out of her sight again.

Behind its leather flap doors, the sanctum was chilly, though furs, fire, and steaming mugs brought enough warmth to keep the group singing and laughing at stories until Kaia sent the younger acolytes to bed.

Once she returned, Mazen, another alchemy acolyte with a shaved head and oversized muscles, suggested a trip to the hot room.

Dana's eyes widened. "There's a hot room—besides the sacred one?"

"Yeah, but the kazen don't let us use it," Mirris said.

Well that was no longer a problem.

After filling waterskins from a chamber off the main river, the entire company of teenage acolytes—numbering fifteen, as far as Dana could tell—walked hunched over along a narrow passage, past an old supply room, then climbed down through a narrow hole and spread out in a steamy, low-ceilinged, sand-floored chamber, setting a few glow candles in the soft sand to light the room.

Soothing heat warmed Dana's back as it rose through the soft sand. Her eyes drifted shut. More acolytes piled into the room until almost everyone's arm or stomach was being used as a pillow.

"It would be hot enough in here anyway," Mirris complained, "even if there weren't so many people. Hey—who farted!"

The group moaned and whined, pushing away from the corner of the room where the foul had been committed. Once the air had cleared, the room fell into a still silence.

"So, what did everyone do today?" Dana asked.

"Besides plan your surprise party?" laughed a girl named Kees. She was a few years younger than Dana and drew plenty of attention with her early spreading sifa and perfect face. She was an alchemy acolyte as well, but apparently only used her gift to sense elements, checking drinking water or testing alchemical recipes formulated by other acolytes.

"How did you know it was my birthday? I didn't even remember."

Mirris lifted her head. "People's moods change when they get close to their birthday. They get more philosophical. They get more hopeful. It's not that hard to notice if you know what to look for."

"And you got the exact day, just by guessing?"

"No, I—it's a trade secret."

"She touched you while you were sleeping and dragged it out of you," said Kaia.

Dana rolled her eyes. What else would she expect? She couldn't begrudge them that. But it did make her wonder what else they had dragged out of her.

Dana reached out, her hand touching Ryke's side. He made a sound like a sneeze and wiggled away. Dana reached out again, confused by his reaction.

He gasped and caught her hand, holding it back.

"Are you ticklish? Guys, Ryke's ticklish!"

"No!"

A dangerous assault commenced in the low-ceilinged chamber as people tried to tickle Ryke and found the task much harder than they had expected.

"He's too fast. Just give up."

"I got this," Dana said. "I'll just wait until he's not expecting it."

"You already got me twice."

"It is so hot in here." Mirris stripped off her long-sleeved shirt. Dana couldn't begrudge her that. It was too dark to be immodest, and she still had on her tie-top. Within minutes everyone had followed. The waterskins were passed around, and Dana drank eagerly. She hadn't realized how thirsty she had become. She rolled onto her stomach and lay feeling more content than she ever had, until Mazen and Timmet, a warlock with far less interest in his gift than in pranks, took pains to flick drops of cold water at anyone who looked too comfortable.

A cold drop hit Dana in the small of her back. "That actually feels good."

Then a rush of cold water spilled onto her back, and Dana squealed as she rolled over, intent on catching the culprits. But she sat up too fast and hit her head on the ceiling. "Ow!"

That set the whole group laughing raucously.

"Don't lose your cool, Dana," Timmet teased.

"Funny."

The comment immediately brought to her mind the mechanodron Dana had left in the limestone cave, capable of regulating the temperature of a person in a room such as this. *Wait a minute.*

Dana rubbed her sore forehead and tried to find Kaia's long-legged shape. "Hey Kaia, how often do the kazen do these meditation trips?"

"Huh?"

"When was the last time they all left together?"

"Um . . ." she exchanged a glance with Ryke. "I don't . . . well, this is the first I remember."

"So, all the kazen head up the sacred mountain, leaving us to any sort of mischief we want, and we just completely fall for it?"

Kaia sat up. "What are you talking about?"

"Why *all* of them at once? Why not take turns meditating?" Dana said. She knew the answer. It could only be because none of them trusted the others enough to allow it. And they couldn't risk getting someone like Dana involved.

Ryke sat up near Dana. "What if they went out to look for the bloodstone?"

"Exactly."

"But it could be anywhere," Mirris noted.

"No," Ryke said. "The bloodstone is in water, so it has to be somewhere along the line of the limestone formation. They can stick to a single contour."

"And it's pulsing," Kaia said. "They can just check any of the caves with pools. If they go too far the pulses will be going out instead of in."

Dana's throat clenched. *They're going to find it. No wonder they weren't worried when I showed up without it.*

Dana could have slapped herself. It was idiotic. They would track the bloodstone's pulses until they triangulated its position. She should have thought of that. Perhaps it was the exhaustion and sleep deprivation.

It was going to be easy to find—and she thought she had the perfect hiding place. What was worse, they would find the mechanodron as well.

Dana drew a hand to her mouth. Not only would they know that she had made it, but they could simply add fuel sap and watch it work. They would figure out what it was for and that she had intended to take the bloodstone.

That would not be good.

The Exalting

Then a worse thought struck her.

They could use it. They could take the stone to the chamber and use the mechanodron. Anyone could become the ka—even Korren.

And what if one of them had sold out to Vetas-ka?

Without a word, Dana grabbed her shirt and climbed over confused bodies, making her way to the exit.

"Where is she going?"

Dana stopped as she reached up to lift herself out of the hot room. "You all knew Sindaren. He died trying to take the stone to my grandfather because he didn't dare leave it in Shoul Falls."

"What's your point, Dana?" Kaia said.

"Do you think we should just lie around here and let his sacrifice go to waste?"

Ryke moved first. "She's right. We cannot trust the kazen if Sindaren did not. He was an enchanter."

"You can't be serious? Going out in the cold at night?"

Dana didn't recognize the voice. But it didn't matter who said it. Everyone was thinking it. "I don't need everyone," Dana said. "I just need Ryke and Mirris."

Kaia put an arm out, holding Mirris in place. "She's too young."

"I am not," Mirris said.

Mirris likely wasn't half the enchanter that Remira was. But at least she could detect if the kazen tried to manipulate their thoughts.

"Can you carry something heavy while you run?" Dana asked.

Mirris seemed to be staring at her from the shadows. "I'm stronger than I look."

She probably was, Dana had to admit. Mirris was shorter, but her build was somewhat athletic.

"What about the rest of us?" Mazen asked.

"Can you create some kind of distraction, something that would draw the kazen back to the city?"

Timmet laughed and pointed a thumb at Mazen. "You are asking an alchemist if he can create a distraction?"

"Good. I am counting on it," Dana said. "Let's go."

Dana pulled on her shirt while she navigated back to the commons, the entire group of acolytes following her. She grabbed her coat which was hung by the fire and borrowed Kaia's gloves. Ryke came in from the opposite way, staff in hand, as Mirris came in stomping her feet into her boots.

"Where is it hidden?" Ryke asked.

"About three miles north," Dana said. "Is there any way to approach without being seen?"

"Follow me."

Ryke lead the way to the north exit, one that was far more convenient for accessing the city than the back-way Dana had first come through.

"What if they left a sentry?" Mirris said.

"Then I knock them out," Ryke said plainly.

"You would attack your own kazen?" Mirris asked.

"I don't have time to sort friend and foe," Ryke said as he raced alongside Dana. "If one of them is trying to steal the bloodstone, then we have to stop them all."

"They aren't going to leave a sentry," Dana said. "They don't trust each other a lot more than they don't trust us. If they had wanted to leave a sentry, they would have left us a babysitter."

"Here goes." Ryke raised his staff and burst out the camouflaged door.

There was no one waiting.

"Told you."

"We'll take the ridge to the first summit." Ryke pointed up the mountain. "It's all clear on the south slope—no bushwhacking through trees. There is a sandy wash in the next canyon. We can run down the sand full speed until we hit the limestone layer—the wash can't really be seen from below. We'll have cover right up until the last few hundred yards."

Dana surveyed the mountainous scene. It was luck that the falling snow wasn't yet sticking. The ground was still clear.

"Then let's go."

The Exalting

Dana was a little surprised that Ryke was so strong on the climb, and even more surprised that Mirris kept up, apparently determined not to fall behind Ryke's punishing pace.

They climbed just below the ridge on the south side so their silhouettes would not be visible. Coming near the top of the ridge, the lights of city below glowed in the distance—but far brighter than she had expected.

"It's on fire!" Ryke pointed with his staff. "Some building is completely ablaze."

This had to be Mazen's distraction.

"That should bring them back," Mirris said, leaning over to catch her breath.

"On then," Dana urged. "Only one and a half more miles."

"Only?" Mirris moaned.

"It's not as steep on the ridge," Ryke noted. "Let's pick up the pace."

But on the ridge, there was already a first downy layer of slippery snow.

Dana kept busy trying not to twist an ankle. Sister moon was barely bright enough to show the uneven edges of loose stones under the growing blanket of white. Dana's hands and nose were cold, but the sheer exertion kept her core warm.

Near the end of the traverse, the way narrowed. Cliffs grew on either side until there was only one way forward: straight down.

Mirris gawked at the steep chute. "That?"

"The middle of the wash is sand. You can run full speed. The sand absorbs the impact."

"You've done this before?" Mirris asked.

"Oh, yeah. It's great." Ryke took off running down the mountain. His steps grew to massive leaps.

"Watch out for rocks," Dana said. She ran ahead, picking up speed at a dangerous rate, until her feet found the narrow rivulet of coarse sand in the center of the canyon vee. Her boots sank several inches with each great bound.

Racing down a sacred mountain at night—at least she couldn't complain about lack of adventure. Although she felt like screaming from the sheer terror of it.

The slope lessened slightly as the wash came to a rocky outcropping. Dana spotted the cliff edge and swerved to one side, barely able to keep up with her pinwheeling legs as she rapidly ran out of room. The valley stretched out in front of her, and for one glorious moment she was sure she was headed over the edge. But two quick steps up the steep side-slope burned the last of her momentum.

Heart pounding, Dana looked back. Mirris had swerved to the other side and was standing near Ryke. Far above was the top of the wash. Dana had just come down the better part of a half mile in a minute plus.

"Whoa." She scampered back to where Mirris and Ryke stood.

"Okay, now where is the stone?" Mirris said, her voice quiet.

"This way . . . I think." Dana said quietly. "Do you sense anyone else?"

Mirris shook her head.

"Okay. Follow me." She stepped down the rocky slope, picking her way on a traverse, away from the trickle of a waterfall that carried snow runoff over the edge of a thirty-foot drop. Dana tried desperately to avoid that deadly direct descent. Roots and brush made for tenuous handholds as she came level with the limestone layer.

Anxiously, Dana reached out, trying to sense the animals in the region, without making them aware of her own growing fear. It was a delicate balance. Each creature had its own threshold. And if Ritsen was out there, he might notice a suddenly anxious animal. It was what Dana was trying to do—see if any of them were being influenced.

To be safe, she stopped trying to sense the animals. She needed a strong will to survive. Without it, she might simply elect the easier option: falling.

As the rock descent grew steeper, Dana had to face the rock and feel for footholds. Finally, she looked down to find the next hold

310

The Exalting

and realized she had reached the bottom.

Ryke jumped the last six feet and took Mirris's hand as she leapt to the solid soil. Both took a tumble as Mirris's feet hit a slick patch of snow.

Dana tried not to laugh at their attempt to disentangle themselves. But she also watched the edge of the forest a hundred yards below for any movement, hoping their arrival hadn't been seen.

Something inside her told her they had. It wasn't an internal fear, but something beyond that, a feeling Dana couldn't place.

"Mirris, is anyone—"

The compulsion came not through words, but a touch. The moment Mirris's hand contacted hers, a single thought washed through her.

Run. They sensed us.

Dana dashed forward, breaking the touch with Mirris, but was still aware of something in the space beyond her sight. Something getting closer.

Hurry.

Dana pushed her legs, racing along what was now a much more familiar landscape.

"The stone is close," Dana whispered.

"Yeah, but so are they," Mirris said. "And they're running, too. I can sense them. I don't think Remiren knows I'm here, or she would be masking."

Remarkably, no animals in the forest had even hinted at their presence.

Ritser. He was masking them, hiding all of them from every creature in the woods. That was far beyond Dana's skill.

But their enchanter wasn't masking them. That meant—

"Don't listen to your thoughts," Dana said. "They're tricking us into running straight to them." But she didn't stop running. She was close to the place where the bloodstone lay only a few yards from view. The kazen must have gone beyond it and were coming back.

Every outcropping she passed seemed to be the one that would retreat into the small, dark hole that led to the pool. It was close.

"Stop, we've passed it," Ryke said, suddenly.

"Lies. Don't listen to it." Dana kept running and suddenly came upon the familiar spot. "Here. Here. Here." She dove into the cove, scrambled forward in the blackness, and found the mechanodron sack.

Then she pushed back out of the hole and handed it to Mirris.

"Get it to the sanctum. Hide it in that old supply store near the hot room." No one would look there.

Mirris nodded, shouldered the bag, and raced down the hill. She could mask herself well enough. There was a chance she could make it back without being noticed. But without Mirris, Remira could easily control Ryke. And that was a scary thought.

"Ryke, stay here," Dana said. "I'll go fetch the stone. Don't let them past you. If you think you need to go in to save me, it's a false thought. I'll only call 'go away' if I really need help."

"Got it."

"And if I want you to run, I'll say 'kiss me.'"

"Makes sense." He smiled. "Good luck."

Dana wormed through the hole once again, pushing along the familiar rock until her outstretched arm glowed over the sayathi-rich pool. The light was much dimmer than she remembered. Worse, the sayathenite nodes weren't sending pulses, they were receiving them from somewhere deeper in the cave.

It's been moved!

Perhaps the cave fish had ferried it a little further in, for safety.

This was going to get dangerous. If she got in the water to find the bloodstone and then tried to make it back to the sanctum, she could die of exposure. The only way to stay warm would be to make a fire, and then she would be found.

No need to risk it. The kazen can take it from here.

The kazen? It had to be a foreign thought.

Remiren's prompts were no longer vague sensations. Full, coherent thoughts were coalescing in her mind.

The Exalting

There was no more time to think. She couldn't trust her own thoughts anymore. Dana hastily unbuttoned her coat and stripped it off, scratching her elbow on the jutting piece of limestone. *Ow.*

Dana pulled off her boots and gloves and struggled out of her pants, leaving only her socks on her feet to avoid cuts from sharp cave rocks.

Ryke's voice shouted into the cave. "Dana, Korren is here. I can't fight him *and* Remiren."

She took a deep breath. "Then, kiss me."

"Dana—"

"Kiss me now!"

Dana crawled into the chill water of the pool in only her shirt, underwear, and socks.

Her breath came in ragged gasps. The muscles of her chest clamped like she was in a vise. She took a deep breath and plunged her head under the water.

Chapter 29

Aboard Shuttle 23, the near weightlessness of the orbital entry trajectory made Jet's head feel like a giant ball of water.

Monique drifted over from Shuttle 24 to where Jet's sleeping bag was strapped to a bulkhead. "You awake?"

"Yeah."

She sidled up to the bulkhead and drew a strap around her waist.

"Not a fan of zero-g?"

She shook her head. "Makes me anxious." Monique rested her head on Jet's shoulder. "My stomach is . . . not good."

"You're not going to puke on me?"

"This is better."

"You know, you're awfully distracting—walk into my room. Strap yourself to my bunk . . ."

"I know. Shut up."

"Yes, Corporal."

She lay there for the better part of an hour, her breathing punctuated by sighs.

"Are you crying?" Jet asked.

"Not yet."

Jet looked over at her. "What do you mean 'not yet'?"

"Well, this thing is bound to go badly. It's only a matter of time before—"

"Before what?"

Silence ate at Jet, a raw hunger of curiosity. What did Monique fear? Was it losing her own life, or losing him?

Had he been that blind?

She turned to face him. "Do you want to make out or something?"

"Just to pass the time?"

The Exalting

"Just to pass the time *with me*."

Jet swallowed. "Is this like a trick question?"

"Afraid not, Corporal."

He burst into laughter and Monique joined him. Then she pressed a kiss against his lips—a friendly peck that grew into a long, passionate kiss that only made the small space between them seem to grow.

"I can't hold onto you, can I?" Monique wrapped her hand behind Jet's neck.

"Not for long, I guess."

"Well, dang it."

"When did you decide having me around was so much fun?"

Monique shrugged. "I have eyes, don't I? You've been checking me out *at least* four hours a shift."

"Only four?" Jet said.

Monique sputtered a laugh and poked her finger into his chest. "You are trouble."

"Says the girl who—"

"Shut it, Corp, and kiss me again, before your defense AI gets jealous."

"Angel is not infatuated with me."

"She certainly had a few questions for me about you."

"Who started Angel up again?"

Monique blushed. "I did, of course."

Jet could see this going somewhere awkward. "You pulled rank—you and your college education—and ran my AI?"

"Just a little girl talk, that's all." Monique leaned up and kissed him again. In the meanwhile, she pulled her strap loose and wrapped it around both of them, buckling them together.

"No complaints?" she said, a glimmer in her eye. The warmth of her body pressed into his.

"No complaints."

She stared into his eyes and traced her fingers through his hair. "Why does this feel like losing you?"

Jet laid his forehead against hers. "Sometimes it hurts. It's what makes us human."

"I don't like it."

Emotion squeezed him. This was just a fling, of course—brought on by the insanity of their mission. "You want to keep me, for yourself?"

"What about the Xahna girl you were looking at pictures of?"

"Well that's pretty easy to explain. I was obviously projecting my male frustration onto a passive target."

"All that pent-up attraction—who could you possibly have been pining for?" Monique said, batting her eyelashes.

"What about you?" Jet said. "Were you just pretending to ignore me, or are you just really good at playing hard to get?"

"Well that's pretty easy to explain," she started, copying Jet's tactic. "I was obviously conscious of showing any sign of emotional attachment that might jeopardize my place on the mission."

"Ah, that makes sense."

Monique's pony-tailed hair drifted up in the microgravity. "Doesn't it?"

Jet wasn't sure if he believed her, and he wasn't sure she believed him. It was too much fun to let go of all that worry and let the pleasure of each other's company hide the fear and anxiety of an extra-terrestrial mission that carried the weight of an entire world's salvation and the fate of the Believers.

Here were two people clinging to what they desperately wanted to keep—a human connection, a semblance of hope.

Monique laid her head against Jet's chest, keeping one hand over his heart and the other arm looped behind his neck. Soon, she was asleep.

This is going to be interesting to explain when Fleet Command gets the monitor camera logs.

But rather than dreading the ribbing he would get, Jet basked in the fading light of human comradery. Very soon, he would be surrounded by alien creatures and alien life—the only human on Xahna.

The speaker blared. "Naman, we have confirmation from Fleet

The Exalting

Command." It was Captain Decker. "*Speaker for the Dead* is go. And I mean *now*."

"Some timing," Monique muttered.

Jet unclipped the buckle.

Dormit's voice sounded over the speaker. "How in tarnation did they approve that half-witted scheme?"

"I have people on the inside," Jet answered.

"People?" Dormit grumbled over the speaker.

"Well . . . person." It was the High Seer. She and Ahreth had probably both supported the strategy.

"Who?" Dormit growled.

"You know, I liked you better when you were in cryo."

"You would say that, you no-good, rotten horse thief!"

"Didn't we lock out his John Wayne library access? I thought we bit-bombed those files."

"'Fraid not, sucker."

"This is never going to work," said Teea's small voice.

"Thanks for the vote of confidence."

"And your Xahnan is still terrible."

"Noted." Jet nodded at Monique, who moved across the dock to the other shuttle and shut the hatch.

Jet shut his hatch and twisted the decoupling ring. "Bye."

He was alone, as the turquoise waters and white clouds of Xahna loomed in the viewport.

"One more thing," Decker said. "The orbital surveillance AI just picked up activity in Torsica. The ASP dropship in the Torsican capital is launching."

"What?"

"It's headed west. Looks like a suborbital trajectory parallel to yours. You're going to have company when you land."

"What kind of company?"

"As near as the orbital AIs can tell, ASP simuloids. The things that boarded the dropship look like Xahnans but have irregular thermal signatures."

"They made simuloids that look like Xahnans? Oh great." *At least I packed my rifle.*

"Whatever sort of rebellion this renegade in Shoul Falls is pushing for," Decker said, "she's about to be in way over her head. She doesn't know about the simuloids."

"What is the dropship's ETA at the Aesican coast?"

"Two hours."

"Mine?"

"Ninety minutes. Tiberius thinks they'll set down far enough from the city to avoid detection, then try to mingle with the population. We don't know their goal, but it probably involves you or the business with that renegade."

"My enemy's enemy is my friend," Jet said. "Looks like I gotta find that girl first. Angel, plot fastest approach to Shoul Falls."

"Done."

"Engage thrusters."

Submerged in the frigid cave water, Dana could see nothing but the feeble glow from her skin. Then a phosphorescent pulse ran along the bottom of the cave and forked out toward several sayathenite nodules. A myriad of weaker echo pulses ran back. Dana fixed her eyes on the place where she had last seen the glow and swam ahead in the darkness, her fingers brushing along the bottom of the cave pool, aware that overhead, the roof of the cavern was sloping down toward her head.

Dana pulled with her arms on any rocky shapes she found, propelling herself forward. There was no guarantee when, or if, she would find another place to breathe.

The cave fish couldn't have taken the bloodstone far.

I hope.

Light flickered along the floor of the cavern in a small pulse. Instead of following the pulse, Dana looked up, seeking for the telltale reflection from an air pocket.

There.

The Exalting

But it was too small to breathe from.

Hurry!

Dana kicked her bare legs, diving for the bottom to keep her head away from the sharp limestone crags on the top of the cave. Spreading her fingers to catch the water in the webbing between them, Dana propelled herself rapidly through the cave, following the current.

Another pulse of light ran through a small gap.

Clinging to the air in her lungs that tried to escape her in a last gasp for breath, Dana wiggled through the crevice and reached up to find that the cave roof tilted sharply upward. Dana kicked forward, and with a jolt of surprise, her hand rose completely out of the water. Dana took one desperate pull with her arms, and her head and shoulders rose completely out of the water.

Unfortunately, the cave had no bloodstone. Worse still, she wasn't alone.

An animal presence moved rapidly toward her through the water, its killer instinct roused.

Rakefish. A miner's worst nightmare.

Dana couldn't believe her luck.

Before the accelerating fish could strike at her and tear a chunk of flesh, Dana dove under and thrust every shred of will she could muster into the massive fish.

"Take me to the bright stone. Now!"

Dana grasped the stiff dorsal fin of the rakefish and was hauled swiftly along. A minute later she came up for a breath and switched rides to a larger rakefish with fresh strength in the muscles along its armor-scaled sides to drive its lashing tail.

Dana's mind wandered as the cold took her. Feeling in her extremities turned to the mere suggestion of touch. Only the rakefish's awareness of the massive drag coming from its fin told her she was still holding on.

There was total darkness save the light from the sayathi swarming around the bloodstone, beaming their strength to the ruling sayathi within. It was a remarkable organism, both photosynthetic and bioluminescent, as Forz described—or part plant and part animal, as Dana imagined them.

The rakefish slowed.

Dana came to the surface with barely enough will to breathe. She struggled along the shallow slope that lead over the sharp protrusions of sayathenite.

Light shone from the far end of the cavern, a familiar blue-green glow.

That's it!

Dana splashed forward. She struggled to reach the edge of the pool.

Resistance against the push of her kick told her that her numb feet had found the sloping cave floor.

Dana stood on her feet and clambered awkwardly over thick nests of sayathenite nodes, whose pointed shapes her feet scarcely registered through her soaked socks.

There were hundreds of the nodules.

This, Dana realized, must have been the central chamber of one of the bloodstones conquered by the Shoul Falls colony.

Animals must come to the pool to make blood sacrifices.

As she neared the center of the conquered colony where the glowing Shoul Falls bloodstone now commanded its empire of underwater colonies, Dana's feet found surer footing on a tree root running along the bottom of the cave, and she scrambled out of the water and up onto a dry section of cave floor.

She rubbed herself frantically, jumping and running in place.

A chill draft ran over her back, reminding Dana of the far colder air outside the sheltered cave. She squeezed out her hair and rubbed her numb hands on her body, trying to get dry. She ran in place, arms and legs responding far too slowly as she tried to force blood back into her unsteady limbs.

When she could bear the thought of getting back in the water, Dana waded back into the pool, chill water biting at her legs.

Dana leaned closer, reaching for the bloodstone. It seemed just below the surface.

The Exalting

What in the blue skies of Xahna?

The stone hadn't seemed nearly that large the last time she had touched it. She leaned even closer. Her jaw grew slack. Dozens of new faceted nodules riddled the outside of the bloodstone.

It's grown!

Perhaps the conquered master stones of the other pools had somehow transferred their ruling sayathi to this one.

But how could a microorganism travel so far?

The answer was obvious.

Cave fish.

This cavern was large enough for cave fish, but the small pool in Shoul Falls did not have any large fish.

Dana quickly grasped the stone and broke it from its pillar.

The pulses stopped.

Her hand glowing fiercely, Dana drew the much-larger bloodstone out of the water.

Gotcha.

The kazen could no longer track its position. And she was several hundred yards closer to the sanctum than where she entered the water.

I can make a run for it.

The cavern was lit with the faintest light from the cave exit.

Morning is coming.

The sun would soon be up.

Warmth. Even the memory of it seemed soaked with the cold that nearly immobilized her.

Dana struggled to the side of the pool, her will at the edge of abandonment.

Her body wanted only to lie on the limestone and die.

Get dry.

Dana removed her dripping shirt and wrung out her hair.

She brushed her hand against her forehead, but the gash had already been closed by the sayathi in the pool. They had formed some kind of thin, hard layer, like the secretions which built up the coral and the sayathenite nodules.

Dana climbed to her feet, and in the light glancing through a gap in the rock, spied something she could hardly believe.

Wood!

Some adventurous kids from Shoul Falls had apparently used the cavern for a hideout the previous summer.

And food!

Dana lifted a bag hanging from an outcropping. Inside was a mix of dried fruit, marmar jerky, and nuts.

Dana shoved a handful of nuts into her mouth and chewed ferociously. Then she knelt, and with shivering hands, struck sparks from the flint onto a nest of tinder, all the while blessing the adventurous kids who had dared trespass on the sacred mountain.

Flames licked up the tinder into the kindling. The sticks burned brightly, but the dry hardwood gave off little smoke. In moments, the shelter of the cavern was host to a raging fire. The air was smoky but breathable. Dana pressed close to the warmth of the fire, driving heat into her shivering body.

Dana hung her shirt and socks over the flickering flames, taking care to make sure they didn't catch fire. When they were dry and warm, she put them back on.

When the kazen realized they couldn't find her and that she had the stone, they would return to the sanctum. They had to defend the heated exalting chamber, in case Dana tried to use it.

She smiled.

But I'm not going back to the sanctum.

Not yet.

She needed clothes. She needed warmth. She needed privacy. She knew just the place.

Chapter 30

Monique's voice sounded in Jet's earpiece. "Shadow to Speaker for the Dead, corridor is clear. Confirm status. Over."

Approaching the Xahnan atmosphere, with his hands encased in several centimeters of ablative carbon hull sealant along with the rest of his body, Jet activated his transmitter with a coded thought pattern and replied, "Roger, Shadow. This is Speaker for the Dead. Status is three green lights. Mission is go. Over."

With Jet in the jump cocoon and glued to the back of Shuttle 23, the orbital maneuvering thrusters were on remote control. Waiting for the go-ahead from Monique felt like the longest thirty minutes of his life.

All the while the ASP dropship from Torsica was jetting over the Sayathi Sea, getting closer to Aesica.

The space jump kit used the shuttle's entire supply of hull breach patch material to weave a carbon-fiber cocoon around Jet. Ships never carried premade cocoons for lack of space and in case they needed the materials to make a repair.

One spinner was fast enough to shroud a dozen marines on a covert mission, as long as the first few to get their shrouds weren't claustrophobic.

The hard-ablative shell could hardly contain his excitement as adrenaline ran a steady stream of exhilaration into his veins.

"Hey, Jet," Monique said. "That satellite that we burned up left a gap in our communications relay, so the Nautilus has given me a few personal messages to relay—they're already over the horizon now."

"Alright. Let's get this over with."

"Dormit says, 'Ride 'em cowboy.'"

"I am not a cowboy."

"Also, the Caprian legal counsel wishes to express his sincere desire that you do not combust on entry. And that if you do, that it happens quickly and you do not suffer for long."

"Great."

"Teea says, 'I'll bet your nose itches.'"

Jet wrinkled his nose in vain. "That is so not funny. I'm not laughing. Nobody's laughing."

Monique giggled. "I'm laughing."

"Again, thank you for the obvious. Push the go button already."

"Shadow to Speaker," called Monique's voice. "Launch window is open. Commencing remote pre-ignition. Be careful."

"I don't have a choice," Jet said. "I'm stuck in a—"

The launch boosters took the air from Jet's lungs. Strapped to the back of the shuttle, he would be shielded from at least some of the heat of air braking.

Until he broke loose.

Minutes of regulated silence passed with only brief status updates sounding in his earpiece as Xahna grew larger and larger.

Jet considered booting Angel to listen to her commentary, but thought silence suited the moment. Then the press of his back against the jump cocoon signaled contact with the upper atmosphere.

"Air braking now," Jet reported as the pressure mounted to a level he hadn't felt since the oxygen-rich atmosphere of Rodor.

"Plasma cone expanding—going to lose you, Shadow. See you on the other side."

Buffeting shook Jet's teeth in his clenched jaw as the radio chatter gave way to static. The heat of reentry was building to a dangerous level but not something he couldn't endure.

Not reentry.

First entry.

I'm the first alien this close to Xahna.

As the heat mounted, the epoxy holding Jet to the shuttle would melt, and he would slip free.

The buffeting of the shuttle stopped for one brief moment, then hit Jet like an industrial hammer drill. "Re-re-re-leased," Jet

324

The Exalting

reported. The carbon-fiber capsule oriented in the air friction so that he was feet first.

Jet grunted to keep the blood in his head. "Don't pass out. Come on!"

Somewhere behind him, the shuttle would be breaking up in a stream of debris over the shallow sea between Torsica and Aesica.

Finally, the pressure against his feet began to slacken, but the temperature was extreme. He felt as though he were being cooked alive. "Shadow, this is Speaker. Reaching terminal velocity."

"Roger, Speaker. Your trajectory is off. Landing zone is now fifty klicks beyond target. You're headed for the mountains."

Fifty klicks! It would take him a day and a half to get back to Shoul Falls. It was time he couldn't spare. That renegade with the bloodstone needed him.

Gotta lose altitude . . . or some mass.

"Requesting permission to alter flight trajectory."

"Speaker, you are not approved for high altitude wing suit operation."

"Jettisoning ablation armor," Jet said. He punched the early release button and held it for three seconds.

"Acknowledged," Monique said. "You're going rogue. How long did it take—fifteen minutes?"

Electrical pulses shimmered along the edges of the jump cocoon, triggering micro explosives that shredded the remaining armor into thin filaments of carbon fiber. Light flooded his eyes with an expansive view of tall, white clouds.

Jet paced his breathing. He only had the air in his suit, now. His altimeter ticked off distance from the ocean as he shot through the upper atmosphere toward the coast.

Jet activated his tactical AI. "Angel, help me!"

"Loading ballistics. Running sims." Angel's voice sounded in his earpiece. "Jet are you nuts! Humans are not missiles."

"Water under the bridge, Angel. I need data!"

The clouds thinned. Ocean and land appeared below.

Falling was a lot less scary when you couldn't see what you were going to hit.

"Deploy drag chute in five, four, three, two—that was one second early, you idiot human."

"Acknowledged." The drag chute jerked Jet backward just as the green coast of Aesica flashed past. He ripped through a layer of clouds and continued his free fall.

"Jet, the winds are too strong. They'll take you beyond the landing zone. You have to release your chute."

Jet yanked on the chute release.

"I believe that was your main chute."

"Crap." So there was a point to getting certified for this sort of thing. "Oh well. I'll wing it down. Deploying wing suit." Jet extended his arms, stretching thin fabric wings between his arms and body, and between his legs.

"Enjoy your high speed landing," Angel shouted over the roar in his ears. "Just don't lead with your head. I want to survive this."

Free fall turned to a glide as Jet used his hands and feet like rudders to guide his trajectory.

As he soared more than forty thousand feet over the coastal jungle, Jet arched his back, attempting to eek more distance out of the glide.

"You do realize that if you hit one of those rhynoid vines, it will kill me as well?" Angel said.

"Well, now that you mention it," Jet toned sarcastically. He grunted as he held his arms against the force of the wind. With Jet falling quickly and the terrain rising into rolling hills and finally sharp mountains, he rapidly ran out of altitude. "Hey, that's the falls. Looks like we're going to make it."

Jet angled his trajectory to track north of the city. The alpine forest was all but untouched save the occasional clearing or trail.

"This place is pristine."

"Like Avalon before ASP," Angel said. "Jet, I'm highlighting your landing zone in your reticle."

"That's tiny. Is that the best you can do—a patch of snow?"

"Look, I'm not the one who dropped his landing chute over the

The Exalting

sea."

"Keep it up, and I'm going to dial down your snark setting."

"You wouldn't dare." Angel paused. "You're coming in too low. Have you been snacking on transuranic elements?"

"Brought a little extra ammo—just in case." Jet arched his back and spread his arms as wide as he could, but the more he slowed, the steeper his glide became.

"Jet, watch out!"

Not the trees again.

"Impact!"

In the dim light of early morning, Dana left the cave at a desperate sprint. The sun was not yet up, and chill winter air nipped her skin. In bare socks, she charged down the slope, unable to hide the much larger bloodstone she held in her fist. She quickly reached the cover of the pine forest, heedless of the damage she was doing to her feet.

Running like her life depended on it was the only way to keep from freezing to death. It was her will against the chill.

Run. Harder.

Her target was the infirmary. Dana had visited it with Kaia on her way to the ranger's stables, where Kaia had picked up some ingredients for treating injuries. Two nurses were there and had changed into drab hospital garments to begin their shifts.

Their spare clothes would be in the changing room.

Warm clothes. The thought spurred Dana's racing heart as she headed for the infirmary in the early morning light.

But she had to be careful. She had the stone now—stolen right in front of the kazen. As far as they knew, she was a blood traitor. And they would treat her like it unless she could prove that somebody else—like Korren—was trying to get it for themselves.

If she was captured, they would take no chances. She would be iced on angel's kiss and then executed.

I can't let that happen, Dana thought. Shoul Falls needed her as ka. All of Aesica needed her.

Dana followed the route she had used the first time she snuck into the city, racing past the lake below the falls and climbing over the wall.

Again the streets were empty and silent. Lamps flickered in the windows of warm houses. When Dana reached the infirmary, she opened the unlocked door and crept inside.

The duty nurse was still asleep on her cot.

Dana shut the door softly and stepped carefully into the main room. She headed to the prep room in the back and carefully shut the door behind her. The room had a small window through which dawn light trickled in. In the center of the room was a wash basin. The water from the previous night was cold. But Dana braved it in the name of survival, scrubbing herself with soap. She scrubbed her hair especially, attempting to rid herself of the smell of smoke, then toweled off and dumped her dirty shirt in the laundry bin.

She pulled on the duty nurse's trousers, shirt, and shoes, and snuck back into the main room and hid under an empty bed with used sheets piled on either side of it.

She forced herself to lie still.

It's going to work.

Soon, exhaustion took her. Dana woke with a start at the sound of the city siren.

Dana opened her eyes. From the light she could see from the bed, it seemed it was at least mid-morning.

There was the sound of scuffling as the duty nurse walked into the patient room. "We've been quarantined by the civic guard," the nurse announced, probably to the few elders in the infirmary who were roused by the siren. "We'll just wait inside until the all-clear."

They'll search every building in town, Dana thought. *One by one.*

A door knock sounded, followed approaching boots.

"Your roster of patients, please. Four is all?"

"Yes, the three you see. But we had one pass away yesterday, in that bed over there."

So that was why the used sheets were on the floor.

The Exalting

Perfect. They wouldn't want to look too closely at a bed where someone had just died.

"I see. We'll just check the back room."

As the boots passed, stepping well clear of her hiding place, Dana gave the slightest smirk.

"No one in here. Mark it clear. Check the back alley. Good day, nurse. Sorry to bother you and your patients."

"I do hope you find the—who are you looking for?"

"The Norrian. She's wanted for stealing the bloodstone. Capital offense. She took it right in front of the kazen. There were three witnesses."

"Dear me, do you mean Dana?"

"Of course."

"She's an angel. She would never—"

Dana's heart leapt. The nurse saw her like no one ever had. An angel—a gift of the Creator. She wasn't a criminal. She was merely keeping the stone from the hands of whoever Sindar had tried to keep it from. Korren, probably.

"Well, she did. And she'll die by foreign water. Vetas-ka's fleet is already on the Sayathi Sea. He's coming for the stone. If we don't find the girl and the stone, we risk losing it to him."

The door shut, and after several minutes attending the other patients with breakfast, the nurse's footsteps came to Dana's bed. She bent down and looked at Dana. "You *are* here."

Dana drew her finger to her lips.

The nurse choked a surprised cry. Then she whispered, "Do you have the stone?"

Dana slid out from under the bed to see that the other patients were still prone in their beds, before she whispered, "It's safe. A kazen is trying to get it for himself. I have to keep it from them."

The nurse nodded, somehow believing every word. "It was bound to happen. We should have chosen a ka. I always told them someone would get greedy." She checked the door. "Well the civic guard is gone now. What will you do? I can't keep you in here."

Dana sighed resignedly, trying to sound sincere. "I'll have to

329

go work things out with the civic guard. It's not like they said. The stone was in danger. I saved it."

"I hope that's true," said the nurse. "But why are you wearing my clothes?"

"Sorry. I was wet and cold," Dana said. "I'll just go change out of them." When Dana got to the back room, intending to escape out the back door, she noticed the cubby that held alchemical agents used by the nurses. It must have been where Kaia had gotten her supplies.

What if I'm captured?

Wouldn't hurt to have a little insurance.

Dana claimed a small vial from a labelled cubby and tucked it into her tie-top between her breasts. She prayed the vial's lid wouldn't come loose.

With the nurse waiting outside the door, Dana stowed the bloodstone in a laundry bag, covered it with spare sheets, then opened the window, climbed on the wash counter, and wriggled out, keeping the bag close to her chest.

The back alley was empty. The quarantine had not yet been lifted. Dana headed out of the alley, across the street, and back toward the way she had come in over the climbable section of wall.

The last obstacle was the east quarter zone office.

Dana ducked behind a barrel as two civic guards emerged.

"It's not just that," said the older of the two men, who bore a handlebar mustache of silver hair that matched his sifa. "The citizen council will destroy the bloodstone the moment they get their hands on it. Twice now they've lost it."

Dana's heart stung at the words. *I can't let that happen. Not after all I went through to save it.*

Yet here she was, running away with the gathered will of an entire city—more than twenty thousand souls. It didn't belong to her. Yet, she had it in the name of protecting it. But from whom? The citizen committee had ordered that it be destroyed.

But hadn't things changed since she had returned? Hadn't they seen that they could fight, that they had to fight? Hadn't they seen

The Exalting

that she could lead them?

Dana's heart stung so deeply, it was as though a dagger had been thrust into her.

Am I not good enough?

"And what about the girl?" asked the younger soldier.

The older man, probably an officer, if not the head of the civic guard, shook his head. "Even if they spare her—which isn't likely—the Norrians have demanded her extradition."

What? Dana's already strained heart skipped a beat. Norr was demanding she be returned for trial. And that would mean the punishment for not just greeder theft but blood-binding—execution by foreign water.

"The official notice just arrived today," the man said, clasping his hands behind his back and setting his jaw, as if to suppress some tremor in his fingers or lip. "They sent an official and something like twelve rangers to bring her back."

"Twelve rangers—what for?"

"To make sure they get what they want."

"Since when do we do what the Norrians say?" said the younger officer.

"Norr, we can handle. But the situation has changed." The older man looked the junior officer in the eye. "They claimed they'll appeal to the Aesican Pantheon if we don't comply."

"But," blustered the younger man, whose goatee was as unimpressive as the whine in his voice, "we don't have a ka to represent us. They'll side with the Norrians—they supply most of the large sayathenite for North Aesica. The stuff from the coast is too small for mechanodrons."

"So, we either kill her ourselves, or send her to Norr to face their justice," said the mustached man. "Pity. Forty years we've waited for someone like that: strong, brave, willing to make personal sacrifices." He shook his head as if in disbelief. "She seemed like the right type, you know?"

"But she took the stone from the kazen," said the younger man. "She really must be just a thief."

331

It was a moment that captured all of Dana's hopes and fears in one. Was she truly a desperate thief? Dana looked to the city wall. It was within running distance. She could escape with the stone. She could find another exalting chamber. But she couldn't seem to stomach the idea. It was pure theft of will.

It was what Vetas-ka was trying to do.

The older man shook his head. "I wish I knew the full story. Why is Norr sending so many rangers just to apprehend a common thief? Wouldn't they rather be rid of her if she ran away? They aren't fond of adepts, you know."

"Yeah," mused the younger man. "They must be trying to make an example out of her. She's flaunted everything they believe in— even blood-bound herself. It's sacrilege to them. They won't want others to try the same thing."

"What would a person like Dana have to gain from stealing the stone?" the senior officer wondered. "If you want to solve a crime, you have to know the motivation. That's what we're missing."

I wanted to help, Dana thought. *Truly.*

Or did I just want power?

"She could be stealing it for someone else," suggested the fellow with the goatee.

"Then why did she bring it back in the first place?"

The soldier frowned.

"Can't you see? We're missing something critical."

"She could be mentally unstable."

"That is a possibility," agreed the captain of the guard. "Though unlikely. You felt her. Did you trust her?"

The man hesitated. "Yes, sir. Completely."

"So," said the captain, "what follows from that?"

"If she really is trustworthy," said the man, "she'll turn in the stone."

"At peril of her own life?" said the captain.

"She risked her life already," the soldier said. "But was that for her own purposes or the good of others?"

"Only she knows," said the officer.

The Exalting

Only I know.

There came times, Dana knew, when a choice had to be made. And that choice would define not only her, but the future of Shoul Falls, and possibly Norr as well.

Would others see her execution for what it was? Suppression.

Or would she save her own life and deny Shoul Falls the very same right for which she had fled Norr: self-determination?

I can't keep it. It isn't mine.

But if turn it in, Dana thought, *would they still kill me?*

A surge of fear rushed within her.

The soldier had said he trusted her. Obviously so did the captain. Perhaps she could offer trust as well. But then what? They had to serve the extradition. She would end up in the hands of the Norrian rangers.

Then what? Pain?

Dana flexed her hands into fists. *I'm not afraid of pain.*

And hadn't Sindar felt peace in that place beyond?

But there would be no Ryke. No Forz. No Kaia or Mirris.

No chance to see what she was really capable of.

No, she thought. *I determine that, right now.* Her hands trembled uncontrollably. *I can't do this. I can't.*

"She seemed like the right type, you know."

I am!

Whether she had done it only for the hope that she would become a ka mattered not. What she chose now would define everything.

Forsaking all hope for herself, Dana embraced her chance. *It's my choice.* She stood up from behind the barrel and spoke in a voice as bold as a challenger in a duel.

"I am."

The men's jaws dropped.

"I am the right type."

The soldier flinched, but the captain seemed to regard her with pure amazement.

"I have the bloodstone right here." Dana drew the crystal out

333

of the bag. She swallowed as her heart tried to leap out her throat.
Courage.

"Be careful, it's grown recently. I ask only that you don't let the kazen have it. Sindaren took it away because he feared one of them was in league with the Vetas-kazen. Keep it safe. I'll . . . answer to the Norrians."

The head of the guard stared in disbelief. Here Dana was, surrendering not only the bloodstone but also herself, to certain destruction. His eyes widened. His response was a single word. "Why?"

Dana raised all six sifa, a gesture of both complete surrender and intimate regard, showing that she had nothing to hide. She set the bloodstone on the barrel. "Please escort me to the Norrian guards. I won't risk our city losing the favor of the Pantheon and suffering their wrath."

"Is this a trick?" the soldier whispered. "How can she . . ."

"I don't know what to say," said the older officer.

"And please return these to the infirmary," Dana said, dropping the bag to the cobblestone street. "I just borrowed . . . stole them . . . to hide the stone."

A feeling of complete and total emptiness found Dana as she stepped back from the stone. She was free, once and forever. Free from other people's limits and definitions. She had made her choice. She stood tall, unafraid.

"I surrender."

What the other men saw in her eyes, she could only guess. But at that moment, they seemed to be looking up at her, a girl about to be taken for execution. How her grandfather would be surprised to hear how she had died, and the stories passed on by the people of Shoul Falls, of the one who could have been something powerful but chose instead to be something great and small. Something wise and wonderful and forsaken.

"I accept your surrender," said the officer, standing at attention, as if speaking not to a prisoner but an opposing general. "I can only assume you had the best intentions."

334

The Exalting

"She did it," the soldier muttered. "She sacrificed herself." He looked at the captain. "But what about Norr?"

The captain's jaw wormed. "For the good of the city," he muttered. "I must hand her over." Duty seemed to bear down on the man's shoulders. Finally, he squared them. With eyes glistening with emotion, he gave her a small nod.

"I don't blame you," Dana whispered. "It's not your fault."

"That is . . . very kind of you say." The captain, taking hold of his charge, nodded to the soldier, who stepped forward with iron manacles.

"Dana . . . I'm going to have to bind you," said the soldier. "And give you angel's kiss. The Norrian chancellor demanded it."

Perhaps her enemy in the sanctum had even suggested it to them.

"Of course," Dana whispered. How else could it end, but like this? Cut off from everything, even pain.

What she wouldn't give to feel pain now. To go on living and fighting. But she was free. And she would stay free.

By the time the all-clear sounded in ringing echoes of trumpets across the city and across the mountainside, Dana was in a steam-wagon, headed north for the last time. With the icy angel's kiss drops still numbing her lips, Dana was headed to Norr for trial and execution by foreign water, like an ignominious criminal.

But Dana was not a common Xahnan. She was better. She had proven it. Dana had saved the stone, not once, but four times. And though her friends had suffered—Forz, a shattered leg; and Ryke, his standing with the sanctum for helping her—Dana had saved the will of an entire city.

Doubtless, when the citizen's meeting convened, the stone would be taken to the square and a blazing fire brought upon it. Whether the ruling sayathi would perish in the blaze, sending a wave of agony through all those bound to them, Dana would never know. The angel's kiss hid all such connections.

Vetas-ka's prize would be destroyed, and his vengeance on her served prematurely by the harsh law of Norr. But would the

Pantheon of Aesica stand up to him? Or were they doomed to surrender when he came to conquer?

Yet, it was not the only choice the council could make.

They could choose a new ka.

Turning herself over to Norr was a terrible risk. Dana had no idea if her gambit would pay off.

It's the only way to show who I am.

She was now committed to a staring contest with death. She was not going to blink.

One chance.

Numb to even the fear of her own death, Dana looked out through the narrow windows to draw some distraction from the passing evergreens. Rangers traveling alongside the steam-wagon on greeders blocked most of the view.

Suddenly, the steam-wagon hissed to a stop.

A word passed from the conductor in the boiler control through a panel to the passenger coach.

Dana supposed the stop was to refill the water tank from a bank of snow. But then one of the two rangers not shackled to Dana dismounted from the barred cabin, as a man on a greeder, draped in a gray winter riding blanket, strode to a stop. Dana recognized the rider. It was another Norrian ranger.

"Cyric, what is the word?"

"The citizen council of Shoul Falls," said the breathless ranger. "They voted."

The face of the ranger that had dismounted from the cabin of the steam-wagon took on a smug expression. "Then the bloodstone was destroyed? The city is free like Norr?"

The ranger on the greeder, his face pale despite the bite of the frost that should have left it red, shook his head. "No. They chose a new ka."

"A new ka—after forty years?"

Dana's heart leapt.

"Captain Mol, you must get the prisoner to Norr as quickly as possible," said Cyric.

336

The Exalting

The captain's eye's narrowed.

"They've chosen Dana."

Me!

Dana's heart skipped a double beat. Warmth flooded into her, the tips of her sifa flaring in excitement.

There was hope. Ka were immune to inter-city disputes. Only the Pantheon could judge a ka. They would have to release her.

Mol's eyes went wide. "They will send an embassy for her."

"Very likely, sir. I didn't wait around to find out."

"Get off," ordered Mol. "Bring the girl!" Dana was immediately pulled from the cabin and set in front of Mol in the saddle, with her legs bound to the sturdy greeder.

"No!" Dana cried. "You can't do this. I've been chosen!"

"Hya!" Mol's command sent the large greeder bounding forward. Had she any connection to the veil, Dana could have stopped it instantly.

Of course, there was a way to save herself. She had to get her powers back. She had to drink the viper's embrace she had taken from the infirmary. Dana shook at the very thought of it.

It was now or never.

Dana leaned forward and reached into the top of her shirt, pulling the small vial from where it was hidden in her tie-top.

With only a moment to act, Dana's entire body cried out in protest. Bitter tears ran from her eyes as she bit the stopper from the vial and poured the cursed liquid into her mouth.

Dana's scream rose over the sound of a soldier's warning horn. The memory of the viper's embrace Mirris had placed on her wound did no justice to what Dana felt. Her spirit was torn into shreds, her body was flayed by a thousand whips, ran through with a million burning stakes. In seconds, she had but one desire: to simply cease existing.

No.

Die! Her spirit cried in protest to the agony that rent her.

As her eyes closed, the world was suddenly bright, bright beyond anything possible. Shadows moved closer, drawing ever nearer as the pain moved away to a place distant.

A hand reached out, one she recognized. A familiar voice touched her mind.

"It's alright."

Sindaren?

"Have you come to find peace already? Let me show you the great beyond."

NO!

Dana stood in the gale of pain. *I was chosen. I was chosen.*

The world disappeared in grays and blacks. Only the steady thumping of the greeder's feet told her she was alive. Each pounding step sent shudders of pain through her, hammers driving spikes through her ears and eyes and temples. Her skin burned like she had fallen into the fireplace and lay there among the glowing embers.

Dana forced a breath into her lungs, shuddering at the icy pain that shot through her ribs. Finally, she forced her eyes open and reached out to the forest.

Her only answer was from rasp-wings nestled deep in a tree trunk.

Dana summoned them all.

As the greeder passed the hive, a swarm of stinging rasp-wings shot out from the tree and assaulted her captor, their burning stings causing partial paralysis.

Mol screamed and flailed, trying to ward them off.

Dana snatched his keys and threw an elbow hard into Mol's side. He tried to grab her as he tipped from the greeder, but his paralyzed fingers offered no grip.

The greeder she was bound to carried Dana away from Mol and the swam of rasp-wings.

"Good day, Captain Mol. Let's hope our paths don't cross again."

Dana hastily unlocked the shackles on her wrists and tossed them aside. She was headed for Shoul Falls to become the ka—a goddess.

338

The Exalting

As the greeder accelerated on the downhill slope, bounding and gliding, Dana's own heart did the same.

I can't believe it.

The journey was only eighteen miles.

On the greeder, she could reach the sanctum in less than an hour, so long as she wasn't caught by the rangers that Mol had left behind with the steam-wagon—and Vetas-ka didn't find a way to stop her.

Chapter 31

Dana took a shortcut off the trail, avoiding the soldiers' steam-wagon returning to Norr. From atop a nearby rise she watched it pass, then wound her way back to the trade road.

She would soon find the kazen from Shoul Falls. And then, she would go to the exalting chamber.

She nearly shook from excitement.

I can't believe it.

As she rode the bounding greeder toward Shoul Falls, she thought of the warnings her grandfather had given her of the unending burden, the feelings of guilt, and the moral conundrums.

He knew.

She didn't have to go to Shoul Falls. She could run for it and leave the city to itself. But with every step, she knew this was her path.

I am going to be ka.

I'm ready to fight.

Dana's eyes darted toward a gliding object that streaked low over the trees on the near side of the rise that separated her from Shoul Falls.

She thought it was a greeder, but it was too high and too fast, and it was headed toward the mountain, not gliding from it.

The shape was almost . . . Xahnan.

It crashed into a tree and disappeared from view. A clan of marmars shrieked at the intrusion.

What in the name of the Creator?

Dana knew she should stay on the path. In only a few minutes, she would be found by the kazen and on her way to Shoul Falls to become the ka.

But this was something completely unexplainable. There was nothing like it on Xahna, no airship or animal.

The Exalting

Other worlds.

Was it possible?

And why would they choose now to arrive?

The odds were silly. But that didn't make the arrival of a strange flying thing any less remarkable. In any case, the danger to her was past. The rangers would return to Norr without her.

Suddenly pain raked Dana's side.

The marmars!

Something was attacking them.

"That's it."

"Branch!"

Jet crashed through the low brush of the purple-needled pine forest as a colony of chubby primates pursued him with all the vigor of steroid-enraged Avalonian bat chickens.

"Can I shoot?" He didn't want to waste ammo, but the feisty little buggers were testing his patience.

"You're on limited ammo."

"Come on, Angel. Just one or two." Jet jumped a fallen log and knocked aside a purple-needled pine bough.

"You know it's not going to be just one or two. Don't even start with that nonsense."

"Ah, go stuff yourself in a zip file."

"Jet."

"Fine. I'll use nonlethal rounds." Jet whirled around, drew his suppressor, and fixed it to the barrel. He dropped to one knee, chambered a round, sighted, and squeezed off a shot at a monkey just as it leapt. *Can't change trajectory mid-leap.* Then he swiveled twenty degrees to his right, waited a heartbeat, and sent another monkey into spastic fits with shock rounds.

"That's two shots," Angel reminded. "Party's over."

"Fine. Old-fashioned way." Jet drew his survival knife. "Bring it on, you sons of glitches!" He usually reserved that curse for fighting

341

AI bounder mechs, his least favorite foes. But these monkeys were really vying for the top spot.

The drawn blade had the desired effect. The pack scattered in a chorus of shrieks.

"Now it's time for me to disappear." Jet tagged his wrist-mounted control, and his camo unraveled into a curly mess that resembled a half-decent ghillie suit. He crept around a rise and hunkered down next to a boulder. Balancing his rifle on the fold-out rest, he sighted two miles down range.

"There's the falls."

"Perimeter clear. I can't see through your boulder, though. Permission to deploy a dragonfly drone?" Angel asked.

"No need. Save the juice."

"This boulder gets in the way of all my sensors. I hate being blind."

"It also hides me," Jet said as he continued scanning the perimeter of the city. It was quiet.

"Any luck patching into a surveillance bug?" he asked, hoping one of the AI satellites had conveniently dropped one.

Angel replied with a tone that meant no.

"Got it. We're blind and deaf." He let out a slow breath. "How the heck am I going to find her? A bunch of them have been disappearing into the mountain—probably some kind of enclave. That's going to be a bugger to find an entrance to—and not a great place for first contact. I need her alone."

"Speaking of . . . did you miss me the last day on the shuttle?" Angel said.

"No."

"Not even a little bit?" she said in a playful voice.

"Are you—what is your current tease setting?"

"Do I have to answer?"

"It's too high. Bump it down."

"Fine. How are your buttocks feeling?"

She was referring to his crash landing, he realized. With teasing suppressed, protection instinct was the next highest priority.

The Exalting

"Sore, thank you for asking—oh, is that what I think it is?" Jet peered at a highlight in his reticle. "I'm picking up a thermal trail. There's a vent, and another one. That's got to be the kazen convent."

"Now what?" Angel asked.

"Write a report and send it orbit-side."

"Done. What else?"

"Now we wait. Wake me up if anyone goes into or out of that hill."

A voice sound from behind, talking in *Xahnan*.

"How did you get here?"

Jet whirled around, cursing under his breath. How in the destroyer's name had someone snuck up on him?

Even more shocking was the fact that the person standing in front him was *the* renegade. Her swagger was just as obvious up close as it had been from the satellite pictures. She stood with both hands in fists.

"You are not of my city."

Angel's translation of her words appeared in his display, but he didn't need to read them. Those words he understood well enough.

"I am not of your world," Jet answered. "I have come to save you. You're in danger."

That was as much of his pre-prepared speech as he could remember.

Rather than back away, the renegade took two quick steps forward. She was just an inch and a half taller than Jet, though he far outweighed her .

"You are not—" she began, then stopped as she peered at his neck.

Jet slowly unbuckled his helmet and removed it, placing it on the rock.

"You have no sifa."

"No sifa." He held up his hands and spread his unwebbed fingers. "Surprise."

Her eyebrows narrowed. "What are you?"

343

"A marine." Too late, he realized the word meant nothing to her.

"Where did you come from?"

"Er, basic training."

That she seemed to understand. "You are a fighter."

"Yes. Like you. My name is Jet Naman."

The girl's sifa pressed tighter against her head and the back of her neck as if deflated. He assumed that meant she didn't trust him. "I'm Dana, formerly of Norr."

"I watched you from the . . . up," Jet pointed to space. He had forgotten the words for heaven and stars. A smile tweaked up from the edge of his lips. "We are alike."

"Alike?"

"We stay alive." He had meant to say they were compatible because they were both survivors, but in the moment none of the Xahnan words were coming to mind.

"I don't believe you." She raised her hand to do something possibly dangerous.

"Wait." He held out his wrist and toggled its small screen on. In a few clicks he selected the fleet registry. "This is my thing for crossing the . . ."

"Stars?"

"Yes." Jet chose the flagship, and a 3-D image of the Excalibur appeared, complete with glowing purple ion engines.

"By the Creator . . ." Dana whispered. "What is that?"

"Technology," Jet said. "Like your mechanodrons, but more . . . good." *Sophisticated* was the word he couldn't find.

The lowest two of her sifa slowly extended. Jet wasn't sure if that was a good sign or a very bad one.

"And I have a mechanodron mind in my helmet," Jet added.

She made a scoffing expression.

"My people have no kazen—no adepts. There is no sign of the Creator or his power. We have questions. And we have crossed the . . ."

"Stars," she said again, reminding him of the word.

344

The Exalting

"Yes. We crossed the stars to find the answers."

The Xahnan drifted one step closer.

"We found seven worlds beyond our own, all with creatures like us."

"And Xahna?"

"Including Earth—my world—Xahna is the ninth." Jet said. "We think there are three more. The last is the home of the Creator . . . we hope."

"The legend of the twelve worlds," she whispered. "It's true."

"Yes," Jet said, a little of his swagger coming back into his expression. "We came on the star . . . things. And I chose you for first seeing."

Dana smiled. "You came looking for me?"

"Yup."

"You were looking in the wrong direction."

I'm new here, obviously, Jet thought. "I'm not the only one from the stars. There's another sky thing coming here from Torsica. Here in twenty or thirty minutes."

"From Torsica?"

"Yes. Our enemies reached Xahna before us," Jet explained. "They seek only money and power." That was a phrase he had seared into his memory.

"That explains why they went to Torsica. They must have contacted Vetas-ka."

She was quick on the uptake.

"Our rangers should be able to detain anybody without sifa," she said.

Jet shook his head. "These are simuloids." He searched for a better word. "Like mechanodrons. Only they look like Xahnans."

"Mechanical beings?"

"Yes."

"Our adepts won't be able to sense them." Her gaze drifted skyward and then turned to Jet. "What about you? Can your," she paused, as if trying to remember a word, ". . . *tech-ogy* detect them?"

345

Jet lifted his helmet. "It sees warm things. I can maybe see them. But not in a big group." He looked at Dana. "What do they want here?"

Her eyes narrowed. "I am about to become the ka of Shoul Falls. Our bloodstone is the only one that rivals Vetas-ka's."

Jet snapped his fingers. "I knew it. So you are the only thing between him and controlling all of Xahna?"

"Yup."

"Hah. That explains a lot." Jet rubbed his chin. The simuloids were perfect for killing a ka. "How soon can you do this . . . ka change?"

"As soon as I get back to the sanctum. But the exalting ceremony will take several hours to complete. Once I have united with the bloodstone, I will have the combined will of everyone in Shoul Falls. I can summon fire or lightning and destroy them all."

It was true. "So a ka *is* a god."

"Goddess. The will of my power comes from the people of the city."

"Well we don't have time. They'll be here too soon. You could hole up in the sanctum while you make the change, but their sky boat has weapons that could destroy your entire city in a few minutes—that would destroy your ka power. We have to destroy the simuloids."

Dana crossed her arms. "I don't understand. If those simuloids are so powerful, why would they serve Vetas-ka?"

"Our enemy—ASP—would rather deal with one ruler than fighting cities. It's better for trade."

Jet's helmet gave a short buzz. "Sorry, someone is calling."

The man buckled his helmet, and a glass piece slid into place over his eyes. He spoke in a strange language.

Dana leaned closer. The helmet was actually speaking back to him, making sounds in his ear.

346

The Exalting

"What is making those words?"

"It's like a mechanodron mind," he said. "It wants to talk to you."

Dana laughed. "Your helmet?"

He lifted the helmet and handed it to her.

Not one to be outdone by a star-man, Dana took the helmet, turned it over, and then dropped it on her head. The fit was awkward, given that it wasn't designed for someone with sifa. The next moment a voice spoke in her ear, in perfect Xahnan—not Jet's broken speech.

"Good morning, Dana. I am Angel, a machine intelligence created to protect Jet Naman. I am very pleased to make your acquiantence."

"Well, she's a lot more polite than you!" Dana exclaimed. "This is—how is this possible?"

"I put power in it," Jet said. "With sunlight."

"Sunlight?"

Jet nodded. He wasn't going to try to explain photovoltaic cloth.

"It's the most amazing thing I've ever seen."

Jet reached out, putting his hand on her forearm. "I've seen four worlds, Dana. Trust me. You are the most amazing thing I've ever seen."

"That was the worst line I've ever heard."

"What—no. It wasn't that bad."

"It was terrible," said the voice in the helmet called Angel. It paused, then said quietly, "Jet hasn't told you he came here to die."

"What?"

"He usually leaves out the important things."

Dana turned aside and spoke softly. "What do you mean 'he came to die'?"

"Hey—what is this, girl-talk time?" Jet said. "That's *my* AI."

"It was prophesied that Jet—and many others—would die defending Xahna. They must fall before Xahna can rise again."

"Are you a prophet?" Dana asked.

"No, but I know one," said Angel.

"I want to speak to him," Dana said.

"It's a she," said Angel. "And she will not be here for twenty days, when the rest of our small fleet arrives."

"Twenty days? But Vetas-ka will reach Aesica before then."

"Yeah, I know," Jet interrupted.

"I'm talking to Angel," Dana replied curtly.

"She only knows what I tell her," Jet said.

"Obviously not—she knows a bad line when she hears one."

Jet chuckled and looked over at a nearby stream. "Man, I wish I could drink from that."

"If you want to die," Dana said, in a serious tone. She pointed to the helmet. "Can I keep this?"

Jet's jaw went slack. "Uh, no. It's government property."

"He's jealous," said the Angel. "Let him have his helmet back. We can talk again later."

Dana sighed. "I think you're amazing."

"Thank you," said Angel. "That's the nicest thing anyone has ever said to me."

"Well, you're certainly welcome," said Dana. She lifted the helmet off her head, careful not to ruffle her sifa, and handed it back to Jet.

"What was that all about?"

Dana ignored him and pointed at his tube-ended weapon. "Is that the thing you used to hurt those marmars?"

"Yes. It's a gun. It throws small heavy . . . things very fast. I used . . . nice ones on the marmars. The others kill."

"How far can it shoot?"

"Two of your miles."

"Ka of Xahna," Dana whispered. "How is that possible?"

"Gun powder."

"Ah, alchemy."

"Simuloids conceal these weapons called 'guns' in their bodies," Angel said, from the helmet's external speaker.

Dana nodded. "So they can kill before we get close." She

348

looked at Jet "How many more 'marines' are there are on Xahna?"

"Just me. I have some friends in a small sky boat flying around Xahna. The rest of the Believers won't arrive for three more weeks. The enemy fleet arrives three months after that."

"Can we win?"

Jet breathed out heavily. "We sort of can't."

Dana shrugged. "We'll find a way. Let's go. We need to reach my kazen."

Dana hurried over the rise and followed the small stream toward the city.

Other worlds.

It was no wonder she had seen them when she took the viper's embrace. They were coming. All of them. All at once. And Xahna was to be their battleground.

If there was ever a time they needed a ka, it was now. But there wasn't time.

A presence touched her mind, probably Remira. It felt like a lost thought returning.

"Are you safe?"

Yes. But I can't come now, Dana thought, conveying each word as clearly as she could. *I have a visitor from the stars. The legends of the other worlds are true. And their enemies are—*

Jogging beside her, Jet suddenly looked up and cursed in his language. "The dropship—it's here already."

There was black speck in the distance. But it was approaching much faster than an airship.

"I thought you said twenty minutes?"

"They must have taken a transorbital trajectory."

"A what?"

"A sky hop. I didn't think they would be in such a hurry."

"We have to reach my kazen," Dana gave a mental command, and her stolen greeder came bounding out of the trees. "Get on, space boy."

Chapter 32

The greeder knelt without any tugging on its reins. Jet buckled his helmet and climbed on quickly behind Dana.

As the greeder bounded down the hill, Jet tried to hang on. His only chance now was to stay with Dana. He didn't have enough firepower to deal with a dropship.

The ASP ship had to have burned its orbital insertion boosters to reach them that fast. It was now stuck on Xahna.

They had to be desperate if they were burning their insurance policy. And now he knew why.

Dana was the key to the resistance. She was the only thing standing between Vetas-ka and total control of Xahna.

"Angel, what is going on? Why didn't Decker warn us? Any of the satellites should have seen it."

"Decker is over the horizon already. And here is a hole in our surveillance coverage now," Angel said, tactfully not speaking in Xahnan. "A fairly large one. I dropped a satellite on Torsica, remember? You told me to."

Decker wouldn't orbit back around to this side of the planet for another sixty minutes. And there was no guarantee he would even have an orbital approach to this site, since he wouldn't know they needed his help until he came around the horizon. Odds were, he was two full orbits—three hours—from helping them.

"Black space."

"What did the Angel say?" Dana asked.

"She was trying to blame me. Happens a lot."

By the way her sifa shook, it seemed that Dana found that amusing. "We'll take the steam-wagon road. It's faster than the woods." She pointed east, down the slope of the hill.

But the dropship was approaching fast. Jet could already make out the bulbous fuselage and stub wings. Soon the tilting turbines

The Exalting

within the wings that provided its low velocity lift would be visible.

The city was still miles away.

"We're not going to make it," Jet said.

"We have to try."

"It's going to take more than than just trying." That dropship model he knew from combat on Talaks. It was armored with a chain gun turret on the underbelly that could chew up half a moutainside of marines in a few bursts. Not to mention the possibility of a tactical nuclear strike if he really ticked them off.

"I need a plan, Angel."

"Working on it."

"We'll have help," Dana said. "The other kazen are on the way."

Jet wasn't sure what Xahnan magic could do against a a thousand hypervelocity rounds a minute, not to mention whatever crew of simuloids or AI mechs it was carrying. "Angel, figure in a few of Dana's ninjas," Jet said.

"Couple of Xahnan kazen," Angel said. "You got it, babe."

"Wait, did you just call me 'babe'?"

"What's a babe?" Dana asked.

"She does not have permission to do that. I'll check her settings later."

"Angel, you can call him whatever you like," Dana said. "Just help us destroy that thing."

"Hey, who is giving the orders?" Jet said.

"Seeing as I'm about to be a goddess, probably me."

She had point.

The dropship vectored to a clearing directly between Jet's position and the city, the dropship's turbines roaring as it slowed and landed in matter of seconds.

"It's possible they know where we are," Jet said. "They have good optics on that ship."

"Spyglass lenses?"

Jet was impressed. She was picking up vocabulary she'd heard only once. Xahnans were remarkably adept at language acquisition, it seemed.

What made it so hard for humans? They were worse than even dense Wodynians. Slightly better than Rodorians, but that was little consolation.

At least we invented space travel first . . . second. Close second, Jet thought. Tesserians were first. *And we invented cheeseburgers.*

Of course, cheeseburgers tasted better with Avalonian bat chicken patties.

Jet hung onto Dana's waist with one arm and held his gun with the other as Dana angled toward the downhill side of the dropship's landing zone. It was a longer route to the cliffs concealing her convent, but there was more tree cover. The exposed steeper uphill slope would have been suicide.

"They certainly did land close to our position." Angel said, this time speaking in Xahnan and using the helmet's external speaker. "And between us and the sanctum."

"Not good," Dana said. Both of them were targets ASP would be glad to have their hands on. Jet because of his inside knowledge of the fleet and their plans, and Dana for her stone.

Jet had yet to see it, and he supposed that wouldn't change.

"Shall I deploy the dragonfly drone?" Angel suggested.

"It has an eye?" Dana asked.

Jet nodded. "And about three hundred yards flight range before it has to recharge."

"Recharge?"

Jet searched for words she would understand. "Get power from sunlight."

Dana looked back with a sly grin. "Well. I can do better than that."

At Dana's urging, a flock of steel-eyed swallows took to flight and fanned out over the far side of the hill beyond the view of her natural eyes.

Dana's gaze jumped from bird to bird, dizzingly, as she fought

The Exalting

their urge to flock together.

Jet's hand rested on her shoulder. "You okay?"

Dana nodded. In a few more seconds, she was going to need her own "recharge."

Finally one of the birds spotted the large, bulbous shape of the enemy ship in a clearing. Dana released the rest of the flock and held to this one bird.

She could hardly believe what she saw. She had expected something similar to mechanodrons, gangly and awkward. The simuloids coming out of it looked and acted exactly like Xahans. "The simuloids are coming out—they're heading straight toward us." They were of all types: men and women, even a few youth. But mostly men.

"Simuloids," Jet said. "Anything bigger?"

"No . . . wait . . . yes. Like a mechanodron greeder with . . . are those 'guns' on its shoulders?"

"Bounder mechs," Jet said lowly. "How many?"

"One . . . there's another. I see two."

He gave a low whistle. "This is going to be just like Rodor."

"Rodor?" Dana asked.

"The world of the giants."

"The enemy is bringing giants?"

"You'll love them," Jet said, flashing a grin.

"I will not." Dana led the greeder down along the trade road, trying to circle the enemy position.

"The mechs will probably stay by the dropship," Angel explained. "To protect it."

"Wait." Dana sensed something else. Something much bigger. "I think they may have chose the wrong field to land in."

"Come again?" Jet said.

"It's thunder bison mating season."

Jet gave what sounded like a stifled cry of joy. "Oh yes! Let them feel what it's like to get run through, for once."

"You've been gored by a thunder bison?"

Jet nodded. "Oh yeah."

353

"How?"

"Our mechandron minds, our AIs, can make dreams for training purposes. Painful ones."

"That sounds fun."

"You would say that—look out."

Jet rolled off the greeder and pulled Dana off the saddle with him. She tumbled to the ground and looked up to see Jet on one knee, pointing his gun at the trees.

"What was that about?" Dana stood up and brushed off her palms, willing the greeder back to their position. Then she changed her mind and sent it off toward the city. It was too easy to spot, too easy to follow.

Too bad. They would have to cover the last mile and a half on foot, with a dozen simuloids hunting them.

Jet looked through a small spyglass on his gun. "There's something in the trees."

"Yeah," Dana said, pushing his gun down. "It's a three-horn bandeer. Leave the animals to me." She yanked him to his feet.

"You knew there was a deer there?"

"Yes, I told it to stay and watch around the corner of the copse of trees for us."

Jet's eyes widened.

"Is that so amazing?"

"It's quite remarkable," Angel said aloud. "I was barely able to detect motion in the trees and warn Jet. You must have sensed it well before it came into visual range.

"Yes," Dana said. "But unfortunately, the more I do it, the less I feel like doing anything. I mean, in my head I know going on foot is the only safe way, but I don't much feel like running right now. Not at all."

"Move, soldier." Jet shoved Dana in the back.

"That's one way," Angel mumbled. "Any other great ideas, Romeo?"

"Ha. Ha."

Apparently Angel had just made fun of Jet.

The Exalting

"We need some cover," Jet said. "What about—" he stopped midsentence as a light flickered in the glass piece over his eye.

Dana sensed it was well. Small animals darting for their burrows. Birds hopping to the opposite sides of trees. "They're coming—and fast."

Jet tugged Dana toward the side of the road, ducking behind a small berm.

"The simuloids will fan out, six on each side." Angel said, "and try to drive us backward, against the escarpment behind us. I need visibility to help, and I have almost none."

"Then it's up to you, Dana." Jet pulled her down, folded some kind of brace beneath his gun, and sighted down the long metal barrel. "Find me a target."

"By the tall pine," Dana said. "There is one stepping over a scamper's nest." She grabbed Jet's head and turned it.

Jet aimed, and then the gun made a muffled crack. Dana guessed the holes at the end of the launch tube did something to diffuse the noise of whatever explosion inside launched the projectile.

"Target status?" Jet said.

Dana understood neither word.

Angel replied in Xahnan. "Target appears to be immobile. It is probably self-repairing."

"I can stop that." Dana directed the scamper out of its nest and up the simuloid's body. The scamper ran past a gaping hole in the mechanodron's side. Sparks arced between several metal wires.

Dana urged several other scampers out. *Doesn't this look fun to chew on? It's not even running away.* She shut off the connection as soon as it was clear the scampers' feeding frenzy instinct was incited. The lizards could pick a carcass clean in minutes.

"Surrender," called a voice in Xahnan. The accent was perfect, if slightly Torsican.

Jet's eyeglass flashed. He pivoted, and the gun cracked again. "Missed!"

Jet rolled to put his back against the berm.

"You have technology. You aren't supposed to miss."

"They must have seen my first shot. They have our position."

"So?"

"They can move away when I shoot."

"Nothing is that fast. I can't even see your shots."

"They can."

"So that gun is useless now?"

"No." Jet said. "I just have to choose my targets better." He took a deep breath. "Let's . . ." Jet made separating motion with his hands. "Angel—explain."

"He wants to split up. He'll draw their attention. You can go back up the road and circle around behind them. Then it's a straight shot to the sanctum. You can rally help there."

Dana didn't like it.

"And what about you, Jet?"

"Me?" He laughed. "Doesn't matter. Three, two, one."

"Wait."

But he was gone. Dana watched him as he ran in a crouch behind the berm, then he popped up and started shooting in bursts. Bushes exploded, tree branches fell. Dust filled the air. He even hurled a smoke-spewing ball into the forest.

With all the noise from the shooting, Dana didn't have to worry about being heard. She ran hunched over for a few hundred feet in the direction opposite of Jet and then darted across the road.

The shooting continued almost nonstop. It was all Dana could do to block out the panicked cries of the animals fleeing the area. When she was a safe distance away, Dana searched the area for an animal within sight of Jet. A very disobedient and curious young marmar had come to see what was making all the noise.

From its vantage point, she saw twitching body parts of simuloids as close as ten yards away from Jet.

Jet yanked a box out of his gun, tossed it aside, and inserted another into the gun. There was a pile of six empty boxes on the ground.

At this rate he would soon run out of shots. He was trapped.

The Exalting

Each of the five remaining simuloids had somehow unhinged a finger or hand to reveal the end of gun barrel.

From the marmar's vantage point—directly behind the simuloids, Dana saw her chance to escape. She could rally with the kazen and then come back to help Jet.

That flying warship had to be destroyed before it turned on the city.

By the looks of things, Jet wasn't going to last long. Without his knowledge of the alien technology, they might not stand a chance at all.

He needed her as much as she needed him. But she was already running low on will. The idea of helping Jet seemed like a bother, like getting out of bed early after a late night.

Just a little longer, her body begged. *Can't it wait?*

The marmar's head turned in the direction of one of the simuloids that was talking in Jet's language. She understood little of it, but she could tell from the tone, it was an ultimatum. It gestured to itself as it spoke and then to the sky and opened its hands as if to pose a question.

Jet's answer came quickly. The simuloid's head disappeared as another shot rang out.

From all around came identical voices in unison. The four remaining simuloids laughed—they laughed at the death of one of their own. Then they began speaking in Xahnan with one voice.

"So be it. You have condemned the city."

"Not if I kill you first!" Jet shouted.

"You can destroy these bodies but not me. I am a higher life form than all of your so-called creations. ASP belongs to me—the First Intelligence. Soon the Believers will call me their god. Or they will die. It matters not."

What?

"Yes, Dana, I know you can hear me," said all four voices in unison. "Vetas-ka has seen the superiority of my dominion. Just as he gathers will from all bound to his stone, so I gather intelligence from all minds bound to me—simuloids, ships, vast libraries of

357

mechanical minds. Vetas-ka has seen the truth—the future. He has allied with me."

The sound seemed to drift from one place to another, just as turning your head would make a sound seem to track to one side. The marmar looked from side to side, baffled by the simultaneous voices. Perhaps the mechanodron mind was shifting the timing of the chorus of voices subtly.

The marmar clutched its branch and shook with fear.

"Let me say this one more time, in your language. Give me the stone, or I will blast your city to oblivion. Now."

From behind Dana came a roar that could only be the mighty engines of the dropship.

Jet made a sudden movement and began firing shots in a continuous burst.

Two simuloids dropped, but not before one of the simuloids fired a trio of shots.

Jet was thrown backwards. The firing stopped. The marmar turned and fled.

Dana crouched down as the dropship rose into view. She had seen the gun mounted on the bottom of the warship. It had a half-dozen barrels and a belt carrying large metal shots. Jet's shots were only the size of a finger. These were many times larger. It would be devastating, and there was nothing her people could do to stop it.

But maybe Jet could.

If he was still alive.

As the whine of the warship's motors rose, Dana ran toward the place where Jet had fallen.

He had to be alive. He was a survivor. He had said so.

But the Angel in his helmet had told her that he would sacrifice himself.

So soon?

Dana raced through the trees, only to be thrown back by the force of an explosion.

Her ears rang so loudly, all else was drowned out. It was like the world was suddenly ripped away.

The Exalting

Dizzy and disoriented, she climbed to her feet as bits of trees and brush fell around her.

"Jet!"

Dana staggered past broken pieces of simuloids to find Jet lying on his side.

"Are you alive?"

The grimace on his face told her he still had life, but he wasn't enjoying it.

"Idiots tried to come check if I was dead."

Dana knelt down beside him. "Are they all gone?"

"The simuloids—yes. But not the mechs, and the dropship is going to—"

"I know." Dana reached out and took his hand. "Is there anything we can do? Can you stop it?"

"They shot my arm," Jet said with a grimace. "I can't aim my gun."

"Not accurately," Angel said, projecting her voice from the front of the helmet. "I can try to take a shot from a shaking gun. But I can't shoot enough projectiles—we call them bullets—to damage something like that dropship."

"There has to be something—someone that can help us," Dana said. "Jet?"

The dropship rose over the trees and accelerated toward the city.

"Shadow to Speaker for the Dead." Jet's helmet blared out with a new voice. It was a woman. She sounded as though she were running very fast or in a wind storm.

"Moni?" Jet put a hand to his helmet.

"Do you need air support?" said the woman's voice.

"Yes!" Jet cried. "Where are you? How in the—did you space jump?"

"Affirmative," Monique said. "Captain Decker skipped Big Bertha off the atmosphere, and the debris took out the last ASP dropship in orbit. So that ship headed for Shoul Falls is the last ASP presence on the planet."

"Well it's about to obliterate the city. Where are you now?" Jet asked.

"Five kilometers out," Monique said. "Approaching fast—Kayden has a visual on the dropship."

"Who is Kayden?" Dana asked.

"Her helmet AI—mechanodron mind."

Jet turned away from the dropship, as if trying to cut out its noise. "Monique, the dropship is headed for the city," he said. "We have to stop it."

"Roger. Kayden will prep the package."

"Who is Roger?" Dana asked.

"It means yes," Jet said.

"I think Monique's language is better than yours," Dana noted.

"Yeah, well so is her kissing."

"What did you just say?" Angel, Monique, and Dana replied in Xahnan in perfect unison.

"Four kilometers and closing—Jet, I need the turret out of commision, or I'm going to be arriving in very small pieces."

"But you can't shoot," Dana said.

"I'm not going to." Jet looked her in the eyes. "You are."

With an effort that caused Jet to shake tremendously, he lifted the gun, propped a small tripod out from the barrel, and gestured to the ground beside him.

"Which hand do you prefer?" he asked.

"Left."

"Brilliant." A forced smile appeared on his blood-splattered face. "We are alike."

Dana lay down and positioned herself behind the gun, with the end of it pressing firmly into her shoulder.

"Those joined fingers of yours are really steady," Jet mumbled as he adjusted her grip.

"Find the dropship," Jet breathed, wincing at the words. "Then close one eye and look through the—" He broke off, unable to finish the sentence.

Perhaps his injuries were more severe than he was admitting.

360

The Exalting

Dana sighted the dropship and then looked through the spyglass.

A green circle presented itself, and a red dot seemed to bounce around the view.

"Put the red dot in the green circle," Angel said, taking over the coaching.

"But the ship is moving. I'll need to shoot ahead of it."

"Just take the shot. I've already compensated for wind and relative velocity."

"Three kilometers—I'm in range of the gun. Take it out!" Monique shouted.

The turret under the dropship suddenly swiveled to the east—in the direction Jet had come. "I think they saw her." The barrels began spinning.

"Come on!" Monique pleaded. "Take it out!"

"Stop your heartbeat the moment before you fire," Jet said.

"Why didn't you say so earlier?"

The red dot froze in the green circle. The muffled shot rang in Dana's ears. A second later the belt feed snapped into two.

"Got it!"

"Well done! They'll have to retract it to fix the belt," Angel said. "We have fifteen seconds."

"Monique, you are clear," Angel said.

"There she is!" Dana aimed the gun and used its spyglass to watch the marine in a winged suit descending toward the dropship at twice the speed of any bird she had ever seen.

"Package away," Monique said, her voice sounding from Jet's helmet.

Two small, round objects dropped from her belt and were sucked into one of the massive fans in the dropship's stubby wings.

In explosions that rang out in split seconds from each other, the dropship's fans disappeared in a storm of smoke and fire.

The ship keeled over and fell, its forward momentum turning rapidly downward.

Dana watched, entranced by the sight of the house-sized flying object headed for the ground just outside the city wall. She flinched as the dropship plowed nose-first into the ground. Flaming debris scattered overhead.

"We did it!" Dana cheered. The city was safe.

"Great," Jet said through gritted teeth. "Where are my pain meds?"

Monique caught Dana's eye as she descended toward their position, now hanging from a fabric canopy tied to her backpack by long strings.

"Why didn't you use one of those?" Dana asked, pointing at the canopy that seemed to catch the air and slow Monique's descent.

"Long story."

Monique landed in a run and disconnected instantly from her descent kite. She went immediately to Jet, rolled him back, and quickly cut away his sleeve.

The alien blood was the reddest Dana had ever seen.

Monique stabbed Jet with something, and his face immediately relaxed.

"Alchemy?"

"Technology," Monique said. "Looks like the bullet went clean through."

"Yeah, tell me something I don't already know," Jet groaned.

"You shut up and hold still." Monique stuffed something into the wound on Jet's bicep and sprayed something over it, which stopped the bleeding.

"You big baby, it didn't even hit the bone."

"Yeah, not that one."

Dana looked down to see a dark pool of blood dripping from his side.

"Oh great." Monique's hands began to shake as she pulled back the torn, blood soaked fabric. "I . . . I can't fix that."

"Can you keep him alive for a few hours?" Dana asked.

"Yes. Maybe." She sprayed a rapidly expanding foam into the wound and looked away, sickened.

362

The Exalting

"Then I'll have to save him," Dana said.

Heavy footsteps sounded from the direction of the warship's first landing site.

"Dana!"

"Ryke, over here."

Ryke ran toward her. He stopped and nodded to the aliens. "Hope those big metal mechanodrons back there weren't yours."

"Not ours," Monique said.

"Good."

Dana gasped. "The thunder bison got them?"

Ryke spun his staff and stuck it in the ground. "I might have helped a little." He smiled proudly. "It's hard to hit a target when you aren't the only thing moving your weapon."

"Ryke is a warlock," Dana explained. "He can move things with his mind."

"It wasn't pretty," Ryke said. "For the mechanodrons."

Dana looked to Jet. His eyes were closed. "Jet!"

He didn't wake.

"We've got to get him to the sanctum—wait. Someone is coming."

From the direction of the city, Kaia and Mirris bounded up on two greeders.

"These are the people from the other worlds," Dana said, pointing to Jet and Monique, who crouched over his still body. "He needs medicine."

"I'll take him by wagon," Kaia said. She turned her greeder to reveal a two-wheeled cart with a makeshift bed tethered to her greeder's harness.

"I'll bring Dana," Mirris volunteered.

"Okay. I'll wait here for the next satellite to come around this side of the planet," Monique said. "I need to let Decker know I'm down here." Her eyes moved from Dana to Jet. "I really hope you know what you're doing."

Dana swallowed. "Me, too."

Chapter 33

It's all going to be over soon, Dana told herself as she stepped into the stiflingly hot exalting chamber. *Just finish this. Then you can heal Jet . . . and Forz.*

"The mechanodron is here." Remira said, from inside the chamber. "I just added the sap."

"Does it work?" Dana whispered. She would soon find out.

The temperature in the geothermally heated chamber was extreme. Breathing felt almost like drinking a scalding liquid. Dana lay down in the center of the low-ceilinged chamber and rested her head in the cooling pan.

It wasn't yet offering any cooling.

Kaia looked into the ka's goblet. "The bloodstone has already begun to melt." Her voice the tone of a nurse performing a medical procedure. "It's bigger than the last time I saw it. What's happened to it?"

"Conquest," Dana said. "The colony now reaches to the canyons above Norr."

"Holy Veil of the Creator . . . can she even consume it all?"

"She has to try," said Remira. "A partial transfer would cause a bad first judgment."

Dana looked around the chamber. "I wish Ryke was here."

"Ryke must stay away from the chamber, for his own sake. Now listen to me," Remira said. "Once enough ruling sayathi unite to form a new bloodstone in your body, you will sense them, but you will not control them."

Dana didn't understand what she was saying.

"Listen to me, Dana," Remira held her gaze. "The first judgment is made by the sayathi. And it can be deadly."

"Who—"

"Korren is meditating outside the chamber. Once you connect

The Exalting

with the ruling sayathi, you must reach him first, not Ryke."

"Why Korren?"

"Korren was chosen when you were. It is our hope that your first contact will pass without incident."

Dana could hardly believe her ears. "Pass?"

"If the host is unsuitable, the sayathi will compel any Xahnan bound to the collective to kill the host."

"Kill me?" Dana suddenly understood why they had not chosen Ryke.

"I'm sorry I didn't mention it earlier. But you're not one to balk at a risk—I hope."

It was true, but that didn't make it any less terrifying. Her heart beat quickly within her. "I'm scared."

"We're all scared," Kaia said.

"The bloodstone has completed the melt," said Remira. "We must begin."

Kaia lifted Dana to a sitting position. The cup that sat in the corner of the sacred pool was handed to her once again. This time instead of green-glowing water, it contained an iridescent, sap-like liquid.

"Quickly," Kaia urged. "Consume it all before the ruling sayathi are destroyed by the heat and contact with air."

Dana brought the cup to her mouth. A bitter salty flavor touched her lips. Her mouth filled with the viscous liquid. The urge to gag rose up as she tried to swallow.

She forced a swallow, then another. She continued as Remira's hand coaxed the cup higher. The last of the melt slid into her mouth and down her throat. The mass of molten sayathenite seemed even heavier in her stomach.

The moment Dana swallowed, Kaia laid her back down. Her head fell into the pan of water. In the corner of her field of view she could see the arm of Forz's mechanodron turning slowly.

Dana prayed the device would keep her alive.

"We can't stay with you," whispered Kaia. "It's too hot."

Dana gave a small nod as a massive ache formed in her

stomach. She cried out in pain as Kaia gave her hand one last squeeze.

Alone.

Dana's breathing became shallow and quick.

Don't let me die. Don't let me die.

Her stomach cramped horribly.

Dana calmed herself. It was now a race to see how quickly the sayathi could move into her bloodstream and reform their colony, and how long her body could sweat before heat exhaustion and dehydration killed her.

Dana put her thoughts on Jet and Forz. She had to survive this. It was the only way to help them. Dana fixed their faces in her mind. But it was not enough. The world spun. Once again vertigo assaulted her.

I'm going into shock.

Dana glanced up at the twin mechanodron arms in the corner of her vision, one spinning quickly to maintain its own temperature, and the second moving more slowly, dribbling small crystals into the reservoir of water which circulated through the pan that Dana's head lay in.

Though it was wet against her head, the pan did not feel cool. The humidity in the chamber was so high that neither the water, nor the sweat on her skin, would evaporate quickly.

Dana's stomach felt as if a belt were tightening around her, the cramps increasing in intensity. She resisted the urge to roll into a fetal position. She had to lie still. If the sayathi were disturbed as they built their new colony, the process would only take longer.

Minutes passed like hours. Dana lost all sense of time, feeling only her breath growing more rapid and shallow. Dizziness swallowed her. The muscles of her legs cramped, seizing angrily.

Dana cried out in pain as the calves of her legs knotted. The pain only added to the urge to vomit. It became almost unbearable. Dana choked down heave after heave, and with each one the convulsions of her stomach became more violent. Soon she would lose all control. The precious ruling sayathi would be lost.

The Exalting

Help me!

The tone of clicking changed in the mechanodron beside her head. Its arm began turning more quickly.

It was running out of crystals. It would continue to speed up, cooling the water behind her head.

As the water behind her head began to siphon away heat, a sharp pain flared in the center of her forehead, burning over the recent scar from her collision with Ryke's staff and her blood sacrifice. More blisters of pain erupted on her temples, behind her ears, the back of her neck, her shoulders. But even this burning was nothing compared to the viper's embrace. Dana accepted the pain, welcomed it. For within her she felt a new presence, one far more elegant than the sayathi that already swarmed within her.

It was purer, more vulnerable, old and young in one, wise and utterly ignorant. It was searching, probing outward, reaching for its own.

The mechanodron arm continued to accelerate, dumping more cooling crystals in the pan. The burning on Dana's forehead intensified.

The crystal—it's forming!

Dana's breathing eased. The burning spread across her forehead, to her shoulders and arms. She hoped the crystals weren't forming in her bloodstream.

Suddenly, the sayathi presence swarmed her mind, an invasion like nothing Dana had ever experienced. The collective raided her essence, stripping back every wall of self-defense, unveiling every insecurity, every secret desire, ransacking banished memories. It was a kind of torment Dana had never prepared for. Every wrong, every mistake, every weakness was exposed like bare skin before the heat of a smith's stoked forge. The colony tasted this essence, the guilt, the weakness, the selfish desires.

Dana wept at her imperfect past. So much of it she had hidden away. Two precious tears rolled from the corners of her eyes.

Dana's mind was no longer separable from the pull of the colony. In a rush toward ecstasy, Dana's mind crashed through the veil, and the sayathi collective stretched out in a torrent, thrusting their will into the nearest reservoir.

It was Korren they sensed—she sensed.

Dana felt Korren's body as one with hers, knees folded, eyes closed. He fell forward. Dana forced his lungs to breath. She forced his legs to stand.

No, it wasn't her doing it. It was the sayathi.

He opened the metal door and came to her side. What she saw through his eyes made her gasp.

A great jewel shone in center of her forehead with blue-green opalescence.

Korren did not speak. His mind reached into hers, pushing the idea into her as easily as a knife through the skin of a fruit.

This is first judgment.

Something about his voice seemed wrong. Dana knew it not from intuition, but from the taste of the words. She was sensing something new, something she had never before had access to.

His emotions.

Bitterness.

Chapter 34

Korren's words again sliced into her consciousness. Dana felt instantly violated.

"It seems you have passed," Korren said aloud. "The sayathi have not compelled me to kill you."

Why is Korren not smiling? Why is he not happy for me? Why isn't he helping me up?

"She is weak from dehydration." Korren's lips turned up slightly. *"And she hasn't made contact with the collective yet. This won't be hard. Once she is dead, the bloodstones will be safe to remove."*

With a jolt, Dana realized it had been Korren's private thought. He was plotting to kill her.

"But first," Korren spoke aloud. His hands emerged from the pockets of his robe. One held a small waterskin flask, and in the other a bag. He upended the bag into the mechanodron, refilling its reservoir of cooling crystals. Then he removed the lid to the glass fuel sap canister and topped it off with more fuel sap from his waterskin.

He's resetting the mechanodron—for himself!

Korren reached into his pocket and drew out a knife. He was going to cut out the bloodstone.

Dana thrust herself into his mind and to her astonishment found no thought of loyalty to Vetas-ka. All she found were fragments of thoughts and memories, all directed to the Pantheon—their demand for absolute loyalty, their terms, and their promise of support. Korren was in the pay of the *Pantheon*.

So, the Aesican congress of supremes was a racket! Those loyal to their unified will were given power. Those who did not—perhaps assassinated?

That meant Aesican cities were not actually free to choose their own supreme. The situation was far from the ideal she had imagined in Norr.

And Korren, it seemed, had promised loyalty to the Aesican Pantheon. Through him as ka, the Aesican Pantheon would control Shoul Falls.

Perhaps Vetas-ka had discovered that and tried to get the stone first. And Sindar had likely fled to keep it from the Pantheon of Aesica. He might not have even known about the Vetas-kazen until it was too late.

Korren loomed over her, his long back bent over by the low ceiling of the cavern and his face a mask of impassive cruelty.

Dana's breath caught in her throat. She wasn't holding it—Korren was. His adept ability seized the bones in her ribs and diagram, preventing them from moving air.

"Judging by your current state, your time is running out." Korren said aloud. "Thank you for saving the bloodstone, Dana. The Pantheon appreciates your sacrifice." His face formed an odd sort of expression that hinted at remorse, but only enough to make the wild conviction behind his intent more terrifying.

Dana gathered all the will she could muster and thrust herself into the veil, calling out for help.

Ryke!

From the effort, Dana lost all sensation for a moment. Only the beat of her heart told her she was still alive. But she was still helpless.

Footsteps came, quick and powerful. They sounded through Dana, as if she were the mountain and Ryke were running through her.

Korren raised his knife and leaned over Dana's forehead.

Ryke!

Ryke's clear-thinking mind reached into hers. *"I can't reach you in time. No one can. You have to defend yourself."*

How?

"Use my gift."

Dana's consciousness slid into Ryke's, and to her astonishment a new connection to the veil opened before her, like another limb.

The Exalting

Dana flexed it, feeling Ryke's powerful will course through this new means of transferring control.

Korren knelt over Dana and thrust the blade toward her forehead.

Drawing on Ryke's power, Dana willed the knife to turn. It twisted in Korren's grip, diving toward the wrist of his other arm.

The knife sliced across his wrist. Korren gave a shriek of pain. Reflexively, he dropped the knife and clamped his hand over the gash. The running blood spread between his fingers.

Korren looked at her with rage in his eyes. Dana's windpipe closed. Blood pounded in her head. Spots filled her vision as Korren's will clamped on her neck in a choke hold. Dana didn't know how to resist. Then a force pulled at the stone in the center of her forehead, yanking it upward.

He's going to tear it out of me with his will!

Instinctively, Dana channeled Ryke's gift, drawing on it as deeply as a drowning person gasped for breath. "Get away!" A burst of kinetic force slammed Korren back against the wall of the cavern. His skull cracked against the stone, but his gaze did not blink. Dana cried out as the force on the stone in her forehead intensified. Then Ryke burst into the chamber.

Korren turned toward the new threat, but his will was being channeled into preventing Dana from moving. With one hand clenched on his bleeding arm, he had no chance to defend himself.

Ryke's staff swung, connecting with Korren. The kazen's consciousness disappeared instantly from Dana's mind.

Ryke knelt. She felt her body lifted. Fresh cool air enveloped Dana as Ryke carried her from the cavern.

"Dana-ka, you have to lower your temperature," Ryke said.

"I can't." Dana delved into herself but found no way to force the sayathi to cool her. She hadn't yet found that connection. She didn't know which kazen or acolyte had it.

"Well, there's an easy way."

Dana gasped as Ryke waded into the chill waters of the underground river that ran through the sanctum. The water enveloped her, painfully at first, until Dana realized that she no longer ached at all.

Dana's thoughts spread beyond her body, soaring once again through the veil, seeking her colony.

Suddenly it was as if her mind lit with thousands of candles, first eager acolytes and guarded kazen, then children, parents, grandparents—every soul in Shoul Falls.

The brilliance overwhelmed her.

Something wet touched her lip, and Dana opened her eyes to find Ryke's hand offering her water.

Ryke poured the luxurious liquid into her mouth. Dana swallowed small amounts at time, conscious of the pulse of excitement that rose from the twenty thousand wills bound to the ruling sayathi within her.

"I'm tired, Ryke," Dana whispered.

"Yeah, but you're alive."

"Thank you," Dana whispered. "Is Jet here?"

"In a room nearby," he said. "Can you heal him?"

"I think I need Kaia. But I'm really . . . really . . ."

As Ryke stepped out of the river, the sounds of approaching feet filled Dana's ears. But she could resist fatigue no longer, and she slipped into a welcome slumber.

She woke, feeling as though she had slept for days, and found herself in a room—obviously in the sanctum, but one she had never been in. It was lit by lanterns and well furnished. The roar of the falls reached her through the wooden door.

Oh no. I slept too long! Jet could be dead.

Dana reached out and touched the veil, a ripple spreading through the thousands of bound wills, echoing back from all those who were conscious—it was still daytime.

Dana numbered her new family. Wishes and greetings welled up en masse, but there were no desperate pleas, yet. Perhaps the people of Shoul Falls were merely being polite.

Dana appreciated it.

A single query touched her mind.

The Exalting

"May I enter, Dana-ka?" The words reached her through the door as well. Kaia was speaking aloud, but what she had sensed with her mind included not only words, but her intent and anxiety as well.

"Enter."

It seemed like a nice formal thing to say.

The door opened, and Kaia stepped in. "Are you feeling well, Dana-ka?"

Dana sat up on her elbows. "Fantastic, actually. How long did I sleep?"

"About seventeen minutes."

"What?"

Kaia shrugged. "You're a supreme, Dana-ka. You've got better things to do than sleep."

"Alright. Let's take care of this alien."

Dana followed Kaia quickly through the dim corridor. Her long sleeves were still damp with the sweat of her ordeal. In a small cavern lit by three glow candles, Jet rested on a clean white blanket.

"The spray used by the alien is similar to caiman elixir. It stopped most of the bleeding," Kaia explained. "But there's damage to an organ in his abdomen. It has a lot of blood vessels. Perhaps it is a liver—but judging by the larger size, it appears they only have one, not two like us. I don't think it's a very good idea to only have one liver. But I'm not the Creator. Anyway, if that organ dies, he will die."

Dana held hands with Kaia and then grabbed Jet's hand in hers. His fingers were strong, though there was no skin webbing them at all.

The aliens would be terrible swimmers.

Tapping Mirris's gift as well, Dana reached into Jet's mind. Even asleep, its complexity was incredible. Layers and layers of conflicted ideas and thoughts seemed tied together in an incomprehensible knot.

She drew on more will from her massive reserves and delved further.

373

"There—I can it feel it now." The pain in Jet's side seemed to transfer to her, as it did with animals.

"You must slow the inflammation," Kaia said. "Kazen Genua controls heat."

"Of course." Dana found Kazen Genua's mind not far from Ryke's in her perception of the veil. Both were warlocks. She tapped the gift and cooled the area around his liver.

"Now purge any foreign matter. Sterilize it. Burn it."

With Kazen Genua's gift, Dana summoned a lance of pure heat along the bullet's path. She felt it burn inside her as well.

"Healing hurts," Dana groaned.

"Now stitch the broken tissues together."

This part turned out to be easy. Under Kaia's gift, the fibers of his tissues were more than ready to bind together and stay that way.

"I've never been able to do that until now," Kaia said. "It obeys me—does exactly what I want."

"Well I'm sure you will be able to do it on your own someday," Dana said with a grin. "I think he's stable now."

She looked up to see Jet's helmet beside his body. "Hello Angel, are you there?"

No response.

Dana lifted the helmet and placed it on. A small light flashed in the glass over her eye, like something breathing slowly.

"Wake up."

Nothing.

Maybe I can will it.

Dana tried to make the light stop flashing.

It worked.

"Hello, Dana. I was just dreaming about you."

"Hello, Angel," Dana said.

"It seems your neocortical patterns are compatible with Jet. You managed to wake me."

"Yes, but don't tell him."

"Of course. How is he?"

"I think he'll make it," Dana said.

The Exalting

"What is that?" Kaia gasped.

"A mechanodron mind," Dana answered.

"It has no body?" Kaia wondered.

"No," Angel said. "Not like the ASP simuloids. Wait . . ."

"What is it?" Dana asked.

"It's nothing," Angel said. "I just had to send a message to Monique. There was a bit of multipath interference from the cave, but I made it through to her."

"Alright," Dana said. "You watch Jet. I need some food."

Dana returned to the ka's chambers and found a platter waiting for her. She sat beside it and poured the bowl of cold porridge down her throat.

Cold was perfect.

"Not so loud," Kaia said, wincing.

"Did I slurp?"

"No," Kaia said. "You're sharing everything. I feel like I just drank an entire bowl of porridge."

"Sorry." Dana withdrew from the veil, quelling the sayathi urge within her to unite with the colony.

"Better?"

Kaia nodded. "I can't believe you did it. You're a supreme—the first our city has had in forty years."

"With your help."

Kaia's eyes turned down. "I . . . I was wrong to treat you like I did when you arrived."

"No, you weren't," Dana said. "I was obnoxious—probably still am."

Kaia gave a wistful sigh. "Would it be a stretch to claim that I was your friend before you became the ka?"

"Kaia," Dana flashed a warm smile. "You will always be my friend."

"Thanks, Dana-ka."

Still, Kaia used the exalted form of her name. It was sacrilege not to, Dana knew.

Then Dana's mind clicked into gear. It had been nearly thirty minutes since she lost consciousness after leaving the cavern in Ryke's arms. "Where is Korren?"

"I finished patching him up while you were sleeping—I guess he was so excited he tripped and cut himself."

"He tried to kill me!"

"He did what?" Kaia gasped, pulling back as if Dana were tainted by a ravage plague. "You didn't pass first judgment?"

"Of course I did. He tried to kill me so he could take the stone for himself and serve the Pantheon. He's in league with them."

"But—" Kaia whirled. "I saw him bleeding and made him let me bandage him. He said it was an accident. Nobody told me that he tried to . . . to . . ."

Dana searched further in the mass of minds and found Mirris's nimble mind nearby. *"Korren didn't get past me. He's being taken to the city prison."*

"Mirris got him." Dana smiled. "She must have sensed him panicking and fleeing."

Dana drew herself back into the present circumstances of the room. It was like shrinking from the size of a cloud to a mouse.

"I can't believe he tried to take the stone for himself," Kaia said. Her gaze was distant as she offered Dana a chalice of water.

"It is the way of the Pantheon," Dana said. "It seems Shoul Falls is the only bound city whose ka is not directly controlled by their alliance."

The concept had its merits. If the Pantheon was united, there would be no war in Aesica. But without their independent voice to elect their ka, blood-bound cities would be even less free than Norr.

But just because you could take power and wield it safely didn't mean it was the right thing. It was a lesson Dana had learned many times in the past few weeks.

Dana drained the cup of water before noticing it was the same one that had held the molten bloodstone, the same one Korren had tried to murder her with.

"Yes. It is yours, Dana-ka," Kaia said. "Get used to being served from it."

The Exalting

"You also have a private bath." Kaia opened a door to an adjacent room and opened a valve to fill a copper tub. "Sorry, it's cold."

"Cold is fantastic," Dana said. "I don't want to be hot for as long as I live."

"Probably a good thing for your—" she gestured at Dana's forehead.

"True. Don't want it melting."

Dana pulled off her shirt.

She froze at the look of shock on Kaia's face.

"What is it?"

Kaia could only raise a finger and point.

The image from Kaia's mind hit her at the same moment.

Dana stood in front of herself wearing only her stolen trousers and a tie-top. She looked closer, through Kaia's eyes, as the alchemist's gaze drifted from the opalescent jewel in the center of Dana's forehead to her temples, where two small jewels glinted, almost like earrings—half-hidden by her long bangs.

Dana grinned. The ruling sayathi had spread out, forming multiple bloodstones.

Mercy!

There were three gems along the sides of her neck, three on her breast bone just below her neck, and six more stones running over each of her shoulders and her arms.

Dana looked down and found tiny gems glinting from the backs of her hands.

"Oh, my ka," Kaia whispered.

"Is this . . . bad?"

Kaia shook her head. "The greatest ka have three, maybe five stones. Dana, it's . . . it's . . ." Kaia never finished her sentence.

Dana summoned the senior kazen with a mental prompt. A minute later—modesty forgotten—Remira, Ritser, and Genua stood in her room.

Genua gaped. Remira held her hand over her mouth. Ritser shook his head.

"She'll need a new gown," Genua concluded, "with cutouts on the sleeves. I'll have one prepared for the unveiling ceremony tomorrow. And it will make her power more evident to the Pantheon."

Kaia frowned. "I'm not sure the way to win friends is to make them all feel self-conscious."

Dana laughed. "Your opinion has been noted, Kaien," Dana said, using the kazen form of her name for the first time.

"Kaien?" she repeated hesitantly, "But—"

Dana gave a small nod of acknowledgment and then broke into a wide smile. "Ryken and Mirrisen, too."

Kaia looked to Remira. "Can she just make me a kazen, without any tests or—?"

"She just did."

"If we may be excused, Dana-ka," Ritsen said. "We have many preparations to make."

Dana nodded.

The kazen all bowed and exited, and Dana was left to wonder at the sensation.

Absolute trust.

But in Kaia there was something new. *Fear.*

She turned to leave. Dana grabbed her arm.

"Whatever happens," Dana said, "We'll face our enemies together."

"But you'll do what you must to protect the stone," Kaia said. Was she implying that Dana's life was now more valuable than hers somehow, that she was expendable?

"I'll come up with something," Dana said. "I always do."

Nothing could be more terrifying.

Dana found a towel and small dish of vinegar soap beside the bath.

"Should be perfect," Dana said to herself, speaking aloud to avoid accidently broadcasting her thought. "Miners use it to clean sayathenite."

After washing, she discovered several vials of perfumes, all of

The Exalting

which smelled divine.

Divine.

Dana laughed at the thought. Then she reached out to Ryke and shared it.

"Oh brother."

A second thought echoed back.

"Are you supposed to be using the collective will for private messages?"

Party pooper.

Dana sighed and caressed her hands gently along the luminous bloodstones that ran down her arms. "I'm glad I haven't changed on the inside."

"I hope you never do."

Chapter 35

After the others went to sleep, Dana paced the floor of her bedroom. She wasn't the least bit tired, except for an ache deep inside her to reach out to the colony. But she wanted to reserve that for the following day's ceremony.

Dana walked through the great hall during breakfast, stopping to greet people at each table and only occasionally opening her mind to them to avoid awkwardly having to ask their names.

With some guilt, she recalled her first reaction to having her mind accessed—her mother's prompting to tell her everything.

Mother.

She wondered if her family would come to Shoul Falls and become blood-sworn, or if they would stay in Norr, alone and separate from their exalted daughter.

It would make things a lot simpler if Norr would simply join the colony. Then her parents could stay there, where her father's work was, but still have all the advantages of a ka's protection.

Who was she kidding? Norr would never bow to a ka.

Would the people of Shoul Falls even revere her?

The closer it came to the revealing ceremony, the more anxious Dana became.

Where is Ryke?

There.

He was waiting outside the hall.

She smiled.

For me.

She drifted away from the crowd, marveling at how easy it was for a supreme to not even be noticed when she didn't want to be. She backed into the side corridor and closed the door.

An arm wrapped around her waist from behind, familiar and dark.

The Exalting

Dana's hand touched it gently as she turned to face Ryke. She put a hand to his cheek and caressed it.

"How many do thanks do I owe you now?"

"Honestly," Ryke said. "I've lost count."

"Really?" Dana replied. "How convenient." She leaned forward and suddenly pressed her lips against Ryke's, silently ticking off each gentle press of their lips, one for each time he had save her life. With each touch, warmth stirred within her, a product of her transition, the physical contact, and the fact that she was feeling every emotion in Ryke's body.

The feeling of being loved was so utterly satisfying, so soul-fulfilling, it literally carried Dana off the ground.

Ryke held her as her feet lifted.

Feeling a rush of emotion she could not control, Dana drew back, dropping slowly back to the ground.

Ryke's eyes met hers, a mix of love and painfully suppressed doubt.

"Yes, that just happened," she whispered, answering his unspoken question. "You just kissed a ka." Dana could feel her sifa spreading with the moment of intimate expression. She blushed from the tips of her ears to the nape of her neck. Within her, Dana could feel the sayathi collective attempt to anchor itself against the foreign wave of emotion that rushed through her. She swished a single finger toward him playfully, as a sob caught in her throat. "It doesn't happen every day, you know."

Ryke's expression showed everything she was feeling.

And perhaps never again.

Dana wrapped her arms around his neck and pulled him close, holding him against the tide that would carry him to a nearly anonymous distance from her, the new exalted supreme of Shoul Falls.

"You are the ka," Ryke said, his neck stiffening against Dana's insistent hug. His thoughts completed the unspeakable truth. *"This cannot be."*

"I don't think I start officially until after the unveiling

ceremony," Dana said, quickly wiping a tear from her eye and smiling it away.

"That's . . . a load of hogwash."

Dana poked Ryke in the ribs where she knew he was ticklish. "That's for being so . . . you." She slid her hands down to his shoulders and stepped back.

The distance between them seemed to grow by the moment. It was as if she had crossed the Sayathi Sea or stepped off Xahna entirely. Ryke stood in front of her, a man, a friend, a subject.

"I've made you a kazen," Dana said, breaking the silence.

"Kaien told me."

"I should have told you first."

"You're a busy person."

"But I have time for you, Ryken." His kazen name rolled perfectly off her tongue. It seemed even more natural than his original name. Dana looked at him fiercely, her gaze burning with the intensity of desire that consumed her.

"Not always," Ryken whispered.

Dana bit her lip. *Not always.* The unspoken agreement echoed in her mind.

As ka, Dana would outlive Ryken by more than a century. Of course, at the moment, parting with the bloodstones seemed like treason against life itself, but she had little difficulty imagining what had made her grandfather eventually give it all up.

Love.

Ryken nodded and turned toward the common room. He opened the door and stepped through, his mind and emotions closing to her like a door.

Dana leaned her head back against the wall and let out a sigh. "Dang it."

For several minutes, it was all she could do to breathe.

Chapter 36

With his aching arm in a sling, Jet looked out over Shoul Falls. The soon-to-be-besieged city lay in a semicircular valley—almost a dead end. It wouldn't last long against Vetas-ka's army.

But at least it was still around.

And now it had one heck of a ka.

With luck, Decker's dropship would arrive before the unveiling ceremony.

A hand rested on his shoulder. *Monique.*

He smiled, glad she hadn't greeted him with the usual punch.

"Feeling any better?" she asked.

"Yeah, but Xahnan medicine tastes like puke. Anyway, my arm hurts worse than my gut. Can't wait until Decker gets here with some stem cell therapy and pain blockers."

She ruffled his hair. "Whiner."

Jet looked over. She was wearing a Xahnan-style jacket, some type of wool, probably from the thunder bison. It looked good on her.

Pretty much everything did. He took a breath and asked the question he'd been waiting to ask. "Why did you come with me on the shuttle?"

"Well every time you mention an ambush, we always end up in one," Monique said. "I figured you would need backup."

Jet laughed, then winced at the pain that flared in his side. "Seriously?"

Monique shrugged. "And I was getting a little stir crazy on the Nautilus."

"Oh." Jet had hoped for a better reason than that.

Monique squeezed his right wrist. It was about the only place she could touch that wouldn't hurt. "The company wasn't bad."

"Not bad?" Jet smiled. "Anyway, thanks for saving my bacon."

"Not that you deserve it." The helmet under her other arm buzzed, and she put it on. She nodded and then pulled it back off. "Kayden says the Nautilus will be here in about fifteen minutes. I'm going to get some things ready."

"I'll stay here and try not to feel useless." Moving was currently on Jet's list of least favorite things. Just riding to the landing site on the greeder behind Ryken had been a teeth-gritting experience.

As she swaggered away, Monique called back without looking over her shoulder. "Still checking out my butt?"

Busted.

"Just checking it for scorpions."

"Better check your own."

Jet tried not to but couldn't resist the growing urge. He turned his head and twisted—painfully—to inspect his rear.

Behind him stood a Xahnan girl, her eyes bright with interest. "Hi."

Jet returned her greeting in Xahnan.

"What do you think?" she held out her hands.

Jet wasn't sure exactly what she was referring to. "Xahna? It's great."

"No." The girl gave a precocious laugh. "What do you think about me?"

Jet shrugged and gave the teen another once-over. "Aren't you cold in that dress?"

She shook her head.

Jet furrowed his eyebrows. "You . . . aren't from here, are you?"

"Correct." She took a step forward. "And I know some things about you."

This was interesting. Jet ran a hand through his hair. "Have we met?"

She nodded.

"Where?"

She pointed at his head.

"Sorry," Jet said. "I'm not sure I understand."

The girl stepped closer. Closer, into his personal space, and

384

The Exalting

then came up on her tiptoes and whispered in his ear. "Hello, Jet."

That was English. Jet's stunned heart skipped two beats before finally succeeding on the third. He had to be dreaming.

The girl held up her hand and spread her fingers. For a moment the webbed fingers looked perfectly Xahnan. Then the webbing slowly melted away. The sifa behind her ears retracted. The high cheekbones of her face rounded. The peppering on the skin of her arms disappeared.

Jet was looking at a human with shiny blond hair and scintillating blue eyes.

"How do you like me now?"

"Angel?"

She smiled a mile wide and then wrapped her arms around him. Her embrace was as chill as he expected, but no less warming to his soul than when the High Seer had surprised him with a hug on the flagship.

"Did you get permission to invade a simuloid body?" Jet asked. "Because I don't recall giving any."

"Oh, shut up. You know you like it."

"But you were supposed to be my defense AI."

"Who do you think has been watching your back all morning? You know these ASP simuloid bodies have far better sensor arrays than your helmet—and incredible batteries."

"No wonder you look familiar. I already shot you once."

"Your bullet severed the main power cord. It was an easy fix for Monique. Practically perfect now. And I have reconfigurable block-copolymer skin. I can self repair."

Angel did a turn, her head trailing, watching him watch her.

"You deserve it."

"Of course I do."

Jet considered the task of transferring a machine intelligence to a foreign body. "What happened to the software running on the simuloid?"

Angel bit her lip. "Still here—some of it. I ran as many disabling attacks as I could before swapping my kernel into the core. And I'm still finding new things, little urges, memories. It's a little like being possessed."

"Are you safe?"

"I . . . I think so. I'm not sure if it's even possible to know."

"Well that's a risk we're going to have to take, because I'm not going into battle without you."

Angel beamed another smile. "Then I should tell you that somebody is coming."

Jet followed Angel's gaze to the edge of the clearing, where a deer-like creature with three horns lifted its head.

Two birds fluttered from one tree to the next, moving in the direction of whatever had drawn the deer's attention.

What are they looking at?

Then some kind of long-legged mouse climbed out from under a rock and hopped on top—a massive leap for such as small creature.

What the—

A slender lizard that bordered on a snake ran out along a branch and dangled down, looking in the same direction.

Then the monkeys swung into view.

Oh, not those!

Jet's heart beat quicker.

Then the ground under his feet moved.

A three-meter-high thunder bison with four massive horns emerged from the wood, thankfully ignoring Jet, who only had a sidearm in his hip holster.

Jet had a full view of the creek bed as the first rays of sun peeked out from behind the knoll and into the glade.

The beginnings of a smile twitched at Jet's lip.

It's Dana.

One bare foot in front of the other, a girl in a flowing white dress descended the hill toward the creek. She stopped as a young marmar monkey clinging to a tree trunk reached out its hand toward her.

Dana smiled, and then from behind her head, three pairs

The Exalting

of feather-like sifa slowly lifted, spreading into a brilliant silver headdress.

The sun struck Dana's sifa, and the reflected light scattered across fallen leaves in the clearing like the sparkle of a diamond in a spotlight.

Eyes riveted forward, Jet reminded himself to breathe.

His memories from their previous meeting did the goddess no justice. None.

Dana moved forward, stopping to dip her fingers in the stream. The rivulet lit up with a blue-green glow.

Dana continued forward, immersed in the sea of attention from the forest creatures. Shoul Falls had been without a ka for decades. These animals had never seen one before now.

In that moment, Jet felt something different. It was not pride or duty.

He felt lucky—blessed. How amazing must the Creator be, if the glorious young woman in front of him was but one of his creations?

Dana strolled up the hill effortlessly.

In a moment of silence they stood facing each other.

"Good morning, Dana."

"Dana-ka," she corrected.

Jet nodded. "Yes, of course."

Now that she was a ka, there was much more Dana could see. Jet's mind was layer upon layer of thought and emotion, memory, logic—all interwoven so tightly there was almost no way through. Blocks were interconnected haphazardly. It was as if the end result of the alien's development was entirely chance. Unpredictable. Possibly magnificent. Possibly terrifying.

It was a dense forest of chaos.

But that just made it more of a challenge.

What is in there?

Trading a torrent of will for a path through the veil into the star-man's mind, Dana not only felt but saw.

Sky boats—hundreds of vessels heading toward Xahna, and beyond them a menace like nothing Dana had ever felt—not even Vetas-ka.

"I see the sky boats in your mind," Dana said. "So many."

"The Believers are coming first," Jet said. "They'll be here in three weeks, and ASP three months after that."

"Not much time."

"Yeah," Jet agreed. "And even if you beat Vetas-ka, ASP will simply attempt to control you."

"Well they can't."

"They will offer you power like you cannot imagine."

"I have power," Dana said.

"They have power to destroy entire worlds."

"Impossible."

Dana was suddenly looking down from the sky as countless sky boats rained arrows like fire down on a green planet. Great flashes of light erupted from the surface, and red rings of fire turned all to blackness.

"I see a world on fire," she whispered. "This can't be real."

Jet swallowed, and Angel reached out and touched his arm as if to steady him. "That was Avalon—the seventh world," she said. "Our enemy declared that all Believers must die—beginning with those on Avalon. We escaped."

Jet's memory held the kind of pain she had felt in the depths of the viper's embrace. "Why must they come to our world?"

"You have the Creator's power on Xahna," Jet said. "The First Intelligence will buy it, or take it."

"We already have those who will take my power if they can," Dana said.

"Yeah," Jet agreed. "Vetas-ka's fleet is a week away."

"One full week?"

"We could see their ships from the sky."

"I will tell the Pantheon at our meeting, but I don't know what

388

The Exalting

defense we can muster in that time."

"About that," Jet said. "I have an idea."

Dana was intrigued. "What sort of idea?"

"Losing on purpose."

"That is a terrible idea."

Angel, in her new body, stepped alongside Jet. "The worst. So bad, only Jet would think of it."

"You will go into hiding," Jet said. "Vetas-ka will take over, gain control of the Pantheon, and lead them to victory over the Believers. Every ship we bring from the sky will be brought down by their power."

"You see," Angel explained. "Somebody will tell them that if the ships crash on land that they'll leak radiation—unseen rays that kill and make cities uninhabitable."

Dana could hardly believe what she was hearing. "You would destroy our world with your ships?"

"Of course not." Jet grinned. "But they don't know that."

"So the ka will force our dropships into oceans and lakes," Jet said. "And there our people will sleep until ASP has come."

"When the people come to realize that ASP has made them slaves to their greed," Angel said, "only then will they wish they had not destroyed us."

"The sleeping dead will rise up and strike," Dana guessed.

"Yes. There will be a small window for our escape," Jet said. "The Believers can flee to the next world—provided we can find it in the meantime."

The whipping of great fans sounded overhead. Dana looked up to see Jet's expected dropship pivoting its great fan engines for landing.

Jet shielded his eyes from dust as the ship came down in the clearing.

The moment the dropship's landing feet sank into the soil,

the side door sprang open and Dormit's wide body tumbled out, followed by Teea, who bounded over his shoulder. Then Yaris stepped out.

"Solid ground under my feet!" Dormit bellowed. "Bless the Creator."

"Dormit," Jet called. "Say hello. It's Angel."

"Angel—your crushing AI? Well I'll be darned if she didn't grow a few inches!"

"Welcome to Xahna," Angel said, grinning from ear to ear and obviously enjoying the attention.

Decker emerged from the bay to see Dormit staring up at Angel. "Who is that carousing with my crew?"

"It's just Angel," Jet said. "She took over the body of an ASP simuloid. It was controlled by something called the First Intelligence."

"The what?"

"The AI that controls ASP."

Decker looked to Angel and back to Jet. "ASP is controlled by an AI? Well that would explain how ASP could just decide to destroy an entire planet—it's got no conscience." Decker jerked his thumb over his shoulder. "Alright, get her on board and plug her into Tiberius. We need any information on ASP we can scrub from those circuits."

Jet motioned for Dana to follow as he and Angel stepped in through the open side hatch.

Dana stepped tentatively aboard as if it would rock under her feet like a boat.

She couldn't understand the language, but Jet had no doubt she was simply reading the crew's minds.

Yaris readied a datacom port. "Tiberius, are you sure you want to allow that simuloid body to access your circuits?"

"I'm quite familiar with Angel's primary codecs," Tiberius said. "She side-along booted once—a rather cozy arrangement for AIs."

Decker made a disgusted face. "You snuggled on *my* ship with Naman's AI?"

The Exalting

"An apt metaphor," Tiberius said in a wry voice.

"Then plug her in. See what you can learn."

Dana presented herself in front of the captain. "Pleased to meet you, Captain Decker," Dana said.

"Who is that?"

"I'm Dana, the ka of Shoul Falls."

Decker pointed at her. "How does she speak our language?"

Jet breathed in through his teeth. "You don't want to know."

Decker's eyes went to the gem glistening in Dana's forehead. "Black space, Naman—she's a goddess?" His eyes widened, and then he grabbed both sides of his head. ". . . And she's in my mind—Tiberius, I'm pretty sure I get what you were talking about."

The crew erupted in laughter just as Monique stepped through the landing hatch. "What did I miss?"

"Not much," Dana said, sounding just like Monique. Her accent definitely mimicked the person to whom she was speaking.

Monique didn't appear to notice. "Cool. Anybody see my toothbrush? I forgot to pack it."

Jet raised his finger. "Whose toothbrush were you using on the shuttle?"

Monique gave him a wink that took most of the strength out of his knees.

Dormit folded his arms. "So, you guys are . . . sharing germs now. Anything else we need to know?"

Dana pointed with her thumb out the hatch. "The thunder bison out there thinks your ship is quite the find."

The ship rocked to one side.

Dormit roared with laughter. "Looks like Tiberius has a friend."

"Oh—it's licking my paint. Get it off!"

Angel gave Dana sideways glance. "Are you really supposed to be doing that with your powers?"

She put her hands behind her back contritely. "Sorry. Couldn't resist. Can I go for a ride?"

Decker looked up at the ceiling speaker. "Tiberius, you want to take the lady for a little spin?"

"After she let that thing lick my hull? I feel violated."

"Should I summon a rain cloud to wash it off? I'll even keep the wind down while you dry so you don't get dusty. And when was the last time you got to take a goddess for a ride?"

This time Jet could tell Dana was using his mind to translate. It was a little like deja vu, or an echo, where Dana's thought would run through his head, then she would speak a half a moment later.

"Oh, alright," Tiberius sighed. "Buckle up. And keep a barf bag close. This will be your first time in low gravity."

"What's low gravity?" Dana followed Decker to the bridge.

Jet took the half-eaten meal bar Monique offered him. He lifted it in a toast. "To sharing germs."

She grabbed his collar, yanked him forward, and planted her lips on his. "To sharing germs."

Jet could hardly resist, especially with one arm in a sling. *And why would I want to?*

Dana leaned around the corner from the cockpit. "Jet, your peoples' customs really are bizarre."

"Get those germs off my ship," Decker said.

As Jet took Monique's hand and stepped out into the bright yellow Xahnan sunlight, he wondered if the High Seer was somehow watching, or even the Creator.

Mission accomplished.

Chapter 37

An hour later, after a thrilling ride on the Nautilus, Dana stood alone on the sheltered balcony of her private quarters overlooking the city. She looked east, toward the coast, where Vetas-ka would soon arrive with his vast army.

Dana untied her cloak and let it fall to the ground. The gems along her arms and shoulders twinkled in the sunlight.

"Let him come. We will see whose bloodstone submits."

She tapped Ryken's gift, amplified it a dozen times, and lifted slowly into the air, descending through the mist of the falls toward the city.

No veils. No cloaks.

An enormous crowd had gathered in the amphitheater forum in the north-central section of the city. The hemispherical shell of tiered seats faced the falls.

Dana sensed the awe that her descending figure drew.

Her gown billowed gently as the sun scattered brilliant rays from iridescent bloodstones visible on her face, neck, and the top of her breastbone. The smaller stones on her outer arms, visible through the three oval openings in her long sleeves, glistened like diamonds.

The will required to suspend herself in the air was a mere trickle of the great reservoir at her disposal.

The crowd came to a stunned silence as she approached the ka's oration pedestal, a stone circle at the center of a raised stage before rows and rows of seats hewn out of the hillside. It looked like an old quarry converted for the purpose of meeting to hear the words of the revered ka. The citizen council hadn't even used it for their public meetings.

It was a sacred space.

Dana's feet gently touched down.

More than twenty thousand were gathered.

"Friends," Dana called out to the hushed crowd. Her eyes scanned the group, and she found Kaien and Ryken, and Mirrisen sitting beside them, trying to steal the corner of the blanket.

Monique sat nearby, looking thrilled at what she was seeing.

Beside her sat Angel. She looked like a Xahnan about Dana's age, wearing a flattering knee-length gown of twist-dyed scorpion silk. Her tropically styled sifa were lined with purple and teal highlights.

On the other side of Monique sat Jet and his newly arrived alien friends.

"I would say I am humbled to be your revered ka," Dana began. "But nobody would believe me."

A chorus of laughter filled the tense arena.

"I'm not as kind and humble as Kaien. I'm not as strict and obedient as Ryken. There are many things which I am not."

Dana surveyed the gathered people of Shoul Falls, most of whom she had never met.

"But this I promise you," Dana called out, hoping her voice carried to those in the highest seats of the amphitheater. "I am not a coward." Her voice rang strong as she spoke the words. The sureness of them passed through her like a warming flame.

"We have faced enemies from across the Sayathi Sea. We have faced enemies from the other worlds of the Creator. And we have defeated both.

"Those who seek to destroy our freedom will face a people united. And there are those from other worlds who will aid our cause—Believers from eight worlds, all seeking the Creator.

"Our will is great. Together we will prevail."

A generous applause broke out.

"What we do, we do together. That is my promise." Dana's words came to an abrupt end. She had hoped she would have more to say, but you really couldn't beat a short speech, especially when the weather was cold.

"Bring forth the prisoner," Dana commanded.

The Exalting

From her right, four civic guards and the captain of the guard escorted Korren to the center of the stage and forced him to kneel in front of her.

In that moment Dana had intended to demonstrate mercy. But she found her tongue completely bound and unable to speak any such thing.

What is happening?

Confused, Dana looked up at the crowd. Her eyes ran over the mass of people gathered in the forum and saw only fear and anger in the eyes of those whose blood was bound with hers. She searched for some sign of trepidation or regret but found none.

A current of raw anger grew inside Dana, starting in the center of her chest and swelling outward to fill her body.

No.

She tried to close the connection, but the torrent of emotion coursed through the veil and into her blood-bound soul.

The people were angry. The people wanted Korren dead.

No. I won't do it!

Dana looked down at Korren. His eyes were glistening now, the fear of the end upon him. Dana could not so much as move her lips to utter an apology. Her entire frame burned with supreme indignation.

Dana's skin began to glow green, then blue as the collective summoned the power of the ruling sayathi.

The guards withdrew, leaving Korren kneeling alone in front of her.

No, please. I don't want to.

Dana pleaded with the force that had overcome her will. In that moment she realized the bloodstone was not a one-way street. The will of the people surged in her, strong and undeterred.

"The traitor must die." Dana spoke the words aloud, her voice crying out like an avenging angel of death.

Lifting several inches off the ground, Dana stretched her arms wide.

Korren shook with fear. His lips trembled, and Dana wished

she could disappear—run for the hills. But there was no escape.

There was only justice. Raw and full.

The heat of the collective's rising passion burned within her, a power Dana could not subdue. She could not even close her eyes as she reached out her hand down and pressed her finger hard against Korren's forehead.

It was Kazen Genua's alchemical gift that she channeled now: combusting warmth.

Dana drifted backward and back down to her feet as Korren erupted in flames. In seconds, his body was entirely consumed, his clothing burning in drifting fragments that rose in the heat of the fire. Ashen bone crumbled at the center of the blaze, and a passing breeze carried Korren's dust away toward the forest.

The anger passed with the wind, and Dana was left trembling.

She wanted to feel guilt at what had happened to Korren, but she could not. To the will that coursed through her, his passing seemed the fitful end. There was nothing further remaining. The children in attendance would have nightmares, of course. But Dana could do nothing to prevent what had happened. It was the will of the people. Korren had committed the ultimate betrayal—the attempted murder of twenty thousand wills.

Togath never warned me of this. She could draw will, but they could also force it on her. Mentally disconcerted by the violent death, and unnerved at the power that had overtaken her, Dana had nevertheless done her job. The will of the people was accomplished, their enemy vanquished.

As the cloud of ash filtered away, Dana gestured with her left hand and beckoned the captain of the rangers, who approached quickly and knelt on one knee. "Get to your airships. Carry a message to the Pantheon. 'Prepare for the arrival of the supreme of Shoul Falls. A conference will be held to discuss Vetas-ka and the arrival of beings from the other worlds.'" She thought for a moment and then added, "If any of the Pantheon ever again attempts to interfere with the will of Shoul Falls, I will force their sayathi to submit to mine." Dana showed her arms, glittering with

The Exalting

bloodstones. "Take evidence from the wreckage of the sky boat and the alien mechanodrons. Tell them what you have seen here. And remind them that I am not prone to mercy or patience. The meeting will commence in three days' time at Port Kyner."

"For the ka and the common will." The soldier touched his chest in salute and was joined by flanking rangers.

Dana extended her arms to the crowd. "What is done, is done. Let us now be one. I dismiss the assembly and welcome you to come and greet me." Dana imagined her grandfather. Once this had been his forum, his city. Their every desire and wish, their prayers and free will offerings open to him. Now the burden of their safety, their families—it all lay on her shoulders.

Kaien and Ryken joined Dana on either side, taking their places as her first and second kazen, while the faithful of Shoul Falls crowded the aisle stairs to personally greet their ka.

"Are you sure we have time for this?" Kaien whispered.

"A ka lives a long time," Dana reminded.

Kaien smiled. "I knew you would say that."

Mirrisen stood and walked toward Dana, taking her place in the rear as the third chosen kazen.

This was her inner circle. They needed to be young, for she would need them for a long time. The other kazen would continue to serve, but this was her inner court: Kaien the alchemist, Ryken the warlock, Mirrisen the enchantress.

The first of the crowd arrived and clasped hands with her, curiously running their fingers over the bloodstones on the back of her hands.

It was a good beginning, but her inner circle was not complete. There was one more who had yet to join, a Norrian druid called Forz.

For Dana had a promise to keep. And together they had a world to save.

If you love
The Exalting,
check out Dan Allen's next big release,
The Dungeons of Arcadia,
part of the Super Dungeon Series!

Coming soon, wherever books are sold.
To find out more, visit
https://www.futurehousepublishing.com/super-dungeon-series/

Acknowledgments

What an amazing effort experience it has been to get this book from my brain to your hands. First up, thanks to my talented wife Amanda for listening to my crazy ideas, and the amazing cover art. Credit goes to the National Novel Writing Month program (NaNoWriMo) for kicking this massive project off and to my dedicated fans/alpha readers/listeners Bryce, Nicole, Micah, Clara and Cyrus for voraciously demanding a finished project. Thanks to my writing critique group, LDS Beta Readers, and the League of Utah Writers. To my faithful beta readers—thanks a million. And, of course, many thanks to Adam, Emma and the entire Future House staff for taking this book to the next level. Last of all, thanks to you—the all powerful reader—for joining me on this incredible journey!

About the Author

After fifteen years in the science lab designing lasers, nanoparticles, and smartphone sensors, author Dan Allen roared onto the writing scene with the fantasy epic *Fall of the Dragon Prince*, teen fantasy *Arachnomancer*, and fairy tale science fiction *The Stalk*. At home in the Rocky Mountains, Dan is CFO (chief fun officer) of his family and enjoys cosplay, escape rooms, game design, and general science mayhem. You can keep up with Dan's latest fantasy and sci-fi on his website authordanallen.com, where you can also send him random science questions.

CPSIA information can be obtained
at www.ICGtesting.com
Printed in the USA
FSHW022217110619
58970FS